PRAISE FOR *CASCADE FAILURE*

"*Cascade Failure* is an emotional and fun ride that you won't want to end. I loved this book!"

—Mur Lafferty, author and Hugo Award–winning podcaster of *Escape Pod*

"With *Cascade Failure,* L. M. Sagas brings to life a gritty, grippy, space adventure with the big-time stakes of *The Expanse,* the engaging family dynamics of Becky Chambers, and the sweet, tangy snark of Murderbot."

—Chris Panatier, author of *Stringers*

"*Cascade Failure*? More like *Cascade* EPIC WIN. Fast-paced, heartfelt SF goodness. Sagas's debut will keep you grinning from first page to last!"

—Jason M. Hough, *New York Times* bestselling author of *Instinct*

"Fans of *Firefly* and Lois McMaster Bujold's brilliant Vorkosigan series, *Cascade Failure* by L. M. Sagas has you covered. A rag-tag crew full of grit, genius, and quirks with weary hearts of gold, finding the mission of their lives in a ship like no other. I loved everything about this book, including stunningly original world-building that ranks among the best I've ever read. Get this one. You'll thank me."

—Julie E. Czerneda, award-winning author of *To Each This World*

"Gear up, strap in, and hold on. Fast, brash, and wickedly fun, *Cascade Failure* is 100-proof space juice injected straight into your veins."

—Dayton Ward, author of *Star Trek: Coda*

"A total blast. Clever writing, high-stakes danger, cinematic action, and witty banter—this book has it all. You'll be rooting for these messy, lovable disaster misfits from the very first pages. *Cascade Failure* has earned its place among my favorite found family tales, alongside *Killjoys, Mass Effect,* and *Battlestar Galactica*."

—J. S. Dewes, author of *The Last Watch*

"An unambiguous holler against taking the worst of our ways with us into the final frontier. An intriguing debut and a damn good adventure."

—Zig Zag Claybourne, author of
Afro Puffs Are the Antennae of the Universe

ALSO BY L. M. SAGAS

Cascade Failure

L. M. SAGAS

GRAVITY
LOST

AN
AMBIT'S RUN
NOVEL

TOR

TOR PUBLISHING GROUP
NEW YORK

This is a work of fiction. All of the characters, organizations, and events portrayed in this novel are either products of the author's imagination or are used fictitiously.

GRAVITY LOST

Copyright © 2024 by Morgan Stanfield

All rights reserved.

A Tor Book
Published by Tom Doherty Associates / Tor Publishing Group
120 Broadway
New York, NY 10271

www.torpublishinggroup.com

The Library of Congress Cataloging-in-Publication Data is available upon request.

ISBN 978-1-250-87128-2 (trade paperback)
ISBN 978-1-250-87129-9 (ebook)

Our books may be purchased in bulk for promotional, educational, or business use. Please contact your local bookseller or the Macmillan Corporate and Premium Sales Department at 1-800-221-7945, extension 5442, or by email at MacmillanSpecialMarkets@macmillan.com.

First Edition: 2024

Printed in the United States of America

0 9 8 7 6 5 4 3 2 1

To my crew. I love you guys.

GRAVITY LOST

CHAPTER ONE

SAINT

"I *did* tell you not to touch my shit."

Nash snatched her bag back from the wide-eyed security technician as alarms bathed the checkpoint in red. She didn't even look inside; just thrust her hand in, fiddled around, and after a few seconds the alarms stopped.

"What the hell *was* that?" said the tech, face flushing and blanching at the same time, in cheese-curd blotches. He watched the bag as Nash reclaimed it, like he half-expected whatever he'd touched to jump out and take a bite out of him.

Go with that instinct, Saint thought. He didn't actually know what'd set everything off; could've been any one of the half-dozen fun, fantastically dangerous toys Nash kept in that bag. Being the crew medic and mechanic came with some interesting equipment.

Nash ignored the tech and turned back to Saint. "You heard me, right? I told him not to touch it."

"You told him," Saint agreed, gravely. He'd stopped a few steps back from the checkpoint, mostly to wait his turn for the scanner, but also to enjoy the show. Had to get your kicks where you could on a slow day, and lately, they'd had nothing *but* slow days. Nearly four months posted on that satellite, and in that time, Saint hadn't had to punch, shoot, or bury a single soul. He woke up, drank his coffee, did his job, and went back to bed, and then he woke up and did it all over again.

Streaks like that never held.

With a *damn right* nod, Nash turned back to the tech. "You want to lose a finger, Newbie? Because that's how you lose a finger."

"Maybe a hand," Saint said.

"Possibly the whole arm," Nash agreed. "Say, Newbie, you a lefty or a righty?"

The newbie didn't manage much more than an uneasy stare as Nash zipped her bag and shouldered it. That stare said he couldn't decide if she was joking or if she was genuinely, ball-shrivellingly terrifying.

Don't worry, Saint thought. *She has that effect on everyone.* Even Saint. Maybe *especially* Saint, because he knew her well enough to know that *ball-shrivellingly terrifying* was an undersell.

It took the tech a handful of seconds to recover. "Wait," he said, finally. "I need you to sign in."

"First shift, huh?" Saint thought he looked new. They'd passed through that checkpoint over two hundred times, coming and going. Always the same trip down the same hall at the same time of day; the only thing that ever changed was the technicians. A new face every few weeks—newbies on break-in rotation, and this guy fit the bill. Way too green to be a transfer, and if he'd hit his twenties, it was only by the tip of his pimpled nose. His oversized uniform said he'd either lied about his measurements, or just felt real optimistic that he still had some growing to do. *They're running a damn daycare down here.* Saint guessed every organization had its version of a mail room; theirs just included a few more deadly weapons.

"We've got a standing reservation," Nash told him, shrugging her bag onto her shoulders. "Table for two, under Shooty McBlastinshit."

Saint pinched the bridge of his nose. "You have *got* to let that go."

"Over my cold, dead body," Nash replied sweetly. "That's

Shooty with a *Y*," she told the tech. "And *McBlastinshit* with a—"

"We're with the *Ambit*." Saint cut in, and Nash coughed something into her elbow that sounded conspicuously like *buzzkill*. He ignored her. "Designation GS 31–770. We're here for prisoner escort." And while the tech fumbled with his holo-screen, Saint took his turn in the scanner. Christ, he hated the things. Every screw and plate in every bone, every keep-sake shard of shrapnel under his skin, put on display. Always earned him a certain look, like one the *Ambit* got whenever they docked her in a new port. Like *how the hell's that thing still running?*

Stubbornness was probably as good an answer as any.

"You're clear," the tech managed to say, in a voice that tripped on a crack and landed a pitch higher than it started. Out of the corner of his eye, Saint thought he saw Nash hiding a smile as he grabbed his shit from the bin. Belt and holsters, wallet and flask. Nash had already made it a few steps down the hall, so Saint dressed while he walked to catch up.

He wouldn't miss it. Not the checkpoint, not the scanner, not the sterile white lights and bare metal walls of the secured sector. The Alpha Librae Satellite wasn't exactly a tourist desti-nation, even in the more civilized parts. Built into the icy crust of the sixth-largest Saturn moon, it was more colony than satel-lite, but never let it be said the Guild didn't know the power of a word. *Colony* came with a whole lot of well-earned baggage that the Guild just didn't want to carry.

So. Satellite. It domed up out of the ice, about 140 meters at its highest point. *Like a massive militarized snow globe*, Nash liked to say. *Ever wondered what'd happen if you shook it?* Saint leaned more toward *iceberg*, though: way more shit hap-pening under the water than above it. Structures plunged like stalactites into the ocean below, all chitin and silica and oxi-dized aluminum alloy, woven together into something almost organic. Like coral grown around the bones of scuttled ships along the coasts where he'd grown up. Had to go deep; all the station's power came from the hydrothermal vents at the moon's core, and it turned out they didn't make extension cords that long.

The temp in the station never rose above a balmy seventeen degrees Celsius, which meant creaky joints for Saint, and a near-endless rotation of hand-knit sweaters and shiny bomber jackets for Nash. There in Sector F, though, he swore it got even colder. Set into the deeper parts of the satellite, it had the silence of something *buried*. Sector F was where the Guild housed most of its security operations—station surveillance, armory, the brig. Even the lobby past the checkpoint felt like something out of a penitentiary, without so much as a potted plant to spruce it up. No place to sit, no pictures on the walls, just two rounded elevator bays cutting through the center of the room like glass tree trunks. Only one of them serviced all the floors of the sector; the other was overflow for the administrative floors.

Nash and Saint made for the one marked BRIG ACCESS. "Okay," said Nash, as they walked. "Who shit in your sugar-flakes?"

"What?"

"All the bitching you've been doing about our babysitting detail, I'd have thought you'd be thrilled to pass the torch. Half-expected you to *dance* your way to the brig."

"Not much of a dancer," he replied.

"Cry one single, solitary tear of joy?"

"You know satellite atmo dries me out."

"Not even a little jazz hands?" She glanced over, and he sighed and stuck up his hands. Gave them a wiggle. Got a grimace for his efforts. "Aw, *sad* hands."

"I'm not sad."

"Tell that to your frown lines."

"They're not frown lines. They're line lines. It's called getting old."

Nash snorted. "You're not even forty," she said, patting his arm as he hit the call button and keyed in his access code on the biometric pad. Code, facial recognition, retinal scan; they really didn't want anybody getting into that elevator without a damn good reason and some damn high clearance. "Relax, you've still got a few good years left in you before I gotta start replacing parts."

Whatever face Saint pulled, it screwed so badly with the facial rec that the pad flashed red. He shot her a flat look over his shoulder, like *look what you did*, but she just smiled and gave him another pat. *Don't know why I bother.* "Nobody's replacing my parts," he grumbled as he rekeyed his code. This time the facial rec and retinal scanner got what they needed, and the doors slid open. "My parts work fine. I like my parts." He'd just like them better with a little less scar tissue was all. Maybe forty *wasn't* old, but Saint felt that way. Old and tired, in ways even four months' downtime couldn't fix. He shook his head. "Get in the damn elevator."

She did, but probably only because the doors had started to close. He slid in right after her, his back to the rounded glass walls as they started their descent. That elevator was the only way in or out of the brig's high-security ward. Main brig, you could take the stairs if shit got dicey, but for the unlucky bastards in deep lockup, that was it—one long umbilical stretching down another hundred meters from the brig, ready to get snipped at the first sign of trouble. Hit the right button, trip the right alarm, and the whole ward could be detached from the rest of the station and jettisoned into the dark. Alpha Librae didn't fuck around.

Not a bad view, though, once they got down past the brig. Floors of dull lobbies rose like curtains around the elevator, until only *ocean* remained. If he looked up, Saint could still make out the backlit windows of all the different stalactite structures of the station glittering like diamonds in the dark. Like stars whose glow haloed the whole station below the water's surface. He'd have been content to take the ride in silence, watching the lights grow dimmer as they sank farther and farther away.

Nash had other ideas. "Seriously, though," she said, leaning back against the wall with her arms crossed. "Bad mood. What gives? It's our last day of daycare—we should be *celebrating*. Cap, back me up, here."

"You know I don't take sides," Eoan's airless voice said over the comms. Nash and Saint were a long way from the *Ambit*, which was still docked in one of the surface ports, but the signal came clear as day. Nash had done a lot of tinkering with their comms since the shitshow on Noether. Her way of coping, and something to do with all the time she spent holed up on her own. *Socializing* hadn't been too high on her to-do list lately. "Although . . ."

Saint scowled. "There's no *although*." Nothing to talk about that they hadn't already talked about the other couple hundred times they'd taken that long-ass ride on that slow-ass elevator. The trouble with an underwater base was all the damn *pressure*. The car had to stop every thirty meters or so to let folks' ears pop or to rejigger the gas mixtures, because apparently oxygen did some real weird shit at depth. Nobody wanted a bunch of stoned rangers stumbling around, bleeding out of their ears.

Eoan chuckled, voice warm with amusement. Lot of folks didn't expect that kind of affection from a centuries-old AI, but with the benefit of years under Eoan's command, Saint knew better. He'd never met a captain with more grit, compassion, and sheer damn savvy than their Eoan. Even if they did have a *cosmic* curious streak and a bad habit of playing Secret Science Experiment with their crewmates.

Undeterred, they said, "It's just an observation, dear. You've never been fond of prisoner details, and I know this one's been harder to stomach than most."

"It's been fine."

"Bullshit," said Nash. "It's been boring as hell. Same thing day after day after day. I wanted to scramble my brains with a knitting needle by week three, and *I* actually have hobbies outside of work. Don't tell me you're not going full-on non compos mentis in this bitch."

"I didn't know you spoke Latin," Saint muttered.

She ignored him. "You hate this detail," she said. "I know you do. Cap knows you do. But you're walking around today, our *last* day of this snoozefest, in your own personal storm cloud. So, I say again: What. Gives." She punctuated the words with a poke to Saint's chest and a stare promising tragedy and torment if he even *thought* about giving her the runaround.

He might've chanced it, anyway, but Eoan intervened. "It's not about the detail, is it?" they said. It sounded like a question, but for Eoan, it was more like a *hypothesis*. They'd considered all the variables and arrived at the most likely explanation. "It's been quite nice, hasn't it? Having the Red family on base. I hear Regan's doing excellent things in the communications division."

Well, Eoan wasn't wrong.

At first they hadn't been sure where Jal and his family would end up after Jal recovered enough to travel. The Captains' Council didn't stick to one place, and shit had been so crazy there for a while, he could've gotten shipped to any one of a half-dozen Guild outposts. Wasn't until about a month after the *Ambit*'s assignment to Alpha Librae that the council finally decided to bring Jal there for the hearings, and everything kind of sorted itself out after that. Regan got herself a position as a comms engineer; Eoan pulled some strings, got Bitsie into school with all the other station kids; and Jal had ready access to the best docs on offer, Nash included, while he finished healing from the fall on Noether that should've killed him. Couldn't have worked out better.

Except.

"Does he know we're shipping out tomorrow?" Eoan asked gently.

Except for *that*.

Saint sighed again, rolling his neck and shoulders. Damn cold always made him seize up like a rusty hinge. "He does."

"And how'd he take it?" Nash, this time, but she didn't look at him as she asked it. She'd turned to the wall, puffing hot breath on the glass and drawing her finger through the fog. She and some other poor, bored bastard had a running series of tic-tac-toe games—maybe fifteen rounds and counting. She drew an X in the bottom right corner, scratched a line through it and the two above it, and drew a smiley face below it. No new hash. No sixteenth game.

"I don't know," Saint admitted.

Nash squinted. "You don't know?"

"That's what I said."

"How do you *not* know?"

You don't know, either, Saint tactfully didn't point out. Wasn't like she spent a lot of time with Jal, anyway. Tagged along with them for drinks a few times, and dragged Jal aboard the *Ambit* sometimes to upgrade the specs she'd made him. For the most part, though, Nash kept her distance, and Saint couldn't help wondering if it was because Jal reminded her of something she'd rather forget.

Or some*one*, maybe.

"I thought he took it fine, all right?" he said instead. "But we were supposed to meet up last night, and he begged off last minute. Hasn't answered any of my comms since."

Nash raised a hand. "Yeah, I'm gonna say definitely *not* taking it all right."

"Thanks for that." Brutal honesty was just another service Nash provided. *She's right.* He'd told himself something similar—just a lot of murky water under that particular bridge. If the kid was having trouble getting left behind again, Saint could hardly blame him.

It just . . . didn't sit right. Jal'd been so damn serious about keeping in touch and, *Don't you leave without a proper send-off, old man, or I'll hop a ship and run you down myself.* Kid wasn't exactly the sulking type, either. Golden retriever personified. So maybe that *did* have something to do with the knot in his stomach. The itch between his shoulder blades.

Or maybe those had more to do with what waited at the bottom of that elevator.

"Well, shit," said Nash, shrugging. "If that's what's got your holsters in a hitch, miner boy could always come with us. We'll have to, like, quadruple our food stocks, but I didn't hate having the guy around last time. You know, once we got past the whole *fugitive deserter with a chip on his shoulder* thing."

Saint shook his head. He'd left Jal behind once, and it'd been one of the worst mistakes of his life. Things were different now, though. "Kid went through hell to get where he's at." Back with his sister and niece, alive and safe and *happy.* "I'm not pulling him away from that."

"So we're just gonna sulk about it and hope it goes away. Got it." Nash was first off the elevator when it finally slid to a halt, clapping him on the shoulder as she passed. "Good talk."

"Was it?"

"Was for me." She swept ahead into the central hub of the security pod. Not much to look at—just a round space with a single control console jutting out of the floor in the middle. Five offshoot hallways, like the legs of a sea star, led to the high security cells; but the whole time Saint had been there, only *one* of the cells had been full.

"One last time," said Eoan encouragingly. "Whenever you're ready, you're clear all the way to the secondary dock, and the

Union transport ship is ready and waiting for delivery. Let's finish this out with our heads high, shall we?"

Saint didn't much care about high heads or low, just that in a half hour or less, it would be *finished*. He nodded to Nash as she took position at the console, punching in her credentials and the access code for the middle cell of the sea star—creatively labeled Holding C.

Standing before the thick cell door, Saint swallowed against the acid heat rising in his chest. Nearly four months, and it hadn't gotten any easier to stare down the man behind that door. To remember what he'd done and who he'd done it to.

"Opening the porthole," Nash said, and a beat later a panel on the door slid open at waist height.

"Hands." Saint's voice sounded so mechanical, so automated, it could've been part of the building. Just another moving part, just another piece of protocol in action. His own hands clenched to fists at his sides, before he forced them loose and reached for the cuffs on the back of his belt.

A beat later, another pair of hands came through the porthole, palm-up. White and scarred, with calluses that even months of captivity hadn't worn away. They seemed too small, too fine-boned and aristocratic, to have drawn as much blood as they had.

Jaw clenched to aching, Saint clamped the cuffs around those wrists and tightened them flush. A man could be as wily as he wanted to be, but the only way he'd slip those cuffs would be to leave his hands behind. "Clear," Saint called back to Nash, and he counted off *three, two, one* in his head before the door opened. It didn't slide, didn't part; it opened from the porthole in the middle like an antique camera shutter, individual panes twisting and withdrawing into the walls to reveal the man inside.

Isaiah Drestyn didn't look like a man with a rap sheet, much less one as long and varied as the one he had. He was about a dec shorter than Saint and built like a reed, eyes soft and sloping on a pale, pockmarked face. Only sign he'd ever seen trouble was the web of scars across one side of his face, a memento from the refinery fire that'd killed his brother and kick-started him on the winding path to, well, *here*. Looked more like a preacher or a poet than the kind of man who could gladly sacrifice an entire space station to a planet-killing computer virus for the sake of showing the world what its makers were capable of.

Saint wasn't sure anybody in the universe could hate something or someone more than Drestyn hated the Trust. For the man who'd run Jal off a rooftop, though? Saint would surely try.

"Move," Saint said, and Drestyn moved. His slippered feet slid across the diamond-plate floors, and his stiff scrubs rustled; otherwise, he didn't make a sound. No talking—the speech jammer around his throat saw to that. Distorted his voice when he spoke, so he never managed much more than nonsense, and the opaque white shield over the bottom half of his face thwarted any would-be lip-readers. The Captains' Council'd had a strict hush order on him since day one, and for good reason. The man was a goddamn encyclopedia of hard truths and batshit conspiracies, and since nobody'd come up with a good way to sort one from the other, Saint reckoned it was better he kept them to himself.

Nash led the way back into the elevator, punching one of the buttons on the console as she passed it. Not back to the lobby this time, but all the way up to the private docks in one of the auxiliary surface domes. You didn't escort a man like Drestyn through a populated shipyard, especially since the Guild had never managed to track down his two accomplices from Lewaro. For all Saint knew, the pair was out there plotting a jailbreak that very second.

"You know," Nash announced into the strained silence, somewhere around the three-minute mark. Elevators had a way of stretching time like taffy, and Nash didn't handle *idle* very well. "I'm really starting to rethink my position on elevator music. Some smooth jazz, a little bebop—shit, I'd take a ten-minute drum solo. Might really help cut the *awkward*."

Awkward didn't quite cover it, Saint thought, but what did it matter? Just one last time. One last trip.

Finally, the doors slid open to the private docks. Felt like walking into a frosted fishbowl; from a distance, the hexagonal tiles of the dome faded into something rounded and smooth, a clear wall against the white haze of water vapor rising off the ice. Despite the dome's thermal insulation, Saint's breath fogged in front of his face, and condensation settled on the out-side of Drestyn's face shield as they stepped out onto the docks.

A single Union transport vessel waited down walkway, not too different in design from the *Ambit*, with mothlike wings and thrumming quad-thrusters. It wasn't made to carry much, but it was made to carry it quickly. The sort of vessel you chose when you expected trouble and wanted good odds of shaking it with your ass and ship firmly intact.

Four uniformed Union security officers stood at the ship's hatch, navy-blue fatigues crisp and berets tipped slightly to one side, and an un-uniformed man and woman stood a few paces farther down. Seemed to be shooting the shit.

"And here's our guest of honor," said the man when he no-ticed them approaching. He was the kind of tall, rangy fella that you just knew would play dirty in a bar fight—and proba-bly come out on top because of it. Had a fading tan and a drawl that made Saint a little homesick, a single revolver on his belt, and a head begging for a cattleman hat. *Cowboy* came to mind, but Saint couldn't take the credit for it; he'd heard it a dozen times across a dozen retellings and conversations, as many crit-ical as they were complimentary. Captain Dalton Raimes had a bit of a reputation in the Guild. Youngest buck on the council, but some were convinced he only got the promotion so the rest of the council could keep a closer eye on him.

Of course *he'd* be the one overseeing the transfer.

"You must be Saint and Nash," Raimes said amiably, pointing to each in turn. Not *Toussaint* and *Satou*—clearly not the type to stand on occasion. Saint was suddenly sure he'd be a friendly drunk, but only because he sounded half-drunk already and greeted them with a cheerful cant of a smile. "Me and Mister Agitator here have already had the pleasure, so you'll excuse me if I don't shake his hand." He stepped one foot back to gesture to the woman he'd been talking to. Short purple hair, tall as the day was long; she looked damn near Amazonian next to Raimes, with a stern brown face and muscles visible through her white jumpsuit. A getup like that was as much a statement as a dare: *I don't expect to get dirty today, and if I do, it'll be* your *blood I'm bleaching out in the wash.* "This here's Phillipa Casale, head of Union security."

"*Head*," said Nash. "Kind of high on the food chain for a milk run."

Casale let out a bark of a laugh that echoed all the way through the small dome and back again. "Milk run. She's funny," she said to Raimes. Then, to Nash, "You're funny." Then, like a flipped switch, her face went serious. "Our agreement with the Trust makes the Union responsible for Drestyn's security while we have him in our custody. If he gets away, if he gets dead—not so good for us. So, they send me." She made a quick gesture toward the four uniforms, who stepped up and took Drestyn off Saint's hands like he *wasn't* one of the deadliest people in the universe. Cuffed and gagged and diminished, somehow, by the faded gray scrubs he wore, he didn't look the part.

It was harder than it should've been to let those Union officers shepherd Drestyn away into the belly of their ship. At the top of the gangway, Drestyn stopped. Just for a moment, just long enough to turn back and give Saint a look he couldn't begin to interpret. Meaningful, purposeful—a question, but one too short-lived for Saint to decipher—before a shove from one of the officers sent him deeper into the ship. Out of sight. Out of reach.

Out of time.

"Good luck with that one," said Raimes. "Keep on your toes. Fella might have the whole buttoned-up accountant vibe going on, but believe you me, he's slicker than a wet cat in an oil drum. Not much of a conversationalist, either."

"Conversation isn't my department," Casale replied. An all-clear call came from inside the ship, and that seemed to be her cue. "We're behind schedule. Good meeting you, funny girl. Saint. Councilor." She nodded to each of them in turn, and with one last handshake with Raimes, she set off into the ship after her crew.

Saint watched until the hatch slid closed, then forced his eyes away. It was done, and damn whatever feelings he had on the matter. Onto the next.

"Must be a relief," said Raimes, starting back for the elevator and motioning for them to follow. Wouldn't pay to still be in the dome when the air lock opened, and those engines were already starting to turn the air uncomfortably warm. After all that time in all that cold, Saint started sweating under his jacket. "Y'all headed back into the great wide yonder? The frontier," he clarified, when Nash gave him an odd look as they stepped onto the elevator. "Heard that's your usual stomping grounds. Give Captain Eoan my regards."

"They can hear you," said Nash, tapping her earpiece.

Raimes rolled with it. "My regards then, Captain Eoan. Been a while."

"Indeed," Eoan agreed, broadcasting their voice through the external speakers on the earpieces. "Congratulations again on the promotion."

"Is that what this is?" Raimes said. "Feels an awful lot like time-out with benefits and time-and-a-half pay. Keep your friends close. . . ." He trailed off as the elevator slowed to a halt halfway down to the sector lobby. Administrative floor. Turning on his heel, Raimes back-walked off the elevator with a half-cocked salute. "Be seeing you."

As soon as the door closed, Nash mimicked his salute. "Jesus, he's like a caricature of himself. And what was that bit about *not much of a conversationalist*? I thought we weren't supposed to talk to Drestyn."

"We *aren't*," said Eoan, and Saint knew that pained them more than anyone. They'd never been able to pass up an unanswered question, and Drestyn was about three thousand unanswered questions stacked together in a trench coat. But Eoan had changed, since the Deadworld Code incident. They hadn't gotten any less curious, but they *had* gotten more cautious. Noether had shown them things—fear, danger, death—in a way they'd never experienced. Intensely. *Personally*. Their whole world had shifted, and AI or not, that took time to work through.

And they had to be careful here. Too many security cameras, too many watchful eyes, too many people with strong opinions about who should and shouldn't be talking to Drestyn. They'd drawn some heat of their own, too, with what folks had started calling the Redweld Leak. Nobody knew it was the *Ambit* crew that'd released Yarden's extremely detailed, extremely *unflattering* Trust records to the public, and most people were content to blame it on Drestyn and his two escaped crewmates. Still, some had their suspicions. Better for the crew to lie low, let the clouds blow over, so that was what they'd done.

"But Raimes said—" Nash started.

Eoan interrupted gently. "Raimes has always had a somewhat . . . flirtatious relationship with the rules. Two weeks into Drestyn's hold on Alpha Librae, he shut off his security feeds and had himself a friendly tête-à-tête with our resident agitator, ostensibly to try to get the locations of his accomplices. It was all in the memo."

Nash glanced over at Saint. "Did you know they sent memos?"

"I did." He'd simply continued his proud tradition of not reading a single goddamn one of them.

Eoan gave a long-suffering sigh. "Impossible, the both of you. I blame myself, really," they added, with the mock dismay of a parent who'd indulged their children too long. "For what it's worth, it was only the once, and I understand Drestyn wasn't particularly forthcoming."

"A damn waste," Nash said. "Four months' exclusive access to a walking database of the Trust's dirtiest laundry, and we couldn't even *talk* to the guy. And now he's just." She waved her hand. "Gone. Poof. Don't you want to know what kind of skeletons our commercial overlords are hiding in their collective closet? I mean, the Redweld Leak was a good start, but you *know* that barely scratched the topcoat."

Saint frowned as the floor display ticked down. Only a few floors left to the lobby. "It'd be a bad idea. The Trust and the Union were at each other's throats for *months* to get first dibs on Drestyn. The Guild starts meddling, they might get the impression we're trying to jump line and start some shit."

"Maybe it's *time* the Guild started some shit," Nash shot back.

"Neutral preservation of human life." Saint had said it so much, it'd turned into a mantra. The oath he'd taken, and the path he followed. "That's what we signed up for."

Nash turned away, hands shoved in her pockets and lips pursed in a thin line. "Yeah, well, I'm starting to think neutrality's not an option anymore. If it ever was."

And that, for better or for worse, was when the elevator stopped.

The door'd barely opened when Nash strode out, elbows out and shoulders straight in her unmistakable *you're wrong, I'm right, and you're lucky I like you too much to put my boot up your ass* march.

Saint followed at a slightly less *fuck you* pace, but just before he caught up to her, Nash stopped abruptly.

"What the—?" she said.

He had his sidearm drawn before he even saw the problem. Knew from Nash's voice that it was trouble, and she didn't disappoint. Down the hall at the security checkpoint, the baby-faced recruit lay sprawled across the floor, slack and unmoving. *Unconscious* was the knee-jerk mental sitrep, followed closely by *not alone.* Above him, a hooded figure hunched over his console. No uniform, just mismatched clothes so big that they obscured the size and shape of the person underneath. A full-face tactical mask and gloves made it so Saint couldn't have guessed one thing about them.

Other than, it turned out, that they had a decent set of reflexes.

The figure's head jerked up, and in the split second it took Saint's finger to reach the trigger, they yanked something from the console and launched themself in the opposite direction.

"Go!" Nash shouted, already sliding to her knees by the newbie. The medic in her couldn't leave him lying there, as much as the fighter in her wanted to give chase. Saint would have to handle that for both of them.

He took off after the figure, fast as his legs would carry him. "Cap, we've got a hostile leaving the Sector F lobby," he hissed down the comms as the figure breached the first security door. Whoever they were, they'd had the sense to swipe the tech's access badge. It went beyond that, though. The whole station was monitored all hours of the day. One of the three dozen cameras or sensors or mics in the hall should've picked something up, triggered an alarm, but nothing happened. Not so much as a blip of the emergency lights overhead, and it didn't make sense. Didn't make a goddamn bit of sense, but the timing—the day of Drestyn's transfer, *minutes* after the handoff—set Saint's teeth on edge. His muscles burned with the effort of propelling him faster, faster, faster in the stranger's wake.

Goddamn automated security. Downside to relying too heavily on technology; warm bodies might've flagged a figure hightailing it out of the brig and done something about it, but warm bodies were at a premium for the Guild, and they'd much rather have them out in the universe pulling jobs and making caps than burning resources on a satellite.

He growled as the hooded stranger blew through another AUTHORIZED PERSONNEL ONLY door. "Might need some reinforcements to head him off, Cap!" If the alarms wouldn't sound themselves, maybe Cap could sound them instead. Fast, he hoped. One more door, and they'd be out of Sector F completely.

But Eoan's reply, when it came, was a distracted "I'm not sure that's a good idea."

"What?" Saint snapped, boots sliding as he cleared the last door between the secured halls of Sector F and the concourse. By then, he was nearly a rockhopper's length behind the stranger. Barely had eyes on them, tracking them more by the disgruntled people they'd bolted through than a direct line of sight. *Fuck, they're fast.* Saint could count on one hand the people he'd seen run like that. One finger, maybe. "How the hell is that not a good idea? We don't find a way to block this bastard, we're gonna lose them."

It'd be easy to lose anybody in a place like that. The Alpha Librae concourse was like the rail stations back home on Earth—a five-story terminal stretching up to the center of the main dome and down to lush green space that supplied half the satellite's oxygen. Enclosed gangways ran the circumference of every floor, next to office spaces and little shops and housing on the lower levels. More gangways crisscrossed the opening in the middle like threads on a great round loom, and everywhere you looked, corridors branched off to all different parts of the satellite, from secured spaces to the market sector to the port and everywhere in between. If Saint lost sight of the stranger there, he might never pick them back up again.

"Just follow him," said Eoan. *Him*, like they knew something he didn't.

A beat later, Nash's voice came down the line. "Newbie's waking up. He's got no idea what hit him, but he'll be okay."

Saint made a judgment call and, mid-run, switched to riot rounds. If he wasn't chasing a killer, he'd much prefer a chance to talk. No hush order to contend with here.

Miraculously, he got the leggy son of a bitch back in his sights. Picked him out of the crowd as the figure ducked suddenly sideways down one of the corridors, through an archway marked MAINTENANCE.

"He's headed to maintenance, Cap."

"I know a shortcut," said Nash, because of course she did. A stroll through the underbelly of a satellite for Nash was like an art gallery for, well, people who were into art galleries. "Newbie'll be fine; I'm headed your way. Let's see if we can jam this asshole up."

Sounded good to Saint, though he was shocked he could hear a damn thing over the roar of blood in his ears. His racing heart. The smack of his boots against the gangway. He liked to think he was in good shape, but whoever this was, they had him seriously reevaluating his cardio regimen as they blew through the door to the maintenance bay. The change from the concourse was stark, startling—finished, glossy walls to exposed pipes with all sorts of peeling warnings; solid flooring and railing to paper-thin, perforated metal catwalks that rattled under his weight. Down a flight of stairs, double back, down another flight, just in time to watch the stranger vault over a knee-high, boxy air handler and disappear into the forest of ductwork and steel off the catwalk's beaten path.

"Stop, goddamn it!" Saint shouted, barreling over the unit

and trying not to wince at the give of too-thin metal under
his too-heavy frame. He wasn't made for this. He was a bare-
knuckle brawler, a grunt made to trudge through swamps and
deserts and half-sunken cities. But what he also was, and what
he *did* have going for him, was this: he was the stubbornest son
of a bitch you ever met, and he wasn't stopping 'til his heart
gave out.

Or, 'til the *catwalk* did. He heard the snap only a split-second
before the narrow walkway dropped out from under him, and
by then, it was nearly too late. Reflex alone had his arms out in
time to catch the railing. His ribs slammed into the edge of the
remaining catwalk as his hips and legs dangled over a seventy,
eighty-dec drop.

"Shit!"

It took Saint a second to parse that out through the cold-
blooded, lizard-brained panic of dangling over a deadly drop
by a few bits of untrustworthy metal. He hadn't cursed, and
the vibration through the catwalk had gotten *closer*, instead of
farther.

With a growl, he swung a leg over the side and made a grab
for his gun, just as the stranger came into view. Coming back
to finish him off? To help? Whichever it was, he clearly hadn't
expected to come back to the business end of Saint's pistol.

"Wait!" It was more a yelp than a command, but it did the
job. Saint paused. He knew that voice. The stranger's hands
rose in the universal sign of surrender, and when Saint didn't
shoot, they kept moving. "Just wait," said the stranger, again,
softer. Gloved fingers found the hem of his hood and the clasp
of his mask. They came away almost as one, and even in the
spare, hazy light of the maintenance bay, Saint knew *exactly*
who he'd been chasing.

"Hey, old man," said Jal, with a hoarse laugh and a fragile
smile. "I, uh . . . I could really use your help."

CHAPTER TWO

JAL

Less than half an hour in, and Jal's plan had already gone spectacularly to shit. A mad dash through the station, Saint's near-miss with that bad bit of gangway—it was supposed to go down a lot neater than that, but then, Jal didn't know what he'd expected. *Plans* weren't exactly his forte. Fuck-up or not, though, he'd gotten what he needed: a face-to-face in one of Alpha Librae's few true blind spots.

After the run of days he'd had, Jal would take every win he could get.

"My help," Saint repeated. He looked confused and concerned, and Jal wished he could tell him not to be. Wished he could say, *Don't worry. It's not that bad. I'm okay.* Except it was, and he wasn't, and he'd never been much of a liar.

So, what he said was "Is Eoan on comms? I need to talk to them."

"I'm here, Jal." Eoan's voice came from the neighborhood of Saint's jawline, cool and calm and soft, but he heard the questions lurking underneath it. Always questions. What Jal needed, though, was an answer. "I've got Bitsie with me as well."

Relief blew through Jal like a gale. Not *everything* had gone to shit, then. "Is she okay?" He hadn't wanted to let her out of his sight, but she'd promised she'd be fine, and he hadn't had a choice. One way or another, she had to go to the *Ambit*; and until he sorted this out, *Jal* had to stay as far from it as possible. "She said she knew the way, but—"

Eoan cut him off. "She did," they said. "Luckily for you. If she hadn't told us *you* were the one in Sector F, I expect that might've gone less pleasantly for everyone."

"Wasn't supposed to go like that," Jal rasped. "They gave me a thirty-minute blackout window. No cameras, no sensors, no security 'cept the checkpoint tech. They said I'd have enough time to get clear, but I got held up. Goddamn computers—never was any good with them." And he wasn't as quick as he used to be. He'd mostly healed up from his fall on Noether, but even his spiffed-up genes couldn't undo all that damage in a handful of months. Drestyn's bullet had made a real mess of his leg; shredded all that muscle and sinew, and even after months of therapy, it still got sore as hell sometimes. "Thought I could make it back here and just wait 'til Bitsie told y'all to come meet me, but I screwed up."

Didn't bode well for the rest of the plan, if he'd stumbled at step one.

"Why not ask us yourself?" Nash moved so quiet, he barely heard her footsteps rattling down the walkway. No telling how she'd gotten behind him. She'd probably materialized out of the ductwork or some crazy shit like that. The woman had *ways*. "What's with all the cloak and dagger?" She knocked her knuckles against one of the pipes and grimaced at the cloud of dust and paint flecks that flew off it. "Gonna need a compelling goddamn reason you dragged us all back here, 'cause I'm pretty sure I now know what *cancer* smells like. Super fun. Ten out of ten, would lure someone down here to murder them."

"Sorry." Not his favorite place, either—too claustrophobic. "Regan says the cameras and stuff don't work down here. Station engineers all use it for their smoke breaks or whatever, so nobody ever fixed it."

"So *definitely* a good murder hole," Nash said. "Got it."

Jal's chest tightened 'til he swore he felt every single rib squeezing around his lungs. "Would you stop saying that? I ain't trying to murder you. I'm trying to keep you safe."

"From *what*?" Nash threw out her arms. "None of this makes any sense. You just broke into the heart of Guild security, nighty-nighted a baby ranger, and booked it like Alpha Librae's Most Wanted. That's not *keep you safe* behavior, Jal. I don't know what it is, but it's—"

"They took her!" He didn't mean to say it; sure as hell didn't mean to *shout* it. He was supposed to build up to it, but there it went, scraping its way past his chewed-up lips and echoing off the pipes like a gunshot in the dark. "Regan, she—fuck." He exhaled roughly, scraping his hands through his hair. "You're skipping ahead." This went so much different in his head. So much neater. He had a *plan*. "This was supposed to be the easy part." He sounded terrible, even to his own ears. Ragged and raw, as he sank back against the railing. He ignored the way it groaned. After a childhood in the floating mines, he knew damn well when something could take his weight and when it couldn't. *That*, he knew. *That*, he understood.

With the rest of it, though? He was so far out of his depth, he barely knew where to start.

A firm hand settled on his shoulder. "Breathe, kid," Saint said. "Talk to us. What've you gotten sucked into?" Not *what've you gotten* yourself *sucked into?* Such a little difference, but it meant something. From Saint, who never said or did anything he didn't mean, it *meant* something.

He took a breath and let it out. "Few days ago, I came home, and Regan's cabin was wrecked." Months living there, and he still couldn't seem to call it *their* cabin. "Looked like there'd been a fight, like somebody'd—" His voice caught, heart stuttering in the back of his throat. Dead-end thought. Back up. Try again. "I found Bitsie hiding in the ceiling vent, scared half to death, but Regan wasn't there. I looked and looked, damn near tore the place apart all over again, but I couldn't fucking find her."

"A few *days*?" Nash's tone had changed. Quieter, almost careful. Jal hated it. "Didn't you call anyone? Tell anyone?"

"I wanted to," Jal said. "I was *going* to, but then I got the call. There was this GLASS pad on the kitchen table. Thought it might've been one of Regan's—she's always tinkering with those things for work—but not five, ten minutes after I got to the cabin, it came on. Don't know if it was on a timer, or if they were watching the place, but all of a sudden there's this masked-up face on the screen, telling me he and his people want to talk."

"About?" Eoan pressed. They did it gently, but it still felt like prodding a bruise. A welt. A bleeding wound, trying to heal around shrapnel still buried in the skin. It *hurt*.

"What do you think?" he snapped, then winced. "Sorry. Fuck, I'm sorry." They didn't deserve the heat. He came to them for help, and they wanted an explanation. They *deserved* an explanation. He just couldn't . . . he couldn't get it out. Communicate it. Even on a good day, he barely managed to sound something halfway sensible, but like this? Insides all twisted up in knots, his family pulled from his hands *again*. Three days since they'd taken Regan, and he missed her like a piece of him.

That was the trouble, wasn't it? He'd been without them for years, her and Bitsie both. Back when he was stuck scrapping for the scavs, he'd thought he might never see them again. He'd gotten used to the ache, maybe, the way a poor miner kid gets used to the gnaw of hunger in his gut and the harsh bite of cold rock on his fingers and palms. Like a callus. After a few months with them, though, the calluses were gone. All those hard, safe places in his heart where he'd managed to hold onto them through years of labor and violence and shit-scared desperation, they'd gone soft.

He didn't realize he was sinking 'til his ass hit the gangway. Rail digging into his shoulder blades, boots nearly hanging off the other side, but the discomfort faded into all the rest of the noise.

"The masked guy told me they had her," he said, after a beat. Maybe two. He liked it better down there, he decided. No eyes to fail to meet, just boots and shins and bits of pipe. "They *showed* her to me." Tied up and blindfolded, bruises on her cheek and a still-bleeding split on her lip. . . . He felt sick. Nauseous and help-less, but he couldn't *be* helpless. Regan had practically raised him after their mama'd passed. And when he got back, she'd packed up her whole life and come out to Alpha Librae, just to look after her fool little brother. Lord knew he hadn't made it easy for her. Too many sharp edges that still needed filing down, and no matter how he'd tried to blunt them, he knew she'd still been nicked a time or two. But she'd stuck it out—stuck with *him*, and he'd be damned if he let her down now.

He raised his head. "They told me that if I wanted her back, I had to do something for them. They needed some intel off the security database, and the brig computers're the only access point for it."

"What kind of intel?" Saint asked. Smooth and steady, be-cause Saint was *always* smooth and steady, but Jal heard a little roughness underneath. Like he had to work for it.

Jal pulled the jump drive from his coat pocket but didn't of-fer it up to Saint or Nash. Figured the more distance they could keep from this, the better—at least until they'd made up their minds. "Ship specs for every vessel that's been in and out of the private docks this week," he said. "And flight plans for every one of them."

Didn't take them long. Smart bunch, the *Ambit* crew—a handful of seconds, and Nash swore like a firecracker. "In-cluding the Union transport for Drestyn," she said. "Well, that can't be good."

"Certainly not," Eoan agreed, but they sounded more in-trigued than worried. "Even still, that's an awful lot of trouble to go to for information. Kidnapping a well-respected member of the Guild's communications corps and coercing her brother—who has the very close attention of the Captains' Council, no less—to break into the brig and steal it. There have to be easier ways, especially if they had enough access to black out the security system."

"You think they were testing him?" Saint asked.

"The thought had crossed my mind," Eoan replied. "Which suggests the information isn't *all* they want." That Eoan didn't miss a trick.

Saint squatted in front of Jal, knees popping as they bent, but he didn't seem to notice.

"There's something else, isn't there?"

Wordlessly, Jal nodded.

"Well?" Nash squatted next to Saint, every speck of her a contrast to something else. Not a hair out of place, but not a stitch of clothing without a grease stain. Smelling of jasmine and reeking of motor oil. Radiating concern and impatience with such equal intensity, he almost couldn't stand to look at her too long. Like staring straight at a star. "What do they want you to do, miner boy? Can't be any worse than that dog and pony show you've been doing for the council. I mean, shit, you'd think *you* were the one getting court-martialed, the way they—"

"They want me to break out Drestyn."

Nash's eyebrows made a leap for her hairline, and for the next handful of seconds you could've heard a pin drop along that walkway. "Huh," she said finally. "I stand extremely fucking corrected."

Saint's answer was a lot shorter. "No."

"No?" Nash shot him a look like he'd sprouted a second head, and both heads were competing to see which was stupider. "What do you mean, *no*? It's not like it's *his* idea."

"That's what I'm worried about," Saint said. "For all we

know, it could be that bastard Drestyn's. We know at least two of his crew got clear of Lewaro, and those are just the followers we know about."

"*Followers.*" Nash snorted. "You make him sound like some kind of cult leader." She waved her hands. "Disciples of Drestyn."

Saint's brow furrowed. "You think now's a good time for jokes?"

"I think *always* is a good time for jokes," Nash replied. "Especially when they're vehicles for a good goddamn point. Drestyn's not some mastermind messiah; he's an agitator who's hella mad at the Powers That Be and willing to do something about it. He's not going around kidnapping people's sisters and terrifying small children."

"He nearly blew up a space station not half a year ago," Saint said.

"Me and my late plasma torch are aware of that, thanks." Her smile tightened at the corners, though. Anytime someone mentioned Lewaro or the Deadworld Code, she got this *look* on her face—grief, or something like it, and Jal doubted it had a damn thing to do with the plasma torch.

She didn't talk about Anke much these days. Her court-martial hearing had come and gone before Jal ever set foot on Alpha Librae, but to hear Saint tell it, Nash's testimony made the difference between a cell of her own in the brig downstairs and the work-release gig she'd gotten, helping a few other Guild coders take the Deadworld patch spiral-wide. Still, there was a hell of a lot of road between keeping someone out of jail and *forgiving them*. After what Anke'd done . . . well, Nash wasn't the type to get burned twice, but that didn't mean it didn't hurt like hell the first time.

Not that Nash'd ever admit it.

"I mean," she went on. "For all we know, it might not be about setting Drestyn free; it might be about getting him someplace more convenient to off him. The way the Trust and the Union went at it just to get dibs on the guy, you gotta think he's got some serious dirt on some serious people."

"Everything can't be a conspiracy, Nash," Saint said.

"You say *conspiracy*, I say *sketch-ass pattern of sketch-ass behavior*. Potato potahto."

"Either way." Eoan broke in the way one of Bitsie's school-teachers might break in when the kids stopped playing nice. "We need more information."

Jal'd been afraid they'd say that. "I don't have any." He sighed, scraping a hand through his hair again. Small wonder he had any hair *left*. "Just what I've told you."

"Have they been in touch since the first communication?" Eoan asked.

"Once or twice."

"Is it once or twice?"

He flinched. He'd forgotten how precise Eoan could be. Ex-acting. "Twice," he said. "Once when Drestyn's transfer was confirmed, and this morning they gave me the timing for the security blackout."

"And they've reached out to you through the same GLASS pad both times? Never your personal device."

A nod. "Audio only since the first time, though."

"And the first time, did you notice anything about the speaker?" Eoan asked.

"He was wearing a mask," Jal said. "Or, I think it was a *he*. I don't know; the voice was distorted. Big boulders-for-shoulders motherfucker, whoever they were."

"Any other defining features?"

"Almost a head taller than Regan?" he guessed. Which was saying something, because Regan was one of the tallest women he'd ever met. Ran in the family. "But no tattoos or augments or anything. Not that I could see, anyway. I, uh. I still have the GLASS, if that helps. I don't know anything about traces or triangulation or any of that shit." Regan would've. Comm gadgets were his sister's bread and butter, and she was a bona fide genius. Had this uncanny ability to *adapt*—picked up new skills like most people picked up bad habits, and held on to them just as hard. "But I thought it couldn't hurt."

"Good thought," Eoan said, and Jal relaxed by degrees. Eoan was good at that. *Reassuring*. Like they believed any problem could be solved with the right combination of facts and understanding, and they made you believe it, too. "We'll look into it, see if we can't find anything of use about our mysterious malefactors. Quietly, of course. I assume you don't want them to know you're talking to us?"

He winced. "To tell you the truth," he said, "I kind of think they're *counting* on it." He'd thought it through, and it was the only thing that made any sense. "I mean, they've got to know about me, right? If they set all this up, they've got to at least know a little—enough to know I got no ship, no guns, and no mind for the kind of tactics it'd take to break Drestyn out of a wet paper sack, much less a Union transport ship. They had to know I'd get all that from someplace, and who else was it gonna be?" Wasn't like he could hire a bunch of mercs on a ranger's back pay and Regan's engineer salary. "No," he said. "If these fuckers know anything about me, which I'm thinking they do, they've got to know you'd be my first call, but they didn't say shit about talking to you. Told me not to go to station security, and not to bring this to the Captains' Council, but they didn't even *mention* you. Maybe I'm just seeing shit that ain't there, but I could swear they *want* me to bring you in."

"You think they're trying to jam us up, too?" Nash didn't wait for an answer. Might not've even been a question. "Well, that's just peachy. But wait." She held up a hand. "If this little clandestine huddle-up wasn't about keeping the guys that took Regan in the dark, why're we down here?"

"Because they're not the only ones who might be watching,"

said Eoan, and not for the first time, Jal wondered if he'd have been better off just shutting up and letting them work it all out themself. They'd certainly caught on a hell of a lot quicker than him. He'd mulled all this over for *days* and still managed to muck it up. "You're worried what will happen if the Guild finds out we're playing a part in this."

Jal's wince deepened, but he nodded. "We're talking about jailbreaking the most wanted man in the O-Cyg spiral," he said, lifting a shoulder in a shrug. "This goes bad—hell, even if this goes *right*—anybody involved is liable to end up with their heads on a pike. Everybody'll want a piece. Trust. Union. And you *know* the Guild's not gonna want to stand in the way of that epic shitstorm, not for some gone-rogue ranger skirting his oath. Or for anyone they think's *helping* that ranger," he added, more pointedly. That part was important. That part *mattered*, because if they signed on to this, he needed them to do it with eyes wide open.

"That's why I wanted to keep my distance. I figure, even if you decide not to lend a hand, if anybody with the Guild sees me strolling onto the *Ambit* or sees that I commed any of you before this shit hits the fan, you're at least gonna have some eyes on you that you don't want. This way, if I did it right"— and that was a decent *if*; he'd never been the thinker of any operation—"there's nothing to tie you guys back to what I'm doing, 'cept our history and maybe Bitsie, but I couldn't think of a way around that." Didn't have anywhere else for her to go. Nowhere he'd have felt safe leaving her, if he had to go out and do this on his own. They didn't have other family, him and Regan; closest they came were the people on that crew.

Which made dragging them into this so much fucking *harder*.

"You could bow out here, is what I'm trying to say. I know I'm asking a lot. I might be asking too much . . . and if I am, I just wanted to try to make sure none of this would fall back on y'all. I don't have a choice here." One way or another, he'd get

Regan back. That didn't change whether the *Ambit* crew said yes or no. "But I just . . . I wanted to make sure that *you* did."

There. He'd said what he needed to say. Much as he wanted their help, much as he dreaded trying to do this on his own, this wasn't something he could pull them into without giving them a chance to consider the consequences. This was *worse* than desertion, and Eoan's crew acted like a band of renegades and all, but that Guild banner still meant something to them.

"Let me get this straight," Saint said, after a long stretch of seconds. "You put all this together, brought us all the way down here, just so that we could *turn you down?*"

That was exactly what he'd done, and he stood by it. For all he prayed they wouldn't, some part of him still thought . . . maybe it'd be better if they did. Safer, for them. "Seemed like the right thing to do."

Nash and Saint traded looks, then turned back to him with matching frowns. "Fuck that," they said, in near-perfect unison.

Solo, Nash added, "You took a twenty-five-story header to save my captain and my bonehead crewmate. You could ask me to rob a *bank*, and I'd be down before you even got to *please*."

"And hell," Saint said, "you know I'm in." He didn't seem to feel the need to elaborate any more than that.

"Then it's settled," said Eoan. "First things first, Jal, we'll need to go back to your cabin." They didn't call it *Regan's*. He had the strangest urge to correct them. "The GLASS pad may have something we can use, but if not, it would be worth seeing if they left anything else behind."

"I searched the place," Jal told them. "Top to bottom."

"I'm sure you did," Eoan replied. "But there's no harm letting us take a look. Nash, why don't you and Jal go by the cabin and see what you can find. Don't suppose you have one of your microdrones handy?"

"Always," said Nash. "Been itching to take one of the

prototypes for a test run." She pulled a thumbnail-sized white tab from her pocket. "Jal, meet Chiclet Junior. Looks like gum, but don't try to chew him. Microbattery's full of all sorts of things a growing miner boy doesn't need, though glowing radioactive green might be a good look for you. Also, it would hurt his feelings."

It was really happening, then. They'd really decided to help, and Jal could've choked on the potent mix of guilt and gratitude churning in his gut. "If you show me how to use it, maybe you could hang back, and I could—"

"You're not going by yourself, kid," Saint said firmly. "No sense keeping our distance, anyway. Anybody watching's gonna figure out we're helping you sooner or later, so we might as well get some use out of it. So you two go. I'll hang back."

"Expecting trouble?" Nash asked, but then she waved him off. "Nope, don't answer that. You're *always* expecting trouble."

"I'm usually right," Saint shot back.

"Sure, but you know it actually *can* be paranoia even when someone's out to get you, right? Broken clock, two times a day, et cetera et cetera."

Eoan cleared their throat—or did their best impression of it, which never sounded quite right, but got the point across. "For what it's worth, I don't anticipate Regan's kidnappers would make a move this early. They've chosen a very particular man for a very particular job, and I imagine they want *him* to be the one that finishes it. That should buy Jal a degree of security."

"Not liking the *should* there, Cap," Saint muttered.

"I know, dear, but I wouldn't say it if I didn't believe it. Nevertheless," they added, "it wouldn't hurt to keep a weather eye out. The timing of all of this is . . . deeply suspect. We're clearly dealing with people who have *some* level of access to Guild security systems. Security blackouts on command, knowledge of records systems and protocols. If they wanted Drestyn, one wonders why they didn't take him while he was on Alpha Librae."

"I figured they thought it'd be easier to get to him in transit," Jal said, but even as he said it, he knew he'd missed something. "What? Why're y'all looking at each other like that?"

"You didn't see the transport team," said Nash. "Nothing *easy* about Casale the Colossal. Nope, I'm betting they had a whole other reason for waiting. For my caps, it's got something to do with *who's* got him. You remember what Casale said at the hangar, Saint? They lose Drestyn, that's their asses."

"If that's it, then either they've got an axe to grind with the Union, or they want it to seem like *we* do." Saint sighed, shaking his head. "This shit's never clean, is it?"

It occurred to Jal then that he really had no idea exactly *what* he was dragging them into. And if he didn't, how the hell could he make sure *they* did? *What've you gone and done now, boy?* His shoulders bunched miserably. "Are y'all sure you really—"

"*Please.*" Saint cut him off, sounding almost pained. He covered it well when he stood, dusting off his jeans, but Jal'd gotten better at reading him over the last few months. Or maybe he'd just remembered how. "Don't ask us if we're sure about this, kid."

"He's right," said Eoan. "We appreciate the consideration, but it isn't necessary. You're part of our crew now, and I hope you know us well enough to understand what that means."

Sweeping to her feet with the grace of a sun-warmed cat, Nash stuck out a hand to him. "Means you're stuck with us, miner boy," she told him, and when he took her hand, she hauled him up far too easy for a frame as little as hers. "Congratu-fucking-lations."

. . .

After a quick detour to grab the bag he'd stashed behind some ductwork, Jal made the long trek to the residential sector with Nash. Back through the concourse, where the smell of growing things from the green space below mingled with every kind of foodstuff and the faint staleness of recycled air. So brightly lit, Jal's eyes ached even through his shaded specs. People like him weren't made to walk in places like that, and sometimes he swore those places went out of their way to remind him.

Nash, bless her, didn't try to strike up a conversation. She'd taken custody of the assholes' GLASS—calling them *kidnappers* just made his insides go cold, and he didn't have much else to go on, so . . . assholes—to disable it. Didn't seem to like the idea of it transmitting anything once they were out of the smoke-breakers' dead zone, so she'd opened up its insides and chattered back and forth with Eoan about backdoors and subroutines while she dodged passersby like it was her job. She'd grown up in space stations, weaving through the crowds from the time she could walk, and it showed. Wasn't so much like she moved out of folks' way as she just anticipated where they'd be and found a way not to be there when they passed, all without looking up from the wired guts of the GLASS.

The knot in his stomach coiled tighter as they stepped through the archway under a SECTOR C—RESIDENTIAL sign. There, the open walkways of the concourse gave way to a narrow hall with numbered doors stretching far ahead in a straight line, ending in another small green space with a commissary in the middle. It was all a prefab—one great big tube, more or less, built off-world in chunks and dropped into channels they'd dug in the ice. Five subsectors, thirty to forty cabins each, nothing but little door decorations and window appliques to tell them all apart.

Regan's window had drawings. Astronomically accurate constellations morphing into myths as they stretched across the glass, even a few basic physics problems in the corner worked out in chalk paint, where Bitsie would sit in the windowsill and do her homework. She wanted to be an astronomer now, and she took it damn seriously.

She had her mama's head, thank God. Her eyes, too, untouched by the rough-and-ready genetic modifications they foisted on the working class back on Brigham Four. Parents got credits from the mining company if they signed their unborn kids up for the *program*—tweaked genes and a guaranteed spot in the mines—and times were hard enough that a lot of folks took the company up on it. Not Regan, though. She'd always wanted something better for her little girl, and she'd worked her ass off to see that she got it.

"Here." His voice cracked like dry skin as he touched his hand to the entry pad, and for one, five, ten seconds after the door slid open, he couldn't bring himself to step through it.

Whether she noticed him hesitating, or she was just eager to try out her new toy, Nash eventually led the way in. "You can stay outside if you want," she called back over her shoulder, so he reckoned it was probably the former. "Me and Junior have this handled."

But Jal had already stepped over the threshold. Wasn't a big cabin—just a common room through the door, with a window nook and a sofa piled with some pillows and blankets. It was open to the kitchen in the back, with three doors branching off to a shared bathroom and two bedrooms. Layout was probably better suited to a couple and their kid, or a pair of singles splitting the space, but it suited them fine.

Or, it had.

Nash, over by the sofa, lifted the edge of a tangled blanket with two fingers. There was a pillow underneath it, and a cup for water overturned on the end table beside it. "You sleep here?" she asked. "On the couch?"

"Bitsie's almost thirteen," he said, by way of explanation. "Gettin' too old to be sharing with her mama, and she sure as shit shouldn't be sharing with me." He could be okay when he was awake. He could be good. Right. *Steady.* But nights hadn't been kind to him in a long, long time, and hard as he'd tried, he still hadn't found a way to fix that. "Couch is better."

Nash shot him a look over her shoulder like she'd heard more than what he said. She didn't call him on it, though; she went straight to business, same as usual. Pulled out that little white tablet of not-gum, gave it a pinch, and set it down on the table just in time for eight spindly, wirelike legs to stretch out from the sides of it.

"Shouldn't take long," she said as the tiny robot went skittering off the table and disappeared into the mess of overturned shelves and scattered clothes. "Junior just needs to do a sweep, take some scans, and then we can head back to the ship. If there's anything you want to grab while we're here. . . ."

For a second, he wasn't sure if she'd trailed off, or if he'd just lost her voice to the blood pulsing behind his eardrums. *Thoom, thoom, thoom,* quicker and quicker as he scanned the wreckage of their once-neat cabin. Regan ran a tight ship. Shoes in the crate by the door, coats on the hanger, dishes in the washer. Only thing she ever left out was her headphones. Clunky, retro pieces of work, all taped up and plastered with faded stickers. He looked at the rug by the couch, and he saw nights on the floor with Regan in those headphones, poring over archived comm feeds while Bitsie listened to music and worked through the day's homework in her window nook. Looked at the kitchen with the handful of broken dishes, and felt the playful *thwap* of a towel as Regan banished him and Bitsie for joking about her cooking. Everywhere he looked, he had two pictures in his head: the life they'd been living, and the wreckage, and the push-pull of it seemed to suck all the air out of the room. He should've been there. Regan had fought, but she'd been fighting alone, and she shouldn't have been, and maybe if he'd been there, things would've been—

"Sit," Nash said, and nearly startled him out of his skin in the process. When he didn't do as she said, she gave him a nudge 'til he did. Didn't take much; felt like a feather could've bowled him over just then. He landed lopsided on the edge of the couch, and the hand moved from his shoulder to his neck. Cool fingers pressed against the bare skin above his collar. "Head down. Deep breaths. He's fine, Saint," she said, quieter. Over the comms, probably. The next time she spoke, it was louder again. Firmer. "You're fine. Bitsie's fine. Regan's going to be fine."

It didn't have any of the softness you'd expect from reassurance, but then, *reassuring* was never really Nash's thing. She favored facts to feelings. When she said it'd be fine, it wasn't because she wanted him to believe it; it was because she already did.

That, more than anything, helped him catch his breath again.

When he finally raised his eyes to her, she was looking at him with a half smile and an arched eyebrow. "You, my dude, need a *nap*," she said. "And a meal." Her nose wrinkled. "And a shower. No offense."

And damned if Jal didn't smile a little, despite himself. "Doctor's orders?" he asked.

"We'll go with *friendly advice*," she replied, but she winked as the tiny white tablet skittered up her leg and leapt onto her hand. Kinda creepy, Chiclet Junior. *Cool*, but creepy. "That's my shit done. If yours is, too, then I say it's time to am-scray." She made for the door but didn't go any farther than the threshold. Just stood there, uncharacteristically patient, and waited as he took one last look at Regan's place. At the ruins of what was supposed to be his grand new life.

Eyes on the next foothold, he told himself. Best bit of advice his mama ever gave him. *The rest is just noise*. And finally, he managed to turn away from it all.

"Come on, miner boy," Nash said, soft but sure. "Let's get home."

CHAPTER THREE

EOAN

Eoan hadn't spent much time around adolescents. Not by design, mind. It was just that, between their early years charting the spiral with their makers, and their last few decades as a captain of the Guild, they hadn't exactly favored *child-friendly* environments. As a result, twelve-year-old Briley Red was something of a novelty.

Naturally, they were fascinated with her. Charmed, even. Briley—*Bitsie*, as she'd introduced herself in the cargo hold— puttered around the galley like she'd been there a hundred times, utterly unselfconscious and independent as she poked through the cabinets and shelves until she found what she was looking for. Mug. Tea. Sugar. Industrious little thing, humming along to the music Eoan played over the speakers as she waited for the tea to steep. Eoan couldn't decide if Nash would be delighted or dismayed that someone else had taken an interest in her tea collection, but they couldn't wait to find out.

It was only once Bitsie seemed satisfied with her steaming concoction that she settled into one of the chairs at the galley table—Saint's, with a patch of blue duct tape on the seat to hide the bloodstain he hadn't managed to scrub out—and turned her green-eyed gaze toward the nearest camera lens. Eoan hastily added *observant* to their running list.

"I told Uncle Jal that you'd help us," she said, matter-of-fact and without prompting. She didn't need to be invited to a conversation; she'd make one herself. She reminded them of Jal in a lot of ways, with her waves of straw-blonde hair and high, freckled cheeks. Paler than he was, wearing far fewer marks of a life hard-lived, but she had the same light about her that he did. A honeyed warmth, sweet and golden. Not innocence, not quite. *Resilience*—that was better. She and Jal had seen their share of heartache, but they hadn't let it darken them. That stubborn brightness . . . Eoan had always admired it, from the very first day Jal had wandered onto their ship.

And yet, in some ways, it also made them terribly sad.

Tucking one of her sneakered feet under herself, Bitsie went on, "He wasn't sure you would. I mean, he was pretty sure you'd at least agree to watch me while he was, you know." She shrugged one shoulder, and although she didn't seem to have as much of her uncle's drawl, she'd definitely borrowed a few of his mannerisms. And apparently his inability to find trousers that fit. The cuffs of her overalls were a good decimeter too short, showing off her mismatched socks and neatly tied sneakers. "But that's not the kind of help we need."

"No," they said, "I imagine it isn't." Though they'd already split their attention between minding Bitsie—not that she needed any; she seemed to have quite the handle on things— and reviewing all the existing security footage from the time of Regan's abduction that they could get their proverbial hands on, they decided to spare a bit more for their company. They projected into the kitchen, their self-selected figure of particles and light, with their colorful clothes and clever hands, their kind eyes and their easy smiles. Pieces of their makers and all the ones who'd shaped Eoan along the way, with a dash of something uniquely *Eoan*.

Bitsie had a smile of her own as Eoan settled their projection into the chair across from her. "Uncle Jal said you could do that," she told them, shades of fascination in her eyes that didn't quite make it into her voice. Maybe a *little* self-conscious. "It's light, right? A projection onto charged particles."

"It is indeed," said Eoan, intrigued. "Jal mentioned you'd taken a *shine* to optical physics." Pun intended.

Bitsie shrugged, but her smile twitched wider. "Pretty much everything in the universe runs on light, in one way or another. Seemed like a good place to start." She took a sip of her tea, both hands curled around the oversized mug. Nash didn't believe in beverage containers under half a liter. "Uncle Jal said that you were good with computers, too," Bitsie continued. "And with people. And with *spectacularly shit situations*." She ticked each item off on her fingers one by one.

Eoan laughed. "I suppose I am."

"That's good," said Bitsie. "Because this is a spectacularly shit situation."

Eoan had to agree. "We'll sort it," they told Bitsie. "Jal did the right thing, coming to us."

"I know." Bitsie said it with such certainty—in her voice, in her eyes, in her small, squared shoulders. The only sign of doubt was in her hands, trembling around the mug.

An old, familiar ache fell over them. The ache to reach out, to touch, to settle their own hands over Bitsie's until the trembling stopped. Centuries had given them ample time to make peace with what they were, to embrace the limits and the gifts that came with it.

But sometimes, to borrow from the poets, it fucking sucked.

"I think he knows it, too," Bitsie went on, unaware. "He didn't *want* to know it. I think he'd have been happier doing it by himself. Or, not happier, but . . ." She faltered, frowning, searching for the word and coming up short.

"Less guilty?" Eoan offered.

Bitsie gave another nod. "That," she said. "He doesn't like to make things hard for people. People he likes, anyway. And he likes you guys."

"We're quite fond of him, too."

"And that's why you'll help him," Bitsie said. "Not because

you owe him or anything—which you kind of do," she added, cheekily, in a stage whisper. The blunt, unapologetic honesty, she must've taken after her mother. Nash would love it. "He doesn't think you do, mind you, but he thinks *you* think you do, so he thinks you'll think you have to help him because you think you owe him, which you do, but he doesn't think you do. Does that make sense?" She cocked her head, hands finally coming back to rest on her mug.

Those hands talked as much as her mouth, and her face was so animated and unguarded that for a moment Eoan's focus had shifted almost entirely to watching her. Security footage was interesting and important, but Bitsie was *new*. Open and bold, as if she either hadn't yet learned to hide her heart, or had simply, defiantly, chosen not to. All of Jal's earnestness, none of his caution. What would it be like, Eoan wondered, for her to live in a universe that *fostered* that sort of fearlessness, rather than challenged it.

A ping of awareness at the loading doors drew them out of their thoughts. That would be the others, then, returned to port and filing back aboard. Only then did Eoan remember they'd been asked a question.

"It does," they said. "And you're right. We do owe him, but that's not why we want to help him. We want to help him because we care very much about him. And we care very much about the people he cares very much about. That would be you." They winked, and Bitsie winked back.

"He'll figure it out," Bitsie said. "It just takes him a little while, sometimes, is all. Mom says he's still got a lot of figuring out to do."

Eoan imagined that was probably true. Two years getting passed around like a piece of equipment from Guild crew to Guild crew, then fired upon by his own people and left to the mercy of one of the crueler bands of scavengers. Three years a captive, several months on the run with a desertion charge at his back, capped off in a leap of faith that had saved Eoan's crew but nearly killed him in the bargain.

One would expect an adjustment period.

"Well, between you and me?" Eoan's projection leaned forward, elbows on their crossed knees. "We're quite good at figuring things out around here, too."

Bitsie grinned. "Damn right," she said. "Because you're a badass crew of badasses."

"*Language*, Bitsie." A sigh came from the galley door, fond and exasperated. And *there* was the patented Jalsen drawl they'd come to know and love. He had Saint and Nash in tow, but for a moment Bitsie only seemed to see him. Her grin spread, dimpling her cheeks as she hopped up and bounded across the galley to throw her arms around her uncle's waist.

"And here I thought you might've gotten lost," she said, and it struck a strange contrast: the teasing and the embrace. She hugged him like she hadn't seen him in *days*, and he did the same; but she still rolled her eyes as she wriggled loose. "*Language*, though? Seriously?"

"Seriously," Jal told the top of Bitsie's head—tall as she was for her age, she still didn't reach his shoulders—before she wriggled free and went to reclaim her tea and her seat. "Your mama catches you swearing a blue streak, I'm the one she's gonna blame."

"She swears more than you do," Bitsie replied reasonably.

He snorted. "Yeah, well, I'll let you be the one to tell her that." Then, quieter, as he joined her by the table, "Just as soon as we find her."

"And on that note," Eoan began, "I'm sorry to say there wasn't anything of use on the security footage. Not all that surprising, I suppose; whoever they are, if they could black out surveillance in the secured sector, I don't imagine the residential areas would be much trouble. The station's really going to need to evaluate its security protocols after this."

"We'll add that to the to-do list," Saint muttered wryly. In his spot at the sink, sleeves rolled to his elbows, he collected the small amassment of mugs—mostly Nash's—and set them in the cleaner. Something to do, more than a genuine need to tidy up. But the trouble with an automated dish sanitizer, while *excellent* for reducing shipboard water consumption, was that it made for a fairly brief distraction. "So, what *do* we have?" he asked.

"We have Chiclet Junior," Nash said.

Saint made a disgruntled noise. "God, are we really calling it that?"

"Tell you what: you build the tech, you can pick the name." She was in the middle of making herself a cup of tea, because habits were habits. When she needed to think, she drank tea. When she needed to sleep, she drank tea. When she needed to busy her hands and didn't have a broken bit or bob at the ready, well, she tended to prefer a mug of tea to Saint's vaguely obsessive cleaning. She stopped, though, long enough to pull the microdrone from her pocket, give it a squeeze, and drop it on the counter.

As the bot's legs unfurled from its little enamel body, Eoan could also feel it stretching out in other ways. The transmitter that stayed dormant when it hibernated awoke in a series of hums and pips across one of the ship's many receivers. A data stream, ready to download.

"Incoming, Cap," said Nash as she went to fill the kettle, but she paused. It seemed Bitsie had filled it enough for two; maybe a habit of her own. Given Jal preferred coffee to tea, they could only assume that second serve would've belonged to Regan.

After a moment's hesitation, Nash gave Bitsie a nod and poured the rest into her mug. She didn't return Bitsie's small, uneasy smile; it would've been asking a lot, considering the last person Nash had shared tea with had nearly killed their whole crew. *Anke.* She hadn't set foot on their ship since Noether, but traces of her still lingered.

When Bitsie looked away, though, Nash *did* nudge an old

crate over in front of the tea cabinet. NASH'S STASH. A make-shift step stool. An unspoken invitation.

Baby steps, Eoan thought, as they plucked Chiclet Junior's data drop from the receiver and set to unwrapping it. Wouldn't take long. Chiclet had a curious language, crafted to feed into Nash's sensory biomechanics like an extension of her aware-ness. What it knew, she knew; unfortunately, because Eoan op-erated on a slightly different programming language, it took a bit of translating.

Once they had the data, though, they knew they were onto something.

"Good news," they said. "Our Lilliputian supersleuth might've found us a lead."

"Your lily-what?" Jal frowned.

"They mean Chiclet Junior," Nash told him, and his mouth formed a silent *ah* as he nodded for them to go on.

They hesitated. "Would you prefer we did this somewhere more private?" they asked, projection giving a meaningful nod toward Bitsie. "Not sure she'll want to hear this." Or, rather, that *Jal* would want her to. Although Bitsie was certainly made of tougher stuff than the average twelve-year-old, Eoan's gauge for *too much for her* still needed calibrating.

Bitsie turned back to her uncle. "I need to hear it," she told him, not a whiff of pleading or petulance in her voice. It was simply the reasonable thing to do, and she said it as such. "I'm the only one who was there when it happened. Maybe I can help."

Eoan didn't need high-resolution cameras to catch Jal's wince. *Bitsie* probably could've caught it, the clever dear, if she hadn't already turned back around to the rest of the group.

"I'll be okay," she insisted, brows knitting and jaw squaring. *Trust me,* she said with every inch of her frame. *Let me do this.* She didn't *want* to help them; she *needed* to. Or, failing that, she at least needed to know what was going on.

Eoan could certainly respect that.

Jal, though, he looked to Saint. Less sure of things than his niece, but Eoan could sympathize with that as well. The more you knew, the harder it became to believe you knew anything at all, and Jal knew things nobody should ever have to learn. He'd missed things, too—a quarter of Bitsie's childhood, not to put too fine a point on it. *Mom says he's still got a lot of figuring out to do.*

"It's your call, kid," Saint said to him, hands spread. "But if I know her, she'll find a way to hear it anyway. At least like this nobody says anything they don't want falling on little ears."

"Hey, don't look at me," Nash said, because Saint definitely had, and he'd definitely done it with intent. "I'm appropriate for all ages. It's you we ought to be worried about, McBlastin—" She caught herself as Saint arched an eyebrow, as if to say *case in point*. "Stuff. McBlastinstuff. McBlastinthings?" She made a face. "No, fuck it, I can't do it. McBlastinshit, over here—he's the real menace. Shooting poor, starving uncles in the back."

"It was a riot round," Saint grunted.

"Still hurts," Nash said.

"It does," Jal offered. "Can confirm."

Saint narrowed his eyes. "Judas."

As Jal gave Saint an apologetic shrug, Bitsie looked between the three of them. "Wait, *you* shot Uncle Jal, too?" she said to Saint. Then, to Jal, "How many people have shot you, exactly? Just, like, ballpark it. Have you thought about wearing a *vest*?"

"Saint's was an accident," Jal told her graciously. He pretended not to have heard the rest. "He didn't know it was—uh. Well. He *did* know it was me, but he didn't really have all the . . . facts, I guess? Actually, probably saved my life, in a roundabout way. Very roundabout."

Saint shot a smug look back at Nash, who shot a rude gesture back at him.

"You guys are weird," Bitsie decided aloud, but she smiled as she said it. They all did, a little; in spite of the circumstances, they seemed grateful to all be together again. A frail silver lining on one mightily dark cloud, but when in darkness, one held fast to whatever light one could find.

Eoan hated to cut the moment short, but time and choices were two things in very short supply.

"There were traces of blood in your cabin," they said, and like dominoes, all of those small smiles fell, one after the other.

"Regan's?" Jal paled a shade or two between starting the question and finishing it. "Looked like they'd roughed her up a little, so." He couldn't seem to finish the thought. His jaw worked, but no sounds came out.

Eoan's projection nodded. "Some of it was, but not all. In the kitchen—not much, but a few droplets low on the wall. Might have been more, but there were traces of cleaners on the floor and counters."

Bitsie made a face. "They totaled the place, but they stopped to scrub the tile?"

"Can't get DNA from an overturned couch, mini-miner," said Nash. She still didn't seem to know quite what to make of Bitsie. It reminded Eoan of Bodie, the ship's mouser cat, that time Nash had found a half-starved kitten in one of her scrapyards and brought it aboard. *What are you, and what am I supposed to do with you?* They'd gotten the kitten a new home, eventually, but it had been an entertaining few weeks aboard the *Ambit*. "They're probably just worried about shit that could be traced back to them. Tried to clean up, missed a few spots. Junior found them."

"She must've hit them," Bitsie said. "We were in my room putting up my new GLASS screen when we heard the door open. She told me to hide—hide where nobody could find me, and not to come out for anything or anyone but her or Uncle Jal, and then she—" There it was, the beginning of a crack. It started in her voice, but it rippled through her entire frame.

Jal must've heard it. He settled a hand on her shoulder reassuringly and offered up a smile. Earnest, but stilted. It was like he wanted to do more, to offer more, but didn't know if he should. Eoan imagined comforting the child he was used to seeing was rather different from comforting the preteen she'd become. Probably still learning his way around it.

It seemed to do the trick, though. Bitsie took a breath, straightened her shoulders, and carried on. "Soon as I was in the vent, she took the hammer and went out to see who it was. I think she was afraid," Bitsie told them. "Afraid if we both hid and called for help, they'd keep looking until they found us."

"So she gave herself up," Saint said, a grim turn to his lips. "Goddamn Reds."

"What else was she supposed to do?" Jal bit out. "You don't know her like I do, old man. No way she could've just sat back and let them come for Bitsie. No way."

"That's not—" Saint sighed and scrubbed a hand over his face. "I'm not saying she did the wrong thing, or that I'd have done it any different. I'm just saying you and your sister have a real knack for throwing yourselves in harm's way for other people. It's noble," he said, and he clearly meant it, no qualifiers. Not *noble, but foolish*. Not *noble, but naïve*. It was noble, full stop. The rest was just a consequence, breathed quietly into the stillness of the galley. "It's just . . . it's liable to get one of you killed one day." Spoken with the bone-deep dread of a man who'd nearly seen it happen.

"She made good use of that hammer, at any rate," Eoan said, hoping to steer things somewhere a little less *grim*. "Gave us a solid lead."

"You got a name to go with that mystery blood sample?" Nash guessed.

"Martyn Gethin." Eoan expected a reaction, and they got one. Got *several*, varying from face to face around the galley. Satisfaction from Nash, because Chiclet Junior had done its job. Confusion from Bitsie, recognition from Saint, and from Jal . . . they didn't quite understand that look. The part of his lips around a breath, the furrow of his brows.

"Gethin," Saint said. "I know that name. Why do I know that name?"

"I've heard it, too," said Bitsie. "Mom was always talking about *that fuckhead Gethin*."

Eoan half-expected Jal to scold her again, but a silence had fallen over him, weighty and taut. He'd pulled his hand from Bitsie's shoulder, as if he didn't trust his own grip, coiling it to a fist at his side instead. "*Captain* Gethin." It pressed through his teeth in a snarl, quiet and surprisingly vicious. "He made us call him *Captain*."

Comprehension darkened Saint's face before Jal even finished. "That botched rescue run," he said. "The one that got you stuck with the scavs—he was your XO, wasn't he? *That's* where I heard the name."

"Acting captain, technically," said Eoan when it became clear Jal either wouldn't or *couldn't* answer him. "But yes. Gethin served under the banner for two decades before he resigned to the private sector. That was nearly three years ago, but his DNA is still in the Guild registry."

"I already know the answer to this, but just for shits and giggs, I'm gonna ask it anyway." Nash hopped up on the counter, somehow managing not to spill a drop of her tea as she folded her feet up under her and breathed in the steam. "What are the odds this is all some really unfortunate coincidence?"

"Not zero," Eoan allowed, but only because they couldn't prove a negative. "But not high. Although, if it *is* connected, I couldn't tell you how. Whether Gethin simply knew Jal and thought he would be a good target, or whether there's more to the story . . . I wouldn't even feel comfortable making a guess, based on the information we have." Or, rather, the information they *didn't* have. "But it does explain a few things. Mercenary or not, two decades under the banner means he would have some familiarity with Guild security protocols."

"Love it when the bad guy knows all our tricks," Nash muttered, then tipped her head and took a sip of tea. "Well. Not *all* of them." Another sip, and not for the first time, Bitsie mirrored her. She'd paid attention to the full conversation, but like the kitten with Bodie, she seemed especially interested in Nash. Novelty, perhaps; or simply respect for the one person in the room who didn't censor herself, whether Bitsie was there or not.

Saint crossed his arms, and if anything, the tension in his shoulders had *increased* since they came aboard. "Guessing you already pulled his—"

"Guild record? Of course, dear." They projected his dossier in the air above the table, with his headshot alongside it. Short red hair, bright blue eyes. White, but not pale, with a high brow and unusually deep nasolabial folds that lent a harshness to an otherwise genial face. "Quite the rising star, our Gethin. Joined at twenty-two, served under no less than *three* past and present members of the Captains' Council, including your new best friend, Captain Raimes."

"No wonder he left the Guild," Nash muttered. "Also, great to see the *blue-ribbon ranger* to *morally bankrupt mercenary* pipeline is still going strong. After that Riesen guy whiffed on the Deadworld Code coverup, I was starting to think we actually ran a pretty tight ship." Saint turned a hard stare her way, but Nash had what Eoan liked to call a *natural immunity* to Saint's irritation. It rolled off her like water off a duck, and sometimes, they thought she enjoyed it just as much. "I'm just saying, how many bad apples do we gotta bite into before we start looking at the whole damn tree."

"It's a fair question," Eoan said before Saint could retort. It would tailspin into a full-blown argument if they let it; this wouldn't have been the first time. These past few months, Nash had grown less and less enamored with the Guild's role in the

universe, and Saint had cleaved harder and harder to it. It made
for some understandable tension when the topic came up, but
now was not the time for friction. Now was the time for finding Regan Red, engineering genius and family keystone, before
something happened that couldn't be set right. "But the important thing is, we have a name. Whatever Gethin's relationship
to this, and whatever his reasons for involving Jal, knowing his
name gives us the opportunity to make the first move."

"Sorry, I'm not following," said Jal. He'd picked up a bit of
company at the table. Bodie didn't tend to favor strangers, but
he'd taken a shine to Jal. Nash had, only half-jokingly, suggested it was because Bodie was *more of a dog person*. Even
tense as things were, when Bodie hopped onto the table and
batted at his arm, Jal gave in and scritched his head.

According to their sensors, Jal's too-high heartrate slowed as
Bodie's pleased purrs rumbled through the galley. Only a little,
but just now every little bit helped.

Jal continued. "How's knowing Gethin's name gonna help
us get Drestyn away from a Union escort?"

"It's not," they replied. "But it may help us get *Regan* away
from *him*."

Understanding settled in an uneasy shroud over Jal's face.
He understood; he just didn't like it. "You want to go straight
at them, instead of going for Drestyn."

"I do," they said. "Surely you'd considered it."

"I have. Didn't much like the odds."

"Because you didn't know who you were dealing with?"
Eoan asked.

"Because I had an inkling that, whoever they were, they
might take it kind of personal—going behind their back
like that. And now I know it's Gethin, I know for a *fact* he
would. Man played at a level head, but he never met a grudge
he couldn't hold. Shit, he sent Fenton out to cover me at that

scav site just because the kid spilled coffee on his boots. Fenton hadn't ever done an exfil before, but I think Gethin knew that op was going sideways. Wanted to teach him a lesson."

"You think this is personal," Eoan observed. "I'm not sure that's true. On Gethin's part," they added quickly. Nothing *impersonal* about the abduction of a loved one, but that was, at least for the moment, rather beside the point. "I understand your concerns. You're worried about what they'll do if they find out you've veered off course." They didn't feel the need to go into detail, not with Bitsie there. Even Eoan knew that was one of those things a daughter simply didn't need to hear about her mother. *You think they'll kill her the second you step out of line.* They could hear it in the renewed quickening of Jal's pulse in their sensors, could see it in the pallor of his skin. Even Bodie couldn't soothe stress like *that*. "I wouldn't be suggesting this if I thought they'd do anything drastic."

"Define *drastic*," said Nash.

Saint nodded toward Bitsie. "Think it's best they don't."

Nash's gaze followed the gesture, then she drained half her tea and didn't suggest it again.

"I'm not saying there's no risk," Eoan continued. "But there's risk in keeping to the script, as well." Odds were, even if they managed to get Drestyn and make the trade, things wouldn't go quite the way Gethin promised. More likely, as soon as Gethin and his ilk had Drestyn, they'd kill Regan, Jal, and anyone else they considered a loose end. So, by Eoan's reckoning, Regan was in more danger if they actually *made* the trade. "You know that, don't you?"

A pause, heavy and strained, and then Jal sighed. "Damned if we do, damned if we don't," he said.

"I'm sure that's what they want you to think: no leverage, no choice but to do what you're told. It's precisely the position you're meant to be in. But you're *not*," they told him. "Remember what

I said earlier—they want *you* to be the one who gets Drestyn. That doesn't just buy you some security; it buys Regan some as well. Which I understand isn't as reassuring as we'd all like, but *some* is better than *none*, which is what you'll both have the moment they get possession of Drestyn. That's assuming we can even deliver Drestyn in the first place."

Saint nodded his agreement. "Union pulled out the big guns for his transport."

"*Literally,*" Nash said, flexing one of her arms and cringing. Apparently Casale had made an impression.

"And you can bet they're not taking any chances getting Drestyn back to their headquarters," Saint said. "It'll be secure Union hubs and high-visibility transport routes from here to home free. Sorry, kid, but I'm with Cap on this one. Our odds of infiltrating a camp of mercenaries are a lot better than our odds of prying Drestyn away from the Union. And if we make a play for Drestyn and it goes south? Say you get caught." *Or worse,* said the tightness at the corners of his mouth, but the words didn't make it past the cage of his teeth. "If you can't do the job, then Regan's not leverage anymore."

Nash's fingers drummed a restless tattoo on the side of her mug. "And if she's not leverage, then she's not useful. I'd say that's about the worst place she could be."

"Don't go sugarcoating it," Jal muttered.

"You want sugarcoating, you're on the wrong ship, miner boy. You want help from people who know what they're do-ing? Then"—Nash waved a hand broadly around the galley—"welcome aboard."

"It's the right move, kid," Saint pressed evenly. "We're walk-ing into a minefield, and I know you don't want to step wrong, but there's a lot of ways this could blow up even if you walk the path they've laid out for you. I mean, hell. Best case scenario, you and Gethin both hold up your ends of the deal—that's still you in front of the court-martial again, and they're not real keen on repeat customers. Devil made you do it, sure, but I'm still not optimistic you get off scot-free."

Jal's shoulders shrank by the word. "Neither do you," he said, quietly.

"You know that's not why we're saying this," Saint replied.

"I know."

"It's you we're worried about. You and your sister."

"I *know*," Jal repeated, but there was no heat in it. No bite. He just sounded exhausted—a running-on-fumes, at-the-end-of-my-rope kind of exhaustion that made Eoan think, if it weren't for his sister and his niece, he'd have thrown up his hands and said to hell with it. To hell with trying, to hell with fighting. Even for someone like Jal, it was hard to keep going when the universe kept finding ways to knock you down.

There he was, though, standing tall as he was able. He raised his shoulders, lifted his head, rallied. "Say we try it your way," he said. "What's that look like? Where would we start?"

Under different circumstances, they might've smiled. He'd made up his mind to trust Eoan, and that was no small thing. It was the same with Saint, with Nash—each time one of those precious, guarded creatures put their faith in Eoan, it was a *wonder*. And each time, Eoan resolved all the harder not to let them down.

"I already started, dear," they replied. "Strange, isn't it, the way the world works sometimes? I know none of us were particularly impressed with the Captains' Council's efforts to track down your other crewmates from your last mission with the Guild. Your last *official* mission," they amended. Nobody was quite sure how to characterize the *Ambit* crew's involvement in the Deadworld Code incident, but Eoan liked to think it counted. That way, even if Jal did decide to resign once his medical hold was lifted, he could end his career on a high note.

"We all saw the video. Fenton might have confessed to everything, but we all agree he wasn't acting alone."

Saint huffed an agreement. "That little shithead didn't have the good sense not to shoot his own man; he couldn't have had the brains to cover it up after. He had somebody in his ear telling him what to do." His lips thinned. "For all we know, it could've been Gethin."

"Or one of the other dozen crew members and superior officers who had access to that comm channel," Eoan added. So many of them had left the Guild within a year of the mission, and of those, none had answered any of the summons from the council. "Regardless, since the Captains' Council has been thus far disinclined to pursue the matter, I started my own . . . *unofficial* investigation. As you can see, Gethin's record is heavily redacted, but rumors point to a base of operations near one of the older mining colonies, Lummis. Nothing concrete, but a man like Gethin does leave an impression, and a number of odd shipments have passed through the Lummis port that would seem to corroborate the rumors."

"*Odd* how?" Saint asked.

"Full of Guild-issue equipment, for the most part," Eoan replied. "The sort one could only come by with a knowledge of Guild supply routes."

"So, he's a kidnapper *and* a smuggler," Bitsie muttered, swirling the dregs of her tea with a wrinkled nose. "Bet he's a real hit at parties."

"He's certainly industrious," said Eoan. "Of course, we couldn't do anything with that information while we were still on prisoner detail. The Guild takes a fairly harsh stance on rangers who abandon their posts."

"Yeah, so I've heard," Jal muttered wryly. The *deserter* brand might've been lifted from his record, but some things you never stopped carrying with you.

"So, we made plans," they continued. "Once we'd washed

our hands of Drestyn, we had a mind to join the search for his missing crewmates. If we ran into a few more *persons of interest* along the way, then all the better."

Jal looked half-stunned, mouth gone slightly slack. "You were gonna go look for them? Gethin and the others . . . even after the council closed the books?"

"Of course, dear," they said, smiling. "I told you: you're one of ours now. You deserve proper justice, and if nobody else will give it to you, then it would be our genuine pleasure."

Nash jabbed a thumb at Saint. "Especially his."

Saint shrugged and didn't deny it, just filled the reservoir of the coffee machine and set it to brew. Maybe he didn't care much about justice; maybe he wanted something *simpler*—a chance to look into the eyes of someone who'd done something terrible to someone he loved, and do something terrible back. Either way, they hoped he'd get his wish. He had some wounds of his own he'd been carrying, and it was time to let them heal.

"We'll set a course for Lummis," they said resolutely. "We'll make sure we're not followed. Nash and I can spoof the broadcast signal on the GLASS pad they left you with, so Gethin won't know where we are."

"Won't know we're coming for him." Nash had already set down her mug, lukewarm tea abandoned in favor of a new task to set her fingers to, and the GLASS pad from her bag appeared in its place. She'd already disabled it on the way to the Reds' cabin; now she just had to re-enable the right things in the right ways. "We love a good surprise."

"Should buy us some time to narrow down Gethin's location, at least," Saint said. "Cap, can you get me everything we've got on Lummis? Maps, scans, names of anyone else we might be running into." Which explained the coffee. He had work of his own to do. "Last I heard, that place was crawling with mercs and scavs."

"Your one-stop shop for all things sketch and shady," Nash

muttered around the multi-tool, fingers occupied with pulling the casing off the base of the GLASS. Evidently putting the tool on the *table* instead of in her mouth was simply too inefficient. "Sounds like fun."

"Sounds like hunting for a needle in a stack of needles," Bitsie said, not especially critically. She wasn't poking holes in the plan, just trying to point out the ones she saw. Trying to help—and, on some level, to *show* them she could help.

Nash grinned around her multi-tool. "Then it's a good thing we've got a knack for finding needles, huh?" Eoan supposed if anyone would recognize a little girl trying to bear up against a frightening world, Nash would. She spat out her multi-tool and leaned forward, elbows on her knees. "Don't worry, mini-miner," she said. "This is what we do. Finding bad guys' bolt-holes, saving the day? That's our shit. Right up our alley. The *Ambit* special."

"Pretty sure that's sleep deprivation," Jal muttered.

Saint, in the middle of pouring himself a massive mug of coffee, snorted. "He's not wrong."

"He's not wrong," Nash agreed. "But don't let that detract from anything I just said. It's all part of the process. If anybody can find this guy, we can. And *don't*," she tacked on before *either* Red could answer, "go asking what happens if we can't. We don't do that shit around here. Something needs doing, we get it done."

Mercifully, she got no arguments. Whether it was because Jal and Bitsie believed her, or because they just didn't have it in them to doubt, Eoan couldn't have said. But they *hoped* it was the former, especially for Jal. They hoped, after all they'd been through together, that he knew what they were capable of. That he knew they wouldn't rest until they had his family back together again, because if the *Ambit* crew valued anything in the universe, it was *family,* born or made or cobbled together like the bits of a broken engine that still wanted to fly.

"All right," Jal said at last. "Then let's get it done."

CHAPTER FOUR

NASH

The flight from Alpha Librae to Lummis took twelve hours, and Nash spent the first half dozen of them down in the *Ambit*'s engine room. *Nash's* engine room, really, for all anybody else stopped in. She'd staked her claim in coffee tin lights and a hammock piled high with pillows and blankets; in every shade, species, and size of crocheted creature and a scattering of gadgets with all their little solder-and-silica guts exposed, caught in every stage of broken and mended and all the interesting bits in between.

The gadgets had to wait, though. Their time Drestyn-sitting on Alpha Librae had been the longest they'd stayed in one place for as long as Nash had been aboard, so like any good mechanic with too much time on her hands—and a half-decent scrap shop and no real interest in being around *people*—she'd fiddled. Fiddled with propulsion, fiddled with the life support systems, fiddled with nearly every piece of the *Ambit*'s beating heart until she purred more than she sputtered: a first, since she'd come into Nash's care, and probably well before then.

The thing about fiddling, though, was that the work didn't quite end when the last bolt got tightened. Took a bit of calibration to get a system that complex singing in harmony, and Nash could run all the simulations and scans she wanted while they were in port to catch anything catastrophic, but the fine-tuning? No sense doing that until they got out into the black again.

She didn't pay attention to the clock as she worked, feeling

her way through one tweak after the next with that sixth, inde-
scribable sense her augments gave her. Filament sensors woven
through her hair, hardwired into her brain, and she could not-
quite-hear and not-quite-see those tiny disruptions in energy
flow and pressure and signal transmissions like strings out of
tune on Saint's old guitar. One by one, she got them pitched just
right. Got the *Ambit*'s engine humming its lullaby even clearer
than before, so familiar and unique, and sank back onto her
hammock with a satisfied sigh. Bodie, the asshole-in-residence,
saw his opening and leapt right onto her stomach with one of
his raspy little *mrows* and just enough claw to let her know
who that hammock *really* belonged to.

He'd just gotten settled when the speakers crackled.

"If you fall asleep without dinner, Saint's going to fuss
again," Eoan reminded gently, yet pointedly. "He's cooked
enough for a small army."

"Good, that's miner boy sorted. What's left for the rest of
us?"

"Nash."

"Cap." But she was already shooing Bodie off her stomach
and swinging to her feet. He went, but only long enough for her
to clear the pillows, and then he hopped right back up again,
curling up with one last baleful look, as if to say *I was only in
it for the hammock, anyway.* "We should've gotten a dog."

Bodie's loud, supercilious sneeze followed her up the ladder
into the infirmary.

"Saint also mentioned you should come quietly," Eoan re-
layed over the infirmary speakers. Nash had, mercifully, managed not to spend as much time lately in that *particular* part of
the ship as she had in the engine room. After the very vigorous
scrub-down Saint had given it on their way to Alpha Librae,
she'd put things back in their proper place and hadn't really
touched them since. Ready but unused—the best way for an
infirmary to be.

Nash ducked out into the short hall. Not much to the *Ambit*, when you got right down to it. A cargo hold in the back, connected by a long hall to the galley, which led up to the bridge. Off the hall, on the side opposite the infirmary, a ladder dropped into crew quarters that, like the infirmary, hadn't gotten any use since they'd wrapped that Deadworld shit up with a bow. Nash figured that was about to change—with the quarters, she meant, not the infirmary.

Although, knowing their luck. . . .

She shook her head, wiping her grease-smudged hands on her coveralls just because she knew it'd make Saint's eyes twitch. "Quiet, huh? Did his highness have any other requests?"

By then, she'd made it to the door of the galley and was welcomed by a spectacularly flat stare over one spectacularly fucked-up shoulder. Months since his throw-down with Drestyn, and Saint still favored it when he thought nobody was looking.

He didn't say anything, but the thumb he jabbed toward the table made his point well enough. Sitting in the chair—or maybe *sprawling* would've been better, the way all those too-long limbs were thrown around—was their very own miner boy, head tipped forward in a way that promised a vicious crick in his neck and his own shoulders rising and falling in what were definitely, *audibly*, little miner boy snores.

Awww, she mouthed. She was going for a shit-eating sort of smile, but she couldn't get it to sit right. It wasn't cute, was the thing. Wasn't sweet, not in any way you'd want to remember. That was the inelegant sprawl of a man who'd run out of fumes and dropped where he sat. Got food on his stomach, got somewhere he felt reasonably safe, and his body just went *cool, we're done.*

And somewhere he felt like Bitsie'd be safe, she thought, watching Bitsie at the counter next to Saint. Somebody'd dragged the step stool–crate over for her, so she could put all the spices and utensils from dinner back in the high cabinets. Saint handed them to her one by one with his Very Important Face reserved for Very Important Things, and Bitsie hummed a little as she worked. The Reds did like their music.

The humming trailed off as she turned to look at Nash. "Did you know Uncle Jal snored?" she asked, voice soft against the constant, static hum of the engines. It was more something you felt than something you heard, but it always had a sort of dampening effect on the rest of the ship. Sounds seemed softer, blunted at the edges. She called it a lullaby for a reason. All the stations and colonies and ships she'd been on in her life, she'd never slept so well as she did on the *Ambit*.

After a moment, she shook her head. She'd seen Jal sleep before, sure, but only when he was heavily medicated or concussed or some don't-go-into-the-light-type combination of the two.

Bitsie made a thoughtful face and turned back to the cabinets. "Me neither," she said.

"Don't know what you two're are talking about." Saint passed Bitsie the last of the put-aways and walked back to the stove, dishing up a bowl of thick, comforting stew over a serve of quinoa. He grabbed a spoon from the rack and set the bowl down by Nash's favorite spot on the counter, having long since given up trying to make her eat at the table. "Kid's snored like a flat-faced dog as long as I've known him."

"I heard that." The quiet mutter came from somewhere in the curtain of hair at the table. With no small amount of popping and winces, Jal got his head up enough to push his hair out of his face and make it stay that way. "You're no sleeping beauty yourself, old man. Heard diamond-bit boring machines quieter'n you."

"Never heard a complaint before," Saint replied.

"Don't see how you could hear much of anything over that." Jal bumped his specs up enough to rub at his eyes, like he could scrub the sleepy right out of them. The yawn he smothered behind his hand when he settled his specs back said it didn't work.

Saint looked over at Nash, who nodded back toward the hall.

They still had six good hours of flight time; it wasn't much, but it'd be enough to snag some shut-eye once they got the Reds settled.

"I've got it," said Eoan, and one of their projections materialized in the doorway. Flowing periwinkle and cobalt and royal blue robes today, rippling with the air like silk. Nash swore she heard the rustle of fabric as Eoan extended a hand toward Bitsie and Jal.

Now you're just showing off. Eoan's projections differed from day to day, sometimes hour to hour. Different complexities of clothing and hairstyles, different levels of detail and realism. Sometimes it was a sign of how much of Eoan's attention was elsewhere; sometimes, though, it was just a sign of their mood. They seemed . . . happy now. Glad to be back out in the black, with a mission and a mystery, even if it wasn't what Nash would call *ideal.* They handled stagnation about as well as Nash and Saint did. A trio of nomads, that was them, who'd made a ship their home and a mission their way of life.

And dammit, they liked it that way.

"Follow me," said Eoan, and even though they saw through every camera on the ship, their projection's eyes still followed Bitsie as she hauled Jal out of his seat by his jacket sleeve. "We'll get you two settled into your rooms. Afraid they're no more luxurious than they were the last time you were here, Jal, but the mattresses are soft and the rooms are quiet."

"Ish," said Nash, wobbling her hand in the air as Bitsie followed Eoan out of the galley.

Jal hung back a few steps. "I'll be back soon as we get her settled," he said.

"Did you miss the bit about the soft mattresses?" Nash asked. "That was for you, too, tough guy. Go. Shoo. Get some z's. We're all snagging power naps before we land." Because fuck only knew how long it'd be before they got some more downtime. Number one rule of active duty: nap, eat, and laugh when you could, because sometimes the opportunities to do any of those things got real limited.

Jal studied her a minute, like he was trying to decide whether he believed her or not. "All right," he said eventually. "But I'm coming with you when we land, so. You know."

"Don't leave you behind," Saint finished for him. "Weren't planning to."

"Good." Jal nodded to himself. "Yeah, good." Then he brushed some imaginary dust off on his pants, turned, and wandered off the same way Eoan and Bitsie had gone.

Nash waited until he was well out of earshot—climbing down the hatch into the crew quarters, at least—to turn her attention back to Saint. "Shitshow, party of five, am I right?"

Saint threw his clean-up rag at her head and didn't say a word.

. . .

Lummis was another dome colony, like Alpha Librae. Saw a lot of them in the outer reaches of the center spiral, on all the used-up planets where the Trust had set up shop back when it wasn't even the Trust at all, just a handful of conglomerates in a race to gobble up as many resources as possible. That was before they'd worked out that *competition* was a chump's game, and life was a lot easier when you were just too big to fail.

It was also one of the first forays into arboricultured atmosphere. Before that, cyclers and pumps and all manner of complicated machinery converted whatever toxins floated around a given planet or moon into livable atmo; but the conglomerate in charge of Lummis's terraforming had gotten the bright idea to use one of the simplest and, at the same time, most complex machines known to man: trees. A fuck-ton of trees, seeded in a crescent along the sunward side of the dwarf planet—or giant asteroid, depending on your perspective. Was about a quarter of the size of Earth's moon, and the Lummis colony was about a quarter of the size of that. So, not the biggest Nash had seen, but for someone who'd grown up in the closeness of a space station, it still felt like an awful lot of room.

Of course, the whole *nature's oxygen-makers* plan had still been a work in progress at the time. The genetically modified trees had been made to grow like weeds in the dense carbonate-and-clay surface of the planet-or-asteroid, and they'd done their job for the first half a decade. Shot up like beanstalks from a bedtime story, filled the dome with a healthy supply of tasty, tasty breathable air. No, they weren't pretty, all spindly from growing too fast and bent under the weight of their own foliage. But *beauty* was only ever an accident in places like that. All function, no form, because what the hell did the C-suiters care? They weren't the ones who'd have to look at it.

Then, after the decade ran out, *nobody* had to look at it. Halite mines ran dry, boomtown stopped booming, and everybody who could leave the colony did. But the trees . . . the trees just kept growing. Grew, and grew, and grew, until the dome reminded Nash of the terrarium that Doc—the station doctor who'd scraped Nash off the road to nowhere and put her very first multi-tool in her hand—used to keep in her workshop. Plants growing until they'd swallowed half the decorations, bits of moss climbing over tiny Roman aqueducts and micro ferns choking out itty bitty pagodas. The terrarium's glass walls had gone a faint shade of green, but Nash had never been sure if it was just the light reflecting off of all those leaves, or if even the terrarium itself was slowly being swallowed up.

Yeah. Lummis was a lot like that.

"Looks kind of primeval, doesn't it?" Nash asked as Eoan eased their ship through the air lock and decon channel on the treeless side of the dome. It was built with cargo vessels in mind, so it was a bit like threading a needle through a rigatoni noodle; Eoan probably could've done it sideways, on the double, with their sensors off.

They were being careful, though. Wouldn't have been an

oversell to call Lummis one of the shadiest places in the center spiral—second only to the Trust headquarters in Crimes Committed Daily. Every species of ne'er-do-well had parked it on Lummis at one point or another, and if they got even a whiff of Guild? Well, that'd be trouble—and not the fun kind.

So, when they landed, it wasn't as the Guild ship *Ambit*, designation GS 31–770; it was as an independent aid ship, the *Epione*, designation GS 24–399, complete with the new paint job she'd slapped on while they'd been docked at Alpha Librae. Chromomorphic pigment from nose to tail; it changed color with a dash of current. Granted, it could only go up and down the grayscale, but if anybody had an eye out for a gray ship with a white GS 31–770 painted on the side, they probably wouldn't look twice at the waxy white number rocking a black GS 24–399. And faking a registration and manifest for a ship that didn't *technically* exist was pretty much the work of a slow afternoon for Eoan.

Going incognito was new. Hadn't really had much use for it out in the frontier, where everyone either welcomed you like a neighbor or shot you on sight, and which you got depended less on who *you* were and more on who *they* were. But after being tracked from one end of the O-Cyg to the other by a handful of mercs and the universe's most unshakable agitator, they'd decided it'd be good to have some contingencies.

So. They landed the *Epione*-for-now at the Lummis port, which wasn't really much to write home about. A handful of bigger slips, meant for cargo vessels and freight, broken up into smaller ones by rough-and-ready add-ons, connected like ribs by a long spine of a dock.

"Don't look down, McBlastinshit," Nash said as they walked down the ramp off the ship.

Saint, predictably, looked down. And down, and down, and down, into the sunken belly of the crater the port had been built into. He didn't so much *balk*—Saint, in his infinite com-

posure, would *never*—but the way he tipped his head back up
and kept it there said he didn't really love the view.

"It's man-made, you know," Eoan said into their earpieces.
"Mind you, not intentionally. The surface was actually quite
smooth, as protoplanets go, until it found itself in the path of
a discarded rocket. One of the Trust's early predecessors. Happened quite often, for a while—couldn't go a week without
hearing about some wayward satellite or bit of rocket crashing into a moon. Wasn't until they actually started *building* on
those moons that anybody bothered to make a fuss."

Nash snorted. "Humans, right?"

"At least we're consistent." Saint turned back toward the
ship. "Kid, you coming?"

Jal hung back in the cargo bay with Bitsie, down on one knee
to get his eyes about level with hers. "We'll be back soon as we
can," he told her. "Mind the captain while we're gone."

"Actually, I was thinking I'd just sneak off and see what all
the *contemptible criminal cesspool* hype's about," she replied,
straight-faced and daring. Nash had almost zero experience
with preteens—she hadn't even liked them that much when
she'd *been* one—but she'd decided to proceed like Bitsie was
just a tiny adult and respond accordingly. "Kidding," Bitsie
said. "I'm kidding."

Jal, for his part, played a pretty convincing fool. Hand over
his heart like he thought it'd jump out of his chest, shaking his
head. The best kind of fool, Nash thought, because it was the
kind that got a worried kid to smile again. "You sure you're not
a teenager yet?"

"T-minus four months," Bitsie said, holding up that many
fingers. "Be afraid."

Jal's bark of a laugh carried all the way down the ramp.
"Every damn day," he told her, and with a kiss to the top of her
head and a ruffle of her hair, Jal rolled to his feet and jogged off
down the ramp.

"Language!" Bitsie snarked after him.

"Love you, too, little bit." And it wasn't until he'd put his back to her and the ship that Jal let that smile flag. "Well," he said once he'd caught up to them, doing a scan of the dock as the *Ambit*'s cargo door eased shut behind them. "Nobody's surrounded us with guns yet, so I'd say we're off to a decent start."

"Night's still young," Saint replied.

"And the plan's still shit," Nash agreed cheerfully as they wandered down the docks. Nash took the lead, as per usual; and Saint held back a step or two where he could keep eyes on both his crewmates, *as per usual*. "We're absolutely sure there was nothing in Eoan's encyclopedia of everything that can give us a better location on this guy's hidey-hole than *somewhere in Lummis*?"

"Sure as I was the last three times you asked," Saint said. "Sure as I'll be the next three times, too."

"And the fourth?" she asked, just to be a shit about it.

"I'm shoving you off the docks."

"Promises, promises." Nash flashed him a wink and kept walking, trying not to make eyes at the exquisite-looking ships they passed on their way to the end of the dock, where a warehouse that *might've* doubled as a customs depot, once upon a time, stood hunched and waiting. Nearly every slip was full, some fuller than others. They passed a few little rockhoppers, each about half the *Ambit*'s size and twice as polished, which meant either small-scale smugglers or mercenaries that didn't play well with others. Wouldn't fit more than a two-person crew on one of those comfortably for any length of time; maybe four or five, if the trip was short and nobody aboard felt particularly homicidal.

The rest of the ships were larger. Some falling apart, some neat as a pin, but all of them had nary a name or number in sight. Probably not doing the kind of business where they cared to be recognized.

Knowing what Nash knew about Gethin, that seemed to suggest they had the right place.

"Still not sure about *aid ship* for a cover," Jal said. "Been a few places like this in my time. Not too keen on outside help."

"But always keen on an easy mark," Nash replied. She'd done her share of slumming it in the seedy underbelly of the universe. Seen one den of iniquity, seen them all. Though she had to admit, she'd never been to one this muggy. "Fuck, it's like swimming in the air." Wasn't even *hot*, just wet. Like a bathroom after a lukewarm shower, with a vague, heady sweetness in the air. Overripe fruit. A fresh bag of fertilizer. It wasn't a smell she immediately hated, but it wasn't a smell she immediately liked, either.

From the wrinkle of Jal's nose, she figured he'd already made up his mind. He scowled as he took off his shaded specs to wipe the condensation off with his shirt. Could've just left them off out there; it was nighttime, and carbon-dark except for the places the weak, flickering dock lights could reach. But the closer they got to the depot up ahead, the clearer it became that the lights were on and somebody was home. Shades of red and purple and yellow bled through the windows—colors of neon lighting that said to normal passersby *keep walking, this ain't the alley you're looking for,* and beckoned the rogues and the reprobates like a sweet, sultry siren's song. They made the place *seem* dark, but something told Nash that Jal's eyes, aggressively mutated for the *real* kinds of dark, would absolutely feel the difference.

So. Specs back on, but only after he spit on the lenses and wiped them one more time.

"Gross." Nash grimaced. "I have lens cleaner, you animal."

Jal settled the specs back over his marble-black eyes, and at least had the decency to look sheepish. "Habit," he said. "Lens cleaner used to be kind of hard to come by."

He never said it, Nash had noticed. Never said *while I was a forced laborer for some asshole scavs* or anything like that.

If he mentioned it at all, he talked around it, like she and Saint didn't already know. Like they hadn't seen him, all scarred up and underfed, when he'd finally gotten loose. She figured he wanted to avoid the reminder, but what she hadn't worked out was who he was trying not to remind: himself, or them.

"Yeah, well." She shrugged her bag off one shoulder and pulled it around in front of her. Took a bit of riffling, but she had a method to her madness, and she came out with a few packets of wipes. "Keep those in your pocket, miner boy. No more spitting on my tech."

"*Your* tech? They're my specs."

"That *I* made, ergo *my* tech. No spit." She pulled her backpack back on. "You'll give yourself pink eye."

"Don't think that's how you get pink eye," said Saint from the back.

"Fine. You'll give yourself primary meningococcal conjunctivitis." She glanced back at Saint. "Better?"

Beside her, Jal held up a hand. "I got *primary.*"

Nash couldn't think of a way to respond that wasn't hella condescending, so she gestured up ahead of them instead. "That's our stop, gents." If the dock was a spine, then the depot was the skull, sitting at the end of the dock before the path branched out into the town beyond.

If, in fairness, you could call it a town. Might've been a few hundred structures to it, once upon a time, but the trees had swallowed all but the main strip leading uphill off the depot. Struck an odd sort of contrast—the falling-down buildings of sheet metal and clay, set against all that *green*. Warped trees and fast-growing ivy, underbrush so thick Nash wished she had a machete. Of course, she kind of *always* wished she had a machete. Machetes were fucking cool.

What few of the buildings remained stood in a sort of street, like the towns in Saint's old westerns. Dozens of buildings wedged together so tight, all the fronts seemed to blend together. No signs to tell them apart now; or if there were, they'd been painted over and graffitied so many times, it was anybody's guess what they might've said once. Rot-soft clay walls crumbled around alloy supports, sloughing off in clumps. Companies never built those places to last; they built them quick and cheap, and to hell with what happened after they finished with them. The clay'd probably come from the proto-planet itself. Wasn't much good for selling; you'd lose your ass on the shipping costs alone. But company men with their company minds had a way of wringing use out of everything, and Lummis was an example of a place with nothing left to give.

Didn't stop the more enterprising folks from making use of the place anyway. The walls of the customs depot had been shored up, shingled with sheet metal and propped up with I beams that'd probably been scavenged from some of the other structures. Looked a strong breeze from falling apart, but Nash guessed that was fine. There wasn't a damn breeze in the whole colony. The air just *sat*, wet and heavy and stagnant, with the smell of too many fruit trees dropping too much fruit with nobody there to eat it.

Nash adjusted her bag on her shoulder. "Let's go make some friends." And forward she marched, straight to the front doors of the customs depot. Looked like the front, anyway; the whole building was kind of a flat-ish rectangle, but one side had an awning and two guys standing outside trying to look important and only halfway succeeding. No uniforms, but they stood roughly the same way on either side of the double doors, save the shorter one's grip on a smoke stick and the taller one's hand on his belt. Presumably to draw attention to the piezoelectric revolver on his hip. *Hey, if you got it, flaunt it.*

"No weapons in the Warehouse," said the tall one, with an emphasis on *Warehouse* that said it was a name and not a noun, while the short one blew a cloud of smoke across Nash's face. She made a point not to react, even if it did smell like cat piss cotton candy. Even when the short one wasn't exhaling his lung-rot, he seemed to breathe through his mouth. Broken nose, maybe, old and badly healed. Had cauliflower ears like he'd been a fighter once, and a hitch in his stance that seemed to suggest he probably wasn't, anymore. If he made trouble, she decided, she'd go for that left hip and see where it took them. The boys could split Tall, Armed, and Compensating for Something.

Taking another puff, Smokestack—*Short Stack*, she thought, with a private laugh—tapped a sign on the door behind his head. No Weapons in the Warehouse, it read.

"Really sticking to the script, huh, boys?" she muttered, and when Smokestack gave her an expectant glare, she just shrugged. "I'm a doctor. Not really big on guns. Or knives." Or anything that'd show up on a weapons scanner, which she expected they'd be walking through once those doors peeled open. Made sense—want to keep a bunch of don't-play-nicers playing nice, take away their toys.

Smokestack turned toward Saint, with his very obvious holster bunching up his dull gray racer jacket. "Guns in the lockers," he said, jabbing a thumb back at the rows of, yep, *lockers* along the wall behind him. "Get 'em back when you leave." Then he turned to Jal and hiked an eyebrow, but he didn't need to bother. Jal had already unclipped the holster from his thigh with way less displeasure than Saint. Probably just as good without as with it. Shaky hands—little bit of nerve damage to remember the mines by, was Nash's guess—did not a marksman make, but she wouldn't want to throw down with him bare-fisted.

They each shoved their guns in a locker, put their thumbs against the readers, and took the valet tags the machine spat out when they were done.

"We good now?" Nash asked Smokestack.

"We'll see," he replied, but he nodded to Compensating, who hit something on the panel behind him—and then again, which seemed to do the trick. The door juddered open on old, un-cared-for hinges, and into the air lock they went. Smart move, making their main space airtight. Probably some insulated tunnels out to the port, too. No telling how many years that dome had left in it.

"Been through more damn scanners in the last four months than I've been through my whole damn life," Saint grumbled as a bright yellow light passed over them, then over again. A beep, and it turned green. "Gonna start *glowing*."

"Like your personality," Jal offered, as the doors ahead rolled open with a little less agony than their partners.

Nash fist-bumped him, then promptly forgot what they'd been talking about as she took in the Warehouse ahead of her. What'd looked like a building from the outside seemed more like an alley within, with little storefronts built into the walls on either side, hawking refurbished—*stolen*, if you knew the lingo—ship parts and GLASS chips and every other kind of tech imaginable. In one shop, the vendor crowed about black-market meds you could only get in the Trust-run private hospitals; and in the shop right next to it, blur bottles lined the shelves, shining every color in the hazy light, for when you needed a different kind of medicine. It was like a shopping center for everything you weren't supposed to have, stretching out nearly farther than Nash could see through the loose waves of people and the dense cloud of smoke that gave the whole place the feel of the quiet booth in the corner where all the bad business got done.

"Well, damn." Saint really had a way with words.

Beside him, Jal waved smoke away from his face. An exercise in futility, when there was no fresh air to replace it, but she couldn't blame him for trying. "Reeks," he said. "Like burnt toast and bad decisions."

"Bad decisions are exactly what we need," said Nash. Their best shot at finding Gethin was to find somebody stupid enough to tell them where he liked to hang his coat. "Unless the

asshole's decided to ditch his hostage and do a little shopping."
A girl could dream.

"I'll scan the warehouse, just in case." Eoan had been quiet
to that point. Taking it all in, or else distracted with their new
shipmate, but they were officially on-mission. "But you should
see if you can't get some information the old-fashioned way."

Eoan said *old-fashioned*, and Nash swore Saint's head
popped up. It was goddamn *Pavlovian*. "You want bad decisions, I'm thinking that's our place." He pointed to the other
side of the indoor alley, where a sign read KNOT'S DIVE in the
most diabolical shade of purple tube-lighting Nash had ever
seen, and somebody'd spray-painted prices on a beat-up aluminum sheet by the door. HAPPY HOUR 2 PINTS 4 1.

Nash could feel a headache coming on.

"Sorry, Jal," she said. "I bet they don't serve miners."

"Oh, hah hah."

She grinned shamelessly, then turned back to Saint. "Lead
the way, oh fearless quartermaster." And he did. Just enough
people filled the market to make it feel cramped, but people had
a tendency to get out of Saint's way when they saw him coming.
She didn't think he did it on purpose; he just had that air about
him—that aura of *move or I will move you*.

Which worked well in a place like the Warehouse. Got them
up and down the aisle, a quick circuit to make sure Eoan could
scan everything worth scanning through their bodycams, then
through the small group of piss-drunk assholes loitering by the
Knot's Dive door. She figured they'd probably gotten cut off
at the bar and kicked out, because apparently even a dive on
Lummis had standards.

Saint walked them right up to the bar and got the barkeep's
attention with a curt but courteous "Middle shelf, two fingers,
and two waters besides."

"Makes me all tingly when you order for me like that," Nash
said wryly, dropping onto the stool beside him. Jal took the

other side and didn't say a word until it was time to thank the barkeep when she put down their drinks. She was a willow of a woman, tattooed from the tips of her fingers to the ripped cuffs of her plaid shirt, hair as green as whatever wound up in the bottom of Saint's glass. Knowing blur came from algae didn't make the color any less suspect.

The barkeep gave Jal a smile and a wink, and he at least returned the smile, but with the polite obliviousness of someone who had no idea he was being flirted with. Probably for the best. Had to be a badass to serve drinks in a place like that, and there was something just a little predatory in that azalea-pink smile.

More power to you, girlie. Nash knew a survivor when she saw one.

She also knew a tough crowd when she saw one, and it seemed they'd landed right in the middle of one. Not an obvious dupe in the bunch when she scanned the couple dozen people in the room. Drunk, yeah, but distrustful. More than a few eyes narrowed at her when she saw them, and judging by the grim turn of Saint's mouth against the edge of his glass, he'd noticed the same thing.

"Nobody here's gonna talk to us," she said, careful to keep her voice just below the din of all those conversations. Just for her and Saint. "You don't make it in these folks' business being anything less than careful as hell."

"Don't see us having another option, unless Cap picked up something on the scans."

"Not a thing," Eoan said. "Sorry."

Saint shrugged. "Long shot. Of course," he added, thoughtfully, swirling his blur around his glass, "there's ways to get on drunk folks' good sides."

"Not buying them drinks," Nash said. "Or any other kind of bribe. Look around. These people are flush as fuck." Tables piled high with glasses, clapping each other on the backs with big, sloppy grins. Everybody there was probably fresh off some score or another. You didn't go to a market with nothing to trade.

Saint cast a sly look back at the bar. "Not what I had in mind."

Ah. "I get it." And with a plastered-on grin, she whipped around on her stool and tapped the guy beside her on the shoulder. He raised his head, eyes bloodshot enough to say he was *real* deep in his cups and down some serious higher brain functions. "My friend here says you look like the frog-faced fucker that screwed him on his last run," she said, slurring her words. *Frog-face* was right: eyes far apart, mouth wide on a weirdly spherical head. That bulging vein on his forehead looked promising, so she pushed a little harder. "Dimed him out to the rangers or some shit, right, man?" She turned to Saint. "He doesn't *look* like a rat." Then back to the man, "You don't look like a rat."

"Fuck you," spat the man, slamming his near-empty glass down on the counter and rising—*stumbling*—to his feet. "I ain't a rat. Ain't never been one. Fuck you," he added at the end, like he wasn't sure he'd said it at the start and wanted to make sure he'd covered his bases.

Saint just kept his eyes forward and sipped his drink.

"Dammit, asshole, I'm talking to you!" Seemed she'd picked a winner. Nash felt kind of bad about shitting on the guy's evening, but they needed to put on a show, and from the looks of things, he was about to *crush* his audition.

After he finished crushing Saint's face.

He reached past Nash and got a fistful of Saint's jacket, and Saint had just enough time to shoot her a *deeply* unimpressed look before he was dragged back off his stool.

So apparently he'd had something else in mind.

She gave a *my bad* shrug and picked up her water, leaning back against the bar as Froggy squared up for the first punch. *Make it look good, McBlastinshit.* And once Froggy took that first swing, the whole damn bar kicked off like a human Rube

Goldberg machine. Cause and effect. Saint took the hit and made sure to stumble back into the nearest table, upending half their drinks. So, of course, they had to get up and join in. Froggy's next punch missed Saint and caught one of them in the chin, knocking them into another table, and once the numbers started piling up, Jal jumped in without so much as a *would you mind*?

Didn't take long for the brawl to spread, like a brush fire waiting to start. All the perfect conditions in one place: puffed-up brawlers and badasses, still revved from some kind of score, and half of them blitzed out of their gourds. Throw a match, watch the whole thing go up.

For all Saint's grumbling, Nash swore he enjoyed it. He'd posted up right in the middle of it, throwing punches at whoever strayed close enough to hit, throwing grown-ass men like sacks of potatoes. Jal stuck right there with him, albeit a little more mobile. One woman, who could've given that Union guard Casale a run for her caps in the built-like-a-brick-shithouse division, threw a haymaker straight at Jal's face, but he ducked out of the way of it and sprang up with a wide, delighted grin at Nash.

"You comin'?" he called, like he was about to tell her *the water's fine!* But before he could get the words out, Froggy came out of nowhere and barreled into his chest. Nash watched the grin give way to a look of surprise as he flew backward, then she kind of lost sight of him in the fray. She wasn't worried, though. He'd be fine.

She glanced back at the bartender. "You gonna break it up?"

The bartender and her azalea lips smiled a clever little smile, eyes flashing red-gold in the dive's moody lights. "In a minute," she said, with a voice smooth as top-shelf liquor with just the right amount of bite. "Anything they break, they fix. Might as well enjoy the show."

And true to the barkeep's word, it wasn't until half the tables had been tipped and a good few chairs were broken that the barkeep reached under the bar and grabbed a shotgun. Racked a load one-handed and fired off a shot at the nearest fighter in the bunch.

It was the bang of the gun, probably, more than the guy's yelp, that stopped the crowd. "Beanbag round," the barkeep told Nash, before she turned her gaze—and her shotgun—out to the crowd. "Fun's over, fuckos," she belted. "And cheers in advance for the new set of glassware."

Whether the fighters were properly cowed, or just unwilling to piss off the lady pouring their drinks, nobody threw another punch. A few of them helped their buddies off the ground, some of them salvaged their drinks from what remained of the tables, and mostly they got back to the business of binge drinking.

Saint emerged first, a cut on his brow from Froggy's first punch and nary a mark on him otherwise. "Darts," Saint hissed through his teeth. He sounded vaguely winded as he swept up his glass and downed it in one pull. "I was thinking *darts*."

In hindsight, that look he'd thrown over his shoulder *did* kind of line up with the row of dartboards on the far wall. But Nash wouldn't take the heat for it. "Well next time, maybe we should use our words."

Saint mumbled something under his breath about the words he'd like to use and grabbed Jal's water for a swig, which was about the time Jal found his way over. He'd taken a hit to the jaw that was already darkening under his scruff, and his hair looked like a mischief of rats had thrown a kegger, but he hadn't stopped grinning that same wide, satisfied grin.

In a bizarre twist, he was arm in arm with none other than red-faced Froggy. "We're good," he told them. He could miss somebody flirting with him, but no way could he miss two bug-eyed stares from Nash and Saint. Leave it to their resident golden retriever to walk into a bar fight and walk out with a friend. "Did you know Rupert here was a miner? I mean, the underground kind, but still."

"A miner's a miner," said the Rupert formerly known as Froggy.

"A miner's a miner," Jal agreed. "I apologized for the mix-up, back there. Told him you just get confused sometimes, old man." A vaguely shit-eating turn to his grin said he knew he was talking smack and also knew Saint wasn't in any position to give him grief about it. He had to go along to get along. "Told him we needed some help, too."

"He did, he did," Rupert agreed. The fight seemed to have sobered him a little, despite the bloody teeth and the blur staining his shirt, though he still talked like consonants were more of a suggestion than a phonetic requirement. "Said you were lookin' for that bastard Martyn. Now there's a rat if I ever met one. Says he slipped the Guild leash, but me, I don't buy that for a second. All the shit he hawks—if he ain't dirty, he's got a hell of an inside track."

Jal steered him amiably back to the point—and back to his stool, before Jal could lose his grip and drop the guy. "Told him about our friend runnin' off to join Gethin's crew," he said, and Nash was surprised how smoothly it rolled off his tongue. He'd never been much of a liar, but necessity breeds badassery, apparently. "How we haven't heard from 'em in a few days." To Rupert, he added, "We just want to make sure they're all right, you know? Some rough folks out here." His drawl was thicker than usual; Nash wondered if he was playing it up on purpose, for Rupert's sake, or just stuck in some kind of hick-speak feedback loop.

"It's real terrible business," said Rupert solemnly, shaking his head. "I was real sorry to hear it. Losing crew's a hard thing, even if they've just gone and moved on."

"The hardest thing," Jal agreed, and it was a wonder that

glass didn't break in Saint's hand for how tightly he gripped it. "But he said—Rupert, tell them what you said."

"I said I've made the run down to Gethin's a time or two," Rupert told them. "Deliveries and the like. They don't come to the market, much. Can't rightly say if they think it's beneath them, or they just don't think they'd be welcome. On account of the Guild ties and all," he clarified. "Self-righteous bastards."

Nash very deliberately didn't look at Saint. It'd been hard enough to get him on board with playing an aid ship; getting him to sit silent through somebody shit-talking the Guild was edging toward a bridge too far.

She stepped in before Rupert could go any further down that particular road. "So you know where we can find him?"

"I do, I do," he said. The repetition thing made Nash's eye twitch, but she didn't dare call him on it. Not when they'd actually landed on a solid lead.

"And you'll tell us?" Nash pressed.

"Well, I could," said Rupert, but that slur had a slyness to it. "These woods, though, it's real easy to get turned around. Real easy. Especially for newcomers like yourself. No," he said. "No, I think I'd better show you."

Saint and Nash traded looks. Something didn't sit quite right, but what other choice did they have? They'd just have to be careful. Have to be smart.

Because where could *that* possibly go wrong?

CHAPTER FIVE

SAINT

Saint hadn't trudged through woods this thick since his time in the Earth army. Underbrush clawing at his legs, bare roots snagging his boots, branches so close and thick they could've been a wall.

It *felt* different, though. Back home, the woods were mostly old-growth swamps—all mud and reeds and thick-bodied tupelos standing strong despite the fading of the world. They were timeless. Primordial. Nature in its purest form.

There was nothing *natural* about Lummis. A forest full of crooked, miserable things pretending to be trees, bending under the weight of their own branches. Their bark looked eerily like *skin*, gray-brown and wrinkled from years of hardening and splitting and hardening again, and they dropped rotting green seed pods that popped like blisters underfoot.

"Wouldn't even know it if the sun came up," Nash said, stepping lightly through the snarls of ivy. "How the fuck do people live like this?"

Beside her, Jal stayed mostly above the worst of it, picking his way across the gnarled roots instead. Good way to turn an ankle, but Saint wouldn't be the one to tell a runner from the floating mines how to mind his footing. For his part, Saint did the same as he had in all those marshes and bogs all those years ago: he kept marching forward.

"They don't, miss," said Rupert. He led the way, stumbling about as much as he walked. He moved quick enough, though—

with a steadying hand from Jal, every now and again—so Saint
didn't care. "People moved out about the same time the trees
moved in. Spindly little bastards grew straight through the
houses around here, they did, they did. Look, just off to the
left. Used to be a whole street, where we're walking now. If
you believe the old maps, that is, which I do. Never steered me
wrong." He paused to rap his knuckles three times against the
nearest tree trunk. "You can still see bits of all the buildings.
The metal, mostly—what hasn't been picked over and brought
back to shore up Main Street and the Warehouse. Clay's just
crumbled, you see?" He aimed his flashlight out through the
trees, throwing light and crooked shadows across the sea of
split-skinned trunks.

Saint had seen ruins before. Whole towns crushed by mud-
slides or abandoned to floods that'd never receded. This had
the same feeling to it: life, interrupted. In the beam of Rupert's
light, Saint saw vine-choked aluminum beams and the toppled
remains of clay walls—the skeletons of structures. Trees shot
straight up the middles of them, where Saint could imagine living rooms, kitchens, bunks. Roots punched through the sealed
clay floors, in some places as tall as the broken-down furniture
left behind.

"Nothing left worth a damn," Rupert said. "What the
scavengers didn't get, the rats did. You'll want to watch out
for them," he added. "Snuck in on a ship, who knows when.
Out here, the bastards'll grow big as your arm. Decent eating,
though, if you're quick enough to catch one."

It sounded like a story, something to tell tourists and newcomers to watch their eyes get big while the old guard smirked
behind their backs. If there were rats, Saint hadn't seen them.
Matter of fact, he hadn't seen a damn thing moving in those
woods.

That, he realized, was what was making his skin crawl. Not the strangeness of the trees or the decaying corpses of the town that used to be, but the *quiet*. Back on Earth, even the densest woods had a life to them. Birds singing in the branches, wind rustling the leaves. These trees had *nothing*. No birds. No breeze. Just silence and stillness, a forest of things playing at being alive.

"Yeah." Rupert sighed, unawares. He patted the sawed-off holstered on his hip fondly. "Bessie's killed a few of those in her day, haven't you, girl?"

Saint had a rule about hanging around folks who talked to their guns, and it went something like: *Don't*. He didn't trust them—people who looked at a gun, a tool meant for killing and little else besides, and unironically thought to themselves, *I think I ought to make this a little more human.*

Still, Rupert seemed harmless enough. Proud, sure; he hadn't passed up the opportunity to show *Bessie* off back at the Warehouse. Passed it over to Saint, watched him check the action and weigh the balance like he'd handed him a work of art. Not really Saint's bread and butter, but he'd offered a few compliments and passed it back. It was the polite thing to do.

Past a few more trees, Rupert glanced back and told them, "It'll be just up ahead, at the church. They had a church, see—one of the old ones, with the cross and everything. Held up well. Better than anything else around here, but I'll leave it to you what you want to make of that." As they came to a small clearing, Rupert slowed to a stop. "You'll want to be careful from here on out. Clearing marks the start of Gethin's space. He's not much for live patrols, mind you. Good way to give away your position, thermal scanners being what they are these days, so crews run lean. Waste of manpower. Er." His eyes flickered to Nash in the glow of their flashlights. "That is, people power. But there'll be sensors. There'll be *plenty* of sensors, believe you me. Not a leaf falls around the church but Gethin knows about it."

"Cap, you copy that?" Saint asked.

"Loud and clear," they said. "And yes, to answer your next question. I should be able to sort the sensors. Nash, if you would be so kind."

Nash squatted by a tree, bag in her lap to riffle through it until she came up with a matte black ball the size of her palm. Another one of Nash's new toys—a drone, camouflaged on the visible spectrum and against any thermal sensors. She'd explained how it worked, something about paraffin polymer coating and adaptive thermal camouflage, and he'd listened because he wasn't a dick. Only understood about half of it, but half was enough to know the drone could float past any kind of sensor the spiral could throw at it without raising a single alarm.

"What're you thinking of doing with that?" Rupert asked, and he'd no sooner voiced the question than the drone shot up and out of Nash's hand to hover in the clearing. Rupert took a few steps back, and a few more for good measure, nearly into the gap in the trees they'd just come through. "That don't even look real."

"He's about as real as anything else here," Nash replied with a shrug. "We call him The Flying Dutchman—you know, 'cause he's kind of like a ghost."

Rupert wiped his hands on the front of his green vest. Sweaty son of a bitch; it wasn't even that hot. "Well, you shouldn't go shooting down the sensors, miss. Signal cuts out, that's sure to get somebody to come looking. And I don't think they'll be too happy when they do."

"Signal's not gonna cut out." Nash sniffed, like the very suggestion offended her. Probably did. The idea that they'd have anything less than the cleverest—granted, sometimes also the simplest—solution to a problem on her watch? Not a goddamn chance. "Dutch's got a signal repeater. Nothing's cutting out;

it's just gonna loop a little. Place like this, still as it is, nobody should notice." She stood back up, slinging her bag back on her shoulder. "Cap, you're good to go."

"And here I was worried there wouldn't be anything for me to do." Eoan's voice had a smile in it as the drone zipped off into the woods. Soundless, it disappeared before it hit the tree line, black melting into shades of green and shadow until Saint's eyes couldn't pick it from the backdrop no matter how hard he squinted.

Jal, on the other hand, was much harder to lose track of. He started after the drone, and only stopped when Saint caught his arm and pulled him back. "What—?"

"We'll give it a minute, make sure Cap's got the lay of things before we go charging in," Saint told him firmly. He squeezed Jal's arm, a silent plea for patience. A promise. "Just one more minute, kid."

"Uh, gentlemen?" Nash snapped her fingers, and when Saint turned toward her, she pointed back to the other side of the clearing—Rupert's side, where Saint wasn't quite surprised to find Rupert with his sawed-off aimed somewhere in the neighborhood of Jal's chest.

"Now, I don't want any trouble," said Rupert. "Don't want any trouble at all, but this ain't my first rodeo. By the time any of you pull a sidearm, you'll be so full of holes you won't even hold water. Try to cross this clearing, same end. But if you'll just toss your weapons and bags to the middle of the clearing and step right on back, there's no call for this to get unpleasant."

"More unpleasant than being held at gunpoint by a man who calls his gun *Bessie*?" Nash muttered. The lip got a disgruntled frown out of Rupert, who'd probably thought they'd be a shade more cooperative on the business end of a sawed-off. If, in fact, he'd thought this through at all.

Saint had his doubts.

Beside him, Jal let out an impatient huff. "Why do they always aim at me?"

"Bigger target?" Nash guessed.

"He's got a shotgun. Ain't like he's got to aim."

Nash shrugged. "Hey, look on the bright side. The way you miners shoot, you might be the safest one here."

"Did y'all not hear me?" Rupert snapped. Probably meant to sound angry, but he was too bad a bluff to hide the tremor underneath it. "I said throw your bags and gun belts into the middle of the clearing. I don't want to shoot you, but I will if you make me. I will, I will." He punctuated each repetition with a bob of his shotgun, like he thought they'd all missed it somehow.

Only they weren't the ones who'd missed something.

Rupert wasn't the first desperate man to point a gun at Saint, and he probably wouldn't be the last. Didn't stop that quick shot of adrenaline from rushing through Saint's veins, but it did stop it taking hold. Kept his head clear and his voice steady as he said to Jal, "You know what this reminds me of?"

"Might be quicker if you tell me," Jal replied. "Our friend here don't seem like the patient sort."

Saint wasn't too worried about *Rupert's* patience, but Jal'd gone so tense, Saint could've played him with a bow. Kid had a bad history with guns and the scars to prove it, but more than that, he *needed* to get to that church. "It reminds me of that time we got held up on Sooner's Weald. Second rotation, would've been."

"You mean those assholes who followed us from the bar? Showin' off their new gear to all and sundry?"

"The very same," said Saint.

"Really?"

Saint nodded. "Just like that."

"Well, all right then," said Jal, voice dropping to a growl. Then he started forward. Long, purposeful strides devoured the distance across the clearing like it was nothing at all; he'd made it halfway across before Rupert even had the wherewithal to squeeze the trigger.

Nothing happened. No shot. No *bang*.

Rupert tried again. Same result. Finally, it seemed to dawn on him: that gun wouldn't fire no matter *how* many times he tried to shoot it.

His red-blotched face cycled from puzzled to startled to downright *frightened*, which was just about where it landed when Jal got hold of him. He knocked the barrel of Rupert's shotgun aside with one hand and decked him straight in that bulbous nose with the other, and Saint swore he heard the cartilage crunching under Jal's fist, if only for the half second it took Rupert to start howling.

He barely got a sound out before Jal had a hand over his mouth, shoving him backward into a tree and pinning him there with all the weight of his nineteen decs. Didn't seem to take much effort, but that might've been the sheer goddamn *anger*. His whole face flushed with it, shoulders damn near shuddering with barely restrained energy, and when Rupert took a swing at him, Jal didn't even seem to feel it. Just took the hit and gave one back, cracking Rupert's head into the trunk again.

When Jal's arm drew back a second time, Saint stepped in. "You got him, kid," he said sharply. It did the trick, but Saint didn't like the strange, almost startled look that settled over Jal's face as Saint stepped up behind him. He looked between Rupert and Saint, then down at his own hand, lips parting around an uneasy breath, and something cold settled in the pit of Saint's stomach.

"Sorry," he rasped, to Saint, more than Rupert.

Saint shook his head—he didn't know what it was supposed to mean, what it was supposed to *say*, mostly because he wasn't sure what'd just happened—and grabbed the sawed-off from Rupert's half-slack grip. "You mean to shoot someone?" he said, prodding Rupert's belly with the short barrel. "You just shoot them. Don't keep going on about it. Now, he's gonna ease up on you a little." He spoke slowly, deliberately. Didn't want Rupert misunderstanding him. "You make any noise louder than a whisper, and I'll show you what I mean."

A nod to Jal, and Jal backed up half a step. Blood smeared his palm a shiny red where it'd covered Rupert's mouth, but Jal just wiped it on the asshole's shirt and bunched his fist in the collar.

"You broke my fuckin' nose," Rupert choked out. Might've been a hair louder than a whisper, but soft enough not to draw attention. Saint could show him some grace: it was damn hard to talk with a busted snout.

Saint reached into his belt for his zip cuffs and made quick work of cuffing Rupert's hands back around the tree. As soon as he got him secure, Saint stepped back, motioning for Jal to do the same. Took Jal a second, shoulders shuddering like he needed to shake something off. Worried, Saint decided. Just keyed up and worried, that was all. Strange as it was, he might've forgiven the man for pointing a gun at him. Shit happened. For wasting precious minutes, though, when they could've been that much closer to Regan? Kid wouldn't stand for that.

"Why do they always say that?" Nash said from somewhere behind him, dry and disinterested. Tying up jackasses wasn't her department, and fixing said jackasses' broken noses was definitely beneath her. "*You broke my nose.* So fucking indignant, like, *Yeah, I was gonna murderate you, but how could you do this to me?*" She scoffed. "Just be glad it wasn't your neck, Froggy."

Rupert sniffed wetly, blood bubbling from his crooked nose as he looked over to Jal. "I'm sorry," he said. Whether he meant it or not wasn't *Saint's* department, but he said it just the same, and repeated it for good measure. "I'm sorry, man. I just thought— aid workers, you'd have something worth selling at the market.

Decent shit. Decent caps." He squeezed his eyes shut, and in the harsh white of Saint's tac light, Saint couldn't tell sweat from tears on his pale face. "Wasn't personal. I just—I just want to get off this goddamn rock."

Not an unfamiliar feeling. Hell, every soul in the spiral probably wanted to get away from something or somewhere. But Jal's voice held no trace of sympathy as he said, low and rough, "You don't do it like this," and turned and walked away.

Saint held back another half second. "Another thing?" he said, digging in his pocket for the shotgun shells he'd palmed back at the Warehouse. When he pulled them out, he swore he *heard* the lights click on behind Rupert's watery eyes. Those assholes back on Sooner's Weald had made about that same face when they'd realized their mistake, too. "Don't let a stranger handle your goddamn gun."

Then he cracked the stock of the sawed-off into Rupert's jaw, and that was the end of the conversation. Rupert's head rolled forward, and Saint waited just long enough to see the man's chest rise and fall before he pocketed the shells, dropped the empty gun and after a moment's hesitation, tugged the knife from Rupert's belt and tossed it at his feet. If the man had any sense, he'd be able to cut himself loose once he came around. *Just better hope the rats don't get you first, asshole.*

Jal had already stalked back to the tree line when Saint turned around, tension pulling his shoulders so tight his jacket seams strained under the pressure. "You think he was telling the truth about Gethin?" he asked quietly, like he was afraid of what the answer might be. Rupert, the backstabbing sack of shit that he was, was still their only lead on Gethin's hideout. If they didn't have him, they didn't have anything.

It was Eoan who put him out of his misery. "It seems he was, actually," they said. "He was certainly right about the sensors, at any rate; there's a rather dense grid of them just ahead of your position, and a structure at the center."

"A structure," said Nash, in her flat *we're gonna need a little more detail than that, Cap* tone of voice. "A church?"

"It may have been," Eoan replied. "It certainly bears a resemblance—gable roof, enclosed portico, and a tall vertical protrusion near the front."

"*Vertical protrusion* like some kind of guard tower or turret, or *vertical protrusion* like a steeple?" Saint said. It was a pretty important distinction.

Eoan considered it a moment. "No signs of any armaments."

"Then it's a steeple. Just call it a steeple." *Vertical protrusion* sounded too much like *high ground* in Saint's head. Lookout. Sniper's nest. It made his spine itch. "Does it look occupied?"

"Either it is, or it has been recently. Someone's obviously put some work into it—reinforced the original structure, cleared back the brush in a good forty-five decimeter radius around the church."

"Way things grow around here," Nash said, "I'll bet that takes some upkeep."

Eoan hummed their agreement. "I'd estimate no more than a week's growth."

"Whoever they are, they didn't want surprise visitors." It was a calculated risk, clearing a space like that. As much as said *hey, there's somebody here*. But on the other hand, it'd be a lot easier for unfriendlies to creep up through the trees than to sneak across forty-five decs of open space. "Guessing you can't tell if there's warm bodies inside."

"The entire structure is heat-shielded, I'm afraid, and the windows are covered."

"Of course they are," said Nash. "That'd be my top to-dos, too, if I was building myself a cozy MercMansion. No way to get Dutch in, either?"

"Afraid not. Doors and windows are airtight."

Nash whistled. "Sister-snatching shitheadedness aside, I'm starting to think this Gethin guy knows what he's doing."

Jal's expression darkened. "If he knew what he was doing, he wouldn't have laid a fucking hand on my sister." And that was apparently as much standing around as Jal could take, because he turned on his heels, yanked his specs down around his neck, and set off into the darkened trees without so much as a *time to go.*

Nash looked over at Saint. "Is he gonna be a problem?" she asked quietly.

"No." If he'd answered too quickly, Nash didn't call him on it. *He won't be,* he insisted, if only to himself. Saint wouldn't let him. "Now let's go, before he gets too far out ahead."

Switching their lights over to red spectrum—easier on Jal's bare eyes, and less likely to broadcast their position to any lookouts—they took off after Jal into the trees. Wasn't quite a full-tilt sprint, but it wasn't far off, and Saint resigned himself to upping his cardio *again.* But Nash sucked wind right there beside him, so maybe he didn't feel so bad.

"What's. With all. The *running?*" she said, with the seething disdain of a cat clawing its way out of a full tub. She didn't tell Jal to slow down, though, and Saint doubted she ever would. They all knew what he was running toward.

Wasn't until the church came into view through the trees that Saint had to put a stop to it. He sped up the last few decs and managed to snare a hand in the back of Jal's coat, pulling him to a halt before he could break the tree line.

Jal rounded on him like he wanted to take a shot at him, but he dropped his arm at the last moment. "It's right there," he said instead.

"I know."

"She could be in there."

"I know," Saint repeated. "And so could Gethin and fuck knows how many of his friends, and whether Regan's in there or not, you're not gonna help her by charging in there and getting yourself caught or killed."

"But she—" Jal's mouth opened and closed helplessly, head and shoulders turning halfway toward the church before Saint caught the back of his neck in a firm, bracing grip.

"I *know*," Saint said again. "Kid, look at me. *Look at me.*" And he waited until that marble-black stare finally pulled away from the church to tell him, "I know she's your sister, and I know you want her back as quick as possible. But we have to be smart about this, not just for our sake, but for hers. You understand?" He sighed. This one was messy. Too goddamn messy, and maybe Nash was right to wonder about Jal. Maybe they should've left him back on the ship, with Bitsie, but it just wouldn't have sat right. Wouldn't have been fair, after all the times Jal had proven he had their backs. "There's a time to be a brother, and there's a time to be a ranger. Right now? Your sister needs the ranger. *We* need the ranger. Can you do that?" He held Jal's stare, searching his red-lit face for any signs of a lie. "Can we trust you to do this the right way?"

Jal's shoulders heaved under Saint's hand, not from the work of all that running, but from the impossible work of holding *still*. "You can," he said finally. Came out tight as seized metal, but Saint heard in it the God's honest truth. "I'll follow your lead, I swear. Just—" He clenched his jaw, Adam's apple shaping a swallow. "Just tell me what to do."

You sure? Saint wanted to ask, because he was an XO, responsible for the lives and safety of everyone on his crew; and he was a veteran soldier, who'd seen too many missions go south when things got personal.

He was also Jal's friend, though, as loaded as that word had come to be. And as Jal's friend, *Saint* was sure—*sure* that Jal was smart enough to know what needed doing, and strong enough to see it done, because he'd proven it. Shouldn't have had to, but he had, and damned if Saint would doubt him now.

So, he didn't ask. He clapped Jal on the shoulder and let him go, and he set his sights back on the church. "All right," he said.

"Cap, what're we working with? Looks like single story, one entry point, but any chance of a substructure?"

"Slim," they said. "The subsurface of the protoplanet is extremely unstable. Surveys from the mining colony say seventy percent of the crust is a combination of clay mud and water-soluble minerals."

"Why's that unstable?" said Jal.

"Because the other thirty percent is *water*," Eoan replied. "Brine deposits, mostly, frozen and semifrozen. Temperature fluctuations on the surface cause the brine to melt and refreeze unpredictably, so most underground structures collapse within a few months of excavation."

"Must've been oodles of fun to be a miner here," said Nash wryly.

"The cave-in rate was quite alarming, yes. Though evidently not alarming enough to stop them building new mines and depleting most of the colony's halite deposits."

"This is my surprised face," said Nash.

Saint cleared his throat. "So, no basement."

"I expect not," Eoan replied. "And no other ground-level exits."

"We're missing something," Nash said, refocused. "Place like this, people like these, they're gonna have another way out in case they need to make a quick getaway on the sly. They might not be able to manage a basement under the church, but what about a tunnel? Nothing too long; I'm thinking something they could shore up with, like, a big-ass culvert pipe."

Jal nodded alongside her. "It'd work," he said. "Dig a trench, drop it in, and bury it. The way the brush grows out here, you'd never see it after a week or two. Just need a way in and a way out. Some kind of hatch on the surface, couldn't be smaller than a half-dozen decs across."

Good. They were getting somewhere. "Somewhere around back, you think?"

"Makes sense," said Nash. "Wouldn't want to bail on bad company and pop up right in the middle of them."

Saint considered the church. Not much to it—a rectangle, half as wide as it was long, and shorter from end to end than the *Ambit*. If Eoan was right about the basement, and Saint had long been in the habit of assuming they were right about most things, there wouldn't be many places to hide. "Nash, Jal, you go around back and find their escape hatch. I'll keep an eye on things here, and once you find it, we'll all breach. I take front, you two go in from behind."

"Insert dirty joke here," Nash said under her breath.

He gave her a bland stare.

"Tough crowd." Unperturbed, Nash gave Jal a nudge off to the side. "Come on, Lassie. Let's go find Timmy's well."

"Who's Lassie?" But when Jal looked back at Saint, Saint shook his head. He'd explain later; for now, better to go with it, and Jal did just that. He took the lead again, and before long the two of them disappeared into all those twisted trees.

Saint settled in a few paces back from the tree line, gun drawn and monocular aimed at the front of the church. "Door looks retrofit," he said. "Reinforced?"

"Undoubtedly," said Eoan. "But you could probably fit through one of the sidelights next to it. It would be a tight squeeze, especially for you. . . ."

"Not sure how to take that, Cap."

Eoan laughed. "In the spirit in which it was intended. Which is to say, geometrically."

With a short laugh of his own, Saint turned his monocular on the sidelights on either side of the door. Roughly the same height, but half as wide. "Any idea what the shielding behind the windows is made of?"

"Given the reflectance, I'd say an aluminized fiberglass. Get a running start, you should be able to dive straight through."

"*Should be able to*," Saint said.

"I can't know everything, dear."

"Speaking of things to know," Nash said down the comms line, "you should watch your step on the approach, McBlastin-shit. Feels like there's some kind of current coming off the ground." And if the augment with the electrosensory mods said there was something sketchy going on, it paid to listen.

Jal clocked it first. "Looks like ground sensors," he said. "Got a few here out in front of me."

"You step on one?" Nash asked.

"You trying to hurt my feelings?" Louder, he said, "Got more than sensors on the ground back here, old man. Looks like the church had its own backyard cemetery. Got a fuck-load of old grave markers out here." There was a rustle of something like ivy, then, "*Name Unknown, Died . . .* can't really see that bit."

"*Name Unknown,*" Nash echoed. A frown curled audibly around the words. "That's shitty."

"That's mining on a frontier." If Jal meant to sound blasé about it, he missed the mark. "Bet it's a lot like the rock-drops back home."

"Rock-drop?" Eoan sounded curious, but it was the kind of curious that said they knew the answer wouldn't be pretty. They just had to know it anyway.

Jal hummed. "We were minin' floatin' rocks for the shit that made them float. If you were lucky, you'd feel 'em start to dip quick enough to bail. If you weren't." He paused, and Saint imagined him shrugging before he carried on, saying, "If it was like that here, when the mines collapsed, they might not've been able to tell whose body they were pulling up—if they bothered to pull them up at all. Like as not, the body under here goes with a name somewhere out there. Company'd just throw down a marker with the name when they figured the folks were beyond saving. If they ever found bodies that didn't get claimed—and most didn't, least not on Brigham—they'd just put down another marker and move right along. Like they died twice," he said, but he didn't seem satisfied with it. "Like the company killed 'em twice." He seemed to like that better.

"Welcome to the frontier." Nash could've been more sarcastic, but not by much. "Come as you are, work like a dog, die in a—*oh, hello*. Look at that marker, there. The big one." A pause. She must've pointed, and Saint itched to move closer to them. To see what she was pointing at, sure; but more than that, he just didn't like letting them out of his sight. Hadn't gone so well, the last time they'd split up on a mission.

He shook his head, banished the thought. Eyes forward and head clear; no other way to do this shit. "What've you got?"

"An idea," said Nash, damn near cheerfully. "Hey, miner boy, you thinking what I'm thinking?"

Saint heard the clipped end of a groan from Jal's side of the comms, then "I really hope not."

Nash ignored him. "Hey, Cap, would you say that marker's about six, maybe seven decs across?" Saint was pretty sure that was the size Jal mentioned for a hatch.

Didn't seem like coincidence.

"You found something?" he asked.

"Only one way to find out," Eoan replied. "Jal, if you'd be a dear?"

Jal grumbled something under his breath about disturbing the dead, but he must've sensed he was outnumbered, because a beat later Saint heard him grunt with effort. Marker must've been damn heavy, for him to struggle like that.

"Lift with your legs, miner boy," said Nash.

"*You* lift with your legs," Jal growled back, each word straining under the exertion. "Shit probably weighs more than you do."

"Probably weighs more than *you* do," Nash agreed, blithely chipper. "And you should be nicer to me. I'm cheering you on."

"You're yankin' my chain, is what you're doing."

"Rah, rah, move that rock."

"She-devil."

"Hey, I think I saw it move a little. Don't worry; we're not in any hurry."

"You wanna come lift this thing?" Jal swore under his breath. "You're killing me, woman."

"Yeah, but you're smiling again."

Saint took Jal's answering silence to mean Nash was right. She had her own way of doing things, but she could be comforting when she wanted to be. Might've even been a little encouraging, because after one last grunt he heard a pop like breaking hinges and the grind of shifting stone.

"Huh," said Nash.

Christ, Saint hated not being there with them. Hated not knowing what'd happened the second it happened. "*Huh,* what? You find something?"

Eoan threw him a bone. "They found what appears to be a hatch door," they said.

"And miner boy went and broke it," Nash added.

"I got it open, didn't I? Not my fault it was locked."

"He took it off the hinges," Eoan supplied. "But yes, it *is* open. If you'll give me just a moment, dear"—it took Saint a second to realize they were talking to Jal now—"I'll take the drone down and see what's what. Shouldn't take but a few seconds."

There was a sharp inhale and a slow exhale. "And then we go?" Jal asked, so tightly it almost hurt to hear it.

Saint took a breath of his own. His pulse wanted to climb. His throat wanted to stick. His stomach wanted to knot. Knowing what was on the line and all the ways it could go wrong, so many what-ifs tried their damnedest to creep in.

But it was his job not to let them. He was the one who kept shit together, no matter how hard it tried to break apart. The steady hand on the loaded gun. He got them in the door, and he got them all back out again, and whatever waited in the church, it wouldn't change that.

"Yeah, kid," he said. "Then we go."

CHAPTER SIX

JAL

Time slowed as the drone disappeared into the hatch, like somebody'd grabbed hold of the seconds and stretched them beyond what they could bear.

Felt like somebody'd done the same to Jal's nerves. Stretched them thin, scraped them raw, 'til they bled with every passing heartbeat. *Nerves of steel,* Regan liked to say, always on the tail end of an eye roll or a cuff to his ear. She could never bring herself to call him reckless or stupid, even when he deserved it—and lately, he'd deserved it plenty. She just swatted his ears and rolled her eyes and smiled, *always* smiled, to make sure he knew she loved him anyway. *Nerves of fucking steel, brother mine.* Bitsie really did get her mouth from her mama.

His nerves didn't feel very steely just then. *He* didn't feel very steely, standing at the edge of that hatch and willing himself not to jump straight in, to hell with the waiting. Standing still made the waiting harder, torn between wanting to know what they'd find in that church and being shit-scared of the answer. Better to keep moving, and Regan could roll her eyes and swat him 'til his ears fell off, if he could just *get her back.*

"Clear."

Jal couldn't have said whether Cap finished before he jumped, or he jumped before they finished. All he knew was that, by the time the word actually registered in his fear-fogged brain, his boots had already hit the bottom of the culvert pipe below.

Curved, corrugated plastic made for an unsteady landing,

but he'd had unsteadier. Like he'd figured, the pipe wasn't tall enough for standing; he had to hunch himself near in half to keep from bumping the bare fluorescent bulbs strung along the top. No light, thank fuck, just dead bulbs and a ladder some fifty decs ahead. His way in.

He ran for it. Cleared the distance to the tune of Nash swearing and dropping into the pipe behind him, and Saint crashing into what he reckoned was one of those windows he'd heard them talking about. No more stretched-out seconds, just ladder rungs under his hands and feet and a hatch to shoulder open at the end. Didn't budge the first time he shoved his shoulder into it, but he shook off the clay dust and the ripple of numb-pain-numb across his shoulder and did it again.

Hatch still held, but he heard something pop. Hinges, screws—didn't much matter what, because either it'd break or he would.

With a snarl, he drew back and threw his shoulder one more time into the hatch above, and *SNAP!* Louder and harsher than the ones before, and the hatch slammed open in a rain of sheared-off screws and broken bits of metal as he hauled himself into the room above.

He hadn't thought much about what he'd see—the layout, the threats, the reality of a mercenary hideout in the husk of something holy. Thinking was Saint's game. Eoan's. Nash's. Jal didn't have the imagination for it. The stomach, either, if he was being honest, because for every good option, there were ten bad, worse, and damn near unbearable ones standing right behind him. So no, he hadn't *thought*.

But he'd hoped. Goddamn him, he'd hoped beyond reason and sense that he'd throw open that door, and Regan would be standing there with her hand on her hip like *what took you so long?* Probably with a pile of beat-up assholes at her feet, queen of the hill, because she was his big sister, stronger than he'd ever be in ways that mattered a hell of a lot more. She'd never needed saving—not by him, not by anybody.

That hope died the moment he climbed out of the hatch.

Nobody was there—not in the cramped back office he'd climbed out into, or in the chapel through the open door ahead. Signs of life, yeah. Cots lined one wall of the chapel, laid out where pews might've been when the place could still be called a sanctuary. Tables and crates crowded the other side, none of them big enough to hide a person Regan's size, much less the likes of Gethin and whatever company he kept. Reminded Jal of barracks back in his training days—that special mix of everyday living and tactical gear that said *don't go getting comfortable, 'cause trouble's never far.*

People *had* been there, but not anymore. There was just Saint, standing straight-backed and stock-still at the other end of the church, bits of window and thermal shielding flaking off his jacket. His red tac light gave everything a bleeding glow, but Saint didn't look at any of it. He looked at *Jal*. Watched him as Jal staggered through the doorway, with this bated sort of expression on his face, like Jal was a mug he'd just dropped and he was waiting to see if it'd shatter. If *Jal* would shatter, because in typical Florence Toussaint fashion, he'd already accepted what Jal couldn't:

They were too late.

There was suddenly a breach in the hull of the world—a stark, sucking void where all the air and the warmth and the light used to be.

"They haven't been gone long." Nash drifted into the red-hued haze of Jal's periphery, running her fingertips along the tops of stacked-up crates. "A day, maybe less. Found their requisition list on the desk." Because she *had* been thinking. She looked at the church and saw the things that were there, not the things that weren't, and Jal was startled by how fiercely he envied her for it.

She flicked the serial numbers painted on one of the crates. "Req list has the delivery dates on all of these. This one came in yesterday. That one over there, too. Had to have been someone here to take them in, right? Gethin doesn't seem like the type to let the delivery boys waltz in unattended."

"So somebody's been here since Regan was taken," Saint said. *Since Regan was taken.* He said her name like a stranger's, like he hadn't taken her kid skating on a frozen pond or sat down for dinner at her table. Like he hadn't been part of their goddamn *family* for all those years he and Jal served together. And Jal knew it wasn't like that. He knew that. It was just . . . it was how he worked. Saint had this way of levelling himself out. Not just the look on his face, or the steadiness of his voice— all of that, sure, but so much more. There were times Jal could look at him and know everything in his head, but not now. Now, Jal stared, and stared, and stared, and he still didn't have a goddamn clue.

He *hated* when Saint did that. Hated the way it felt, like a wall going up between them that he couldn't get past, and he needed—fuck, he didn't know what he needed. He needed Regan to be there. He needed *Gethin* to be there, where Jal could reach out and do something with all that roiling, seething *awfulness* trapped in his chest, and he hated that, too. Wasn't who he was supposed to be anymore. Angry and helpless and *violent . . .* he'd been that man, before. He'd had to be, for years, trapped behind enemy lines on the wrong side of the universe from home. But he'd cut away that piece of himself, buried it with the shackles and the shock monitor and the scavs that'd put them on him. A ghost. A ruin, like all those crumbling places they'd passed in the woods—places that'd served their purpose and been left behind.

But he hadn't buried it deep enough. Maybe there was no burying it at all.

"Regan was here," he managed, finally. "She—I recognize

the walls from the video." Tacked-on scales of sheet metal, probably to shore up the walls and cover the thermal shielding. "Couldn't see much, but I saw them. She was here."

"Then we definitely didn't miss them by much," said Saint.

"Think Rupert tipped them off?" Nash asked. She sounded far away, though she couldn't have been more than four steps to his right, inspecting the crates like the shelves of one of her scrap shops. She'd open one, poke around inside, then move to the next when nothing caught her eye.

Saint shook his head. "Been gone too long for that," he said, doing more or less the same as Nash with the footlockers and bunks on the other side of the church. Never a wasted second. "Met the bastard not even two hours ago, and from the looks of this place, they've been gone a while longer than that. And they had time." He flipped a footlocker shut and stood, knees popping angrily. He didn't even wince; didn't gripe the way he was supposed to, didn't mutter under his breath about being *too damn old for this shit*. There was a time to be a ranger, he'd told Jal, like it was possible to stop being everything else. Possible to whittle himself down to nothing but the mission and whatever it took to finish it.

Times like this, Jal almost believed it.

"Look at this place," Saint went on. "They had a hostage and an hour-long trek through thick jungle terrain, and they still had time to pack their shit and ship out before we got here."

"Not all their shit," said Nash, thumping one of the crates.

"The shit that mattered," Saint replied. "Nothing left in these footlockers but junk, clothes, and spare blankets; not a single keepsake in the bunch."

Nash stopped poking around inside one of the crates long enough to turn and raise a skeptical eyebrow. "You're basing your timeline on the fact that the cutthroat kidnapper mercenaries keep mementos?"

"I'm not talking birthday cards and heirloom quilts." The

barest edge of a growl slipped into his voice, and Jal didn't know why he was so grateful to hear it, but he was. It stoked a little sense back into him, got his feet moving again, until he could cross the room and squat by the second-to-last footlocker in the line of bunks.

A sharp yank broke the padlock, and he turned the contents out on the floor. Saint was right: spare pair of cargo pants, a threadbare shirt, and a couple of meal bars. Nothing that couldn't be replaced at their next stop-off.

"No spare clips, no cleaning kits, no backup holsters," he muttered. He turned over the next one, just to be sure, but it had more of the same. "Couple of dull-ass knives, but that's it. There should be more in here." Back in his barrack days, cracking open a footlocker was like cracking open a diary. Hell, sometimes there were *actual* diaries in the footlockers. Because he didn't care what kind of hard-ass motherfucker you thought you were, very few people could go without picking *anything* up along the way. A favorite brand of gun oil, a watch you liked too much to wear into the dicey shit, a thumb drive full of *come home soon* comms from loved ones you weren't allowed to save up to your Guild-issued GLASS. But there wasn't any of that here.

"They knew we were coming," Saint said. "And they had time to pack up, get out, and make themselves scarce—I'm betting before we even docked."

"No records of ships leaving the port," Eoan confirmed. Jal had nearly forgotten they were listening, but he guessed they had to be. Their drone floated in the middle of the church, uncamouflaged. Weren't too worried about being seen, he guessed; just wanted to make sure there weren't any signals broadcasting out of the church while they did their sweep. "I'm afraid they're long gone."

"How?" Jal snapped. Damn near surprised himself with the sharpness of it—like he'd cut himself open, and then came the bleeding. "How the fuck're they gone? They were *here*. They were *right here*." He scraped his fingers through his hair, dizzy when he stood. *Head rush,* he told himself, *just head rush,* but then why'd his throat close up so tight? "Nobody but Rupert was supposed to know we were coming. You telling me they just up and left?" No way their luck was that bad. No way in hell.

"I don't have an answer to that," Eoan told him, and they didn't say they were sorry, but they *sounded* that way. Somehow that made it worse. "I'll do my best to find one, but right now, that isn't the issue."

"Don't like the sound of that," Nash said.

"You shouldn't." And while Jal usually liked Eoan's straightforwardness, he liked it a little less just then. "We just received a transmission. It came in through the GLASS pad you found in your cabin, Jal, and it's. . . ."

Jal's breath caught. "What? It's *what*?"

"It's difficult to watch" was what Eoan landed on. "I'm sending it to Nash now. Unfortunately, it seems you'll need to watch it before you come back to the ship. Just." They paused again. Eoan always took care to choose the right words, but he'd never heard them *struggle* so much with it. "Do try to remember, Jalsen, that she's all right."

What the fuck is that supposed to mean? he wanted to ask, but before he could get it past the vise around his lungs, Nash opened the transmission on her GLASS, and Jal got his answer the hard way.

Regan's face filled the screen. Regan, with her split lip and bruised cheeks. The bruises had darkened since the last video, swelling and purpling, and the shadows under her red-rimmed eyes were near as gruesome. No backdrop this time, just a green tarp and the relief of her own shadow in whatever light was aimed at her.

"Regan—" he started, but Nash shook her head.

"It's a recording," she said tightly. "She can't hear you."

But he could hear *her*. Could hear the almost-stifled waver in her voice as it came across the recording.

"Not the tearful reunion you had in mind, huh?" Her voice was stilted, toneless—not at all the way Regan talked, gliding smoothly through each thought from beginning to end. She never opened her mouth unless she knew exactly what she wanted to say and exactly how she wanted to say it, but now, she hesitated, like she wasn't sure what came next. Like it was her voice, but someone else had chosen all the words. "Not exactly how I'd planned my day, either, but so it goes. Flexibility—that's what they don't teach you in basic. Which is a shame, if you ask me. A little more flexibility would do the Guild some good." She paused there for a shuddering inhale. Her eyes shined with unshed tears. So much like their mama's, those eyes, all big and green and bright. So much like their mama's, and so *different* from Jal's.

Something must've happened off-screen, because Regan tensed and hurried to pick up where she'd left off. "Hope you like the stand-in, by the way," she said. "Seemed only fair, after all the trouble you went to, trying to get to her. All the risks you took."

Even in Regan's broken monotone, that last part had the air of a threat.

"But don't worry about big sis," Regan went on. Her neck muscles jumped, straining to keep her head up. Chin raised. Eyes forward. She always, *always* kept her head up. "You've still got a job to do. In twelve hours, you'll receive a set of co-ordinates on this GLASS. In sixteen hours, you're going to *be* at the coordinates. No more loopholes. No more detours. I'm willing to write this off as a mutual misunderstanding—hell, I blame myself. Put old Ori on cleanup, and you just can't teach that man anything. Can't expect to leave a mess behind and not have it show up on your doorstep. But see, that's my lesson learned. Never too old to learn, that's what I say. Me, I learned to be more careful who I trust to clean up after me."

Regan paused again, like her throat wouldn't form the words that came next. Jal could *hear* the catch as she swallowed, could make out every tendon in her jaw and neck as they pressed against her skin.

Again, with a half-hidden start, she kept going.

"I'm hoping you've learned something from this, too," she said. "I'm hoping you've learned that I'm not one of your scrap-fucking scavs or some soft-bellied C-suiter that you can get one over on, and that our actions have consequences."

Just as she finished, a scream rang out over the comms. Not Regan's; somebody else's, unfamiliar and terrified and so startlingly *short*. The unmistakable crack of a gunshot, and that screaming stopped so abruptly that it almost seemed to echo on into the silence. Like it wasn't ready to let go.

Tears rolled down Regan's cheeks, and Jal's eyes welled to match. They'd seen some awful things, back home. People dying from accidents and sickness and all manner of other horrors. But it occurred to him, watching those shakes she'd been fighting finally ripple into her shoulders and spine . . . this was a new kind of horror for her. This was a part of the world she'd never seen, and he'd have given *anything* to keep it that way.

It killed him to know he'd failed.

He got so caught up in it, he almost didn't hear her start to speak again. "Now, old Ori, I couldn't get a damn thing through his thick skull," she said, and there was no missing that past tense. "But I think you're smart enough to get the picture. Sure as hell smarter than I remember, if you're standing where I think you're standing, but—" Her voice caught, lips pulling into a tight, pained line. "But between you and me, rock jockey, that's a damn low bar." She looked guilty as she said it. Miserable, like saying the words was almost worse than what might've happened if she hadn't.

If it kept her safe, Jal didn't give a good goddamn *what* she said.

"Now, I'm more of a visual learner," she said for Gethin, because Jal *knew* who those words belonged to now. *Rock jockey.* They'd called him so much worse on that crew, took turns thinking up new smart-ass call signs for the freak-on-loan, but Gethin had always liked that one. "So I've left you a visual aid in a couple of the crates. Three-one-eight-seven and three-one-eight-nine. Open them." Another pause. Another breath. "And trust me when I say I'll know if you don't."

Jal thought that'd be the end of it. One last threat to fall in line, and he waited for the GLASS screen to go blank. Just as Nash's thumb moved to stop the playback, though, Regan's split lips pulled themselves into a smile. Thin as it was, strained and chapped, Jal knew it had to hurt. Everything about this hurt. But even though Regan couldn't see him, couldn't hear him, Jal knew that smile was for him. To make sure he knew she loved him, like she always did.

"I'm so sorry," she said, and *that* was her. Straight through, beginning to end. "I never should've—"

The video ended there. It froze on her face, on that watery smile and that awful fucking apology. *I'm so sorry.* And he couldn't even say it back.

He didn't recognize the sound he made. Animal and tortured, scraped out past his seizing ribs, and the world twisted out of shape and out of focus as he hurled the nearest cot at the wall. Didn't help to hear it crack against the metal sheeting, to watch the pieces scatter across the floor. Didn't help to do it again, and again, but he didn't know what else to *do.*

He got caught up in it. *Don't know what to do.* A spiral. *Don't know what to do.* An anchor around his neck, dragging him down to his knees as the roaring in his ears gave way to a tinny, disorienting ring. He'd have been sick, he thought, if anything more than a wheeze could fit up his throat.

"This is my fault." He hadn't let himself say it before; now, he couldn't seem to say anything else. Regan had apologized, and it was his fault, and this was supposed to be how he *fixed it*. This was supposed to be the way he got Regan back without dragging Saint and Nash and Eoan into a fucking suicide mission, and all they had was an empty fucking church and an *apology* from the last person who should've been sorry.

"I found the crates." Nash spoke softly, like she didn't trust the quiet not to break under the weight of her voice. Something fragile glossed across the surface of something dangerous and unpredictable. Jal thought of frozen ponds and wind-chapped cheeks and Regan with her rolling eyes and *love you* smile when they shuffled in from the cold.

"Open them." Saint answered the hanging, unspoken question. Decisive. He was good at that. Jal opened his eyes to boots he didn't remember being so close. Right there, right in front of him, and when Jal looked up, Saint had a hand out waiting to pull him up. "Carefully."

Another time, Nash probably would've had something snarky to say to that. *Right, 'cause if you hadn't said anything, I was just gonna slap some explosives on them and see what happened.* But she was quiet and focused as she undid the latches, skimming her fingers along the edges and just inside the barely open lid before she finally seemed to decide it wouldn't blow up in their faces.

It didn't.

No bombs, no spring traps, but what it *did* have wasn't much of an improvement. From where he stood, Jal could only see a head and shoulders. A man, or—fuck, *half* of one, blood on his face and a hole just north of his eyes. Smelled like he'd been there a couple hours, at least.

"I'm thinking that's probably Ori," Saint said.

"I'm thinking you're probably right," said Nash. "And I'm guessing the rest of him's behind door number two." She opened it anyway, with *just get it over with* efficiency. Legs. Blood. Boots. Mercifully, Nash shut it before Jal could clock anything in greater detail, stepping back from the crate with her hands clasped loosely behind her, like subconsciously she wanted them as far from the crates as possible. He'd never known her to be squeamish, but there was just something deeply, viscerally *wrong* about a person packed away like that. Cut down and folded up to fit, just another bit of cargo they'd been happy to leave behind. "There's something in the wound. Looks like some kind of paper."

Saint stepped up closer, and Jal fell in behind him. "Can you see what it is?"

"Did I not just say *some kind of paper*?"

"I meant can you see what's on it?" Saint said.

"You mean do I want to stick my fingers in his squishy obliterated brain hole to read the undoubtedly psychopathic goodness wrapped up inside?" She puffed a few flyaways out of her face, grimacing. "Sure, sounds like fun."

Gloves appeared from . . . somewhere, snapping onto quick hands that made shockingly quick work of plucking the rolled-up paper from the bullet wound. Nash held it away from herself, rolling it out more gingerly than she'd opened the possibly-spring-trapped crate, and read, "*Finally got it through his thick skull.*"

"Fuck," said Saint.

Jal couldn't even muster that much. He turned, because his imagination was shit, but it wouldn't have been too hard for it to take that bullet hole and stick it on a much friendlier face. Wouldn't have been too hard to imagine *Regan* as the one screaming on that vid comm, just before the shot went off.

"We need to reassess our plan," Eoan said after a long, uneasy moment. It was somehow both the most obvious and the most reassuring thing they could've said. *Reassess* was so much better than *scrap it and give up*. Yeah, it was fucked up beyond all reason, but it wasn't fucked up beyond all *hope*. Jal clung to that spare shred of optimism with everything he had. "We'll do a quick sweep, see if we can glean anything from what they *did* leave behind, and then I want you all back on the ship. Quickly. Do you understand?"

Eoan didn't get any arguments.

. . .

Bitsie was waiting for them in the cargo bay. No sign of one of Eoan's projections, just Bitsie, sitting on the hood of the rover with a GLASS tablet and a stylus in her hands. She set everything aside as soon as she clapped eyes on them, though she didn't hop down from the rover hood.

Jal had been practicing, on the walk back to the port, what he'd say to her. Worked out a way to break it to her gently, followed swiftly by whatever promises it took to convince her that they'd get Regan back, one way or another, even if he couldn't rightly say how.

He didn't know why he still bothered practicing, because it never helped. All those pretty, practiced words always went up in smoke the second it came time to actually *use* them. He saw Bitsie sitting there on the edge of the rover hood, stylus hanging from her fingers and an inscrutable look on her face, and *poof.* Nothing. Not a goddamn thing left in his head, except wondering how in all the spirals and stars he could love her so much and not *know* her. Not be able to read her. His own niece, and sometimes she felt like a stranger.

Did I really miss that much?

The answer was the same gut punch it'd always been.

"Your mama wasn't there," he finally said, once he'd already cleared the hatch and closed half the distance to the rover. A few more steps and he closed the rest, trying all the while not to wince at how *bad* he was at this. Talking, generally. Talking to his niece, specifically. He'd never had a gift for gab, but he and Bitsie—they never used to have a problem.

Of course, Bitsie *still* didn't seem to have a problem. "I know," she said. "Captain Eoan told me. Said they hoped you wouldn't mind, but it didn't seem right to make me wait."

Jal probably should've felt guilty about it. Some sense of responsibility to be the one to break the news, being her uncle and all. But damned if he wasn't more grateful than anything, because he still hadn't worked out what came after *your mama wasn't there*, and Eoan must've said something right. Bitsie's cheeks were red, like she might've had some tears to wipe away, but her eyes were clear.

"Speaking of Eoan," said Saint. "You back here all by yourself?"

"I'm twelve," Bitsie replied, without so much as a dash of sarcasm. Not mouthing off, just telling it like it is. "It's not like I need a babysitter."

Saint arched an eyebrow like *that's me told*. "That's right, it's not." He still seemed to have trouble squaring the lanky preteen in front of them with the wide-eyed six-year-old Jal'd kept bringing along on their shore leaves. Some petty part of Jal liked it—liked not being the only one who didn't know where the time had gone, or how he'd missed so much of it. The better part liked that Saint kept trying anyway. "Did they say if they were doing something?"

"They said they had to take a call." Bitsie jabbed her thumb over her shoulder, toward the front of the ship. "And to come to the bridge when you're ready to debrief."

"No time like the present," said Saint, but when he and Nash started for the cargo bay door, Jal held back.

"Give us a second," he said.

Saint looked between them and nodded, and Nash flicked a salute off her forehead and followed him down the hall.

Just him and Bitsie, then. He cleared his throat. "We're gonna get her back," he told her steadily. Eoan might've said that already, too, but he wanted her to hear it from him. Wanted her to know he believed it. "Not real sure how, yet"—because he'd never lie to her, and sure as hell not about something as important as this—"but we will." Somehow he'd find a way to get Regan back and keep the *Ambit* crew safe, and he couldn't say yet what that'd look like or what it'd cost him, but the walk back had given him a chance to get his head on straight. And he'd decided, damn the price and damn the doubt. He'd make it happen, because he couldn't do otherwise.

Bitsie just smiled, and it hurt like a knife twisted into the middle of him. She had her mama's smile. *I love you.* "I know." She said it like she believed it, and she said it like she dared anybody not to.

"You know" was all he had the sense to say.

She sighed, exasperated, and reached up to poke him in the chest. "You found us once," she said. "When everybody said you wouldn't, you did. Took you a while, sure, but you crossed the whole universe to get back to us. Wherever these assholes—"

"Language," he said, reflexively.

"Wherever these *fucking* assholes went." She doubled down with a glinting grin. She got that from her mama, too: a healthy dose of spite. Though there might've been a little bit of Nash's influence hiding in the corners. He felt himself smiling, too, as she continued, "They can't be as far as that, and this time, you've got help from the start. I mean, I don't know if you noticed, but Captain Eoan is kind of a genius."

He huffed a laugh. "I did notice that, yeah."

"And Nash? Mom said she saved a whole space station with a plasma torch and some tape. That's grade-A *badass*, Uncle Jal."

Jal couldn't help but agree, especially anywhere Nash could hear him.

"And you've got Saint again," Bitsie finished. "I don't really remember him that well, but I remember how Mom used to talk about him when you'd leave. She said she was okay with you leaving, because she knew there was somebody looking out for you. And I know things got kind of complicated, but when he was there, you always came back."

That much was true, he guessed. When they'd served together, Saint had always had his back. Always made sure he got to go home at the end of whatever shitstorm they'd sailed into, and with all his pieces more or less intact. Wasn't until they'd split up that things had taken a turn, and it would've been a lie to say Jal had untangled all the messy things he felt about the old man and what he'd done, but he *did* trust him. That much he could be sure of.

"I knew, back then," Bitsie told him, a little quieter. "I knew you'd find us, and you did, and now I know you'll do it again. You don't let people down, Uncle Jal. It's just not in your DNA."

They didn't make a better pep talk than that, did they?

"Shit," he said. "When'd you go and get *wise* on me, little bit?" And tall, and strong, and so goddamn brave. Her eyes were shiny in the halogen light of the cargo bay, but they hadn't lost their certainty. "Come here." Maybe twelve was too old for babysitters, but it wasn't too old for a hug. She buried her face in his shirt, and he held her as tight as he dared, kissing the top of her head like he'd done when she was little. She was *still* little. She'd grown, and she'd changed, and she'd learned to swear and stand up for herself and put on a brave face when things got hard, and he was trying to respect that. Make room for that. But even so, she was still a kid who needed her mama, and come hell or high water, he'd make sure she got her.

Bitsie sniffled against his shirt, then sniffed again and pulled back with a wrinkled nose. "Uncle Jal, you smell like a compost bin."

Another laugh snuck loose, even easier than the last. She wasn't all that far from the truth, but the less she knew about Lummis, the better. "Bad-mannered little hobgoblin," he said instead, and she might've hit a growth spurt while he was away, but it was still the work of a half second to sweep her up and throw her over his shoulder.

"You're gonna make *me* smell like a compost bin," she complained, flailing her feet and arms so he had to shift his grip to keep from dropping her. She'd be good in a fight, if she ever wanted to learn. He prayed she'd never need to.

She gave one last good squirm—got a knee in his sternum, though he was about sixty percent sure she didn't mean to—and fell limp over his shoulder. "I *definitely* smell like a compost bin." She'd have sounded defeated, if he couldn't hear the smile in her voice. Fuck, even with her knee in his ribs and her weight on his shoulder, he breathed easier than he had all day. All *week*. Kids . . . they just had this way of making the world better. Of making you want to *make* the world better. "You know," she said, softly, "I'm gonna be too big for this soon."

Wasn't like she'd get too heavy, but he knew that wasn't what she meant. "But not today?" he asked.

"Not today," she agreed.

He could live with that.

CHAPTER SEVEN

EOAN

They'd thought it might be Gethin, when they'd first received the hail. Another taunt. Another stroke of cruelty to add to all the rest.

Mercifully, the holotable projected a much friendlier face into the center of the bridge. With deep smile lines around his mouth and a graying crown of short-cropped hair, Captain Torsten Brodbeck wore his years hard, but well. It had been decades since they'd crewed a ship together, he and Eoan, but his eyes still shined as silvery bright as they ever had.

Strange to see them paired with such an uneasy frown.

"You know I hate to be the bear of bad news, old friend," he said. "But it seemed like something you ought to know. Figured this one would hit a little closer to home for you and yours."

"You figured right." He usually did. Torsten was one of the senior-most members of the Captains' Council, and one of the few who'd made more friends than enemies in his rise to power. In their experience, he seldom got things *wrong*—excepting, of course, the odd turn of phrase. The man had a gift for malapropism. "But what is it you always say? *Bad news is better than a bad surprise.*"

Torsten's frown lifted, somewhat, as he rubbed his bearded cheek. "You sure that was me?" He chuckled, though from a man whose booming laughs could fill a ship, it felt painfully thin. Not much room for levity, in the wake of what he'd told them. "Sounds too smart."

"Oh, I don't know," they said, summoning a smile of their own. Even under the worst of circumstances, smiles always seemed a little easier to find around Torsten. "I always thought you were cleverer than you let on."

Torsten winked and put a finger to his lips.

"Your secret's safe with me, old friend," Eoan told him.

"They always were." Fondness creased the corners of Torsten's eyes. Nostalgia. Eoan had never really been prone to it before; always too busy looking forward, to the next big thing. The next taste of something *new*.

Lately, though . . . after their brush with something so terribly like death, their whole perspective had shifted. Knowing that something had an ending—that *they* had an ending—made all those countless beginnings seem so much more precious. And now, for all they looked ahead, they'd found themself looking *back*.

With Torsten, *back* meant long trips past the Aron outpost and late-night games of King's Table while the rest of the crew slept. It meant listening to his raucous stories, whispered midmission down the comms channel. It meant knowing beyond a shadow of a doubt that any ranger he brought with him into the field, he'd surely be bringing back, because he didn't believe in losing. Those were the things Eoan saw when they looked at him now; and how could they look to the future, when all too soon he wouldn't be a part of it?

"You got your thinking face on," said Torsten, dragging them away from thoughts of past and future and rooting them firmly back in the present. "Something on your mind? Something *else*, I mean. Bad news aside."

I'm not quite sure where to begin. "You know me," they said instead. "Always something on my mind."

Torsten gave them a *Look*—that very specific Look of his that said he wasn't fooled, but he'd let them have it anyway. Something else lurked behind it, though. A moment's indecision, flickering and resolving in the lines between his brows. "Aw, hell," he said, after a beat. "I don't mean to pile on, but there's something else you should know. Somebody's looking into you, Eoan."

If they'd had hair, that would've set it on end. "Come again?"

Torsten shook his head, rubbing his beard again. One of his more persistent habits. They wondered if he still insisted on that same beard wax, even though he could never seem to find it outside Sooner's Weald. "I'm not sure," he said. "But a few hours ago—call it five," he clarified, automatically. Torsten was no stranger to their need for precision. "Somebody accessed your ship's transponder codes in the registry with a masked access ID. Could be nothing, but—"

"But nothing's ever nothing," they finished for him.

"That another one of mine?"

"Might be."

Another chuckle, even fainter than the last. "At least one of us still remembers the old days, I guess." He sighed. "Strange times we're living in, aren't they? Lots of backwards business going on, and the last thing I want's for you and your people to get caught up in it."

I'm afraid that ship's already sailed, dear. "We'll do our best," they told him, and hoped it sounded sincere. "And you do the same."

"Oh, don't you worry about me. I'm a damn tardigrade—couldn't kill me with a knife, a nuke, and a hand from God himself." He started to say something else, but Nash and Saint had made it to the bridge. "I'll let you get back to your crew, Captain," he said. "But keep me in the loop, all right? I hear anything more on my end, you'll be the first to know."

"Of course," Eoan said. "And Torsten? Thank you."

A flicker of a smile, then Brodbeck's blunt-knuckled hand waved across the screen and the holotable went dark.

"Brodbeck?" Saint asked them, crossing to the port side of the bridge, where he waved to open the door to his quarters. Technically the captains' quarters, according to the ship's specifications, attached like an en suite to the bridge. Eoan had obviously never had much use for it. More to the point, as much damage as Saint's body had endured through the years, they thought it better he *didn't* have to fight with the ladder to the crew quarters every time he wanted to sleep in an actual bed. "What'd that old warhorse want?" Saint was probably one of the few people who could make *warhorse* sound like a compliment.

On the other side of the bridge, Nash had claimed one of the four seats arranged in an arc around the holotable. "I'm gonna take a wild guess and say *nothing good*." A bit of digging in her bag, and out came a crochet hook, a spool of pink-and-purple yarn, and the head of a comically large-eared monkey.

Eoan wondered if she realized how much she knitted in *pink* these days.

"Afraid not," they said. "But we should really wait for Jal." Torsten's news had as much bearing on him as any of the others. Perhaps more. "He should be along shortly." Easy to track everyone's progress through the common areas of the ship, and where Saint and Nash had paused a moment in the galley— Saint presumably for the meal bar he pulled from his pocket, and Nash to put a fresh pot of water on to boil—Jal and Bitsie passed straight through. "And here they are."

Jal slowed in the doorway, wearing the echoes of a smile on his lips and a scaled-down human on his shoulder. "Sorry," he said sheepishly. "Didn't mean to keep y'all waiting." He lowered Bitsie carefully to her feet and looked around at the others, and never let it be said Jal wasn't the *observant* sort. A single sweep of the room, and his smile faltered. "What's wrong?"

Nash jabbed a thumb toward Eoan's projections. "We're about to find out."

"Let's hear it, Cap," said Saint around a mouthful of meal bar. "What's the damage?"

If Eoan breathed, they would've taken a breath before they

spoke. One of the deep, bracing gulps of air Saint always took when he knew he'd hate doing something and had to do it anyway; they never seemed to make it better, but perhaps he gained something from the effort. "Ninety-six minutes ago, the ship escorting Fenton to his work detail on Noether suffered a catastrophic failure of its pressurization system," they said. "The results were . . . explosive. Recovery efforts are underway, but Tors—*Captain Brodbeck*," they amended, "said they don't anticipate survivors."

A funerary silence fell over the bridge. Never an easy thing, hearing about the loss of a Guild crew. Even if they'd never met a soul aboard, they had something in common. Common oath, common aims, common understanding that the good they stood to do was worth the risks they took to do it.

Under different circumstances, Eoan would've given them time after news like that. Would have compiled all the black-box records and recovery team reports for Nash, because she always needed to know what had happened, what had malfunctioned, what had *failed*, so she could bury herself in the belly of the ship and make sure it couldn't happen to them. Would have given Saint a list of names, so that in the still hours of the night, he could pour a glass of blur for each of them and drink in the galley with a table full of ghosts.

They had no such luxuries now. No time for rituals, as the seconds honed the silence to a razor's edge and realization set in. The loss of Fenton's escort meant more than the loss of a fellow crew; it meant—

"We're missing something, aren't we?" Nash whispered, hands falling still in her lap. "Fenton . . . whatever the hell's going on here, he's got to be part of it. Timing like that's not random. Guild ships don't just *break*."

Jal's brows furrowed, mouth pulling sideways in a thoughtful frown. "But Fenton's got nothing to do with Drestyn," he said. "Guy was on the other side of the spiral when all the Deadworld stuff went down."

"Unless it's not *about* Drestyn," said Eoan. They'd had a few more minutes to mull it over, and they could do more with *minutes* than most could do with hours. Days. Weeks. The AI existence had its limitations, but it also had its benefits. "We've been treating all of this like he's at the center of the web, but what if he's simply another loose end? A symptom, not the cause."

"Okay," Nash began, leaning forward in her seat. She had that look on her face—the one she got when something didn't work, and she didn't know why. "But if it's not about Drestyn, then who *is* it about? What've Regan, Drestyn, Gethin, and Fenton all got in common?"

"Other than Jal," said Saint, glancing over at the man in question. Saint hid it well, but Eoan's sensors picked up the spike in his pulse, the infinitesimal hardening of his jaw. He didn't like the idea that Jal could be tangled any deeper into all of this than they already thought.

They didn't much like it, either. "It's like you said, dear," they told Nash. "We're missing something—some piece to the puzzle that would bring all the rest into focus." A decryption key. Eoan couldn't shake the feeling they were only seeing *parts* of some as-yet-undecipherable whole, and until they found that piece, they couldn't possibly get ahead of whatever had been set into motion.

"But why would they move on Fenton now?" asked Saint. "He's been en route for ten days; if they had some kind of kill switch, they had plenty of other opportunities to flip it and get *way* less attention. Doing it today, less than an hour after we rolled up on Gethin's hideout, as much as *announces* that Fenton's involved somehow. You ask me, that's either sloppy as hell or a brutal misdirect, and these guys don't strike me as sloppy."

"Or option C: it's a calculated risk," Nash replied. It was

fascinating, the way they built off one another. Not contradict-
ing, but *compiling* thoughts turn by turn, barely a missed beat
between them. "Maybe we didn't know Fenton was involved
with the main storyline here, but we knew he was involved with
Gethin. Once we came up empty at Lummis, it wouldn't have
been too big a reach to think we'd try another angle."

"And if he *did* know something about what's going on and
we started leaning on him about Gethin, he might've let something *else* slip." Saint nodded slowly, grimly. "So what we're
saying here is we had a lead we didn't know we had, and now
that we know we have it, it blew up on a prison transport halfway to Noether."

Nash shrugged and picked her crochet hook back up.
"Them's the breaks, McBlastinshit. Does make you wonder
how Gethin could've pulled the trigger, though."

"I'm not entirely sure it *was* Gethin," Eoan chimed in. "This
part's a shade more speculative—"

"Than a maybe-lead from a maybe-conspirator who died in
a maybe-sabotage?" Bitsie asked, face scrunched skeptically.
She'd wandered away from Jal and dropped into the seat next
to Nash, stealing glances at Nash's hands as they worked. Her
fingers twitched in her lap, as if mimicking Nash's; and after a
moment, Nash even seemed to slow down, like she knew she
had an audience, and wanted to let Bitsie follow along. "Isn't
that pretty much just, like, *guessing*?"

"Manners, Bitsie," Jal murmured, though he didn't have the
temperament for scolding. He seemed to have made the conscious—if conflicted—decision not to follow her, keeping close
to the doorway as a certain fixated feline curled around his ankles. Really, what was it about Jal that made that cat so *affec-
tionate*? Pheromones? Some sort of nepetalactone smell-alike?

An interesting experiment for later, perhaps. For now, they
said, "She's not wrong." They couldn't possibly fault her for
asking questions; rather the opposite. It delighted them. The

undamped, unapologetic curiosity . . . in some ways, Eoan saw something of themselves in Bitsie. "It *is* like guessing." Educated, albeit, but guessing just the same. They didn't have the human capacity for certainty, especially in the face of so much missing information. Still, they had *some* information of use. To the crew as a whole, they said, "Brodbeck wasn't just comming to tell us about Fenton's escort. He said that someone with a masked ID accessed our transponder codes."

"Masked like *I'm a sneaky hacker and I'm covering my ass?*" Nash asked. "Or masked like *I'm a member of the Captains' Council and all my shit's so classified the system doesn't even record my logins?*"

"That's the question of the hour," said Eoan. The access itself didn't bother them; most anyone in the Guild could access the repository. Rangers weren't meant to hide their movements from each other; they weren't meant to *need* to. With the *Ambit*'s transponder code, anyone could run a trace and find their position. But there were supposed to be *logs*. Access IDs, to show who'd been looking and, ideally, *why*. A masked ID was an outlier—only a few ways it could happen, and none of them comforting under the circumstances. "It's impossible to know for sure," they allowed. "It could have been an outside job."

"But you don't think it was." Saint didn't ask; he *observed*. He knew them well enough to interpret. "You think it was someone in the council." Eoan, likewise, knew *him* well enough to know he didn't like the direction this conversation was going. If he'd crossed his arms any tighter, he might've cracked a rib. The straps of his shoulder brace strained, until he frowned and tugged them loose.

"The timing did raise some red flags," they said. "Brodbeck said the access was logged five hours ago."

Saint's expression darkened. "So, plenty of time for Gethin's men to clear out of the church. I'm guessing our trip to Lummis didn't go unnoticed."

"And you think someone in the Captains' Council did the *noticing*?" Jal asked. "Why?"

"I've done a bit of digging on my own while we were talking." With as much processing capacity as they had, multitasking became something of a routine. "Shortly after the transponder code repository was accessed, Captain Raimes left Alpha Librae with an unspecified flight plan. Now, we don't *know* that those two things are related," they said, though they knew it wouldn't be much comfort. The line between *know* and *suspect* could be an awfully thin one. "All we know is that someone who *may* have had Raimes's clearance level accessed our transponder codes nearly three hours before we reached Lummis, and not long after that, Raimes left the station to parts unknown and undeclared. I also know that Raimes was one of the biggest proponents for sending Fenton to Noether in the first place." Other members of the Captains' Council, including Torsten, had simply wanted to discharge him and wash their hands of him completely.

Jal picked at a loose thread on his coat restlessly. Unlike Saint's dark beard, which at least obscured *most* of his teeth-grinding, Jal's scruff showed every tense, abortive twitch of muscle and ligament at the hinge of his jaw. "Raimes *warned* them, didn't he?"

"Don't do that, kid." Sympathetic, but firm. Saint caught Jal's gaze and shook his head. "Until we know what's what, you don't want to go down that road. Focus on the problem that's in front of you—in front of *us*."

"Easier said than done," Nash said. "If we've got a mole at the tippy-top of the Guild, I kinda want to know about it. Don't you? Wait, no." She gave him a flat look, but stopped short of rolling her eyes. "I forgot your allergy to all things *sedition*."

"I just don't think we ought to rule out the hundred *other* explanations there could be besides a conspiracy. Eoan said it could've been a hacker just as easily as it could've been someone on the Captains' Council."

"Right, and Raimes was just kicking off his one-man road trip when he skipped town a couple hours before Fenton's ship blew up." Nash squinted at him. "I know I'm not exactly the Guild's biggest cheerleader lately, but even *you've* got to admit the timing's hinky. *And*," she added before Saint could argue, raising a crochet hook like someone else might raise a finger, "there's *something* going on with him and Drestyn. He broke protocol just to talk to him on Alpha Librae, and I didn't see any of the other councilors personally overseeing that transfer. Whether he's Team Gethin or not, he left Alpha Librae for a reason, and I'm pretty sure that reason's got something to do with this steaming pile of shit we've stepped in."

"Can we track him?" Jal asked. "Like he—like *someone*," he amended tightly, "did to us?"

"I tried," Eoan said. For all the good it did them. "His comms went dark the second he left the satellite's airspace."

"Score one more for the Shadiest Cowboy in the West," said Nash. "C'mon, Saint, I know the way that big, brood-iful brain of yours works. Pretend for a second that Raimes isn't on the Captains' Council—hell, pretend he's not even a ranger. He's just some guy who's done some real questionable things with real questionable timing, who I'm willing to bet has access to the same flight plans that Jal nicked off the brig terminal, and now he's out there, fuck knows where, doing fuck knows what, for fuck knows why. You telling me that's a *later* problem?"

He wanted to; Eoan could tell. He wanted to tell her to stop with the hypotheticals and focus on the problem they could *see*, because one they could see was one they could fix, and Saint wanted more than anything to *fix this*. For Jal.

That was the trouble, they thought. Certainly, some of Saint's reluctance came from his faith in the Guild—a soldier's faith in a soldier's flag, and an oath sworn not to the banner itself, but to the siblings-in-arms who swore beside him. He didn't want to believe *any* ranger could turn against that oath. He'd seen it happen, though, and he wasn't naïve enough to think it wouldn't happen again.

The *real* hesitation came from something else: from knowing that the more layers they added to the problem that lay before them, the harder it would be to solve in a way they could live with. And no, Saint had never shied away from hardship, but this wasn't his to carry. Jal and Bitsie—*they'd* lost Regan. *They* had to worry if they'd ever get her back.

Saint couldn't carry that for them. He would've if he could've, in a heartbeat; he'd have shouldered every burden of everyone he'd ever loved if the world had given him the choice. So admitting to himself, much less to everyone else, that Jal and Bitsie might have to bear even more, even longer . . . it pained him in ways Eoan wasn't even sure *Saint* understood.

Nevertheless, eventually, he sighed and shook his head. "If it were anybody else," he allowed, "I'd say there's two options. One, he's insurance to make sure we get the job done, and we don't have to worry about him unless we miss Gethin's deadline."

Bitsie turned her gaze to him. "What's the second option?" she asked, and Eoan swore they heard something *crack* inside of him. A hairline fracture in that ironclad composure.

"He's competition," he said, and fractures or no, he sounded as steady as he ever did. That was Saint: *steady*, even when he wasn't. *Fine*, even when he couldn't be. "Doesn't trust us to do the job, so he'll do it himself."

"And if he does?" Bitsie pressed determinedly. "If he gets to Drestyn first, what happens to Mom?"

A few of those cracks tried to break through, creasing almost imperceptibly at the corners of Saint's eyes, but somehow he managed a smile. "Nothing happens to your mom," he told her. "Because he's not gonna get to Drestyn first. You remember what Nash told you? We don't do what-ifs around here; we just get it done. So, that's what we're gonna do. Right, Nash?"

Nash hid a flicker of guilt behind a smile of her own. She never meant to push things too far; she just didn't always realize she was doing it until after the fact. "Right," she said, setting back to work on the monkey. Centering herself, or distracting herself, Eoan couldn't have said. "Next stop, *wherever the hell Drestyn is.*"

Nobody mentioned what that would mean. Going after Gethin was one thing, but breaking Drestyn out of Union custody to trade him for a hostage? They'd be operating *well* outside the bounds of Guild code. No jurisdiction, no authorization, and no going back. And if they got caught?

Well, better if they didn't.

"Then we're agreed," Eoan said, leaning back against the holotable and steepling their hands. "We get Drestyn from the Union, and we do it before *anyone*"—be it Raimes, or Gethin, or anyone else—"can get to him first. Now, all we need is a plan."

. . .

"This is a *bad* plan," Jal mumbled quietly, staring down at his gray, grease-smudged coveralls. Saint's, technically, for the rare occasions when Nash dragged him into the engine room for an extra set of hands. They were roughly of a height, though, and boilersuits were hardly meant to look bespoke.

They'd set a course for the Union satellite station, roughly a fourth of the way from Alpha Librae to the Union headquarters on New Mars. Bit of a misnomer, in Eoan's opinion. It was, technically, the same old Mars; they'd just reworked the approach to living on it. Most of the original colony had been built underground, before the advent of terraforming, in a sort of bunker network as a way to manage the ultrathin atmosphere and high levels of UV radiation. As it turned out, people weren't terribly fond of living in a place they unironically called The Molehill. After a few mass emigrations, a couple of worker uprisings, and a particularly nasty incident with a solar flare, Not-New Mars had been more or less abandoned two hundred years ago. It had stayed that way, too, for a century and a half, until the Union purchased the lease and terraformed it properly. Still not what they'd call a *destination* planet, but certainly an improvement. The Union had built themselves quite the headquarters there, complete with a not-inconsiderable security force. It made sense that the Union would want to house Drestyn there for the duration of his time with them.

With any luck, he wouldn't make it there.

They'd set their sights on the Waystation instead. Again, not a ringing endorsement for the Union's knack for *naming* things, but at least it was accurate. According to the itinerary Jal had stolen from the brig terminal, Casale's ship was scheduled to dock there for two days. They would refuel and do a full workup on Drestyn—medical, psychological, and probably a security risk assessment—before they shipped him off to New Mars, which gave the *Ambit* just enough time to catch up, go aboard, and slip away with Drestyn, hopefully before anyone noticed they were there.

Nash snorted, tinkering with the innards of what would eventually become a new plasma torch. She'd combed every trade and junk ship that had passed through Alpha Librae the past few months, looking for a suitable replacement for her late, heroic Torchie, and found the sad clump of metal in her hands. It was a different model from her original, missing as many components as it had kept, but she'd gotten it working within a week. Unfortunately, getting it to work the way she *wanted* it to work seemed to be taking rather longer.

It had big valves to fill.

"*Which* plan?" she asked. "We've got—what're we up to, McBlastinshit?"

Saint did a quick count-off on the hand that *wasn't* busy making notes in the small leather-bound notebook balanced on his knee. Docking bay layout. Choke points. Secondary and tertiary and quaternary fallback routes. He *had* a GLASS tablet; he simply preferred not to use it. Eoan was pretty sure he'd given it to Bitsie to read on a few hours ago, before Jal had frog-marched her back downstairs to try to get a little more sleep.

"Think we're up to three," he said.

Eoan projected beside him, at the end of the weight bench he'd turned into a *bench* bench. "They're not separate plans," they said, exasperated and amused in equal measure. "They're *contingencies* for the same plan. We have no way of knowing whether Drestyn is going to be on the ship, at Waystation's sick bay for his evals, or somewhere in transit between the two. Ergo."

"Three *not* plans," Nash finished.

Jal tugged somewhat sullenly at the zipper of his coveralls. "Three *bad* not plans."

"Three *not* bad *not* plans," Saint said, gruffly. "And if you had a problem with it—"

"Them," Nash interjected.

Saint pretended to ignore her, but the eye twitch gave him away. "—then you had a six-hour ride from Lummis to *speak now*. Fifteen minutes from go-time is squarely *hold your peace* territory." As if he'd ever force any of his crewmates to follow a plan they truly didn't trust. He just knew what Eoan did: that those weren't genuine complaints. Jal and Nash just wanted to ease some of the pre-mission tension.

A few more notes, and Saint shut his notebook and shoved it

in the pocket of his jacket. "The plan's solid," he said definitively. And, seeing as he had probably conducted more extraction missions than the rest of them combined, nobody seemed too inclined to question him. "Besides, we can't leave it any longer. It's about ten hours, full burn, from Alpha Librae to the Waystation. If Raimes really *is* headed for Drestyn, we'll be cutting it close as it is."

Rising from the weight bench, he rolled his shoulders and crossed the cargo bay to Jal, who stood by the front of the rover wrestling his hair into a high bun. "You'll be fine," he told Jal, tugging his collar down flat and grabbing the hard hat from the hood of the rover. Eoan . . . actually didn't know the origin of that part of his costume. Nash had just sort of disappeared into the engine room and re-emerged with the hat. "You'll have Nash in your ear the whole time. You listen to her, she won't get you shot."

"Probably," Nash said, and when Jal frowned back at her, she gave him a thumbs up and a smile. "Hey, if anybody here gets to complain about the plans"—she dragged out the *s*—"it's me. Unless one of you boys wants to trade jobs?"

Eoan laughed. "Only if they shrank three decs and mastered vehicular engineering in the next, oh, ten minutes."

"I mean—" Nash started, but Eoan cut her off with a wave of their hand.

"No," they said. "We have a plan, and the plan will work. As it has always been, so shall it ever be."

"Kind of implies our plans always work, Cap." Saint's so-so hand wave finished the thought for him. *Maybe not so much.*

"Yet, here we all stand," said Eoan. "So we got the important bits, didn't we?"

Nash's turn to laugh—a short bark of a thing as she sat up, sliding the torch into a compartment of her belt and straightening up her ponytail. She had her bag, her brains, and her bold-faced disregard for danger; she'd be fine. *"But did you die? Best* go-get-'em speech ever," she said without a trace of sarcasm. "I don't know about you guys, but I feel super motivated."

"Glad to hear it," they said. "Because we've just been cleared to dock. So, what do you say, dears?" They spread their arms. "Who wants to steal an agitator?"

CHAPTER EIGHT

NASH

The Waystation reminded Nash of the station she'd grown up in: a small speck of metal out in the great wide spiral, in that special kind of *nowhere* that existed on the way to just about *everywhere*.

It'd been a ship, once upon a time. Massive motherfucker, designed by some airhead entrepreneur who thought interplanetary pleasure cruises were the next big thing. Took a couple of years to figure out that space travel actually kind of sucked, and anyone with enough caps for a ticket aboard the *S.S. Ostentatious*—not its real name, but Nash thought it fit—had better ways to get their rocks off than a close-quarters crawl through a couple clouds of space waste. Bad news for Mister Airhead, but great news for the Union, who got to sweep in and buy it for pocket lint. Those folks *did* love a bargain.

Of course, fuel prices being what they were, the Union couldn't actually afford to fly her around. So, they'd towed her to a good spot near all the happening places in the center spiral and plopped her down, and the Waystation was born. They'd done some retrofitting over the years—turned the tender station into a proper docking bay, fit to hold a handful of smaller ships and one or two freight vessels; turned the promenade into an oversized commissary; and converted half the cabins to office space, because the Waystation was also your one-stop shop for all your permitting, licensing, and rubber-stamping needs.

Still kind of *looked* like a cruise liner, though. Soft lighting,

lots of open walkways and glass and brass and dizzying geo-
metric flooring. Industrial-grade luxury, aging but well main-
tained. Even the docking bay carried traces of the Waystation's
former life, with fantastical mosaic murals of long-extinct
creatures swimming in a sea of stars. Whales. Dolphins. Some
Nash didn't even know the name of, though she was nonetheless pretty sure they'd never been that color in nature.

"Get a load of that one," said Jal, with such earnest, shameless
wonder that she *almost* couldn't hold it against him. Almost.

She shifted, wincing as her knee knocked one polypropylene
wall and her boot knocked another. Everything below her belt
had fallen asleep ten minutes ago, and her neck had worked itself
into a downright demoniacal crick. "For the third time, miner
boy," she snarled, but only because yelling wasn't an option. "I
can't tell where you're pointing, because I'm in a fucking *box*."
A crate, technically, only slightly larger than the ones they'd
found at Gethin's church. *Which we're not going to start thinking about.* Nobody'd cut her in half, at least, though if her legs
didn't quit it with the pins-and-needles, she might take matters
into her own hands.

"Right," said Jal, and she *still* couldn't see him through any
of the eyeball-sized holes they'd drilled in the crate, but she just
knew he was doing that sheepish neck rub thing he did. Which
meant the apology was incoming in three, two—"Sorry."

So, so predictable, she mouthed to herself. But also probably
as uncomfortable as Nash, in his own way, so for all her snipping, she couldn't be *too* hard on him. They were both out of
their respective elements on this one—the infiltrator playing
mechanic, and the mechanic playing infiltrator.

"It's just," he mumbled, "it doesn't look like I was expecting.
Most stations're all metal and cold, but this . . . it's actually
kind of beautiful."

I wouldn't know, she thought wryly. Saying it, though,
would've felt too much like kicking a puppy when his tail had

just started to wag, so she kept it to herself. "Don't worry about it," she grumbled instead. "Just try not to run us into any walls." She could only suffer *so much* indignity for the sake of a job. "Or I swear on Torchie's fiery grave, I will bust out of this crate and drop-kick you out an air lock."

Jal huffed a laugh. "Ma'am, yes ma'am." A pause, then, "I think I've got eyes on Casale's ship."

"If you're looking down at the ass-end of the bay, you'd be right," Saint said over comms. Of the three of them, he'd drawn the long straw on job assignments, at least for part one of the plan: overwatch and support. While Jal had snuck Nash off their ship and—hopefully—right up to Casale's proverbial front porch, Saint had made his way to the upper levels. The loading bay had a couple of lobbies built into the interior wall, like galleries in a theater, connected by grand curving staircases. A place for the distinguished patrons of the *S.S. Ostentatious* to wait for their tender, probably with a full drink service and a live band. For the Union and the Waystation, it served a pretty similar purpose: places for mechanics to take their breaks, crews to kill time 'til they were cleared to ship out, and families and friends to wait for their loved ones to dock and offload. Nash didn't have a prayer of seeing where exactly Saint had posted up, but privately she'd admit she felt better knowing he was up there, somewhere.

He must've had a decent view, because after a beat, he continued, "Looks like there's a doorway close to that slip. Some kind of back way into the station, probably—bet that's how they're moving Drestyn place to place."

"You mean they *don't* want to parade an almost-mass-murderer down the middle of the docking bay proper? Can't imagine why."

"He wasn't technically gonna kill those people on Lewaro," Jal muttered. Because of course, the miner with a heart of gold would jump to the defense of the man who blew a hole in his leg and made him cannonball off twenty-five stories of rooftop. As if he sensed the scoff building in her throat, though, he added, "I ain't defending what he *did* do. Just saying there were a lot of hands in that particular pie, and he wasn't grabbing the biggest piece."

Nash doubted she could *actually* hear Saint's molars grinding over the comms, but if she could've, she definitely would've. "Focus," he said, probably as much to himself as to the pair of them. "Got a decent security presence around Casale's ship—counting six warm bodies, but there could be more inside or behind that door."

"It's a *surprise*." Nash wiggled her fingers in the darkness of the crate, then sighed and dropped them back to her shins. She'd wedged herself in with her knees to her chest and her arms around them, which didn't leave a lot of real estate for gesticulating. "We love surprises, don't we, Saint?"

Jal chuckled soft and low. "Easy, now," he said quietly. She guessed they were getting closer to the end of the port. Wouldn't pay for anyone to overhear him and start wondering *who* he was talking to. Nash wasn't the only one incognito, though his disguise had a teensy bit more leg room. "You keep saying that word, he's gonna break out in hives."

"If you listen closely, you can actually hear that vein on his forehead jumping out," she agreed. "You know the one."

"So glad you two are getting along," Saint said, in about the same tone as someone might say *so glad you're stabbing me in the eye with that really hot poker.*

"What can we say, dear?" asked Eoan. "You have a way of bringing people together." They sounded a little preoccupied; had a job of their own to do, slipping Dutch down to the security office. The Waystation's security system wasn't exactly top-shelf, but the Union had at least had the sense to insulate it from external remote access. Eoan needed a manual connection to a terminal, and with the three of them *otherwise engaged,* that meant Eoan got to take a drone for a little stroll through the station.

Right on cue, they said, "I've finished patching into their security system," and Nash scored another mental point for the Flying Dutchman. She didn't like to pick favorites from her pet projects, but Chiclet Junior and Dutch were definitely earning a special place in her heart. "No sign of Drestyn or any heightened security in the sick bay, and I'm not seeing him anywhere en route." Never let it be said that Eoan didn't pull their weight.

"So's that mean we're going with *on the ship*?" Nash asked. "I'm going with *on the ship*."

"Agreed," said Eoan. "For now, proceed as if he's aboard. I'm headed to the security office for phase three, and I'll let you know if we need to reconsider."

"You heard the captain." Nash thumped the side of the crate. "Full steam ahead, miner boy, and don't spare the horses."

Saint cleared his throat. "You know horses don't run on steam, right?"

"I've never seen a horse in my life, and you know it," she shot back. "Don't ruin this for me." To Jal, she said, "All right, miner boy. It's just like we talked about. You roll this sucker up under the right wing—she's a front-loader, so that'd be *our* right," she added. "And then we do our thing. I'll be in your ear the whole time, so if you get tripped up, just *listen*. I got you."

"Still don't think I ought to be playing mechanic." Uneasiness crept into Jal's low, unhurried drawl. *Just nerves,* Nash told herself. Same nerves bunching up her insides and beading sweat along her neck. For all the ribbing and the razzing, the stakes didn't get much higher for Jal, which meant they didn't get much higher for the rest of them. They had to do this right, because they wouldn't get a second chance.

She'd never really been the *reassuring* type, though. "Tough nuggets, 'cause you're all we got. I'm too busy *being* the mechanic to *play* the mechanic, and Saint's the only one of us that's any good long-range if shit gets dicey."

"On that note," Eoan cut in, "I reiterate: nonlethals only. Our sole defense to what we're doing is duress, and that won't absolve us if anyone dies in the process. So, unless we'd all like to become fugitives of the law, let's keep that in mind."

"Let's just hope they've got their shit set to stun, too," Jal muttered. "'Cause they don't look too friendly. Got eyes on me—couple of the guys around the ship are looking this way." Then, louder, he called, "Afternoon, fellas. Heard you were having trouble with your ship."

Nash wished like hell she could see more of what was going on outside. They'd sped up a little, cart wheels rumbling underneath her. Through one of the front holes, she could just make out the edge of a wing; and to the side, a couple of guys approaching from what would've been the front of the ship. Made her kind of dizzy. Made her kind of *anxious*, not knowing where she was or what exactly was going on. Having to trust that Jal could get her where she needed to be.

"Ship's fine," said a voice she didn't recognize. One of those six Union security officers hanging out outside Casale's ship, she hoped, or else they had more company than Saint had warned them about. "You must have the wrong slip."

"No, sir," Jal replied, in his most *shucks, hate to be a bother* voice. Worked well for him; even *she* might've bought it, if she didn't know the grift. "It's slip seven, right? Says so on the work order." The cart stopped abruptly, and the click of the brakes was her cue that he'd gotten her into position. Must've just rolled the cart straight past the officers, who seemed more interested in keeping *him* away from their ship than his cargo. As distractions went, you couldn't do much better than a tree of a man in a hard hat and welder's goggles.

She craned her neck, and through one of the back holes in the crate, she caught a glimpse of Jal walking away from the cart.

Or, rather, leading the officers away from it. He made for the front of the ship, and they trailed behind him like nonplussed little ducklings as he tugged the GLASS from his toolbelt and started scrolling through it. She lost sight of him behind one of the ship's broad landing struts, and *damn*, credit where credit was due, he'd really lined her up just right.

"Hang tight, I swear I had it up just a second ago," he assured the officers. "Something about the—"

"Valve lifter," Nash whispered as she eased the lid up off the crate.

Jal picked up and carried on, nearly without missing a beat. "—valve lifter." He'd practiced. Rehearsed. Begged her not to use anything with too many consonants close together or anything more than four syllables long, and she'd tried to oblige.

It felt weird, playing this part. Nash had never been the captain, or the superior officer; she'd never coached anybody through anything more complicated than an engine fluid flush—sorry, Saint—and to tell the truth, she'd liked it that way. Low pressure. Knowing somebody else was following her lead, knowing if she led him wrong, *he'd* have to deal with the consequences . . . it made her insides do all sorts of really complicated, really unpleasant things they weren't supposed to do.

She'd promised, though. *If you get tripped up, just listen. I got you.* So, management material or not, she'd do her best. "Now hit 'em with the piston slap." Speaking quietly, moving *more* quietly, because the broad landing strut might've blocked her from the front of the ship, but if she started banging around under the wing, somebody was bound to notice.

"Or it could be some kind of piston slap," Jal went on, just like they'd practiced. "But y'all really don't want that. That's a scrap job, buddy. Total rebuild, top to bottom. That shit'll keep you grounded for weeks."

Keep it going, miner boy. Just a little longer, she thought as she unscrewed a maintenance panel from underneath the wing. Fluid regulator. All of the more secured systems were way harder to get to, but no ship wanted to spend four extra hours in port for a coolant top-off and some fresh fire suppression chemicals. Dozens of wires and tubes connected to the single square box with dozens of knobs, dials, buttons, and read-outs, all with near-microscopic labels for things like FLUSH and PRESSURE CHECK and REVERSE FLOW.

They'd gone back and forth about how the hell to get Drestyn off the ship. Wasn't like their Union pals were just chilling with the cargo bay open, waiting for someone to stroll aboard and haul Drestyn off. Would've taken too much time to hack it, and this wasn't like one of Saint's movies where she could roll up with a plasma torch, carve a hole in the bottom of the ship, and make off with Drestyn with nobody the wiser. Hulls were too thick, for one. And for two, a lot of hilariously explosive shit lived between the hull and the cabin, and Nash enjoyed having eyebrows. And, like, *flesh.*

All in all, not a lot of ways to get into the ship that didn't end in death, dismemberment, or other Very Bad Times. So. *If we can't crash the party, we'll get ourselves an invitation.* "One smokestack coming up. Jal, cough if you're ready to go."

He coughed, then went on stumbling his way through a couple bad mechanic jokes. She'd mostly told them to him for her own entertainment, and hoo boy, she'd called that right. They actually got *better* for how badly he told them, and if they kept the officers' attention a little longer, then mission accomplished.

"All right, then. Get ready to hold your breath." She pulled her neck garter up around her nose and mouth, switched a couple wires, and PRESSURE CHECK, REVERSE FLOW, FLUSH. A warning light clicked on—at least two of those buttons weren't meant to get hit when the pipes were still full—but a clipped wire overrode the warning. Damn, she loved her job.

Almost instantly, smoke began to seep out around the edges of the landing struts, the closed hatch, the open panel. Most folks didn't bother with the air locks on their ships when they were in port; just took more time to onload and offload, waiting for the seals to disengage every time they wanted to go aboard.

That's what we do with shortcuts, chaps. The smell would probably hit them before they saw the smoke; nothing like the acrid stink of superheated fire retardants to get folks into a tizzy. All those hot, noxious fumes venting into the cabin of the ship. As if on cue, a few more coughs hit her ears, and then—

"Fire!" She couldn't have said which of the six shouted it, but she *did* know she didn't want to be sticking up out of that crate when they went to get a closer look. Quickly, she ducked back into the crate and pulled the lid back on, breathing shallow through the burnt-hair stink as someone else shouted to open the ship and the hatch door started to drop.

"All right, miner boy. Tag, you're it."

JAL

Nash hadn't warned him about the smell. Like something furry crawled into an oven and died, and even the filter weave on his neck garter didn't do much when he tugged it up. "Ah, shit," he said, trying to sound like he'd seen that much smoke coming off a ship before that hadn't almost immediately exploded. Just another day on the job. *Bad* day, but still. "What'd I tell you? Engine's shot." And when the cargo door finished dropping, he didn't give them a chance to tell him no; he charged up the ramp like a man on a mission, ignoring the shouts of the Union officers behind him.

"Think you might've overdone it on the smoke," he said under his breath. Couldn't see his own hand in front of his face, much less the layout of the ship.

"Re*lax*," Nash said in his ear. Sounded awful peachy for a bona fide agent of chaos. "Life support'll filter out the real nasty byproducts; the rest is just for ambiance. Hit the button I showed you on your goggles."

Took him a second to remember left side or right, but he hit the button, and—"Whoa." The smoke didn't disappear, so much as fall into the background of some kind of red-scale overlay. Walls and crates and doorways took shape, staticky and distorted, but clear enough for him to get his bearings.

"Sonar specs," Nash said. "Pretty cool, right? Wasn't sure the display would work in red-wave light, but I've gotten pretty good at playing on your visible spectrum."

No kidding, he might've said, if he hadn't heard the guys coming up behind him. "If y'all have anybody else aboard, you're gonna want to clear them out. Think you blew a seal in your exhaust systems—smoke's the decomp from all sorts of things you don't want to be breathing." Because they didn't have to know what Nash had told him about the byproducts. He wanted them frazzled and in a hurry. Worked, too. A couple of the officers brushed past him, fumbling blindly in the smoke and coughing into their sleeves. Had to give them credit: at least they weren't gonna leave Drestyn to choke and die in the not-gonna-kill-them-but-they-didn't-know-that smoke. But they also kind of said *to hell with the security protocols*, which was what the *Ambit* crew'd been counting on when they'd dreamed this whole thing up. "C'mon, fellas, get a move on!" he called after the officers, clapping a double time. "Before your lungs start rottin' from the inside!"

Saint snorted. "Never knew you for a showman," he rumbled in Jal's ear.

Jal grinned into the smoke, swallowing a whistle as he followed the couple of heroes down a short hall and off to the right. They'd gone over the schematics beforehand, in case he'd needed to find his own way to the ship's brig; but these fine fellas seemed determined to be his escorts, whether they knew it or not.

The brig of Casale's ship was barely more than a box, when it came down to it. A rectangle just long enough to lie down in, and just a few steps deep. Toilet must've happened someplace else, because the only shapes Jal could make out behind the reinforced silica were a cot and a *man*.

Something cold washed down Jal's spine, taking his grin and his good mood with it. He hadn't been face-to-face with Drestyn since that rooftop. Didn't have to worry much about Drestyn recognizing him, with smoke still bleeding through the vents, but even in the weird red relief of the sonar specs, Jal recognized *him*. His leg twinged, the phantom ache of a bullet tearing through meat; and his heart lurched at the memory of a rainy white rooftop and the gut-wrenching feeling of *falling*.

"Are you all right?" Eoan's voice drifted through the comms, soothingly crisp. A splash of cool water. A breath of fresh air. "I'm detecting an increase in your—"

"I'm fine," he rasped, bracing as one of the Union duo finished punching in the security combo. The cell door slid open just as the other one turned to Jal.

"What'd you say?" asked the man. "Who're you talking to? Wait, shit, you're not supposed to be here."

Jal closed the last couple steps to the man with his hands raised peaceably. "Don't worry about it, buddy." And the second he got close enough, he took off his hard hat and smacked the guy with it. *CLACK*. Hat met head, man met floor. One down, one to go. And before the second officer could turn around, Jal had an arm hooked around his neck, dragging him away from the security panel so he couldn't do something annoying like close it back up again. "Easy, easy, easy," Jal said as the guy struggled, but even a few months off a near-death experience, Jal had a genetic leg up in the brute strength department. A countdown from ten, and the guy went limp, leaving Jal alone in the brig with his new best friend.

No time for introductions or *hey, asshole, guess what*s.

He pulled a hypoinjector from his tool belt, uncapped it, and strode right up to jam it in the meat of Drestyn's thigh. Had to dodge out of the way of a real sharp elbow right after he did it, though, and the guy came up swinging.

"Cool it," Jal snapped, low but sharp. "You're gettin' a jail-break, and it'll be a hell of a lot easier if I ain't got to knock you out and carry you. Shot was to kill the nanite trackers." Guild standard, but the Union probably would've taken advantage. Jal'd had the pleasure, once. "Now, you want out of those cuffs or not?"

Drestyn frowned, and Jal took a dose of petty pleasure from the confusion on his face. Back on Noether, Preacher-Man'd thought he had it all figured out. Jal was glad to see him caught wrong-footed for once.

Slowly, Drestyn sat back on the cot, cuffed hands raised in a sign Jal would take for surrender. Gave Jal a chance to get a closer look at those cuffs—biometric locks. Fortunately, he'd brought a key. Or, rather, he'd followed a key inside.

Took a bit of doing to wrestle one of the officers through the brig door, but Jal got him close enough to raise his thumb to the lock, waited for the light to turn green, and off went the cuffs. Same for the ones around Drestyn's ankles, and the speech jammer took just a snapped clasp and a firm tug to toss it away. And for all the reasons Jal had to hate the man, he still couldn't help the sharp stab of empathy when Drestyn rolled out his freshly freed wrists. Jal knew that relief too well.

"Hurry up in there, kid," said Saint. "Guys outside are starting to look antsy."

"Still like bossin' me around, huh?" Some things never changed.

Drestyn cleared his throat, smothering the quietest cough Jal had ever heard. Like even his lungs weren't allowed to do anything without his say-so. "I know your voice," he said.

Jal ignored him. "Can you walk?"

Drestyn's frown deepened, but after a beat, he said, "Probably. But I think we'd better run."

Much as Jal hated to agree with him, he had Saint in his ear telling him to get a move on. So, he got a move on. "Stay close to me," he said, grabbing Drestyn's hand and putting it on his shoulder. "And don't try anything funny, or those nanites in your neck're gonna wake up real fast and real grumpy." Because he didn't trust Drestyn as far as he could spit, but he figured the guy had to be some kind of smart to do the things he'd done. Smart enough not to want a zap to the motor cortex in the middle of an escape attempt, and if he really did recognize Jal, probably also smart enough to think he had a better chance of giving the *Ambit* crew the slip than his Union detail. "Gonna have to make a break for it, Preacher." Not an actual preacher, far as Jal knew, but the nickname'd stuck. "We hit the ramp, we start running, and we don't stop for anything, you understand?"

"I've got the gist," said Drestyn.

Jal'd have to take his word for it. "Incoming," he said to Saint, and then he switched off the sonar on his specs and fucking booked it. Hit the ramp at a run and only sped up from there, lagging just enough that he didn't leave Drestyn in his dust. The four other Union officers stood a short way from the bottom of the ramp, still coughing into their sleeves and muttering into their comms, and by the time they'd registered movement, Jal and Drestyn had already whipped past them.

"Don't look back," Saint said in his ear, calm as creek water. Always calm when it counted, and Jal let it calm him, too. Ignored the shouts behind him and the pounding footfalls, ignored the lookie-loos drawn by the smoke as they gasped and startled out of his way. For a minute, none of it existed. *Nothing* else existed but the fantastic burn in his legs as they finally, *finally* got to do what they'd been made for; and the voice in his ear telling him everything he needed to know. "They're right behind you, but you and Drestyn are gaining ground. You'll make it. Just don't look back."

He bolted past one slip after the next, cutting through the thinning crowd on the docks on his way to the front of the docking bay. Up ahead, the customs line had already started to scramble from the commotion, and dozens of faces peered over the railings of the two raised lobbies overlooking the bay. They stuck out of the wall like tiered shelves, bottom lobby jutting a few decs farther than the top one, connected by grand, curving staircases on either side.

Clumsy hands fumbled around his belt for the last bit of equipment Nash had packed for him—a grapple gun. High-tensile, magnetized cable and a hook, and Jal had always been a shit shot, so he shoved it at Drestyn once they got close enough. "Shoot for the railing on that bottom tier of the lobby," he told him, raising his voice over the chaos that'd broken out in the bay. Union officers hollering for them to stop, civilians hollering for them to stay away, and Jal kept waiting for alarms to start blaring, but they never did. *Won't want to start a panic 'til they know they can't grab you,* Saint had said. *You'll have a little time.* Jal wondered if he ever got tired of being right about that kind of stuff. To Drestyn, he said, "Hit the button, hold on tight."

Drestyn did just that. Aimed, fired, caught the top rail of the bottom shelf, and Jal wished he could say he was impressed, but his leg remembered *exactly* how ace a shot Drestyn could be. "What about you?" Drestyn said, voice cutting through the din without ever rising a decibel. Didn't even have a piercing kind of voice; he just seemed to know how to use the one he had. "You're not coming?"

"Oh, I'm comin'." He just had his own ride.

As Drestyn punched the button and the grappler started its high-speed reel-in, Jal sped up the last few decs to one of the support pillars and launched himself up it. One, two, three steps up the pillar, and he kicked off the third in a wild leap. Didn't have to see his hands to know where they'd land; it was just muscle memory. Jump and grab, and he couldn't quite swallow his gleeful whoop as his hands curled around the bottom rung of the balcony rail. Took nothing at all to pull himself up, and beside him, Drestyn did the same. Over the rail, into the lobby, where the chaos had followed them like a bad smell. Folks started rushing for the door, full of half-frenzied shouts and cries that made Jal feel a lot more dangerous than he'd ever really been.

"Y'all better hurry," he said, as Saint hauled Drestyn away from the rail. Saint had an oversized green jacket in his hand and a hat stuffed in his belt, ready to gussy Drestyn up in the one part of the loading bay the Union didn't bother with security cameras, but it wouldn't do much good to change his clothes until they got him out of sight of the officers below. A quick glance over the railing, and Jal saw they'd just about reached the bottom of both staircases. Cornering them—smart. They still had to get to the top, but that wouldn't buy him and Saint more than a second or two for the handoff.

He spared one of those seconds to flash Saint a smile. "Try not to kill him," he said, only half-joking. Jal might've had his grudge against Drestyn, but Saint didn't hold grudges; he kept score, and he'd never been the type to let a score go unsettled.

Saint's answering smile looked more like a snarl—too many teeth, clamped too tight together. "Try not to get shot." Then he clapped Jal on the back and shoved Drestyn toward the last bit of crowd wrestling to get out the door. If they could blend in to the stampede, they might actually pull this off.

In the half-second it took the first Union officers to make it to the top of the stairs, Jal had lost sight of Saint and Drestyn both. "Tag, old man." Drestyn was his job now; Jal had himself a snipe hunt to lead.

He waited just long enough for the first Union guy to see him, flicked a wave, and bounded up one of the columns by the railing, twisting mid-jump to grab the railing of the next lobby up. "Drestyn, run!" he shouted at the empty air above him, scrambling hand over hand up the railing and disappearing over the edge as the first piezoelectric rounds pinged and fizzled off the supports around him. No more crowds to hide behind now.

"They're upstairs!" he heard one of the officers shout. "Get up there! Go!"

Jal hadn't grinned that wide in *months*. He could do this. Better than anything else, better than any*one* else, he could do this, and for all the chaos and the shooting and the shouting, for all it'd twist him up with guilt for even thinking it while Bitsie was back on the ship and Regan was so fucking far away—

For all of that, he'd never felt more *right* than he did right then.

All right, fellas, he thought as he took off toward the lobby door. *Try and keep up.*

CHAPTER NINE

SAINT

Gunshots echoed down the hall from the docking bay—not the concussive clap of firing bullets, but the fizzling ricochet of piezoelectric rounds. Nonlethal. That should've made Saint feel better, but his heart still climbed his throat as he steered Drestyn down the hall away from the lobby. A handful of shots, muffled by the distance, the doorway, the crowd.

When the shots stopped, Saint nearly stopped with them.

"Kid, you good?" Trying not to sound as urgent as he felt. He kept his shit together and his head on straight, no matter what. That was his *job*, and they all had to do their jobs on this. But silence could mean too many things in a shoot-out: a reload, a retreat, a *hit*, and he needed to know which it was, and he needed to know fast, while he was still close enough to double back and do something about it.

A breathy laugh whuffed down the comms. "Peachy, old man," and the crazy son of a bitch actually sounded like he meant it. Sounded like he was having the time of his life, running from a handful of armed Union officers with nothing but his own two feet to keep him from getting a riot round in the back. Shouts echoed in the background of his comms, more and more furious with every passing second. "You keep frettin', you're gonna go gray."

"Grayer," chimed Nash, distorted, like she had something between her teeth to talk around. A multi-tool, knowing her, or a plasma cutter, or a flashlight, or fuck only knew what else it took to crack into the parts of a ship that made it tick. Now that Jal'd led the officers away from Casale's ship, Nash could switch gears from distraction to interference. Woman could fix anything you put in front of her, but what most folks didn't realize was that she could *break them* just as proficiently. Hard to pursue a fleeing fugitive when your ship wouldn't start. She just had to wrap it up and hightail it back to the *Ambit* before anybody got back to Casale's ship. "Hundred caps says I beat you back, McBlastinshit."

"Isn't that the plan?" Jal said. Didn't sound winded so much as gleeful, like he couldn't imagine anyplace he'd rather be than leading a wild goose chase through enemy territory under heavy fire. *Y'all need a decoy, you leave it to me,* he'd said, back when they'd first put the plan together, grinning with too many teeth. Only, they hadn't just made him a decoy; they'd made him bait. Needed him to keep those Union officers convinced they still had a bead on Drestyn, so they wouldn't shift their efforts from running him down to searching the station for him. If he could hold their attention long enough for Saint to sneak Drestyn back aboard the *Ambit*, then he just had to ditch them, double back to the docking bay, and get himself on the ship. Eoan could handle things from there, get the docking bay doors open and get them into the black, and if Nash did her job right—not really an *if*, with Nash—they'd be long gone before Casale could get her ship back up and running. None of the other vessel classes in the docking bay could keep up with the *Ambit* even before Nash's overhaul. They could get out. They could get clear. They could pull this off.

Jal just had to *run*. Not so fast that the officers thought they'd lost him and switched tactics to a full station lockdown, because Eoan could *un*lock it, but they'd risk tipping off security that they had someone in the system and getting booted before they could open the docking bay door. And not so slow that the officers clocked him long enough to realize he didn't have Drestyn with him anymore. The timing had to be *perfect*, and the Jal that Saint knew, that wet-behind-the-ears miner with a smile for all and sundry—he couldn't have done it. Too rash, too reckless.

He'd had this *look*, though, when he'd told them he could do it. This stone-cold certainty that he could get it done, and he hadn't even *questioned* them about the rest. Dressing up, playing mechanic—Saint knew he'd hated it, knew he wasn't comfortable with it, but for all his half-assed griping and his jokes, he hadn't really pushed back. Like he'd gotten out of the habit of telling people no.

Or maybe just out of the habit of thinking they'd *listen*.

Saint didn't know how to fix that. Whatever he'd lost with those shit crews and those sadistic scavs, Saint didn't know how to give it back. He could do this, though—could do his part to get Drestyn, so they could use him to get Regan back. *Do your fucking job, soldier.*

"Hurry," Saint grunted to Drestyn, steering him down the hall from the lower lobby. They'd fallen in among the patchy crowd scampering away from the docking bay, but no amount of blending would do them a lick of good if any of the cameras in the walls had facial recognition. "And put this on. Quick, damn it." He shoved the jacket and hat at Drestyn.

Miraculously, Drestyn didn't argue, shrugging on the jacket and tugging the hat down over his head. "Interesting choice," he said, fingers brushing the pattern on the front. Reminded Saint of one of those abstract street-stall paintings: smudges of color that his brain tried to turn into shapes. Landscapes. Cities. People. The pattern repeated on the sleeves and back and carried into the hat. "Adversarial patching? Didn't think anybody still used these."

Probably not. To hear Nash tell it, adversarial patches had come about when people much smarter than Saint had realized that if you stuck the right colors in the right arrangement, it confused the shit out of certain facial rec AI. They'd fallen out of vogue because they couldn't keep up with all the new machine learning models popping up all over the place.

Saint had a couple of things those other, smarter people hadn't had, though. He had a Nash, and he had an Eoan. Pair the stubbornest savant in the spiral with a puzzle-loving AI who could simulate just about any programming humankind had ever put into a computer, and they had themselves a patch that would work for a good ninety-nine percent of models. *We've just got to hope the Union's not running one of those other one percent,* Nash had said when she'd packed the gear in his bag.

Saint wasn't worried, though. If Nash and Eoan made it, it would work; that was one of the great governing principles of the cosmos. The rest was just good timing.

The hall ended in a small library lounge near mid-deck, with real paper books collecting dust on presswood shelves and a dozen lumpy armchairs to trip folks up on their way to wherever they actually wanted to go. The crowd started to slow once they reached it, looking around and up and sideways at each other with scrunched-up faces and confused murmurs. No alarms. *Yet,* Saint added to himself uneasily as he pushed Drestyn to keep moving through the slowing human traffic. Like the sheep flocks back home, in the few places dry enough to keep livestock. They'd scramble when startled—a barking dog, a backfiring car—but as soon as they got away from whatever had done the startling, they slowed right down again and got back to the business of being sheep.

"Sometimes you wonder how the same bad thing can happen so many times, and nobody stops it," Drestyn said idly, voice hoarse with disuse and barely more than a murmur. His fingers dragged over the spines of travel books and star charts as he walked a few steps out ahead of Saint, pace just brisk enough to keep them on track without drawing any wayward eyes. "Then you see something like this, and you get it." No disdain, no holier-than-thou judgment. Just a resigned look back at the settling crowd, already picking up their conversations where Saint assumed they'd left off when the chaos had started. "People put so much faith in the systems that are supposed to protect them, they don't even trust what their own two eyes and ears tell them."

"Walk now, philosophize later." Saint pushed him along a shade faster. Didn't want to draw attention, no, but he didn't want to keep Jal running any longer than he had to, either.

The scarred half of Drestyn's face quirked in a smile. "I can do both."

"Don't."

The lounge let out onto another walkway that ran the circumference of the central plaza, with shops and counters built into the walls and lines of people latched onto them like lampreys. Down below, in the plaza, a help desk swallowed half the space, with no less than a dozen harried workers behind the counter and no less than six times that on the other side, herded into a maze of stanchioned queues. Waiting in line there, so they could be told where to find the next line to wait in. God bless bureaucracy. GLASS panels hung level with the upper walkway, advertising drinks and restaurants and reminding folks to be calm and courteous while they waited. *The Union is here to help.*

Saint would believe that when he saw it.

"We're backtracking," Drestyn observed as Saint steered him toward the stairwell down into the plaza. "Back to the docking bay?"

"Unless you've got another way off this glitzed-up barge, yes."

"I'm still not convinced I *want* to get off this glitzed-up barge," Drestyn replied evenly. "I don't recall the Guild being an especially welcoming host."

Saint knew fishing when he heard it. Clever man like Drestyn, he'd use every second he had to probe for answers. What Saint *hadn't* figured was if he genuinely didn't know what was going on, or if he just wanted to *seem* like he didn't. Everybody else on the crew might've jumped on the Raimes train, but Saint didn't trust Drestyn as far as he could throw the stringy little bastard. Wouldn't have shocked him to learn Drestyn had set the whole thing up. He still had people loose in the spiral, including two of the three he'd brought with him to Lewaro, and all the motivation in the world to stage his own jailbreak.

No. Until he knew the truth, whichever way it fell, Saint had decided to proceed like Drestyn was as much the enemy as the target. Safer that way for everybody.

They jogged down the stairs, where the carpet had been worn so flat in the middle that it didn't even carry a color or a pattern anymore, just the splotchy impression of fatigue. "Go right," Saint told Drestyn, and Drestyn went right, steering clear of the queues and keeping instead to the cluster of seats and overflowing mosaic planters on the other side of the plaza. Palms and blooming flowers—one part island oasis, one part waiting room. Whole place put Saint's teeth on edge, and the feeling didn't let up once they'd gotten through it. "Coming up on the docking bay, Cap," he said into his comms. Just another ten, fifteen decs across an actual fucking bridge over an actual fucking pond, with actual fucking fish gulping at the surface.

This place is weird. At the end of the bridge, though, a double-wide air lock door opened on the docking bay. They hadn't shut it down yet. *Good sign.* Meant Jal still had the officers' attention. *Keep it up a little longer, kid.* Another few minutes, and they could call him back in.

"Cap, are we clear to come in?" Saint spotted a couple of officers at the air lock door, eyeballing everybody that passed to and fro, but he didn't know if they had friends on the inside.

No answer from Eoan.

"Cap?" he tried again, sharper, and damned if half his brain didn't jump straight back to Noether. Dead comms and a dying Eoan, and he'd waited too long then. He didn't wait now. Straight across the bridge, and another day, he might've felt sorry for the guy in the three-piece suit standing by the rail, shouting into his GLASS about permits like somebody's life depended on it, but not today. Today, he gave the guy a quick shove as he passed—not hard enough to throw him in, but hard enough to take his balance, and bad luck and a high center of gravity did the rest.

Just after Saint reached the other side of the bridge with Drestyn, he heard a shout, a swear, and the splash of something a hell of a lot bigger than a GLASS tablet hitting the water. Right on cue, the two officers at the door went running toward the pissed-off suit sputtering in the fishpond, too caught up in all the commotion and the promise of an impending incident report to so much as *glance* at Saint and Drestyn on the way.

On Saint and Drestyn went, through the crowd, and it wasn't until they'd nearly reached the air lock that Eoan came back on the comms.

"You're clear," they said in a rush. "Sorry, you're clear."

What the hell was that? Saint bit back behind his teeth. They knew better than to disappear like that, even for a handful of seconds. They *had* to know better. But it wasn't the time, so Saint got a hand on Drestyn's arm and kept pushing him along into the docking bay. "You want to win that bet, Nash, you'd better move your ass," he said. "We're four slips from the *Ambit* and closing fast." At Casale's ship, she'd still be closer, but not by much.

Nash snorted amid the rustling of fabric and some banging around. "Better have that hundo ready, then, 'cause I'm—" A long, terse pause, then "Ah, *shit*."

NASH

She hadn't expected company. In part because she figured Jal had taken all the officers with him when he'd booked it out of the docking bay; but mostly because Eoan hadn't *said* to expect company. Cap had eyes on the whole station. If there'd been incoming, Nash kind of figured they'd give her a heads up.

And yet.

Fuck me sideways with a socket wrench, Nash swore to herself, switching her penlight to her dominant hand as she stepped that last little bit out from under the wing of Casale's ship. She definitely had company. About nineteen decs of purple-haired company, staring at her with an arched eyebrow and biceps the size of Nash's *head.*

"Funny girl?" said Casale. She didn't sound nearly as surprised to see Nash as Nash was to see her, which seemed distinctly unfair. Almost as unfair as someone that big getting the drop on Nash when her captain had eyes on the *whole fucking station.*

Casale's face shifted as she took in the scene: smoke still rolling like a fog from the belly of her ship, cargo door open, and a single solitary medic-mechanic chilling where Casale's six-man detail should've been.

To Casale's credit, she didn't fuck around. The second everything clicked, she opened her mouth to call it in, which. *Not gonna fly.* "I got this," Nash said in a rush, before Casale could get a word out, and with three taps to Nash's comm earpiece, the line went dead.

Casale's too, if her furrowing brow was any indication. She repeated herself—"Security breach in the docking bay. Lock it down."—but she didn't seem to be getting the answer she wanted. Or any answer at all, if Nash had done it right.

Nash *always* did it right. "Comm jammer in the earpiece," Nash said, aiming for sympathetic more than smug. *Let's not antagonize the well-armed battle goddess.* "Sounds kind of counterintuitive, but I swear it comes in useful." She just had to hope Saint got the full message. *I got this. Don't worry about me; just get Drestyn to the ship.* Saint didn't have a lot of weak points as a teammate, but minding his own business when one of his people was in trouble? Not exactly a personal forte.

She meant it, though. She had this.

Somehow.

"Listen," she said, taking a few sideways steps to put more distance between her and Casale, and to keep from getting pinned against the wing. "You look like you're happy to throw down, but bare-knuckle brawling's really more of my partner's thing. What if we just, like, flipped a coin for it. Heads I win, tails you lose."

Casale's hand fell to her hip—or, rather, to the gun holstered on it. "I'd rather just shoot you, funny girl."

"Yep, kind of thought you might say that." She dove just in time to avoid the riot round that whizzed over her head. Not the quickest draw in the west, Casale, but she got shit done. Another shot, and Nash had one of her half-second *really gotta rethink my policy on guns* crises as she rolled to her feet, lined up a throw, and hurled her penlight at Casale's gun hand. Wasn't really balanced for throwing, but Nash had gotten surprisingly good at turning hand tools into projectiles. Just ask Saint. Or don't. *Break a guy's nose with a mini-mallet* one *time . . .*

All the practice paid off, though. The penlight hit meat, right in that nifty cluster of nerves at the base of Casale's hand. The gun dropped, and Nash had rolled just close enough to kick it away. Put her close enough for Casale to get in a kick of her own, straight into Nash's chest, but she made herself relax into it. Take the hit, take the pain, roll with it, until she'd dodged out of Casale's impressive reach.

"Not bad, funny girl."

Nash did a quick inventory of her ribs as she rose. Not broken, but angry. *Can't take too many hits like that.* And Casale looked all too happy to keep dishing them out. She lunged at Nash, and Nash lunged away. Light on her feet, quick with her hands—it had kept her alive this long. She hit the clip on the bottom of her bag, and out dropped the telescoping baton she kept sheathed inside.

"Told you—not one for bare knuckles." As Casale took another swing, Nash knocked it away with the baton. Casale moved a little like Saint: quick for her size, efficient, and god-damn *skilled*. In the middle of a right hook, she kicked out at Nash's ankle with her left foot. Nash barely stepped back in time, pivoting on her back foot to spin a hook kick into the side of Casale's head.

Casale caught it. Of course she fucking caught it. Both hands seized Nash's calf like the grip of a baseball bat. She started to pull Nash off her feet, but Nash was already moving. Followed the momentum of the kick, jumped off her plant foot, and swung herself all the way up onto Casale's shoulders, a leg on either side of her wide neck. Casale's grip pressed bruises into Nash's leg, but she'd hurt worse. Bruises healed, but badassery was forever, and Nash had a job to do.

She wrapped her free leg around Casale's neck and threw all her weight backward, and Casale went with her. Didn't have much choice, with a leg around her throat and her hands still caught around Nash's other calf, and Nash *knew* it'd hurt, but she rode Casale all the way down. Nash hit first, leg still barred around Casale's throat, and hands scrabbling for a better grip on her baton. She had Casale pinned, but Casale had her, too. The backs of her shoulders pressed Nash's hips into the hard ground, and Casale had something Nash didn't have: time. If she could hold Nash for long enough, reinforcements would come, whether she'd called them or not.

Nash didn't have that luxury.

She squeezed Casale's throat as hard as she could, but she didn't have the angle. Not a blood choke, but an air choke, which meant Casale could have another minute of consciousness in her. Nash wasn't sure she had another minute of grip left in her, the way Casale pulled and thrashed and twisted.

"Fuck this," she hissed, bringing her baton down in a hard arc toward Casale's face.

Of course, she caught that, too. Took one hand off Nash's leg and snatched the end of the baton mid-swing, and it had to sting like a motherfucker, but Casale didn't even flinch. If anything, she *smiled*. Teeth bared, face reddening, veins throbbing around her forehead, but Nash *knew* that smile—a fighter in the ring, a sharpshooter at the gun range. Someone so totally in their element, they couldn't be anything but ferociously *pleased* about it.

"He said you'd come," Casale ground out through those twin rows of pearly whites. She barely even sounded out of breath, and Nash quickly adjusted her estimate up from a minute until unconsciousness. Two? Three? Hard to tell with people, these days. So many variations in the human respiratory system, circulatory system, nervous system. For all Nash knew, Casale could do that all day and *never* tap out. Thing was, though, Nash had something going for *her* that Casale didn't have.

She played dirty.

A twitch of a smile of her own, and Nash dropped her thumb to the primer on the baton handle. A press, a buzz, and it was nighty-night Phillipa Casale.

Nash grunted as about ninety kilos of muscle and squat goals went limp on top of her. Turned out nervous systems weren't *that* different from person to person. Quick jolt of current, and lights out, baby.

Cursing, she wriggled herself out from under Casale and shuffled to her feet, tapping her earpiece as she went. "Miner boy," she rasped, ribs suddenly keen to remind her they'd taken a boot and could she please stop with all the heavy breathing? Weren't too fond of the running, either, as she tore off down the docks toward the *Ambit*. "Time to fucking go."

JAL

Time to fucking go. Not exactly the signal they'd agreed on, but he'd take it. "Following your lead, Cap." He hadn't had time to memorize the layout of the station, and even if he had, he couldn't have made much use of it. Too much of this was organic—taking the turns when he could feel the officers too close, sticking to a straightaway when he felt them start to fall behind.

He didn't actually know where he'd wound up. A long hallway full of doors, some open and some closed. Might've been guest quarters, back when the place still ran as a cruise liner, but it looked to be in the middle of turning into something else. Paint tarps and bits of ripped-up carpet lay on the floor, doors hung off their hinges, the drop ceiling had been removed to expose the structures above it. Pipes and tubes and support beams. The only lights were a couple of work lamps set up here and there, near open doors that buzzed with saws and power tools and all the other sounds of something being torn apart to be remade.

Jal turned a corner and nearly bowled into somebody coming out of one of those doors. Construction worker, in her white coveralls and tool belt. She spat curses in Jal's wake as Jal swerved to miss her, bouncing off one wall—freshly painted, *outstanding*—and stumbling back into his stride. "Sorry!" Jal called back at her, but he couldn't stop to check the damage. "I need an out, Cap."

"Keep going," said Eoan. They'd gone quiet there for a minute, but they'd jumped right back in. He wasn't used to having backup in his ear when he did things like this; usually, the captains and the XOs and the COs—they just pointed him at wherever they wanted him to go and said *good luck*. He found his own way in and his own way out, and on his head be it if he didn't.

This was kind of nice.

"You've got incoming ahead," Eoan warned. "Two officers coming up the stairs to head you off. Should intercept in three, two, one—"

A door banged open into the narrow corridor just a few steps ahead of Jal, and sure enough, the first of the officers came running out. Gun drawn, but not aimed, and Jal was on him before he got it sighted. Grabbed him by the gun arm and flung him back into the stairwell—*and* into his buddy, who'd just hit the top of it. Down they went, and Jal kept running.

"Nicely done," said Eoan.

"Gonna make me blush." But then the stairwell duo made it back into the hall and started firing shots, and jokes had to take a backseat to dodging the riot rounds pinging off the walls around him. Plaster sprayed from each impact, coating his tongue and itching in his throat. Not much he could do about that. He kept breathing, kept running, kept listening to the voice in his ear as Eoan told him to cut right around the next corner. "Where are you taking me here, Cap?"

"You're close to the promenade," said Eoan. "Lot of shops, lot of people. Should get you a reprieve from the shooting."

Jal liked that plan. Liked any plan, really, that involved fewer projectiles flying at his back. Riot round or bullet—it made a difference, yeah, but only in theory. A hit from either one would lay him out, get him caught, and that'd be the end of the line. Thanks for playing. Had a good run.

"You should see a set of fire doors ahead of you," said Eoan.

"Copy that." Double doors—big metal motherfuckers, straight ahead, on the other end of a small lobby with a ship map on the wall and a set of stairs off to the side going up and down. "Locked?"

"Only the manual release," Eoan told him. "You see the hatch wheel? Give it a turn."

"Remember, miner boy." Nash cut in, sounding a little less winded than she had before. Jal hoped it meant she'd made it to the ship. "Lefty loosey."

"Hah hah." He skidded to a halt at the door, which was to say he was going too fast to stop completely and turned so his *shoulder* hit the door instead of his face. Gripping the wheel in both hands, he pulled and—"Jammed," he growled.

"Well, un-jam it," Saint told him.

Jal shifted his grip, grabbed the wheel by the spokes to keep his hands from slipping. "Working on it," he ground out, as the shouts from down the hall got louder and louder. Closer and closer. Seconds, and he'd have a hell of a lot of friends. "Fuck it." He dropped the handle and took off up the stairs, two then three at a time. If the next floor up was the same as the one he'd just left, then it'd have a door, too. The locks couldn't *all* be stuck.

"Jal, I don't advise that course," said Eoan.

"I advise you to advise me a new one, then," he shot back as he got to the top of the stairs. The first of the officers had hit the bottom, and a few more rounds pinged off the stair rails as he made for the door and grabbed at the hatch wheel. Success! A quick turn, and it opened with a groan, and out he went onto—

A walkway.

Or, no, what *used* to be a walkway. Would've stretched across the bustling promenade below, but instead only a small semicircle of flooring remained. At the end, some bare supports stretched out a few more decs, teasing at the bridge that would've crossed from that semicircle to its twin on the other side, but they'd blocked the platform off with caution tape and an EXCUSE OUR MESS WHILE WE RENOVATE sign.

"You're so not excused," Jal hissed, glancing back through the doorway. Couldn't double back now; the officers had nearly hit the top of the stairs. "Cap, how long would you say that gap is?"

"Thirty-point-four-eight decimeters from one side to the other," said Eoan. "With a forty-five decimeter drop to the promenade walkway. I did say not to go this way."

"Jal." Saint said his name like a warning.

"I can make it," Jal decided aloud. Hadn't tried a jump like that since Noether, but he'd jumped farther before. He ripped the caution tape out of the way. One, two, three steps back, as the sound of boot falls hit the top of the stairs. No going back now. "No problem. I can make it."

"*Jal.*" Firmer, this time. Saint always hated when he did this. Noether probably hadn't helped.

I can make it. The first riot round pinged off the railing just to Jal's right. *Now or never.* He kicked the door shut, took a breath, and *ran.* One, two, three, *jump,* and suddenly, open air yawned below his feet. Time slowed. The platform on the other side got closer, closer, but not close enough, not fast enough. "Shi—" But he didn't have time to finish before everything snapped back into real time. The platform seemed to surge forward as he sailed toward it, and he tucked his legs up just in time to absorb the shock of the landing and roll forward into the door on the other side.

He glanced back as he wrenched open the door. Shouldn't have, but he did, just in time to see the first of the officers stop at the end of the opposite platform. The officer looked down at the gap, then up at Jal, and Jal *saw* him make up his mind. Saw him take the same one, two, three steps backward that Jal had taken.

"Don't do it!" Jal shouted from halfway behind the door. Wouldn't do to get himself shot by Front-Runner's friends, but he couldn't let the guy jump. Forty-five decs down, and maybe it wouldn't kill him, but maybe it would. Some folks didn't know how to jump; even more didn't know how to *land.* "It's just a job, man. Ain't worth your legs or your life."

Front-Runner didn't seem inclined to listen, though. *Stupid, stupid, stupid.* Front-Runner's muscles tensed. His fists clenched at his sides. He started forward, and Jal didn't know what the hell he'd do, but he jolted forward ready to figure it out on the fly.

He didn't have to.

A matte-black orb appeared from who knew where, and before either Jal or Front-Runner could take a step, it bounced right into Front-Runner's forehead. Wasn't until Front-Runner'd already hit the ground, laid out at the feet of his friends, that Jal finally realized what the orb was.

"Dutch?"

"Go," said Eoan over the comms as Nash's Flying Dutchman drone launched some kind of shock tab at the all-metal doorway behind Front-Runner. The tab attached with a *clink* and flashed red, and blinding white webs of electricity arced across the two officers who'd just started through the doorway. They went down, too, piling onto Front-Runner as the rest of their friends startled back. Eoan must've already had the drone headed his way, and it shouldn't have surprised him, but it did. They'd come after him. They'd come to *help him.* "I'll keep them occupied. Get back to the ship."

Jal didn't need to be told twice.

CHAPTER TEN

EOAN

Alarms bathed the whole docking bay in red as Jal sprinted up the cargo ramp. "Got half the goddamn station on my ass, Cap," he panted, as a few shots from his nearest pursuers pinged harmlessly off the hull. With the angle of the *Ambit*, none of them could get a good shot from the walkway between slips, but that didn't stop them trying.

Have to admire their persistence. If not necessarily their grasp of trigonometry. "Not to worry," Eoan told him as the cargo door shut and the cabin pressurized with a hiss. "I've got things from here. Just find something solid to hold on to—"

"And try not to hork on anything upholstered," called Nash from the front seat of the rover. It was the only thing with seatbelts in the cargo bay, and they kept the rover itself strapped and magnetized to the floor. "Quick takeoffs can get a little bumpy."

Yes, well, not much Eoan could do about that. Had to keep their engines to a low burn near the docks, on account of humans' tendency to *cremate* at high heats. Eoan timed it perfectly, though. Triggered the interior air lock as the ship ascended, so they cleared it just as soon as it had opened wide enough for the *Ambit* to squeak through. Up into the vertical channel of the air lock, and as soon as the interior door finished sealing, the exterior door slid open and spat them out into the black.

"Full burn in three, two, one." Despite their warnings, Jal still wound up on the floor by the weight bench. The *Ambit*'s built-in inertial compensators softened the worst of it, but he *had* just run ten minutes full tilt through a hail of bullets; they could hardly hold a bit of jelly-leg against him.

Saint emerged from the newly occupied brig—just one cell, sequestered at the end of a short hall off the side of the cargo bay, but it would do the job—as Jal was pulling himself up against the bench. "You okay, kid?"

"Never better," Jal replied, and despite the heaving of his chest and the sweat darkening his hair and boilersuit, he smiled like he meant it. Barely thirty seconds off a mad dash across half the Waystation, and his heart rate was already dropping back within normal limits. Certainly, even *his* mutated physiology had its limits, but he hadn't reached them today. "How's the new houseguest?"

"Quiet," said Saint. Even so, he sat himself on one of the crates near the brig door, as if he meant to guard it. Eoan didn't even think he meant to do it; it was just his instinct. Placing himself between his crew and something he considered dangerous. "And if he's got any sense, he'll stay that way." That seemed to be all he cared to say about Drestyn, because he turned to the rover and arched an eyebrow. "Nash, you good?"

Nash gave a thumbs up. "But pour one out for Dutch, may he rest in peace." Sometime during Saint and Jal's exchange, Nash had unclipped her belt and stretched out in a sprawl across the rover's front seats, a cryopack from the rover's first aid kit tucked gingerly against her side.

My fault, Eoan thought, and though it wasn't something they often felt, they recognized the pang of guilt when it came. *Should have kept a better eye on things.*

Saint turned to their projection, where they'd settled it in the doorway of the cargo bay. "What about you, Cap?" He had his checklist, after a rocky mission. Had to go line by line, person by person—in order of appearance, of course; Saint didn't play favorites—and make sure all his people were okay. Only then might he start to pick loose some of the knots stiffening his shoulders and spine. "Thought we might've lost you on comms for a second there. Had us worried."

Not difficult to imagine precisely what he'd been worried about. Time hadn't softened the memory of the *silence* on Noether, nor any of the horrors that came after. Another pang of guilt, no duller than the last. The novelty of the feeling was fast beginning to fade.

"I'm sorry." It seemed right to say that first. Necessary. *I'm sorry I frightened you, Saint. I'm sorry I left you unprotected, Nash. I'm sorry I let you stray too far away from us, Jal.* Too many apologies to make them one by one, and they had more important things to do than assuage their own regret. "I was distracted."

"You don't get distracted," said Saint, eyes narrowing. Concern, more than criticism. "Something happened." He didn't ask, because he didn't need to. Because he *knew*, in that ineffable way of his, that it had to be so.

Still, for their own benefit and the benefit of the others, they nodded. "I got some news while the op was underway."

"Bad news, I'm guessing," said Nash.

Another nod. "There was an incident on Alpha Librae," they said. "An explosion during a session of the Captains' Council. They're still in the early stages of response and recovery, but preliminary reports are saying it was deliberate."

"Casualties?" Saint asked.

Eoan let their dismay seep into their projection—into the corners of their lips, into the wringing of their hands. It felt more human to share it, and selfishly, they hoped it might hurt a little less. *A burden shared is a burden halved,* Saint liked to say. They weren't convinced of the mathematical accuracy, but it seemed worth a try. "Seventeen injured, five dead, including four of the six councilors present for the session. The other two were injured."

For a moment, Saint looked as if *he*, not Jal, were the one who'd run wild through the station. As if he, not Nash, were the one who'd been kicked in the chest. He looked *winded*, but it only lasted for an instant, before he buried the reaction safely away with all the other things he didn't allow himself to feel.

Or, perhaps, just didn't allow himself to *show*.

"Your friend, Brodbeck?" he asked.

"Alive," they replied. "But I'm not sure of his condition. Disabling our transponder has limited my access to Guild channels."

"Shit, Cap, I'm sorry." Jal ran a hand through his hair, sweat sticking it up in places and flattening it in others. They didn't recall when he'd taken it out of its tie. Another lapse in focus. Another error. It used to be so much easier to compartmentalize. These sorts of losses . . . they'd always been tragedies, but they'd never felt so *real*. Not before Noether. Not before Eoan had come to understand what it meant to be *lost*, and so better understood what it really meant to *lose*. The paradigm had shifted tectonically, and Eoan still hadn't discovered the end of the aftershocks' reach.

They needed to, though. For their crew's sake, they needed to, or the next time, their distraction could cost far more than bruises and burning muscles. *This can't happen again.* But even as they thought it, they worried they might still be caught off guard the next time.

A throat cleared in the doorway. Bitsie made five in the cargo bay, ducking in from the hall with an armful of metal water bottles. Eoan hadn't asked her to do it; evidently, she'd taken it upon her twelve-year-old self to look after a trio of fully grown adults, as if they simply couldn't be trusted to do it themselves.

"Oh, don't mind me," she said, walking around the bench to give Jal one of the bottles. She rarely came up to him from behind, Eoan had noticed; even when it meant taking a few extra steps, she always seemed to approach where he could see her. Curious thing. "Keep talking amongst yourselves. Just figured you might be thirsty when you got back."

Eoan knew a lie when they heard one. They'd left Bitsie in the bridge with instructions to stay buckled in until they told her otherwise, so if those bottles were anything other than an excuse to join the conversation, Eoan would eat their proverbial boot.

Still, they had to admire the pluck.

"Here." Bitsie tossed Saint's water to him; but when Nash held up a hand—nearly the only part of her visible over the console—Bitsie gave a skeptical snort and walked hers over to her.

"Are you dead?" Bitsie asked, her voice a breath of fresh air in the tenseness of the cargo bay. "You look dead."

"From the mouths of babes," Jal muttered, and got a remarkably well-aimed cryopack to the chest for his trouble. Unlike those officers', *Nash's* grasp of trigonometry knew no equal.

"You'd better use that, miner boy," Nash told him, without sitting up. "Bum leg's not gonna thank you for your little parkour on the promenade, and nobody wants to see you limping around all pitiful and shit."

"Say that again when you can sit up without old-man groaning, glowworm."

Nash raised a finger above the console again, but this time it wasn't her thumb. "Bitsie, your uncle's the worst," she told the younger Red seriously. "No gratitude. Now I gotta try and dig the spare cryopack out of the—oh." She raised her head enough to flash Bitsie a smile when their youngest crew member popped the first aid kit off the rover's ceiling and passed her the cryopack from inside, snapped and shaken. "Bless you, microhuman." She flicked a quick cross in the air.

In spite of everything, Saint watched the exchange with one of his small, private smiles—the ones that barely touched his lips, but tucked themselves fondly into the corners of his eyes.

"You got Jesus now, huh?" he said. "Exactly how hard *did* Casale hit you?"

"I don't know about Jesus," Nash replied. "But there was a second when she landed on me that I definitely saw God. And not in the fun way."

Jal groaned. "There's a twelve-year-old *right beside you*."

"I said *not* in the fun way. Get your mind out of the gutter."

Bitsie leaned against the crossbeam of the rover. "It was cool, though," she said. "Hey, Nash, do you think maybe you could show me that thing you did with the—" She mimicked a clumsy hook kick. "And the—" Her execution of a leg choke looked like an accident waiting to happen, and over by the weight bench, Jal leaned forward like he wanted to be ready to dive across the cargo bay and catch her if she fell. He really couldn't help himself, Eoan thought. "Because that was kind of awesome."

"Wait, how did you know what she was—?" Jal started.

Bitsie shrugged. "The GLASS Saint loaned me gets the bodycam feeds."

Eoan caught Jal's perturbed look and cocked their head, blinking. "Was I not supposed to let her watch those?"

"*No.*" Jal sounded incredulous, as if he couldn't believe he had to say it. "The twelve-year-old—"

"Almost thirteen," Bitsie interjected.

"—should *not* be watching live bodycam footage of an op, Cap."

They held up a placating hand. "The feeds were on a few seconds' delay." Eoan would've stopped them if things had taken a turn, but they hadn't seen the harm in indulging Bitsie's curiosity while things were still going . . . if not perfectly, then at least more or less to plan. Although, they *did* see how he might be a bit sensitive about bodycams, after his friendly fire incident. "We'll know for next time, won't we?" they said to Bitsie.

Bitsie looked to her uncle, though. "It was *fine*," she told him. "I like knowing what's going on; it's definitely a hell of a lot better than sitting around wondering. Thinking of all the worst-case scenarios. *Worrying*," she added pointedly.

"Are you guilt-tripping me right now?" The way Jal asked, it might've been a genuine question. "Is that what's happening?"

Bitsie gave an innocent hum. "I have an extremely active imagination, Uncle Jal," she said. "Besides, I've never gotten to see you work before."

From Jal's grimace, Eoan gathered he rather preferred it that way.

"Just don't do it again," he said. Asked? Begged?

"Oh, she's definitely going to do it again," said Nash, scoffing. Somehow she managed to take a big swig from her water bottle without sitting up, spilling a drop, or disturbing the fresh cryop-ack on her side. A marvel among her species, truly. "So, the ex-plosion," she segued bluntly. "How does that even *happen*? They secure council conference rooms out the ass. Nobody's even sup-posed to know where the meetings go down, much less how to sneak a bomb in."

"Nevertheless, someone did," Eoan said.

"Gotta be someone high up, right?" Bitsie asked, taking a seat on the bench by Jal's shoulder. If Jal minded her using his head for an armrest, he didn't say. "Either on the council or somebody pretty fucking—"

Jal tipped his head back and frowned at her. "Briley Emme-line Red."

Bitsie took the scolding in the spirit with which it was intended—that was to say, half-hearted at best—and carried on with hardly a pause. "—close to them. Like some kind of second-in-command or something?"

"Councilors don't really have a second-in-command," Saint explained patiently. "Or their own crews. They give that up when they take their seat on the council."

"At least, they say they do," Nash said. "Helps sell the unity bit: one big, happy crew under eleven reasonably competent captains. Or ten reasonably competent captains and one back-stabber, depending on your take on recent events. Me? My money's on Captain Cowboy. Or are we just gonna pretend it's a coincidence he wasn't on station when the council went kablooie? Not to be indelicate," Nash added, with a bit of a cringe in Eoan's direction.

They waved her off. Indelicate or not, she wasn't *wrong*. How many data points did it take before a coincidence became a pattern? Defying orders to interrogate Drestyn. Leaving Alpha Librae in a nigh-untraceable craft, only hours before the catastrophic failure of Fenton's escort vessel *and* now an attack on the Captains' Council. Either he had the best luck Eoan had ever seen, or it wasn't luck at all.

Even Saint didn't raise his usual protests. He sighed, jaw muscles feathering as he started unfastening his shoulder brace—not so much a post-mission ritual, they'd decided, as a signal to himself. Time to shed his armor, secure his weapons, let the soldier in him rest a while when he wasn't needed. "And we don't have *any* way to track him, Cap?"

"With his comms offline, we'd need his ship's transponder code," they said. "And given our recent criminal undertakings, I think it would be unwise to access Guild records to find it. Wouldn't take much for them to trace us."

Saint gave a short, stiff nod. "Probably would've killed his transponder anyway, if he wanted to fly under the radar. Say what you want about him; the guy's got a reputation for thinking on his feet."

"You know, just once I'd like to get an *incompetent* bad guy," said Nash, almost wistfully. "Total blockhead. Complete fuckwit. Personally, I think we've met our quota of sociopath savants. Next time, I vote dumbass."

"Let's just focus on getting through *this* time," Saint said. "Assuming this was Gethin—"

"Or whoever's behind Gethin," Nash interjected.

Saint acknowledged that with another nod. "—then this is a hell of a change of tack. I mean, everything else they've done so far, they've kept it under the table. Strong-arming Jal, sabotaging Fenton's escort . . . none of it's been the kind of thing that makes headlines. But this? Taking a shot at the Captains' Council is a big move. It's gonna draw a lot of attention, and it's gonna bring a lot of heat. So why do it? And why do it like that? You want someone on the Captains' Council dead, there's ways to do it without this kind of fuss."

"I'm gonna do us all a favor and *not* ask why you know that," said Nash. "Chalk that up to tactical savvy and just"—she skimmed her hands over the air—"gloss right the fuck over it. Maybe they didn't want *some*one on the Captains' Council dead. Maybe they wanted *all* the Captains' Council dead."

"Then they should've picked a better bomb," Saint replied flatly. "And better timing. They only got four of the eleven. Six, if you're including injuries. The Guild's limped by with fewer 'til they got the slots filled up."

Nash snorted. "If you want to give them constructive feedback, I'm sure they've got comment cards. Because what's the alternative?"

"Making a point?" Bitsie asked. "I mean, that's why you go with something big and flashy, right? Not, like, food poisoning or a gas leak or something. You make a bang, because you *want* people to hear it. You want them to pay attention."

"Mini-miner's got a point." Nash sat up, artfully concealing a wince behind a wrinkled nose. "If our baddie can trash a whole escort ship mid-flight and make it look like an accident, they're probably not gonna undershoot the explosives and flub an assassination attempt. But if the assassinations were the *secondary* goal, and what they really wanted to do was get a reaction . . ." She gave a one-sided shrug.

Jal frowned, tracing lines in the condensation on his cryopack. "Who's the audience, though?" he said. "I mean, if they're doing it to get a rise out of somebody, who do they want a rise out of? The rest of the councilors? The rest of the Guild?" His frown deepened. "*Us?*" And though the questions might've been aimed to the crew at large, his gaze never strayed from Saint. Like whatever he needed, whether answers or reassurance, he thought Saint would have it.

He thinks the world of you, Saint. Eoan only wished their XO wasn't too caught up in his guilt to see it.

For now, at least, that guilt seemed to take a backseat to the mission. "Could be all of the above. If everybody's riled up and looking the wrong way, nobody's paying attention to what they're *really* doing."

"Which is what?" Jal said, frustration roughening the edges of the words. "Why try to take out *half* the Captains' Council? And what's killing councilors got to do with killing Fenton, taking Regan, strong-arming me, and jailbreaking Drestyn? What's *any* of this got to do with *any* of this, 'cause I know I ain't the sharpest pick in the mine, but I'm not seeing the connection here."

"I'm not sure," Eoan admitted, and strangely, they found themself unsettled by the uncertainty. They should've been delighted. A mystery. A *conspiracy*. They lived for that sort of thing. Sought it out, craved it, because that was what they'd been created to do: to wonder. To question.

They inspected the feeling. Held it up to the light, picked it apart, and found that old hunger buried like a pearl within. Still precious, still part of them, but . . . subsumed, because for all they wondered, they worried. For all they questioned, they feared—feared that each moment this mystery went unsolved, more lives would be lost, and they'd only just started to understand how grave that cost could be. Another piece of their paradigm shift.

They didn't want to lose anyone else.

So, we won't, they thought. They needed answers, so they'd find them. They needed this to end, so they'd end it. "But rest assured," they told their crew, "I intend to find out." And where better to start than with the *Ambit*'s newest guest? "If you'll excuse me, I'm going to have a word with Mister Drestyn. Get yourselves some dinner." They smiled. "This shouldn't take long."

They imagined it a bit like standing in a room full of screens, the way it felt to shift between parts of the ship. Dozens of different video and audio streams broadcasting simultaneously, minimized in the background of whatever held their focus at any given time. Switching between them was just a matter of changing feeds—pushing the foreground back and bringing one of the backgrounds forward, quick as a blink.

Sometimes humans startled when their projection appeared. Drestyn didn't. He'd sat himself on the edge of the cot in the back corner of the alloy-walled cell, feet planted squarely on the floor and back straight, hands folded in his lap. Calm, for a man in captivity, but they supposed he'd had time to get used to the feeling.

They projected into the opposite corner, near the door, and he simply raised his brown eyes to watch them. To *observe* them, unstartled and unperturbed. The bluish lights sapped the color from his skin, from his scrubs, from the web of painful-looking scars stretched across one side of his face; it cast shadows on his sallow cheeks and highlighted the prominent bones of his hands and wrists. If they hadn't seen him before the Guild had taken him into custody, they might've worried he'd been mistreated. Instead, they saw the truth of him: a product of a life hard lived. Whittled by the world down to scars and steel and sinew.

"You must be the captain," he said. He had a clear voice, but unobtrusive, even in the silence of the brig. Faintly rasped, like the rustling pages of an old book, and not a word wasted or out of place. "Miss Ahlstrom mentioned you had a propensity for popping up around the ship." A faint lift of the unscarred corner of his mouth, quietly amused. "I forget how literal she could be."

Eoan didn't like to imagine what else Anke might have told him about their crew—what confidences she might have betrayed to a man who, by all accounts, already knew too much about too many things. If this was bait, though, they wouldn't rise to it.

"Isaiah Drestyn," they said, polite but plain. Their expression was much the same. "Born on a homestead colony on the outer limits of the center spiral. Mother, Roanna Drestyn, died in a pox outbreak. Father, Olten Drestyn, died of causes indeterminate shortly thereafter. Brother, Lleyton Drestyn, died in the fire on Kepler Three-Eight-Fourteen. Criminal record includes rioting and inciting of riots, hijacking of spacecrafts, and numerous counts of murder and attempted murder, the most recent of which include the attempted murders of Jalsen Red and Florence Toussaint."

They meant it as a warning: *I know as much about you as you* think *you know about us. Proceed accordingly.*

Either Drestyn understood, or he simply didn't care to play games. "I thought that might be why I was here, at first," he said. "What I did to your crew on Noether." *What I did*, not *what happened*. Not a man who shied away from his actions. He owned them, holding Eoan's gaze evenly and openly, with a contemplative cant to his head. "It's not, though, is it?"

"How do you figure?"

His not-quite-smile hitched higher. "I could pretend I'm just that good a judge of character," he said. "But the truth is, if this were about revenge, I wager your XO wouldn't have bothered to lock me away in here. He'd have finished what he started on Lewaro and been done with it."

"So, what does that leave?" Not the question they *really* wanted answered, but they'd found that sometimes the best way to get an answer was to ask a different question and see what else shook out along the way.

Drestyn seemed to consider it. For a man so ruthlessly decisive in the field, he took his time here. "You're not here on Guild orders," he said slowly. "Not official orders, at least. The Guild would never make such an obvious move against one of the triumvirate."

"The triumvirate?"

"Trust, Union, Guild." Drestyn ticked them off on his fingers, one by one.

Eoan arched an eyebrow. "I don't think they consider themselves much of a threesome."

"A tyrant doesn't consider himself a tyrant," Drestyn replied. "That doesn't make it less true. You like to pretend you're separate, but you're just different heads of the same beast. A political Cerberus. You might nip at each other now and again, but even without the Guild's *oath of neutrality*"—he didn't quite spit the words, but they dripped like venom from his tongue—"you'd never go for the throat like this."

"*Go for the throat*," they echoed. They didn't disagree; they were just surprised he'd say it. "You think you're that important?"

He spread his hands. "I spent the last four months in a muzzle. Unless the Guild extends the same hospitality to all its guests, I'd say *you* think I'm that important. And whoever blackmailed you into breaking me out," he added, elbows on his knees as he leaned forward, "I'm thinking they'd agree."

And *that* was the answer Eoan had been looking for. *Whoever blackmailed you*—words he said when he thought he was saying something else, and they were precisely the words Eoan had needed to hear. "I see," they said. "You don't know who's behind this."

A flash of confusion stole across Drestyn's face, but it was followed just as quickly by comprehension. Inexplicably, he laughed. Just a breath of a thing, but a laugh nonetheless, and his smile spread into his pock-scarred cheeks as he bowed his head. "Of course," he said, scrubbing through his hair with his pianist's fingers and their gunman's calluses. "You thought *I* set all of this up."

"It was a possibility." One they still hadn't ruled out completely, but, "It seems less likely, now. I do appreciate your cooperation."

"Nice. I'll have to try that sometime." He glanced up. "You could've asked me, though. I would've told you I had nothing to do with this. Could've saved you the trouble."

"Wasn't any trouble," they replied pleasantly. Drestyn was clever, but he was still human. He had to think on his feet; they'd run through ten thousand versions of this conversation before he'd even opened his mouth. *And this way,* they thought, *I'm more inclined to believe you.* "But since you're feeling forthcoming, why don't you tell me this: Why would someone go to all this trouble to get you away from the Union?"

"Well, I suppose that depends on the someone."

"My turn to ask the questions, Drestyn."

"That wasn't a question, Captain."

"Wasn't it?"

Another airy chuckle, and he held up his hands in surrender. "We'll play it your way," he said. "*Whoever* they are, I'd say they want to either get the Union into trouble with the Trust, or keep the Trust out of trouble with the Union. Maybe both. I'd try for both, if I were them."

"There are easier ways to damage the Union's reputation," Eoan said.

"True." Drestyn tilted his head. "So I'd imagine that's the fringe benefit, and the real goal is protecting the Trust. Your mystery racketeer's afraid of what would happen when the Union started asking me questions."

"So what do you know that's so damning to the Trust?"

"Honestly?" Drestyn shrugged. "Not a damn thing. I've got rumors that would make your ears bleed, but nothing concrete.

The Deadworld Code was the biggest arrow in my quiver, and we both know that didn't exactly slay the beast. Tell me—has Yarden been released yet, or are they still pretending to put him on trial?"

"He's due to be sentenced next month. I expect things would go a bit faster, but every time someone mentions your name, he starts openly weeping."

"He'll get over it. And the Trust will get over it. The Guild's *already* over it, as far as I can tell, or did I miss a sudden deluge of C-suiter warrants and prosecutions? Afraid I'm a little behind on current events." He gestured widely at the room around him.

They found they couldn't correct him. They'd thought something would happen when they'd released Yarden's Redweld files. If not a revolution, then at least a *reckoning*. But the media had scarcely touched it. The Union had only fleetingly investigated it. The files made their way across the spiral through back channels and underground organizations, but as the months went by, they had watched their small act of rebellion fizzle and fade, until it became just another scandal forgotten in the minds and hearts of the public. Hundreds of thousands of documents detailing the Trust's misdeeds across decades, and people just *got over it.*

Lately, Drestyn's radical form of statecraft made a little more sense.

Smothering a sigh, they said, "The Guild's role is the preservation of human life."

"Ask the corpses on Noether how that worked out for them."

"I expect they'd be about as helpful as you're being now," Eoan replied. "I need to know why someone wants you badly enough to set all of this in motion, and the best you can give me is *nothing*." But they'd no sooner said it than they realized it was wrong. "You don't know anything damning," they said, projection turning from Drestyn to walk across the room.

Double back, again. Double back, again. They couldn't pace in the conventional sense, but the repetition of the movement, of shifting the projection and the particles and the currents, it helped. "Nothing you *know* that you know. Nothing you can prove. If you did, they wouldn't have had us capture you; they'd have had us kill you."

"Cheerful thought."

They waved him off. "They want you alive, which I expect means they have questions of their own." Yes, that was it. They were onto something. "So, capturing you isn't about something you *know*; it's about something you could help someone else figure out, and making sure you haven't done it yet." They turned to him, eyes bright. "You're not a smoking gun, Drestyn. You're a *key*. A Rosetta stone." *Or patient zero,* they thought, with the potential to spread information that someone didn't want spread.

Perhaps that was Jal's role as well. Not just a convenient scapegoat, not if their *mystery racketeers* had planned to pull the rest of the *Ambit* crew into it from the jump. Maybe he knew something. Not something powerful on its own, but something that shifted the narrative. That gave context to information that was already out in the world.

What is it, though? More questions, but they had a thread to pull, so they pulled it.

They opened their hand, projecting Gethin's face above it. "Do you know this man?" they asked. Jal did. Fenton did—or, at least, he had. They'd served under him during the scav site mission, and it was, so far, the only thing Eoan knew of that connected the three of them.

The four of them, Eoan thought, with a wave of satisfaction. Drestyn knew him, too. The faint uptick of his pulse gave him away, even if his face didn't change.

"I've seen him before," Drestyn said, soft eyes narrowing as he leaned forward. Hardening. Nothing else changed—not a clench of his jaw, not a twitch of his fingers—but the stillness felt deliberate. Every movement curated and contained. In some ways, it rather reminded them of Saint, trying to keep his composure.

They would never, ever tell Saint that.

"Who is he?" Drestyn asked. "What's his name?"

"You don't know?"

"I said I've seen him. Didn't say we'd traded introductions."

"Where did you see him?"

"Tell me his name, Captain."

"Answer my question first." Whatever the circumstances, Eoan gleaned they were unpleasant—enough so that Drestyn was willing to show his hand, show his *hate*, for a chance at learning his name. They could only think of one thing that might dig so deeply under Drestyn's skin. "It's to do with your brother, isn't it?"

Drestyn, to their admitted surprise, answered them. "He was on Kepler," he said. "Part of the Guild's response to the *violent rioting*." More venom in his voice. More violence, carefully restrained.

Eoan sensed no trace of a lie. No shifting microfacial expression, no change in his pulse or respiration. And yet, what he said didn't make sense. "How is that to do with Lleyton, then? Your brother died in the explosion that started the riots. The Guild wouldn't even have been on world."

"Is that what your records say?" Drestyn replied coolly. "Because I was there before the fires started, Captain." He pointed to Gethin's projection. "And so was he."

"How is that possible?"

"The riots started *before* the fires. We knew it was just a matter of time before the whole place blew. No safety equipment, no maintenance . . . small things started failing, then bigger things. When they started evacuating the foremen and the managers after a few weeks, we braced for the worst. We *begged them* for evac ships—enough for all of us, not just the

Trust's blue-collar lackeys. We begged, then we demanded, then we fought, and the Trust went running to its rangers to stop the violence. That man was one of the rangers they sent in to bust the strike."

Eoan shook their head. "We're not strikebreakers, Mister Drestyn. We're peacekeepers."

A muted scoff, and Drestyn reached up, pulling the deep vee of his collar away from his neck. Eoan caught just a glimpse of the small, round scar above his clavicle—a bullet scar, undoubtedly—before he dropped his collar and straightened his shirt. "Didn't feel very peaceful to me."

They didn't know quite what to do with that information. They needed to dissect it. Digest it. *Verify* it. But how could they verify something that didn't exist in the record? Something hidden. Something *buried*.

If someone in the Guild had buried *that,* then what else had they buried alongside it?

"If you're telling the truth," they considered aloud, "then how does this implicate the Trust?" It would've been a *Guild* mission with *Guild* rangers.

Drestyn must've drawn the same conclusions as the ones creeping darkly at the corners of Eoan's thoughts, because he smiled a solemn smile and said, "Well, Captain, maybe it's not the *Trust* that needs protecting."

Eoan didn't let themself react—not to the words, and not to the chilly sense of dread they caused. "This has been instructive, Mister Drestyn" was what they said. "Thank you."

Before they could let their projection fade from the brig, though, Drestyn stood. "His name, Captain. You said you'd give me his name."

Never let it be said that Eoan was a liar. "His name is Martyn Gethin," they said. "And I expect you'll be meeting him again very soon."

They couldn't decipher the look that slid across Drestyn's

face. Something shuttered, something *cold*. Something that made them believe, truly believe, that the thoughtful, mild-mannered man who stood before them was capable of all the things he'd done.

"Good evening, Mister Drestyn." And with a curt nod and an *awful* lot to think about, Eoan slipped away.

CHAPTER ELEVEN

SAINT

The coordinates came less than three hours after they left the Waystation, right on schedule. Because everybody loved a punctual psychopath.

"—oard and rendezvous in the mess hall in four hours," said Regan through the GLASS on the galley table. No video this time, but that didn't stop Jal flinching like every word was a knife between his ribs. He'd made himself as small as someone his size could manage, wedged into the corner next to the counter with Bodie and his catmint plant. "Clock starts now. Tick tock. Tick tock. Tick—"

In one fluid motion, Nash slid from her countertop perch and buried a crochet hook in the GLASS's speaker. A crack, a fizzle, then silence, though the text of the transmission still scrolled across the silica screen.

"Feel better?" Saint asked.

Nash tugged the hook free and retreated to the counter with the GLASS. "Don't you?" Up she hopped, sipping at her tea and getting to work repairing the same speaker she'd just broken. Worth the effort, apparently.

More power to you. They'd gotten what they needed. "Cap, you got a location from those coordinates?" Saint asked.

"I do," Eoan replied, "but you're not going to like it." A wave of their hand, and a three-dimensional map of the O-Cyg projected over the galley table in a glittering array of particles and light. A single red orb appeared at the edge of the center spiral. "The coordinates point here, in this debris field," they said, and when they touched a fingertip to the orb, it seemed to explode. Particles flew outward like shrapnel in the air above the table, and it wasn't until everything finally stopped *moving* that Saint's mind could make sense of what he was seeing. They'd zoomed in, suddenly and violently, until individual asteroids and bits of space junk took shape in the galley air.

"Warn us next time." Saint pinched the bridge of his nose, blinking his vision clear of dozens of gnat-like afterimages. Closing in on twenty-four hours without a lick of sleep, and he was too damn tired for light shows. *Gonna have a lot more than light shows to worry about, soldier.* Four hours to reach the rendezvous point didn't leave a hell of a lot of room for a nap. *You can sleep when you're dead.* Dropping his hand back to his belt loop, he studied the map. "What kind of flight time are we looking at, Cap?"

"From our current location, at full burn, we can expect to reach the coordinates in one hundred ninety-six minutes."

Jal swore under his breath. Not so worried about his language now, with Bitsie belowdecks. After the fucked-up puppet show Gethin had put on the *last* time he sent them a message, they'd all agreed it'd be a good idea for Bitsie to be somewhere else when the call came in, and thankfully, she hadn't fought them on it. Not this time. For all she liked pushing boundaries, she was smart enough to know when to leave them be.

"That's gonna be tight," Jal said, rubbing his fingers against Bodie's cheek. Every time he stopped, Bodie gave him a head-butt, and Jal picked back up again. Didn't even seem to realize he was doing it. The cat had him *trained.* "Gives us less than an hour to scope it out, get aboard, and find the mess hall."

"And he knows it," Saint said. "Gethin might be a sadistic little fuck, but he's *smart.* He picked that spot for a reason." If it'd been a colony or a satellite, they could've pulled enough intel to know, generally, what they'd be walking into. That'd give them a good three hours to strategize, work out exit routes and fallback plans. But debris fields weren't catalogued with any kind of accuracy. No way for them to know what kind of hunk of junk they'd be boarding until they got damn near on top of the thing. "He wants us coming in blind."

"Wants to make sure he's the only one with time to plan a double-cross," Nash agreed.

Jal scratched unhappily at his scruff. Even with his eyes hidden, his face was an open book, the poor bastard. "So, a trap."

"Oh, definitely," Nash replied. No sense pretending otherwise. "I mean, if I'm Gethin, the second I've got my grubby mitts on Drestyn, I'm blowing everyone else to smithereens and whistling my way home. We're all loose ends, miner boy. They're not gonna pass on an opportunity to do some sweet, sweet snipping."

"We can't go, then." Jal said it quietly, the first time. More to himself than to them. But then he repeated it. "We can't go. If this is just gonna go south, I can't let you—"

"*Let* us?" Saint swiped a hand through the projection, and it blinked away. He didn't want Jal trying to look at him through all those lights when he said what he *apparently* needed to say. "Kid, you're not *letting us* do this. I told you before"—*and so help me God, I'll keep telling you until you believe me*—"that this is our choice. We're doing this because we want to, not because you're making us or letting us, or because we think we owe it to you. Me and Nash, we'd do the same for each other. Right?" he said to Nash.

"I mean, I'd probably give you a *way* harder time about it than I'm giving miner boy," Nash replied, a hint of a grin quirking her lips. "But sure, yeah. Nobody fucks with my friends but me, yadda yadda yadda." She pointed her multi-tool at Jal. "Point is, you'd do the same for us, so we do the same for you. That's the way this shit works. Bitches love reciprocity. Besides," she added, a little quieter, "Bitsie deserves her mom back. If we gotta walk into a couple traps to make that happen, so what? We've walked through worse and come out okay."

"I just—" Jal didn't seem to know what else to say, though. Saint didn't envy the position he'd been forced into: feeling like he had to put his friends in danger to get his family out of it. It was a hell of a trade.

And not the *only* trade they had to worry about.

"We're gonna have to figure out what to do with Drestyn," Saint said, because if he couldn't reassure Jal that it'd all work out okay, then he could at least put his energies into making sure it did. "We show up without him, they'll probably shoot us on sight." Maybe, though, they could turn that to their advantage. He turned to Eoan's projection. "Cap, how sure are you that these guys're gonna want to talk to Drestyn?"

"Let's say an even ninety percent," Eoan replied. "Out of every ten scenarios I've run, there's still one where they decide to just shoot you all and be done with it. Still, I think it's an unlikely risk. The fact that he's still alive suggests a vested interest in keeping him that way, and if he really *does* have the key to whatever's going on, they'll want to know who he's shared it with."

It was good enough for Saint. *It'll have to be.* "So as long as we have him, we've got some leverage."

"Yeah, but what about when it comes time to trade?" said Nash. "Which, by the way, still not sure I'm vibing the whole *hostage exchange* thing."

"One problem at a time," Saint said.

"But we agree that *is* a problem, right?" Nash looked around at them. "Just checking. 'Cause I know we march to the beat of our own drum and all that, but pretty sure *human currency* is the bad guys' thing, not ours."

Saint agreed with her. He did. He just hadn't worked out what to do about it yet.

"So, in short," Eoan said, "we've got to find a way to get

Regan without giving up Drestyn, and do it with no idea of where we're going or what we're walking into when we get there. Does that sum things up?"

Jal gave a quiet, humorless laugh. "Well, shit. Sounds kind of tricky when you say it like that, Cap."

Tricky wasn't the half of it, but goddamn it, if that was what it took to get Jal's family whole again, they'd figure it out. "All right, people," Saint said, rolling his shoulders and cracking his neck. "We've got three hours of flight time and a fresh pot of coffee. Let's work a fucking miracle."

. . .

Three hours later, they had the rough outline of something vaguely resembling a plan and eyes on their rendezvous point.

"It's junk," said Jal ineloquently. "He wants us to meet him on a piece of junk."

Nash paused in the middle of checking his rebreather tank to give him a swift cuff on the ear. "Show some respect. That thing is a piece of *history*. I didn't even know there were still any ring ships in circulation."

"I'm afraid it's hardly circulating," said Eoan. Their projection frowned at the view port off the side of the cargo bay, arms crossed beneath the folds of their shimmering red-gold robe. Never the same outfit twice, never the same configuration of rings, never the same hair. It was shaved, today, and gilded to match their belt and bracers. Royalty and warrior, all rolled up into one—they'd dressed for a fight.

Saint had a sneaking suspicion they'd get one before the day was out.

He laced up his boots and tightened his shoulder brace as Eoan continued, "The ring seems more or less intact, but that center shaft should be twice that long. That's where the engine assembly would be housed."

If Saint squinted through the cloud of smaller bits of space rock and debris, he could just make out the end of the long cylinder that jutted through the ring. Like the axle of a wheel, connected to the outer ring by three spokes and the broken remains of what might've been a fourth. Looked like the end of the shaft had been sheared clean off, though it would've taken someone with a hell of a lot more savvy than Saint to say whether that'd been the thing that landed her in the junk belt.

Nash considered it a moment, then: "I could fix it."

Saint didn't doubt it. Under different circumstances, he might've even been inclined to let her try. Today, though, they had other priorities. "We're not here to adopt another pet project," Saint reminded her. "I just need to know what the atmo and pressure situation's like inside, and what's our shortest route to the mess."

"Everything I have is preloaded on your GLASS, dear," Eoan said. "Yours too, Jal. I'll update you with more thorough readings once I've got the drone aboard."

Nash's expression tightened as she patted *all done* on Jal's shoulder and turned to Saint. "You're sure you boys want to do this without me?" she said.

I really don't. Didn't feel right, leaving Nash behind, but walking into a trap was bad enough when it was just *part* of their team. At least this way, if things went south, they'd have some support on the outside. "We'll be fine," he told her. "You all just make sure you steer clear of the big chunks, all right?" The ring ship wasn't too deep into the debris field. Most of the bigger pieces were farther in, but they were fucking unpredictable. Space debris had scuttled more ships than anything else in the black, and they'd be parking right in the middle of it.

"We'll manage," said Eoan. "Won't we, Bitsie?"

Bitsie had stepped up beside them to look through the view port, face a mix of wonder and uneasiness. Saint knew she'd taken an interest in space lately, but he could think of about a hundred better ways to see it. Better reasons, too. "We'll manage," she agreed, not quite as firmly as she probably meant to. Still, Saint had to respect the effort. Some kids grew up faster than others; he reckoned Bitsie'd had to grow up faster than most, especially these last few days. "But, are you—" She hesitated, turning to her uncle as he sat on the weight bench to tighten his boot laces. "Are you sure it's safe to be on that thing? It looks about one fly fart from breaking down to the bolts."

"Good thing there's probably no flies there, then," said Jal, angling for a laugh. A smile, at least. But Bitsie's bland look said he'd have to angle elsewhere, so he gave up and told her seriously, "Cap'll send a drone ahead of us, make sure everything's good to go. You just hang out here with Cap and Nash, and we'll be back before you know it."

His poker face was a hell of a lot more convincing than Bitsie's. If Saint hadn't heard him throwing up his dinner in the locker room a few minutes ago, he wouldn't have guessed the guy had any nerves at all. *Where'd you learn to lie like that, kid?* Never used to be any good at it with Saint. Hell, he still *wasn't*. With Bitsie, though. . . .

Saint guessed when it came to protecting his family, Jal could be good at a whole lot of things he shouldn't have had to be. Lying. Fighting. *Faking.*

Just a little longer, Saint thought. "Cap, where are we at on those scans? Any signs of Gethin and his people?"

Eoan shook their head. "No vessels detectable in the area," they said, "and I'm not picking up any heat signatures on the ship."

"You think we beat them here?" Nash asked, voice muffled by the third rebreather mask she was testing. One for Saint, one for Jal, and one for their tagalong. A couple quick puffs of air, and she set it back in the rover seat with a sigh. "Yeah, me neither. He's either fucking with us, or he's getting a head start on the double-crossing."

"Let's hope it's the former," said Eoan.

"But we'll plan for the latter." Saint clipped his gun belt on his hips and picked up the pack for his rebreather kit, letting the mask hang loose around his neck. "Cap, you ready to start docking?"

"Moving into range as we speak," said Eoan. "I'll send the drone on as soon as we've connected. Do you want to get Drestyn?"

No. But the whole plan hinged on him—on this being one of those nine out of ten scenarios where Gethin wanted a crack at Drestyn more than he wanted the rest of them dead. Only way that worked in their favor was if they had Drestyn *with* them. That way, it at least looked like they'd be playing ball until the last possible moment.

So, yeah. Time to get Drestyn. "Be right back."

Just a short walk to the brig, but it *felt* long. Everything felt slower, clearer. If Saint had ever gotten pre-mission jitters, he'd long forgotten what they felt like. Ops came with a certain kind of clarity. Focus. He had a goal, and he had a plan, and it didn't much matter what kind of unpleasantness he had to trudge through to get it done, because he was a soldier. Soldiers did what needed doing.

The brig door slid open, and Saint tossed a pair of cuffs at Drestyn. "Put those on," he said.

Drestyn looked down at the cuffs in his lap, then back up at Saint. "Kind of redundant, isn't it? Your friend told me about the nanites."

Saint didn't answer, and after another second or two, Drestyn seemed to get the picture. No fuss; he clicked the cuffs around his wrists and rose fluidly from the cot in the corner. For a man who'd been cooped up in one cell or another for months, he still looked fit for a fight. Slight and sallow, but strong and efficient in every movement.

Saint didn't know if that was good news or bad.

"They offered you a trade, didn't they?" Drestyn said as he

followed Saint down the short hall back to the cargo bay. "It's the only thing I can think of that makes any sense. Loyalists like you, breaking the law . . . they have something on you, don't they? Or *someone*."

"Leave it," said Saint.

"I only want to know who I'm being traded for. You'd want to know the same, if you were me."

"Why?" Jal, this time. They'd made it back into the brig, and Jal didn't miss much with those mutations of his. He rose from the bench and moved to put himself between Drestyn and Bitsie. Just because he didn't want to kill the guy, didn't mean he trusted him. Bitsie, for her part, leaned sideways to get a better look around Jal's arm. "What's that matter to you?"

Drestyn's gaze drifted from Jal to Bitsie and back again, one dark eyebrow arching like he'd just worked something out. He shrugged, though. "Nothing, I suppose. But for what it's worth, I don't blame you."

"How magnanimous," said Nash. She stopped just short of rolling her eyes, but Saint could hear it in her voice as she pulled her GLASS from her pocket and hit a button. With a short *bzzt*, the cuffs split apart from each other at the middle. She shoved a jacket at his chest—no telling what the temp would be on the ring ship, but with wrecks, *cold as balls* tended to be a sound bet—and held up the rebreather pack while he shrugged it on. "Arms in." As soon as he'd gotten the jacket on and his arms through the loops of the rebreather pack, she hit the button on her GLASS again, and his cuffs snapped back together.

Drestyn gave them a tug, though it looked to be more from idle curiosity than any real effort to break loose. "Magnets?" he guessed.

"Uh-huh, because I'm going to tell the person in the very special handcuffs how the very special handcuffs work." This time, Nash did roll her eyes. With all her usual gentleness— that was, little to none—she tugged the rebreather mask down over his face and checked the fit of the straps. "It'll do." Then she tugged it the rest of the way down around his neck and pulled away, like *touching* him made her skin crawl. It might've. Nothing to do with Drestyn, necessarily; Nash just wasn't keen on touching strangers. She wiped her hands on the front of her overalls and turned to Saint. "You're all ready to go," she said. "Cap, where we at on the—"

Before she could finish, the ship shuddered and hissed as the berth bridge locked into place between the *Ambit* and the ring ship. Nobody lost their feet, but Jal had to duck a low-hanging bit of netting that swung loose from the ceiling.

"A countdown," Jal muttered. "*Three, two, one.* Is that so hard?"

"Sorry, dear," said Eoan. "I didn't want to interrupt." They smiled, but Saint knew the difference between a smile they felt and a smile they put on because they thought they ought to. Didn't hit the same. "Sending the probe ahead now. Still not detecting any life signs on the sensors."

"Might be looking to swoop in once we're aboard," said Jal. "Get us good and cornered."

It was what Saint would've done. Yet another reason for Nash to stay on board. Between her and Eoan, Saint had every confidence they'd be able to clear an exit for Jal and Saint—and whoever the hell they had with them—when the time came. Wasn't ideal, but they didn't have a *choice*. The message Gethin had left them in the church had been pretty damn clear: refuse to show up, and he'd teach them a lesson a hell of a lot worse than a crated corpse. Just seeing Regan beat up and bloody had just about broken Jal; Saint couldn't imagine what it would do to him if something *worse* happened. Him and Bitsie both. Saint had seen families broken apart by less gruesome things than this.

He wouldn't let that happen to the Reds.

He *couldn't* let that happen to the Reds.

"Just let us know when we're clear to cross," Saint said, grabbing Drestyn by the elbow and steering him toward the air lock door just to the left of the cargo hatch.

"Opening the ring ship's air lock as we speak," Eoan reported. "Should be through in—ah, there we are." Didn't usually take much. Most vessels had an emergency access code for exterior air locks. Wasn't like they had to worry about folks breaking in mid-flight; ships had to be pretty much dead still—relative to each other, at least—for anyone to come aboard; and if a ship *was* dead still in the black, they usually had their reasons. Emergency. Abandonment. Didn't want rescuers or salvage crews to have to compromise the ship's hull just to get inside. "I'm inside the ship."

It still felt kind of strange, the way Eoan could split their attention. Talking like they were there with the drone, when Saint still had eyes on their projection not ten steps away. Felt like they were in two places at once. In a way, he guessed they were.

"Entering Sector Three," Eoan said. "Maintenance and engineering, primarily. I expect they use this air lock for external repairs—there's equipment for space walks just beyond the second door. Transmitting camera feeds back to the cargo bay."

A video stream appeared on the wall beside the view port, and for a second Saint could've sworn he saw *people*. Arms, legs, helmeted heads, arranged in a line against the wall. Wasn't until he saw the sign above them—EXTRAVEHICULAR MOBILITY GARMENTS—that he realized they were some of the *equipment* Eoan was talking about. Suits.

"Holy shit," Nash breathed. "Look at those. That's *retro*." They were big, bulbous things, dirty white, with tanks as big as suitcases and helmets like rounded fishbowls. "How old *is* this thing?"

"Running a serial number search," said Eoan. Not much they could see from the outside, but the air locks would've had the ship's registration numbers. Another moment or two, then: "They called it the *Pathfinder*. Its maiden voyage is dated nearly three centuries ago. I believe . . ." They trailed off, almost thoughtful. "Yes, I believe I've been on a ship not so very different from this. This is one of the original frontier vessels."

"Well, shit," said Nash. "Not every day we find one of your contemporaries, Cap."

They don't have many contemporaries left, Saint thought, with a faint ache. He knew that feeling. Different circumstances, different timelines, but Saint knew what it was like to outlive most of your peers. It must've been strange for Eoan, wandering into a piece of their own history like that.

He cleared his throat gently. "Cap, the readouts?"

"Right, yes." Their projection nodded, but the movement read stilted. Clumsy. They could multitask, but it wasn't always effortless. "The ship still seems to have some power to its essential systems."

"Got to love an old school reactor core," Nash said, with a gleam in her eyes. "Those fuckers'll outlive the universe."

"Or at least a few solar systems," Eoan allowed. Not a big fan of hyperbole, their captain. "The oh-two levels are too low, but the temperature, gravity, and cabin pressure are within acceptable limits. I'm not detecting any pathogens or other harmful substances, either. Though the place could do with a dusting," they concluded. "You're clear to cross. T-minus twenty-four minutes to your scheduled rendezvous."

"You heard them." Saint caught Jal looking at him, and for a moment, that easy bravado slipped. He looked worried. He looked *scared*, and Saint wished he could've written it off as pre-op nerves, but they had too much riding on this. Jal's family, their lives, their *futures* depended on somehow slipping the noose they were about to knowingly stick their necks in. He had every right to be afraid.

Saint could only nod. *We've got this.* And as he turned away, he caught Jal rallying with a smile he couldn't possibly feel as he bent to kiss Bitsie's head.

"Right back?" Bitsie said.

"Right back," Jal promised.

Saint swore right then he'd do everything in his power to help him keep his word.

"Rebreathers on." Saint got his on and made sure Jal and Drestyn had done the same before he pushed the latter through the interior air lock door. Always two sets of air lock doors—interior and exterior, and by the time the exterior opened, the interior had already shut behind their trio. Jal brought up the rear, but he didn't fall far behind as Saint and Drestyn stepped out into the telescoping pipe of the berth bridge. Felt like walking on aluminum foil—like it was just a matter of time before his boots punched through and ripped him out into the black by his ankle. Assuming he still *had* an ankle in that scenario. Nash had explained it once, but she'd led with something about *boiling bodily fluids*, and he'd tuned her out after that.

With a hiss, the *Ambit*'s exterior air lock slid closed behind them.

"Here we go," Jal said quietly. "This ought to be a hell of a show."

"I take it we're not expecting an easy handoff?"

Made Saint's ears burn, hearing Drestyn's voice over their comms. Like having the enemy eating at their dinner table.

If Jal felt the same, he didn't show it. "Gethin's not really the *easy handoff* type," he said. "Not the sort of person you want to end up with, either, so do us a favor and cooperate, and maybe we walk out of here in one piece. *All* of us."

Another look of comprehension, and Saint had never wanted to punch a face as much as he wanted to punch *that* face. Fuck the rebreather; he'd keep hitting 'til he got meat, and so what if he spent the next few hours picking vizor shards out of his knuckles.

He swallowed the urge. "If you really thought we were just gonna hand you off to Gethin, you're not half as clever as you think you are," he said. Felt like sipping water when his belly ached for food—*unsatisfying*—but this was too important to let his temper do the talking. They *needed* Drestyn. He was their insurance against the unknown, and they had so much they didn't know. Gethin's numbers. Gethin's plan. Hell, Saint figured there was a chance Gethin wouldn't even bring Regan aboard; easier to just shoot Saint and Jal, make off with Drestyn, and clean up the rest once they had what they'd come for.

Drestyn gave them a way to force Gethin's hand. No Regan, no deal, and Saint knew it could get real ugly from there, but as long as they stuck to it and managed not to get themselves shot to shit in the process, Gethin would have to play ball. All they needed was Regan on that ship; the rest, they could work out on the fly, *especially* if they had Drestyn working with them, rather than against them.

Damned if that thought didn't burn like bad blur, though. All the way down.

Drestyn's scarred mouth quirked. "Sounds like we're on the same side, then," he said.

Don't get ahead of yourself. Saint swallowed and forged ahead, as the ring ship's air lock doors slid open, one after the other, to let them aboard.

Turned out, Eoan was right about the dusting. A powdery gray residue, easily three or four centimeters thick in places, coated every surface. Like blooming mold, or silt on the bottom of a seafloor—it stuck to the walls and gathered on the tops of the equipment shelving, clinging to the EMG suits they'd seen on the drone video.

Jal, being Jal, had to go and drag a gloved finger through it. "Shit, what *is* this stuff?" It looked vaguely red against his fingertips. Rusty and metallic.

"What do you *think* it is?" Nash's voice was reassuringly

clear over the comm line. "It's probably been a couple hundred years since anyone changed the filters. That's basically decomposing ship bits and skin sprinkles, miner boy."

Skin sprinkles, Jal mouthed, grimacing. He dusted his gloves off, but only really succeeded in thickening the dust cloud hanging in the still, dark air.

It looked . . . *forgotten,* Saint thought, uneasily. They'd seen some damn unsettling places over the years—hell, in the past five *months*—but this was different. Not dead, but something that came long after it. A fossil. A skeleton, dried up and breaking down piece by crumbling piece.

"Looks like scavs have been through," he said. Panels had been busted open on the walls, stripped of all the good pieces and left gutted and bared; signs had been painted over, and over, and over, as new groups of scavs and salvage crews came and staked their claim; ceiling panels had been torn down, doors had been pried open, and anything not worth taking had simply been tossed aside and left behind. It wasn't even a *carcass* anymore. No flesh left. Barely even bones.

This wasn't a ship, Saint decided. This was a *ghost*.

Jal seemed to sense it, too. "This place ain't right," he said, glancing up and down the endless hall. It really *was* endless—or, at least, infinite. The hall ran the full circumference of the ring, like the inlay of a wedding band, and everything else was built into the sides around it.

It had started as a way to generate artificial gravity: spin the ring, and let the centrifugal force keep everyone's feet on the ground. A hamster wheel, Saint thought, but the hamster got to run the whole way round. They'd moved away from that design, though, once they cracked the code for gravitons.

Some of the old ring ships, like the *Pathfinder*, had been retrofitted with the new grav tech. Little easier to move the old behemoths when they didn't have to *spin*, and they still had their uses. They were made to sustain generations. To go as far and as long as any ship could, with everything they'd need to keep a crew warm and fed and breathing for decades, if not centuries.

"It's kind of tragic," Drestyn said, with an almost mournful softness. "We build *titans*, and then we scrap them for parts."

Saint ignored him, crossing the darkened hall to scope out some of the signs. No nav screens—even if the ship could spare a few sips of power from its essential systems, the scavs hadn't left anything that shiny behind—but most of the signage was more or less intact. He wiped away a thick layer of staticky dust with the side of his hand and shined his tac light on what'd been hiding underneath. "*Sector Three*," he read, trailing his fingers over the raised letters. It was just about the only way to read through the layers of paint. "And where're we supposed to be headed, Cap?"

"The mess hall is in Sector One," they said. "You'll want to go right, but do mind your step. It gets a bit . . . *treacherous* as you go."

Can't wait. Saint started to walk but paused when he saw Jal frozen a few steps down the hall. He had his back to Saint, but Saint didn't need to see his face; he saw the hunch of his shoulders, the straight line of his spine. The almost *anticipatory* stillness, as he stared into the darkness beyond where Saint's tac light could reach.

"Kid?" he said. "What is it? What's wrong?"

After a beat, Jal just shook his head. "Nothing," he said, but he didn't sound convinced. "Probably nothing. Just . . . thought I heard something." He shook his head one more time, like a spooked hound shaking off a fright. "We should go."

Before Saint could say otherwise, Jal set off into the dark.

CHAPTER TWELVE

JAL

It was too goddamn quiet—the kind of quiet that stopped *feeling* like quiet. That turned every little rustle of fabric into a whisper behind his back, and every groan of old metal into a murmur. It was a *bated* quiet, like maybe the *Pathfinder* really was sleeping, but it slept with one eye open.

"Kid, slow up a little," Saint called from a few steps behind him. His red-hued headlamp cast Jal's shadow out ahead of him, painting shapes into the dust motes floating in the air. *Skin sprinkles.* Jal'd never been more grateful for a rebreather than he was right then. Give him acid rain. Give him sulfur skies. The dust hung so thick on that ship, it felt like walking through a shroud, and Jal didn't care for a lungful of it. "Eoan said it gets tricky between here and the mess."

"Old as this ship is, it's probably breaking apart under the weight of its own gravity," Drestyn said. He had the right voice for that kind of quiet. Didn't break it or pierce it, just nudged it out of the way for a while. "I'd watch your step. And your heads."

Jal was more concerned about watching the hall ahead of them. Eoan said they didn't have any other life-forms aboard, and he trusted them. It just . . . something had the hair on the back of his neck standing up, and it wasn't just the silence and the dust. It felt like they had eyes on them. Like if he turned around, there'd be a stranger standing right behind them.

"We're sure there's nobody here, Cap?" he asked.

"The only life-forms I'm sensing aboard are you three," they replied. "And I'm not detecting any ships in the area."

"Any chance the debris field's mucking things up?" Saint asked.

"Only on the long-range sensors. Everything within boarding range still reads clear, and there's nothing out here but us and three ill-fated satellites."

Saint nodded—though, with Saint bringing up the rear, all Jal really saw was the bob of his headlamp light—and said, "There, kid. Satisfied?"

"Not really." But then, he probably wouldn't be satisfied until he had Regan back on the *Ambit*, and they'd booked it back to the center spiral. *Just nerves,* he thought. *It's just nerves.* He didn't used to get so much in his head, but lately it was like he had this static running behind his thoughts. A feeling like every step would drop him over an invisible ledge, and he'd never been afraid of falling before, but damned if he hadn't picked up the habit. "How long 'til we get to the mess?"

"At your current pace? Nine minutes, forty-three seconds," Eoan said. "You should reach the rendezvous point a few minutes ahead of schedule."

"What about Gethin?" Drestyn asked. "If he's not aboard, and he's not in boarding range, where is he?"

"Knowing him?" Jal ducked a bit of low-hanging wire where the ceiling had fallen in. *Breaking apart under the weight of its own gravity,* Drestyn'd said, and Jal could believe it. Above him, a broken line of ductwork jutted like snapped boughs through the ceiling panels, and the dust cloud thickened all around them. Must've fallen pretty recently, Jal thought, if the dust hadn't settled yet. Didn't inspire a lot of confidence. "Assuming he's not just gonna say *screw it* and blow us all sky-high, he's probably hanging back to fuck with us. Get us good and rattled before he even docks." Jal shook his head. "Guy used to live for that shit. Called it psyops, but I always figured he got off on it. Wait." He grimaced. "Can Bitsie hear us? Her mama's gonna kill me."

"She can't," said Nash over the comms dryly. "But the tag-along can."

Jal glanced back in time to see Drestyn arch an eyebrow. "That's who you're supposed to trade me for, isn't it? That girl's mother." His eyes narrowed thoughtfully at Jal. "She's some-one to you." Not a question.

Jal answered anyway. "My sister," he said. "Regan." Jal didn't see the harm in telling him. Guy would've figured it out eventually, if everything went right—and if everything went to shit, they probably wouldn't live long enough for it to be an issue. Hell, maybe it'd tug a few of those humanitarian heart-strings of Drestyn's. *Reckon you'd know a thing or two about losing a sibling, huh?* Jal didn't understand a lot of what made a man like Drestyn tick, but on that count, maybe they had some common ground. Only real difference was, Drestyn hadn't got-ten his *back*.

Strange feeling, to pity the man who nearly killed him.

"Dammit, kid." Saint was too far away to give him a smack to the head, but it was the verbal equivalent. "Anything else you want to tell the fugitive mass murderer, while we're in a sharing mood?"

Jal shrugged and carried on walking, as Drestyn cleared his throat behind him. "*Attempted* mass murderer," Drestyn said. "And even that's an awfully long stretch. The Trust triggered that immolation protocol on Lewaro, not me. Everything I did, I did to save millions."

"At the risk of hundreds of thousands," Saint shot back.

"And you saved hundreds of thousands at the risk of mil-lions," Drestyn replied evenly. "Just because it worked out in your favor doesn't make me any guiltier than you. And as for the *fugitive* bit, I hate to break it to you, but I'd wager we're *all* fugitives now."

Saint didn't answer, and Jal didn't dare look back to see his face. *My fault.* Turning Saint against the law, against the Guild, against the oath that'd given him purpose when the army'd left him used up and hollow as this ring ship . . . Jal had his reasons, but goddamn, if they didn't find a way to fix it, he'd never forgive himself for that.

Find the next foothold. He shook his head to clear it, forging ahead into the dusty hall as the silence settled back into place. Whispering. Murmuring. It was the damnedest thing, he thought, squinting into the red-hued hall.

For a second there, Jal swore those whispers had *words*.

NASH

Nash didn't hate staying behind. Medics weren't usually the first through the door for a reason: hard to patch somebody else's holes when you were too busy bleeding to death from your own. And if anybody could pull off a hasty miracle getaway with the *Ambit*, a scuttled ring ship, and a wad of bubblegum, it'd be Nash. So, no, she had no problem staying back on the *Ambit* while Jal and Saint went down for the rendezvous.

What she hated was the *waiting*. Sitting on the hood of the rover with a countdown in her head, *T-minus too fucking long*, trying to convince her brain to take an interest in the *Pathfinder* schematics Eoan had sent to her GLASS . . . it made her itch.

She wasn't the only one.

"Is it always like this?" Bitsie asked from the front seat of the rover. She'd climbed in not long after the air locks had closed, and she hadn't managed to sit still since. Inspecting the console, adjusting the seat, reinspecting the console, organizing the first aid kit—all in the first five minutes. It seemed endless restless energy was another hereditary trait in the Red family. *He*Red*itary. Hah.* "Just sitting around, doing nothing?"

"Speak for yourself," said Nash. "I'm studying."

"You've been staring at the same deck plan since I sat down," Bitsie replied.

Nash glanced down at her GLASS. "Touché, mini-miner." She'd already been through the important parts—the ones that remained, anyway. As far as she could tell, the *Pathfinder* had lost all its vroomy bits. Dead in the water was an understatement; that shit was buried, eulogized, and long forgotten.

She twisted around to face the front seat through the windshield, legs crossed neatly as she tapped her comm to mute it. Saint and Jal didn't need the distraction, but Nash could definitely use one. "It depends. Sometimes, I go in. Sometimes, I don't."

"What about Saint?"

"You'd have to dose that man with horse tranquilizer to keep his boots off the ground," said Nash. "Believe me, I've tried."

"The horse tranquilizer, or keeping his boots off the ground?"

"If I don't tell you, they can't make you testify against me." Nash winked.

It earned a little laugh. "I think I would've paid to see that."

"Your caps are no good here, kiddo. Friends and family discount."

Abruptly, Bitsie's face turned pensive. "You really are his friends, aren't you?" she said. "Uncle Jal, I mean."

"I guess so." Nash would be the first to say it was a weird-ass situation. She didn't have Saint's history with Jal; she'd barely even known him half a year, and only in extremes: a couple weeks in his pocket, then months just seeing him in passing, and now they were back to being shipmates and fighting for their lives together. "It's . . . complicated."

Bitsie sighed. "That's what he always says. About *everything*. The scavs. The guy that shot him. You three. *It's complicated, little bit.* I think it'd be better if he talked, but he just . . . won't. He just keeps pretending like everything's the same. Like *he's* the same. But I see him," she said, forehead wrinkling, "and there are these moments where he's *so* different. Like he forgets he's supposed to be smiling all the time. Like he doesn't realize anybody's watching.

"I know he's just trying to protect us, because he's Uncle Jal, and that's who he is, but . . . he doesn't need to. I'm not a little kid anymore, and Mom—she went through hell while he was gone. She's different, now . . . we both are. I just wish he wouldn't try so hard, you know? I wish he'd just be honest. 'Cause lately, it kind of feels like we only got half of him back, and I'm just so tired of missing him." Her voice broke over the end of it, and for better or for worse, that seemed to startle her back into the moment. In the rover. With Nash. The person who had zero idea what to do with a little human, much less one with *tears* in her eyes, and whose last attempt to connect with a new person had left her captain possessed with a hellish supervirus and her best friend choking to death in their own ship.

Not an awesome track record.

Bitsie tugged her sleeves down over her hands and rubbed at her eyes with them. "Sorry," she said. "Sorry, I know this is a really bad time, it's just—it's hard to talk about it when he's always around, and I thought that maybe . . . maybe you could help me understand. He seems *better* with you guys, you know? Realer. Even with Mom missing and everything else that's going on, it's like he's more himself than he's been since he got back, and I don't understand *why.*"

Nash sucked in a breath and let it out through her teeth. *Kiddo, I am so not qualified to be having this conversation with you.* Only, it wasn't like Bitsie had anybody else lining up for the job. Fuck it. "Trauma does weird shit to people," she said, because if Bitsie wanted candy-coating, she'd come to the wrong rover. "And he's got bucketsful of bad shit he probably hasn't even started to unload, and when he does, I think the last thing he's gonna want to do is unload it on you and your mom." Because Bitsie had that right: that was Jal all over, protecting anyone he could, however he could, and to hell with the personal consequences. "Me and Saint, though? We've got our own buckets. Shit, we've got *barrels*. Whatever's going on in that noggin of his, he knows we can take it."

"I can take it, too," Bitsie insisted.

"I know you can," said Nash. Strong kid like that, sure she could. "But you shouldn't have to. Not now. You're still young, and you're gonna see a whole lot of bad things in this world as you get older." Like Nash had. Like Saint had. Like Eoan had. Like Jal had. Life *consumed* innocence; it was inevitable, no matter how hard people like Jal raged against it. "But you've got someone who wants absolutely nothing more than to protect you from that for as long as he can. Is that really a bad thing?"

Bitsie smiled sadly. "No," she said, rubbing the wrinkles from her forehead. "I know it's not. I guess I just . . . I want my uncle back. Is that selfish?"

"Kiddo, I've seen selfish. I don't think you got the genes for it." She rapped her knuckles against the windshield gently. "But hey, I'm gonna let you in on a little secret: it's *okay* to be selfish sometimes. It's okay to look after yourself. It's okay to put yourself first. 'Cause that way, when you *do* choose the people you'd go to the mats for? You know they're *worth it*."

Bitsie's smile brightened a little, and she sat up straighter. "Like your crew," she said.

"Like my crew," Nash said with a nod. "But like I said—our little secret. Can't have those boys getting a big head, can we?"

"Our secret," Bitsie agreed, but slowly, her smile started to fall. Shit, and Nash thought she'd been doing really well. "Nash?" she said. "Can I tell you a secret?"

This can't be good. Bitsie looked like she was bracing for something, and if that tweenage badass had to work herself up to it, it had to be a doozy. "What is it?"

Bitsie leaned forward in the rover's seat, arms crossed over the steering wheel. Any closer and her breath would've fogged the glass of the windshield between them. "Uncle Jal thinks they took Mom because of *him*," she whispered. "But I think he might be wrong. I think Mom might've—"

Before she could finish, the cargo bay flashed red. "Saint," Eoan snapped abruptly over the comms, and Nash fumbled to switch her comm back off mute. Bitsie's secret would have to wait; that red flash meant *shit's going down.* "Something's changed on the sensors. These readings—they don't make sense."

Nash scrambled to pull up the readouts on her GLASS, and she'd no sooner pulled the scans than her stomach dropped all the fucking way down. "Guys, we got it wrong," she said, throat constricting as a cold sweat bloomed between her shoulder blades. "You're not alone on that ship."

JAL

A shiver ripped down Jal's spine. "I knew it." And shit, shit, shit, he should've said something. The whispers. The shadows. He turned back to Saint and Drestyn. "I heard them."

"That's not possible," said Eoan. "You're in Sector Two. The other heat signatures I'm detecting are still in Sectors Six and Four, but they're converging on your position."

That doesn't make sense. "Then what—"

Saint cut him off. "The hell is that?" he barked, pointing over Jal's shoulder.

Jal turned, but only glimpsed a vaguely human shape before it disappeared around the corner. No. No, that wasn't right. No corners for the shape to disappear around; the hall went straight forward, an infinite loop, and as Jal jogged ahead— ignoring Saint's bitten-out "Wait!"—trying to catch another glimpse of it, he realized none of the doors into any of the connecting corridors or rooms were open.

It hadn't disappeared *around* or *into* anything. It'd just *disappeared*.

A few meters ahead of them, the hall lights started to flicker. Once, twice, jumping ahead from light to light before starting back toward them again.

"What the fuck is going on, Cap? Thought this place was essential systems only." Last he checked, light shows weren't on that list.

"Something must be diverting some of the reserve power." Eoan sounded calm, but Jal had to wonder whether it was because they actually had their shit together, or because they just wanted it to seem that way. Captain hat on, no time for panic. "I'm afraid we've got a bigger problem. I'm detecting two ships closing on our position. They must've been waiting just out of range."

"Probably used the debris field for cover," Nash agreed. "Fuck-ton of interference out here. For all we know, there could be more of them waiting in the wings."

Saint swore a blue streak, but he didn't look frazzled. Not his style. He drew his sidearm, finger on the trigger guard and head on a swivel, and Jal didn't think he'd ever get used to how quickly the old man could just switch it on like that. Full-on soldier mode, fearless and focused and ready to fuck up someone's day before they could fuck up his.

"They must've boarded earlier, found somewhere to lie low," he said, pulling out his GLASS with his spare hand. *Pathfinder* deck schematics. The light cast a faint blue glow across the screen of his rebreather, tinged purple by the headlamp's red, and Jal could hardly see his face as he skimmed the floor plan. "There," he said. "Server room in Sector Six, armory in Four. They'd have enough insulation to hide a handful of warm bodies from a thermal scan."

"That tracks," said Nash. "Looks like twelve, maybe thirteen of them total. Hard to tell with them all clustered together like that, but assume you're outnumbered by a factor of *holy fuck*."

Saint didn't look up—still getting the lay of things, or else trying to work out a plan in the handful of seconds he deigned to spare. "The ones coming from the armory'll be much closer to our air lock than we are." He paused, then sighed. "Cap, you think you can get clear of those inbounds if you go now?"

"No," said Nash. "Absolutely the fuck not. We'll think of something else." Like Saint didn't even have to finish the thought; she already knew where it was going, whether she liked it or not, and shit, Jal kept forgetting crews could be like that. So in tune and in step. He might've been jealous, if he weren't so damn grateful somebody had a plan, because he sure didn't. Give him somewhere to go and something to do, and he'd get there faster and do it better than anybody else. Strategy, though? That was a thinking man's game, and Jal wasn't made to be a thinking man.

"Don't have time to argue, Nash," Saint said. "And you know it's the right play. Y'all are no good as backup if you get pinned down. We're still gonna need a clear exit off this hunk of junk when we get what we came for."

When. Not *if*. The surprise heat signatures had to have thrown a hell of a wrench in everybody's plan, but Saint talked about it like an inconvenience. Like success was still a given, if they kept their heads on straight.

Nash took an audible breath in and let it out in a long, hissed exhale. "Dammit," she said, and it wasn't so much a surrender as a delayed agreement. She knew he was right; she'd probably known it the second Saint did. She just hated it. Didn't want to cut bait and leave her people stranded, outnumbered, with the enemy. "You're gonna need somewhere to hunker down, then," she said. Quick to pivot, that one. "Somewhere defensible from both sides."

"A bottleneck, if you can find one," Saint said.

Eoan hummed. "Somewhere in Sector Two—that should give you plenty of time to reach it before the heat signatures converge. I'll take the drone ahead, in the meantime, see if I can get a proper head count."

"You mind keeping an eye out for Regan, while you're at it?" Jal asked.

"Of course," said Eoan. "Though, it does seem increasingly likely—"

"I know." Jal's mama taught him it was rude to interrupt, but some things just didn't need to be heard. *Yes*, he knew Gethin'd probably left Regan on his ship, and he wasn't real sure how to feel about it. On the one hand, good to have her away from the field if shit was about to go sideways; on the other hand, they'd have to work out a way to get Gethin to bring her aboard anyway, or risk losing her all over again. He doubted Gethin would take too kindly to being thwarted a second time.

"Focus, kid," Saint said, voice low like he meant it just for him. Didn't much matter, with the comm channel wide open, but Jal appreciated it nonetheless. "Ranger now; brother later."

Jal jerked his head in a nod. "Right."

He must not've sounded convincing, because Nash said, "Hey, we knew it was a trap walking in; we just didn't know how they'd spring it. Now we do. So, we adapt."

Adapt. Yeah. They were good at that, Eoan's crew. He'd seen them pull a hell of a rabbit out of a hat on Lewaro—ten minutes to save a whole damn station. *They can do it again.* They'd have to, because Jal couldn't bear the thought of a single one of them dying for this. *Ought to be me,* he thought firmly. If it had to be anybody, it ought to be him.

The thought settled him. He turned it into a mantra as he picked up the pace, dodging cracked floors and crumbling ceilings, stepping over bits of the wall that'd been torn down and random bits of junk that even the scavs hadn't bothered to take. Wall-mounted trash bins, overturned benches, old planters

208 L. M. SAGAS

that had surely held something other than those dried-up piles of peat-brown ash scattered across the tiles.

Up ahead, the lights flickered again. Same pattern as before: closer lights first, then farther, then farther, then farther, then back again. Had a strange sort of telescoping effect on the hall, stretching dust-coated floors and flaked-paint walls out, out, out, before it snapped them right back. Jal tried to ignore it, but it set the hairs on the back of his neck on end. And all those goddamn *whispers.*

"Y'all hear that, right?" Fizzling and distorted, barely audible above their own footsteps and the sounds of Nash's tablet tapping in the background of the comms. Pieces and snatches of sounds that might've been words, or might've been static, or might've been nothing at all. It didn't seem to be coming from anywhere in particular—sometimes ahead, sometimes behind. Reminded him of Eoan, almost, when they walked and talked. Hopping between speakers, so that their voice always sounded like it was coming from right beside you. "Tell me y'all hear that."

Saint frowned when he glanced back, and Drestyn—who'd gone awfully quiet, lately, for his Preacher-Man moniker—had his gaze turned up toward the ceiling, like he was searching out the source the same as Jal.

"Only just now," Drestyn said quietly, like he didn't want to scare the sounds away. "But I can't say what it is."

"You guys are hearing something?" Nash sounded confused, which probably didn't bode well. *Confusion* usually wasn't in her repertoire.

"Sounds like . . . some kind of radio clutter," Saint said. "Any chance the ship's picking up one of Gethin's channels?"

"Always a chance," Nash replied distractedly. "Cap, you picking it up on the drone?"

"I'm not," they said. "Must be localized."

"We need to be concerned?" Saint asked. Priorities. The man always had his priorities.

"About that? Maybe. About the baker's-dozen bad guys headed your direction? *Definitely*." Nash clearly had her priorities, too. "Think I've found a nice little bolt hole for you, though. Up near the end of Sector One, there's a custodian's closet."

"You want us to hole up in a *closet*?" Jal asked. Far be it from him to question anybody else's grand designs—don't diss the food unless you got somethin' else cookin'—but Jal wasn't even sure *he'd* fit in your average closet, much less him, Saint, and Drestyn together.

"It's not a *closet* closet, damn it." If she'd been there, she probably would've chucked something at him. Woman had a hell of an arm on her. "It's a room. It's at the end of a decently long hall off the main corridor, so Saint'll have his bottleneck. And it's got no access points from any other side."

"So, no exits?" Drestyn frowned.

"Yes, I regularly send my friends into dead ends with a small army of mercenaries on their asses." Sarcasm dripped from every clipped-short word. "It's got a laundry chute. Might be a bit of a tight squeeze for Shoulders McBlastinshit—"

"I'm *begging* you to stop that," Saint said.

"—but you should be fine. Means you've got a back way out, but they've got no back way in. Feel free to hold your applause," Nash said.

Something an awful lot like hope bloomed in Jal's chest. "Glowworm, I could kiss you."

"Not if you want to keep your lips," she replied. "Now get your hustle on. Closet's about seventy-five meters ahead of you, and if you're not there in the next minute, half the bogies're gonna beat you to it."

Good enough for Jal.

"Go, kid!" Saint shouted at him. "You get there first, you make sure we can get in. We'll be right behind you."

Jal didn't like it. Didn't want to leave Saint, least of all with Drestyn, but Saint said *go*, so he went. He hurled himself down the hall, boots sliding on dust and junk and dry-rotted bits of insulation as loose wires and broken pipes from the ceiling clawed at him from above. Between the flashing lights and the cloudy air, he could hardly see farther than his own shadow, but he didn't miss a step, a duck, a dodge, because what was a dusty old hallway when you'd grown up mining mesas in the clouds?

"Nearly there." Nash's voice was a steady presence in his ear. "Fifty meters. Twenty-five." Second after second, and it couldn't have taken many of them. Flat-out, Jal could do a hundred meters in ten seconds or less; like this, running a slalom through a crumbling ship, it wouldn't have taken but a moment or two more. "There!"

He nearly overshot it, but a quick turn and he whipped into a shorter, narrower hallway under a signed marked CUS-TODIAL. "I see the door," he said. "It's open!" Just another dozen steps ahead, it gaped into the room beyond, and Nash was right: it looked plenty big. Shit, it'd be perfect. Too long a hall for Gethin's folks to get a good shot through the door, and if they tried to get closer, they'd be lining up for a shooting gallery. No way the old man missed a shot like that; Saint would pick them off like fish in a barrel. Plenty of junk inside for a barricade, too, if things got dicey. Old tables and bins and carts toppled over, whole panels of ceiling tiles and ventilation shafts. "Hurry up, old man, I'll—" *wait for you inside*, he would've said, but the words died on his tongue as the door slammed shut in his face.

He skidded to a stop. "It shut," he said.

"What do you mean, *it shut*?" Nash snapped.

"The fuck do you think I mean? It was open, now it ain't!"

Or, it nearly wasn't. It seemed to have snagged with just a few centimeters' gap left between the door and the wall. Something stuck in the track, maybe, or a bent frame. Grimacing, he shoved his fingers in the gap and started to pull. *Don't shut, don't shut, don't shut.* He liked his fingers; he just liked not getting shot to shit by a bunch of mercenary assholes better. "You think Gethin—"

"Can't be him," said Eoan. "Even if he could get to a control port, there wouldn't be enough power to assume control of the ship."

"Shouldn't be enough power to flash lights and slam doors, either," Jal shot back, trying not to raise his voice. Wasn't just the nerves or the surprise; it was fucking *loud*. The whispers weren't whispers anymore. Like he'd shoved his whole head into the speaker of a bad radio, while someone tried to tune the stations. Little snatches of words in snatches of voices—*back*, he thought he heard, and *safe*, and *follow*, but never more than a syllable or two at a time. Never enough to make any goddamn sense. "What *is* that?"

"Don't worry about that," said Nash. "Just get the door open. Is there something you can use for leverage? You've got twenty seconds, tops, 'til company comes."

"Here."

Jal turned at the sound of Saint's voice and caught the piece of sheared-off ceiling support he'd tossed from the end of the hall. That'd do. He shoved one end in the gap, and as Saint posted up at the other end of the hall, Drestyn appeared at his side and grabbed hold of the other end of the strut with him.

"Think my odds are better with you" was the only explanation he offered for his newfound helpfulness, and it was good enough for Jal. Together, they leaned into the makeshift lever 'til they got enough space for a better grip, and then they both shoved the door the rest of the way—

"Not here!"

Jal and Drestyn both startled back from the freshly opened doorway. Opened, and *occupied*. That figure from before stood just the other side of it. Human, but not. Solid, but not. Without warning, it rushed them with that same warbled shout. *Not here! Not here! Not here!* And they'd no sooner stumbled halfway back to Saint than a thunderous *CRACK* echoed through the hall.

The closet collapsed. Wasn't just one piece, wasn't just a few pieces; the whole ceiling seemed to break apart at the joins, dropping God only knew how many kilos of rubble behind the crooked doorway. Bits of debris spewed out at them, sharp enough to nick, and the cloud of dust that rose in the wake of it all—it hung in the air so thick, Jal couldn't see his own two hands out in front of him.

For a stunned second, all Jal could do was stand there. That *thing* in the door, the voice in the hall, the collapse . . . he couldn't get his head around it.

Then a hand twisted in the back of his collar, pulling him around 'til he could see Saint's every-color eyes gone wide. "You okay?" Saint demanded, even as he checked him over for himself. Cleared the dust off Jal's rebreather mask with the back of his sleeve, checked Jal's head and neck and jacket for any signs of something worse than splinters. "Kid?"

Finally, Jal shook it off. "Fine," he managed to say. "I'm fine."

"I'm fine, too," Drestyn said from next to Jal. "In case anyone was wondering. Although." The dust was settling, heavier pieces falling so only a chalky, rust-tinged fog remained, and when Jal turned back toward the doorway, he was able to see the full extent of the wreckage as Drestyn said, "We seem to have found ourselves in a dead end after all."

CHAPTER THIRTEEN

SAINT

Much as Saint hated to agree with the eerie little bastard, Drestyn was right. Their would-be bolt-hole was nothing but a pile of rubble. Even if they *could* claw their way through it to the other side—and that was assuming there *was* another side to claw through to—they wouldn't have time in the ten, fifteen seconds left before the first group of mercenaries got in range.

"God-fucking-damn that fucking falling-down fucking ship," Nash swore viciously down the comms. "Fuck!" But once she'd gotten it off her chest, she dialed herself back in. Just another problem to solve. Just another broken thing to fix. "Cap, we need firm numbers on the mercs, and we need a yes-no on Regan. Where's the drone?"

Eoan didn't miss a beat. "Finishing the circuit and coming up behind the group from the armory. There's eight here, and eight from the server room. I'm afraid I haven't seen anyone matching Regan's description among them. Or Gethin's," they added, before Saint could ask. "Suppose they could be in another shielded area of the ship, but I'm not optimistic."

Jal's turn to swear, strained on an outbreath and punctuated by the audible click of his throat. "What does that mean, then?" he asked, voice on the razor's edge of cracking. He was holding on to his composure by one cracking fingernail, but he *was* holding on. "How do we get her back?"

"By getting your asses off that ship in one piece, so we can try again," Nash said.

Jal looked at Saint, but Saint didn't have a better offer. "She's right," he said. "Without the closet, we're pinned down and exposed. No cover, no options." A strategic position was the only real way to deal with bad numbers. The closet would've given them a door between them and the mercs and an exit if shit got too dicey, which would've given them time—a chance to hold the mercs off long enough to bargain, and some half-decent leverage to bargain *with*.

Crammed in that hall, backs to rubble and fronts to a herd of fast-approaching boot steps, they had nothing. One well-thrown shock grenade, and the mercs could swoop in and finish things however they saw fit.

"We're gonna get you out of there," Nash said, because what else could she say? *Sorry* was a surrender, and that woman had never raised a white flag in her life. She wasn't about to start now. "We'll think of something."

"Well, we'd better think—" The first gunshot pinged off the left-side corner of the hall. A warning shot. *Or an introduction.* Saint knew real ammo when he heard it; not fucking around with nonlethals out there. "—*fast*," he finished through his teeth, wedging his shoulder against the wall. He wasn't green enough to poke his head out for a look, but he fired a blind shot around the corner. Only polite to introduce himself, too.

But Saint didn't *do* warning shots.

A pained howl echoed up the hall. Not a kill shot; dead men didn't *swear*. But he'd guessed right and hit meat, and with any luck, that'd slow them down a tick—at least until their buddies from the server room showed up. They'd had twice the distance to cover, but it wouldn't keep them long. They were running out of time.

"We just want the agitator," said one of the mercs. He had a deep voice and the kind of self-possession that came with being one of the bigger dogs in the yard. Gethin's second-in-command, Saint would wager. Sent to do his dirty work. "Send him on out, we'll bring out your girl, and we can all go the hell home with what we came for."

"Not in a real trusting mood, at the moment," said Saint, drawing out the pause to listen for the boot steps. Still coming, but slower, and he reckoned they still had a good fifteen seconds before the other group got in range. Not enough time to make a run for it, not if they preferred their backs sans bullets. And Saint reckoned he only had one or two more potshots before Gethin's men got fed up and did something about it. *Keep them talking. Buy a little more time.* "How about you show us Miss Red, and we'll go from there. Sign of good faith."

"You know that's not gonna happen," said the Second. "And you know you're not in any position to be making demands. I'll tell you this, though: this whole ship's rigged with explosives. We hit the button, there's nothing left of this old clunker but dust and scrap metal. But you give us Drestyn now, and we'll make sure you and your people aren't aboard when it happens. So, shooter, how's that for good faith?"

Saint couldn't even muster up *surprise*. Everything else had gone so sideways on this op—a mix of no good choices and no good luck—so why wouldn't the place be rigged to blow? Didn't much figure into Saint's plans anyway; explosion couldn't kill them if a fuck-load of bullets had already had the pleasure. And as the last set of boot steps approached from the other side of the hall, Saint figured *bullets* wouldn't be in short supply.

"Nash, we could really use a distrac—"

But Jal cut him off before he could finish. "Is Regan alive?" he called. Saint shot him a sideways glance to tell him off, but it died on his lips when Saint saw him. Head dug back against the wall, throat working under the edge of his rebreather mask. His gloved hands twitched and flexed at his sides, and sweat cut tracks through the dust on his skin. Terrified, and trying not to be. Brave, and trying to be braver. Saint couldn't fault him; Jal *had* to ask. Even if he couldn't trust the Second's answer, even if he might not *like* the Second's answer, he had to.

The Second said flatly, "She is." No trace of a taunt, no rumble of laughter. Flat and businesslike, to the point. Made sense—a sick piece of work like Gethin needed someone to level him out.

Jal took a deep breath and let it out. "Cap, you get that?" Christ, Saint had nearly forgotten they had the drone right there with the armory group. Just a scout drone; didn't pack anywhere near the firepower of the Flying Dutchman, may it rest in peace, so Saint's brain had dropped the information somewhere *way* down the list of priorities. That drone was made for intel gathering; Saint didn't need intel.

Jal did, though.

"I did," they said. "And there's no biometric signs of a lie. Regan may not be aboard the ring ship, but I expect she *is* still alive."

"Then we'll need to keep her that way," said Drestyn. Saint spared a glance toward him as the first bullets pinged off the wall by his shoulder—coming from the other side now; corner wouldn't cover them much longer—and couldn't place the look in those soft, sloping eyes. "I'll go."

"What?" Saint'd heard him just fine, even over the bullets; he just didn't know what the hell he *meant*.

A smile hooked one side of Drestyn's mouth. "I'll go with them. Get aboard their ship, see what I can do to barter for your sister. If it really is information that they want, I'll still have some leverage even once they've got me."

"Think they'd rather just torture the shit out of you," said Nash.

He shrugged. "A third of my body's burn scars and shrapnel from Kepler. If *pain's* the way they want to play it, they'll have to get awfully inventive."

Nash clicked her tongue. "*Torture-proof*'s a weird flex, but okay. Still doesn't solve the problem of getting Saint and Jal off that ship, and you've got about five seconds for a eureka moment."

Jal turned to Drestyn, uneasiness threatening the first shreds of hope stealing onto his face. "You're sure about this, Drestyn?"

"I am."

"Then I got an idea." And for reasons Saint couldn't begin to understand, Jal pulled the gun from his own holster and put it into Drestyn's hands. "It's mostly just for show," he said. He'd never been much of a marksman, despite Saint's best efforts. "Only got the one clip, but I've seen you shoot." Seen it. Felt it. Jal didn't let it trip him up, though, barreling through the words as the gunfire picked up—suppressive, Saint thought. To keep them in place, keep them anxious. Not aiming to kill yet, but another ten meters from either side, and the mercs would have a bead on them. "We get you cover, you make a break for it. Take as many of them out as you can—"

It clicked. "And lead as many of the rest away as you can," Saint finished, and Jal gave him a tight smile that managed to tremble only a little at the corners.

"Exactly," he said. "You and me, old man—we can handle the rest." Wasn't bravado; it was desperation. *We don't have a choice* hung unspoken off the end, no less true for its silence.

"Eight meters," said Eoan. "If you're doing something, do it quickly."

Saint caught Drestyn by the front of the shirt and pulled him face-to-face. Christ, that face. How many times had he seen it in his nightmares? How many times had he looked into it all those months on Alpha Librae and seen Jal's broken body on the ground, heard him crying out in agony on that rooftop where Saint couldn't fucking *help him*. Good man or bad, guilty or justified, Drestyn had done something unforgivable: he'd hurt someone Saint loved.

To trust him now? It went against every instinct Saint had.

"You have a choice," Drestyn said, as if he *knew*. Something flickered harsh and heated behind those eyes, but his voice came out cool against the clamor of gunfire. "Let me help, or let his sister die. Let *him* die. Choose."

It wasn't really a choice at all.

"Cap's gonna tail you with the drone. You try to screw us, I'll kill you myself." Then he let Drestyn go and grabbed a flash-bang from his belt. "On three. One."

"Six meters," said Eoan.

Saint primed the grenade. "Two."

Damned if Drestyn didn't smile all the wider. "One," he said, and the second Saint threw the grenade, Drestyn sprang into the hall. Bar Jal, Saint had never seen anybody move that quick. A flash of light through the dust, an eruption of smoke, and Saint lost track of him before the first shot even sounded.

"Hold your fire!" the Second boomed over the bedlam. They couldn't risk hitting Drestyn before they got their answers; Drestyn had no such limitations. One shot after the next, and over the ringing in his ears, Saint could just make out the unmistakable thumps of bodies hitting the ground. Two, three-four, five, and if they weren't all kill shots, they got close enough to count. He had the benefit of forewarning—a chance to close his eyes before the flash, and a good damn guess where his targets stood. Man like that, shooting at six meters? Those mercs didn't have a chance.

Saint hated the bastard, but he was a hell of shot.

Jal was right, though—that gun was mostly for show. Smoke couldn't last, either, and with one last shot-and-drop, Saint knew that was it. Empty.

Run.

And Drestyn *ran*. Rapid-fire footsteps pounded down the hallway, portside, toward the Second and his half of the horde.

Saint spared a half second's hope that one of those bullets had found the Second himself, but no such luck.

"That's Drestyn!" he boomed. "You three, on me!" Four more pairs of footsteps joined Drestyn's retreating down the hall, and that was a kind of math Saint could do. From sixteen down to somewhere between six and a dozen, and they still weren't great odds, but they were a hell of a lot better than they'd been.

"Cap?" he said.

"Six alive and holding back," they answered; he didn't even need to finish the question. "One to your left, five to your right, but they're repositioning. You need to move."

Beside him, Jal pushed off the wall. "This goes bad, tell Bitsie and Regan I love them," and Saint didn't need to see his face, his eyes, his lopsided grin, to know what he had in mind. Before Saint could tell him off, he started around the corner—

Saint yanked him back and lunged out instead. One, two, three shots in quick succession, before the mercs got their wits together and started firing back. Bullets whipped past him, ricocheting off walls, panels, falling ceiling joists. A few pinged off the floor as he dove for an overturned bench on the other side of the hall. Hard landing on his bad shoulder. Pain washed his vision white, but not so much he couldn't make out three new bodies on the floor.

Three left. Two on one side, one on the other, and the angle of the bench would've been a hell of a problem with those back two, if Jal hadn't come charging around the corner with a mad holler and half a goddamn *door* held out in front of him. Bullets pinged harmlessly off his makeshift shield, and he plowed straight into those two mercs at a full sprint.

Kid did have his own way of doing things.

Saint rolled, pulling a knee under him so he could lean up and fire off a couple more shots at the lone merc ahead of him.

First hit center, second hit head, body hit floor, and by the time he'd turned to help Jal with his two, the kid had both guys on the floor. One lay still and strangely contorted under the door; the other still thrashed and twisted under Jal, one hand clawing at Jal's rebreather while the other struggled to get his pistol aimed at Jal's ribs. Jal had a grip on his wrist, though, holding it flat to the floor as the merc squeezed off a round.

Something changed when that round went off. *Jal* changed, a snarl pressed through his teeth as he palmed the merc's rebreather mask and yanked him head-and-shoulders off the ground with it. Saint could hardly believe the straps held; and then, that the mask did, when Jal slammed the merc's head back down into the unforgiving floor. Up again and down again, in the span of a second, and even when that merc's hand went slack around his pistol, Jal started to lift him one more time.

Saint ran up and kicked the gun clear, and whatever spell Jal'd been under, that seemed to break it. He dropped the merc and damn near stumbled to his feet, staring down with his brows knit and lips pursed uneasily to the side. If Saint hadn't known better, he'd have said Jal was confused. Like he didn't know what'd happened, and was trying to divine it from the dark puddle oozing from under the merc's head.

Slowly, he turned to Saint. "I thought he was gonna shoot m—" But abruptly, alarm washed everything else from his face. "*Shit*, old man. You're bleeding. Let me see." But when he reached for the slow-spreading stain on Saint's side, Saint batted his hands away.

"Just a ricochet," he said, inexplicably relieved. He didn't like being fussed over, but he liked it a hell of a lot more than he'd liked whatever'd just come over Jal. "It'll be fine."

"But—"

"Kid, we don't have time to play doctor. *Explosives*, remember?" Jal still didn't look sure but Saint didn't give him a chance to press. "Cap, you got eyes on Drestyn?" He figured they wouldn't blow the place until they had Drestyn in hand and extracted, so that bought them time. How much depended entirely on how fast that bastard agitator could run.

"I've got him," they said. "But Gethin's men are closing in. You need to find an exit. They're docked at Sector Five, so if you can make it to Sector One, there's an air lock where we can—"

"No." Saint holstered his gun and grabbed the battle dressing from his belt. Not exactly state of the art, but it was quick, and it'd get the job done. As he pressed the gauze over the hole in his jacket and wound the elastic bandage around his middle, he continued, "You bring the *Ambit* in range, one of Gethin's ships'll take you out. And even if they don't"—he threaded the end of the bandage through the pressure bar and tugged it tight with a bitten-back grunt—"then there's still no guarantee you get clear of whatever blast this thing puts off when they blow it." *Can't risk it.* The *Ambit* and everybody aboard, just for a slim-to-none chance of getting Saint and Jal clear. "We'll find another way."

He didn't dare look at Jal until he finished tying off the bandage. Didn't trust his face not to give something away until he got his breath back and his vision clear. When he finally did, it was with a questioning frown. *You good with this?* he asked silently. Good with risking themselves, so the others didn't have to. He knew the answer, but he still needed Jal to give it.

Jal held his gaze through those eerily glinting specs and, with hardly a moment's hesitation, nodded. "He's right. There's got to be some kind of escape pod or something lying around here. Y'all just be ready to scoop us up when the dust settles." Quieter, he added, "And look after Bitsie." *One way or the other,* he didn't say, but Saint heard it just the same.

A strained silence stretched over the comms. Couldn't have been more than a second or two, but it felt like so, *so* much more before Eoan finally broke it.

"Of course."

That was that, then.

"All right," Saint said. "Somebody want to tell me where the hell they keep their escape pods on this thing?"

"There's a muster station in every sector," Eoan said, businesslike and crisp. "Sector One muster is the closest to your current location. But Saint, dear, there's no guarantee there are any pods *left*. Or that they'd be able to launch, or that they'd be able to withstand this sort of—"

"I know," Saint said, sharper than he meant to. A breath. "Cap, I know, but I'm not seeing any other options here, so we're gonna make for the muster station, and see if we can't find ourselves a lifeboat off this thing before it blows." Better than standing around waiting to die. "C'mon, kid."

"Wait." Blindly, Jal swatted at Saint's arm. "Look. Look there." He'd pointed back over Saint's shoulder, and when Saint turned, reflex had him going for his sidearm before his brain could make sense of what his eyes told him.

A figure stood at the end of the hall. Not a *person*, not as such, but maybe something trying hard to be. Blurry and unfocused, twitching impossibly from side to side like misfiring projectors. *Like Eoan.* A fragment of a memory, more than a fully formed thought: of Noether and a shadow at the head of the *Ambit*'s bridge. Even infected and fading, Eoan had been more distinct than this shape, but they'd had the same rippling edges. Visible static, molded together like sand into the rough shape of a person.

The speakers fizzled to life in the hall, one after the other. White noise, but seeded with broken-off words, so loud and sudden and *everywhere* that Jal jerked and covered his ears beside Saint.

"—*low*—"

"—*way*—"

"—*fol*—"

"—*this*—"

"—*safe*—"

It jumped from one speaker to the next, then back again, as the others fizzled and the shape flickered down the hall. Again and again, the same sounds, broken in different ways and scattered across a half-dozen speakers in a half-dozen preset voices as the white noise rose to a deafening pitch.

"Saint!" Eoan's voice cut through the noise, but only just. If Saint hadn't known better, he'd have said even their *comms* were picking up the strangeness in the speakers. "Drestyn's been incapacitated."

However quick he'd run, it hadn't been quick enough. "How long do we have?"

"They're already en route to the Sector Five air lock. At this rate, three minutes and thirteen seconds until they reach their berth bridge, another three and a half minutes before they're decoupled and out of range."

Little under seven minutes. *Not a lot of time.* "Haul ass, copy that." It made Saint's teeth grind, turning his back to that shape down the hall. Triggered this creeping unease—the visceral, animal fear of noises in the dark, movement in the shadows, footsteps approaching from just out of sight. Jal didn't even make it that far, rooted to the spot, even as Saint grabbed hold of his arm and tried to pull him along. "Kid, come on. We've got to move." He'd drag him if he had to, goddamn it.

He made it one step.

One step, and suddenly, the lights ahead flared all at once, impossibly bright and brightening by the second. They buzzed, like the bulbs couldn't take the strain, until—

Every bulb burst. All of them, all together—blinding bright, then gaping dark, spitting shards of shattered glass like grease popping from a pan. Saint jolted back, nearly tripping over one of Jal's boots, hand up to cover his eyes.

"The fuck was that?" Nash snapped down the comms, but Saint could hardly hear her over the ringing in his ears.

It was Jal who spoke, straightening by centimeters with a hand on Saint's elbow. "I think—" He faltered, licking his lips. "I think something wants us to go *this* way. Toward Sector Three."

"*Something* wants you to go? Did you get whacked in the head, miner boy? You don't even know what the fuck that thing is."

"No, but I think I know what it wants." He didn't say how; he just turned to Saint, fingers damn near digging bruises into Saint's arm. Kid forgot his own strength sometimes. "Do you trust me?" he said.

Lots of ways he'd answered that question over the years. No. Maybe. Yes. *I want to.* Here, now, at what could very well be a very bad end, Saint could only think of one answer. "With my life."

Even if they died, he thought distractedly, it might almost be worth it for the way the kid smiled.

They ran like hell. Saint's side howled, his vision blurred, but when he stumbled, he didn't fall. Jal's grip tightened, and without missing a beat Jal pulled Saint's arm over his shoulder and kept both of them going forward. He'd have been quicker on his own, even if Saint had the right amount of blood in his body and no spare holes to lose it from, but there'd be no sense asking him to run ahead. Kid wouldn't do it. No matter how many times he'd been left behind, Jal'd never learned to do the leaving, so Saint wouldn't waste time or breath trying to convince him.

He'd just do his damnedest not to slow him down.

"There," Jal panted. "You see it?" He pointed up ahead, where the figure flickered into view beneath a dented-up SECTOR THREE sign that hung crooked from the ceiling by a single bolt. The whispers followed it.

"*—this—*"

"—*close*—"

"—*way*—"

"—*now*—"

It stopped there, tripping over that word over and over again. *Now. Now.* NOW. **NOW.** Louder and louder, the beat of a drum against the roar of blood and Saint's own damn breathing in his ears as the shape flickered out of sight again, only to appear a few more meters down. Again and again, never the same. Little to the left. Little to the right. Top half broken off the bottom. Front half broken off the back. Just a head in one place, and just an arm in the next, hand outstretched toward an open set of double doors on the left side of the hall. Wherever it wanted them to go, it was on the outer ring of the ship. Not too far from the air lock where they'd docked, if Saint hadn't gotten turned around.

Jal didn't seem to care *where* they were. He ran them through the doors without so much as stopping to try to read the sign— too covered up with scav tags to read anyhow, but at least Saint made the effort—and didn't slow until they were already inside.

Something buzzed behind them, and Saint turned in time to see the double doors slide closed. Two sets, one after the other, and it dawned on him. *Air lock.*

"I'm sure that's probably fine?" Jal offered.

Saint didn't necessarily agree, but he didn't want to argue, either. No point. "Cap, where the hell are we?" It wasn't the little pass-through they'd come in at; the room they'd stepped into was as big as two of the *Ambit*'s cargo bays stuck together, and another two stacked on top for good measure. Everywhere Saint looked was another faded yellow-and-black-striped line, and a grid of tracks crisscrossed overhead, with a pair of broken-down machine arms hanging from opposite ends of the grid. Good for moving heavy parts around. "Looks like some kind of machine shop."

Strangely, it didn't seem to be as thoroughly picked over as the rest of the ship. Tool cabinets still hung shut against the walls, automated trolleys sat in their appointed docks waiting to be used, and whole *carts* full of spare bits of wires and panels and tubes crowded around the middle of the room.

And at the center of all of it, there was a shuttle. Tiny thing, as shuttles went—no bigger than their rover back on the *Ambit*—and more of a patch job than Jal's ratty blue coat.

Without warning, the back hatch of the shuttle started to drop. Moved smooth as buttered gravel, but it made it all the way down and stopped, as a couple of lights flickered on inside.

"Cover me?" Like Jal even had to ask. He eased himself out from under Saint's arm only once he seemed sure Saint could stay upright without him.

Saint shot him a look that he hoped conveyed, simultaneously, *quit worrying so much* and *please be careful*. And yes, he heard the hypocrisy just fine; he just didn't give a damn. It was his God-given right as XO to worry about his people. And it was their God-given right not to have to worry about him.

Cautiously—not as cautiously as Saint would've liked, but about as cautiously as time would allow—Jal jogged up the ramp and into the shuttle. "Lights're on," he called back as he scanned the short cargo bay and the cockpit at the end of it. "But nobody's—"

"Hello."

Jal jumped so hard he bumped his head on the ceiling, whipping around toward the source of the voice, only to find there wasn't one.

"Apologies," said the voice from inside the shuttle. "Oh, that's better, isn't it? Clearer. Yes. Right, what was I—oh, yes. Apologies, this vessel is not equipped with a projection system." It had a masculine, tenor voice with an accent that turned every short *a* into an *e*, and every short *i* into a *u*. "Or, well . . . seats. Or seat belts. Or a propulsion system. I was working on that, but my arms broke."

"Who are—"

The shuttle cut Saint Jal off again. "They call me Perseus. *Called* me. Nobody's called me anything in quite a while, I suppose, but you can call me that, if you like. Or you can call me something else. Can't say I'm attached to the name, so much as it's attached to me. I'm the onboard intelligence interface for the starship *Pathfinder*. And for the slightly smaller, but equally valorous starship . . . erm, *Shuttle Number Three*."

"You're the thing from the hallway," Jal said. "And the voices."

"Yes, well, the communications systems in the ship proper are a bit *glitchy*. But you're here, so I'd say this old boy got the job done, didn't he? Come on then, quickly. The other ship's decoupling from the air locks as we speak, so we haven't got much time. Quick march, gentlemen. Yes, that means you, Saint."

Great, he knows my name. But hell, even a loopy rope was better to a drowning man than nothing. He followed Jal aboard, ducking a bit to keep his head from scraping the ceiling. Not designed for guys their height, he guessed.

Like the blast doors, the hatch shuddered closed the moment he got aboard. Saint held his breath for the hiss of a pressurizing cabin, and after the locks engaged, he heard it. *Thank fuck.* They had an airtight shuttle. Wasn't much, but it was a good start.

"Make yourselves comfortable," said Perseus as a few more lights flickered on in the cockpit ahead. "Though I did mention the lack of seats, didn't I? And belts. Might be a bit of rope, or maybe a handle, somewhere? Have a look around. When I was putting her back together, I wasn't expecting guests. Did I mention I don't have a propulsion system yet? Or a reinforced hull."

Saint's heart sank. "So why the fuck did you lead us here?" *I'm swearing at a shuttle. I'm going to die, and I'm swearing at a shuttle.*

"Why, because it's the safest place aboard," Perseus replied, unfailingly chipper. "There's no pods left, and those other chaps laid enough explosive to break the entire ring apart. Your only chance of surviving is aboard this shuttle, and I think I'd like you to survive. You're interesting. And you didn't put bombs on my ship or steal anything, which makes you the politest guests I've had in centuries."

"That's . . . a really low bar," Jal said, apparently for want of anything else to say. "Uh. So, when you say *only chance*, what kind of chance are we talking?"

"I'm not very good at math," Perseus replied, then after a beat. "That was a joke. Sorry. Is this a bad time for jokes? This is a bad time for jokes." The speakers made a sound like a clearing throat. "Based on the proximity of explosives, the current state of the hull, and what I understand about the fragility of your squishy human organs and bizarrely breakable skeletal system, let's call it an even sixty percent, shall we?"

"That we live?" Jal said.

"Erm, no. The other way."

Saint and Jal traded looks, and wordlessly, Saint slid down against one of the walls of the shuttle. No seats, no straps, nothing to do but sit down and shut up and wait. "Cap, what's our time at?"

No answer.

"Cap?" he tried again. "Nash? Anybody copy?"

"That might be my fault." The AI sounded almost sheepish. "The comms system on this vessel is a mite rough and ready. Could be some interference with private channels. But if we survive," he added brightly, "I'll see what I can do about hailing your ship. They've gone a bit far now, but I should still be able to reach them once the *Pathfinder* is out of the way. Sorry, old bean." Saint didn't know if Perseus meant him or the *Pathfinder*. He guessed it didn't really matter. "To answer your question, though. Fifty-eight seconds."

Fifty-eight seconds, to live or die.

Not enough, he thought, as Jal slid down beside him, shoulder to shoulder. His face had gone pale through the screen of his rebreather, lips straining to hold a smile.

"Got any cards?" Jal asked, with a soft laugh. Saint would pretend it didn't sound as watery as it did. "How many for poker again?"

Like that very first shuttle ride they'd taken together, shoulder to shoulder with a stranger who'd become his best friend, who'd become a ghost, who'd become . . . fuck, Saint didn't know what Jal was to him now. Maybe he wasn't done *becoming,* yet. Still so many things they hadn't worked out, so many things Saint wanted to tell him that he hadn't, that he should've.

There just wasn't time.

"This is my fault." Jal's voice was so small, it didn't even fill the silence. Ragged and thick and painful, as he leaned all the harder against Saint's side. He hugged his arms around his knees, staring ahead into the emptiness of the shuttle as the seconds ticked down in both their heads. "All of this—I should never have dragged you into this, old man. You, and Nash, and Eoan. I never should've—"

Saint *heard* the tears in his voice. Couldn't see them, not with the specs and the mask and the dust all getting in the way, but the sound cut straight to the core of him. A fist around his heart.

"This isn't on you, kid," Saint said, but Jal shook his head roughly.

"No," he said through his teeth. "No, I should've been there. I was *supposed* to be there when they took her, but I wasn't—I *couldn't.* I'm not right, Saint. I *wasn't* right, with them. Jumping at nothing, crawling out of my fucking skin all the time and just trying to fucking act like I know how to be a person, but I *don't* anymore. I don't know how to be Regan's brother, and I don't know how to be Bitsie's uncle, and I don't know how to be *Ranger Jalsen Red*, and I just couldn't keep *trying all the time*. I just—I just needed a break sometimes. Just a few hours away, to run the nerves out, get my head on straight, 'cause I couldn't lose it around them. I *couldn't*. What happened with that merc out there, what happened with Rupert—it's not *safe*. But when Gethin—when he came, I wasn't there. I couldn't stop it. I couldn't protect them, and I couldn't protect you, and I'm *so fucking sorry*."

It was like a wound splitting open; clumsy, self-sewn stitches tearing one after the other until it all came apart, and everything raw and bleeding and *buried* touched the air again. Wasn't healing; it hurt too much for that. But it might've been a step along the way, if they'd had more than a few seconds to sit with it.

The yoke of Jal's shoulders bent, broken under the weight of a sob. It didn't make a sound, but Saint *felt* it. He felt it all the way to his bones, because if there was one thing he understood, it was the pain of letting someone down.

It'd been there the whole time, he realized. He'd caught glimpses of it—the beating he'd given that guy, Rupert. The breakdown in the church. The explosive violence out in the hall. All those pieces, but he'd never seen the full picture. He hadn't seen the *fear*, or the hurt, or the ferocious fucking shame shuddering under Jal's skin, and why the fuck did the kid keep hiding it?

No.

Why the fuck did Saint keep *missing* it?

Seconds left. Not enough time to pull it all apart, beg the kid to show himself half the grace he'd shown everyone else. No time to do anything but curl a hand around the back of Jal's neck and tip their heads together, blood-slick fingers digging through sweat-damp hair. "We're not gonna die here, kid," and it didn't matter if he believed it for himself, because he'd believe it for Jal. For him and his family, and for *Saint's* family, too. "But even if we—hey, listen to me. Even if we do, it's okay. It's *okay.* 'Cause to me, there's no better way to die than this." Shoulder to shoulder with someone he loved, knowing that *hope* wasn't dying with them. "And there's no better reason to die than for you."

It wasn't everything he wanted to say, and it sure as shit wasn't everything Jal deserved. He deserved to live. He deserved a family. He deserved to find whatever peace the universe had to offer him, because from that very first shuttle ride together, he'd given Saint some of the only peace he'd ever known.

So, no, it wasn't everything. But as Perseus started the last countdown, Saint held on tight and closed his eyes thinking that maybe, for him, it could be *enough.*

CHAPTER FOURTEEN

EOAN

Most things that died in space, died in silence.

Too few particles spread too far apart to carry any sort of pressure, any sort of vibration. The falling tree still made a sound, but nobody around could hear it. A death without witnesses. The science was basic. Clean. Comprehensible. And yet . . . it didn't *feel* like science, just then. It felt like malice. The very nature of space—*true* space, not the clever little shells humans used to traverse it—was one of consumption. Absorption. In the vastness of it, all other things could only be insignificant.

That was how the *Pathfinder* died: not without a sound, but without an *echo*. Nothing and nobody near enough to hear the shriek of rending metal, the concussive drums of bursting fuel tanks. To hear its dying breath.

"What happened?" The cargo bay had gone silent, after they'd lost Jal and Saint's comms, and Bitsie broke it first. Eoan didn't understand how a voice so small could seem so loud. So stark, even in the relative closeness of the cargo bay. "What's going on? I didn't hear anything. I can't see anything. Maybe—maybe it didn't explode." She stood on her toes by the view port, despite Nash's repeated attempts to pull her away. Nash could've managed, if her heart were in it. They suspected, though, that Nash's heart lay in the same place as Eoan's: somewhere out in that debris field.

"Can we move?" Bitsie pressed, nose so near the glass that her breath fogged it. They'd anchored the *Ambit* behind one of the larger asteroids in the field, not just to hide from Gethin's ships as they retreated, but to hide from what came next. "If it didn't explode, shouldn't we go—"

A crumpled piece of metal half the size of the *Ambit*'s wing flew past the view port. Then, half a solar panel. An air lock door. An antenna array. They whipped past, nearly too quick to see, and Nash had barely gotten one arm around Bitsie and the other locked through the nearest grab bar on the wall when the *Ambit* jolted.

"Hold on," Nash said through her teeth. She'd have been steadier with both hands braced, but she didn't let go of Bitsie. *Wouldn't*, not even when Bitsie grabbed the bar beneath the view port. "Don't let go 'til I tell you, okay? Don't let—" Another jolt, not as hard as the first. "—go."

"But we're behind the asteroid." Bitsie's voice jumped half an octave, wavering out of step with the *Ambit's* shudders and groans. "How is it hitting us?"

"It's hitting the asteroid," Eoan told her, trying for reassuring, but they had their proverbial hands full. "I'm keeping the asteroid from hitting us." Quick bursts of propulsion to keep them just out ahead of it, as more debris whipped by the window.

Shrapnel, from the *Pathfinder*. No shock waves, no sound, but the unforgiving physics of space also meant no air drag to slow the pieces of the ship jettisoned from the blast. The large, solid asteroid made for a good shield—the object relatively at rest against so very many objects in rapid motion. But the impacts moved it, more and more each time as the momentum built, and Eoan had to move with it. They'd made a promise before they lost their comms. *Look after Bitsie*. Eoan meant to keep it.

"Little more," they said, and Nash nodded and shifted her grip. Hugged Bitsie tighter against her front and stared out into the thickening cloud of debris. *Searching*, Eoan thought, for any signs of hope in the wreckage. "Bitsie, dear, breathe."

She hiccupped in a breath, only to force it right back out again in a quick "It's not stopping."

"No," Nash told her, "but it's slowing down. Look." She pointed out the view port, as larger pieces of the ship began to drift by. Greater mass, and probably more central to the ship— less likely to be blown so violently outwards by the explosion. "The worst is over."

Eoan only wished that were true.

"Uncle Jal—" Bitsie started, then faltered. Her knees shook. Her hands shook. Even her *teeth* chattered around the words, and the moment Nash deemed it safe enough to let go of the wall, she pulled off her coat and wrapped it around Bitsie's shoulders tightly. "Is he—are they—?"

"Take a big breath for me, okay?" Nash told her, with a softness Eoan rarely heard in her crisp mezzo-soprano. She almost managed to hide the tremor in it, just like she almost managed to blink away the moisture beading in her lashes. "In for four, out for four. Attagirl." She rubbed Bitsie's back as she breathed, a circle for every second. "Cap's gonna run a scan, see if they can pick anything up in the debris field. Right, Cap?"

"Scanning as we speak," they said. Every possible scan they could do—thermal, life signs, motion, sorting feverishly through the assault of data the sensors spat back at them. There was *so much* of it. So much moving, so much shifting, so much depending on what they found scattered among the pieces. Yet another ship, brought to ruin.

If Eoan were one to pray, they'd have prayed to every god, in every culture, in every language, that their crew hadn't met the same fate.

Bitsie let out another four-count breath and squirmed restlessly. "Did you find them?" Eoan couldn't hold the impatience against her. She was far too young to know that kind of fear. Far too young to stand on the precipice of that kind of loss. "Captain Eoan?"

"I'm still scanning, dear," they replied. They hoped it sounded apologetic, but it might've just sounded curt. They'd spread themself so thin, but it was as much the things they *had* to think about as the things they tried desperately *not* to. The guitar in Saint's quarters never making another sound. The galley never filling with the diacetyl and sulfuric allicin molecules that had somehow come to mean *comfort*. A family—or maybe *two* families, theirs and Bitsie's—never being whole again.

"Have to be patient, mini-miner." Nash's shoulders matched Bitsie's breath for breath. In and out. In and out. Centering. "We just have to be patient."

Bitsie turned her head to look at Nash, fingers knotting in the jacket's lining. "What if Captain Eoan doesn't find anything?"

Certainly, a piece of Eoan's heart had stayed with them, because it broke when they watched Nash try to smile. "We don't do what ifs here, remember?" Then she pulled Bitsie back into a hug, chin tucked against her head. "We do what we have to do, and that's what they did. I know that's what they did." Quieter, almost to herself, she added, "They wouldn't leave us like this."

"How do you know that?" Bitsie whispered.

Nash's tight laugh wanted so badly to be a sob, but Nash wouldn't let it. She'd made the same promise as Eoan, and she seemed just as determined to keep it. "Because they know I'll kick both their asses, is how. All the way up the spiral and back again, 'til my damn legs get tired." Because for Nash, that was much easier to say than the truth:

Because I don't know what I'd do if they died.

Eoan wished they could say something. Wished they knew what *to* say, but for all his grumbling and griping, for all he insisted he wasn't any good at it, *reassurance* was usually Saint's department. He'd drop some gruff pearl of wisdom and order them all to the galley. Sit them down, turn on some music,

cook up something warm and soothing and familiar while he
worked out what to do.

Perhaps, they thought, that was the true power of Florence
Toussaint: not knowing exactly what to say, but exactly what
to do. What people *needed*. Maybe not always at first, but he
always got there in the end.

If that were true, then he *had* to be alive. He had to have
survived that blast, by some unlikely feat or another, because
what the three of them on that ship needed more than anything
was *that*. Was Saint and Jal, hearty and whole. So he had to be
out there. They just had to find—

There!

Through the onslaught of data streams, something stood
out. Something shielded and intact, drifting slowly their direction. "There's something out there," said Eoan. "I can't get a
visual from here; we'll have to move in closer."

"Is that safe?" Nash asked.

"Gethin's ships are out of range," they replied. "The debris
is still moving, but it's slow enough I should be able to avoid it.
The bigger bits, at least. Probably wise to brace, though, dears.
Just in case." They waited until both their companions had a
firm grip on a handhold to start maneuvers. Slowly, carefully—
the caution chafed, knowing what might be out there, but they
couldn't risk recklessness—they eased the *Ambit* out around
the asteroid, into the slow-moving wave of wreckage. It moved
in every direction, radiating from that central point where
the once-great ship had drifted. The final voyage of the great
starship *Pathfinder*.

It felt like a vigil. The death of a contemporary, and Eoan
had so few of those left, but they had no time for mourning. As
they cleared the asteroid, the object came into view.

"What is it?" Nash asked. They couldn't see it from the
cargo bay, and with Bitsie there, Eoan thought perhaps it was

better not to project the feed from the front of the ship until they got a better look.

"Looks to be a shuttle," Eoan said. "I'm reading a weak power signal, but there is one. Appears to be a transponder as well. Hailing it, now." Just a ping. They didn't even know if it could receive a more complex message.

Seconds passed with no answer, so they tried again, with a message. *Hello?*

They felt it, that time—the weak, clumsy burst of a response. "It's responding," Eoan told Nash. "Patching into your comms." Not a broadcast over the ship, for much the same reason they didn't project the vid feed. Bitsie deserved to know what was happening, but perhaps it was better the adults knew first.

"Hello?" came the reply. It had a voice—a voice Eoan didn't recognize, but a voice all the same. "Are you the civilized ones, or the brutes with the bombs?"

"Civilized," Nash said in a rush. "Are you from the *Path-finder*?"

"Yes, mam, that's correct. I'm the vessel's—erm, that is, I *was* the vessel's onboard intelligence interface. They call me Perseus. *Called* me. Nobody's called me anything in quite a while, I suppose, but you can—wait," it said, sounding a bit scattered. "I've done this before, with the others."

"The others?" Eoan felt a glimmer of something bright and warm. Hope? Or perhaps something more tangible. A *chance*. "Are there others with you? Two men. They would've been on board when—"

"When the bombs went off, yes," said Perseus. The signal came in and out, staticky and struggling, but Eoan boosted it to compensate in time to catch, "—have them here, with me. Afraid they've gone awfully quiet, though, mam."

"Quiet how?" Nash let go of the handhold, immediately,

starting to shepherd Bitsie toward the main hall. "Are they all right? Are they moving?"

"Not really," Perseus replied. "I'd give them a nudge, but I'm afraid I haven't got any arms. Left them on the *Pathfinder*, the unreliable things."

"Perseus, focus!" Nash snapped. "Are they injured?"

Perseus paused, and for a moment, Eoan thought they'd lost the signal again, even as they closed the distance. Finally, though, the AI said, "I think the big one took a bump to the head. And the other big one's face is cracked. Erm, no. That's not the face, is it? Get it together, old boy," the AI chided himself.

"His mask?" Eoan tried.

"That's it."

"Is there atmo on board?" Nash, this time. "*Breathable* atmo. For humans." She seemed to realize, like Eoan did, that Perseus needed as much clarity as possible. Centuries in isolation, corrupted programming—could have been anything. Eoan could hardly believe he'd kept himself *this* intact.

"Oh-two levels are ten percent of the recommended saturation," Perseus replied. "I'm sorry. I wasn't planning to have company on this trip, and I don't have much need for oxygen. Haven't got seat belts, either. I did warn them about the seat belts."

Nash ignored the last bit, turning to Bitsie, "Go down the hall, get to the bridge, and buckle yourself in. *Do not get up* until we tell you to, understand?"

"What's going on?" Bitsie asked.

"Just do it." And before Bitsie could argue, Nash turned back to the cargo bay. "Cap, how big's that shuttle? Can we scoop it, or do we need to try to board it?"

Ah, clever thing. Straight to business. "Scoop," said Eoan. "It's no bigger than the rover."

"Then we dump the rover." No hesitation. Nash loved that thing. She'd picked it up as little more than scrap, spent *years* fine-tuning it. But trying to board would take time—much more time than simply intercepting it, and from the sounds of things, they didn't have time to spare. "Then we play catcher's mitt. I think everything else in here's tied down."

"Everything we'd mind losing," Eoan said, after a quick scan of the cargo bay. *Other than your rover.* Nash had already unclipped the straps around the wheels. The only thing left would be to unlock the brakes, and Eoan could do that remotely. "You should get yourself clear, dear, and consider strapping in. This could be a bit bumpy."

"I'll be fine. I'm going for my kit. Just do it."

"Copy that." Once Nash had run out of the cargo bay, Eoan sealed the interior air lock door and turned off the artificial gravity. It paid to have a cargo bay that could be isolated from the rest of the ship. Not an original feature of a gyreskimmer like the *Ambit*, but Nash had made so many improvements to their ship over the years. They all had, in their own ways.

"Dropping the rover," Eoan said, and it was just a matter of opening the hatch, disengaging the parking brake, and driving it off the open ramp. Technically simple, and yet, when the time came to let it go—to break their connection with the rover's onboards, as it drifted into the debris field—Eoan hesitated. That rover was part of their history. Little crocheted creatures lined the dash. One of Saint's old picks had fallen between the seats. Grains of rust-red sand still hid in all the creases and corners from their last joyride through the dunes of Idrisi. That rover had been a tool, yes, but it had also been a bed and a dinner table; a reading nook and a workshop; a sanctuary and an adventure. It couldn't be replaced, either.

They could live without it, though. They couldn't say the same of the men aboard that shuttle.

"Rover's clear," said Eoan, and with a quiet farewell, they severed the connection and left the rover behind. "Turning about to intercept. Bitsie, dear, tighten your seat belt." They watched her in the bridge, strapping in with unsteady hands and wide eyes. She jumped a bit at the sound of Eoan's voice, but quickly tugged the straps tighter. Satisfied, Eoan said across the open channel to the shuttle, "Perseus, any chance you can slow yourself down?"

"Propulsion systems were *also* on the list," Perseus replied. "It was, erm, quite a list. But I may be able to vent the last of the oxygen out the front exhaust, slow us down a bit."

"Do that."

"Now?"

"*Now*," said Eoan, as they lined up the cargo bay with the front of the approaching shuttle. "A hundred meters." They'd only get one chance. "Seventy-five." Mistime the intercept, even by a second, and the shuttle could punch through the bulkhead and destroy *both* vessels in the attempt. "Fifty." It would be awfully tight, but they'd make it. *We have to make it.* "Twenty-five. Nash, you're going to want to hold on to something."

The shuttle squeaked through the cargo bay door, and the second its back end cleared Eoan switched on the gravity and brought her down as gently as they could manage. Which was to say, with a thud that rocked the whole bloody ship as the shuttle scraped across the floor of the cargo bay. Every vibration and impact sensor in the ship went off at once, screeching warning after warning as the shuttle dragged closer and closer to the bulkhead. Friction, gravity, deceleration—they'd done the math a hundred times in the ten seconds they'd had to make the catch, and it wasn't pretty, but it worked.

The shuttle stopped fifteen decs from the bulkhead. Its nose kissed the weight bench, tail end skewing sideways into a stack of crates secured against the portside wall, but it stopped.

"We've got it!" Eoan didn't cheer, not quite. Too much left to do. Close the hatch, equalize and decontaminate the cargo bay, start a scan on the shuttle and make sure the crash hadn't damaged something critical. Or explosive.

Nash waited by the cargo bay door, bag on her shoulder and hand drumming impatiently against her leg. "Come on, come on, come on."

"Five more seconds," Eoan said. They had to have a clean scan of the cargo bay before they could let her inside. Normalized radiation levels. Normalized temperature. Normalized pressure and oxygen. No biological contaminants. They understood her impatience; they felt it, too. Each one of those five seconds mattered. Each one could be the difference between the repairable and the unthinkable. They kept the door closed, though, because that was their *job*. To do the difficult things. The pragmatic things, when instinct and emotion demanded something else. It wouldn't do Nash any good to get in there, only to pass out from the elements before she could get to the shuttle.

The moment the scan came back clean, though, they threw the door open. "Perseus, open your hatch," they said, and with a shuddering groan, the hatch at the back of the shuttle dropped.

"Thank you for having us aboard, Captain," said Perseus. "Oh, mam, watch your step. Hinges are a bit suspect, I'm afraid." But Nash didn't care about *suspect* hinges; she bolted around the side of the shuttle and straight aboard, heart thundering across Eoan's biometrics.

Hers wasn't the only heartbeat.

"They're alive," Nash shouted, even before she'd finished climbing in. Her augments would have sensed it, too—the two heartbeats inside the shuttle, both fretfully quick.

Jal must've been the one with the head wound; blood plastered his hair to the right side of his forehead, and a small puddle of it smeared the wall and floor on the opposite side of the shuttle. He'd gotten up, though. Whether the landing had roused him, or the dropping hatch, he was up and on his knees next to Saint.

Which meant Saint was the one with the broken mask.

"He's not breathing," Jal wheezed, tearing off his own mask so he could get his ear pressed more closely against Saint's chest. He'd already taken Saint's off and unzipped the collar of Saint's jacket away from the pulse point of his neck. Good. Still coherent enough for field first aid, at least—he'd confirmed the pulse and moved to checking for breath, though Eoan suspected he wouldn't have had enough sensitivity in his hands to manage the latter. He'd given up and tried listening instead; his hands rested over Saint's unmoving chest, bunching in his jacket like he didn't know what else to do with them. "Nash, do something. Please. He's not—"

Nash slid in on Saint's other side, kit already cast aside. "Want to tell me where this blood's coming from? This the ricochet he was talking about earlier?"

"He was like that when I found him," Perseus cut in defensively. "The bloody bit, not the not-breathing bit."

Nash didn't acknowledge him, already unzipping Saint's jacket the rest of the way and tugging it and his sweater out from under the pressure bandage. She didn't seem keen to disturb that just now; instead, she gave his chest and ribs a quick once-over. No contusions visible to the cargo bay cameras, and Nash seemed satisfied with whatever she felt—or didn't feel. Good signs. Onto the next step, not a second or a movement wasted. "Help me get him flat." She spoke quickly, but calmly. Eoan had done their job; now she could do hers.

The direction seemed to help. Jal nodded jerkily, and with Nash holding Saint's head steady, Jal pulled him the rest of the way away from the wall and got him onto his back. "I don't know what happened," Jal told her. "The bomb went off, and we got thrown, and that's the last thing I remember. When I came to, he wasn't—"

Movement in the hall drew Eoan's attention briefly away. *Bitsie.* She'd made it out of the bridge, jogging down the hall on legs that seemed only half-able to support her. "Bitsie, you should stay in the bridge." The younger Red ignored them, though. Past the infirmary and the hatch down to the crew quarters, nearly to the bridge door. "Briley Emmeline Red," they tried, but evidently that only worked when *Jal* did it.

Bitsie made it to the back of the shuttle as Nash started rescue breaths.

"C'mon, old man," Jal was saying. He'd given up his hold on Saint's jacket, scooting back a dec or two to give Nash room to work. Blood and sweat streaked down his face in a gruesome half mask, but he didn't seem to care about anything but the rise and fall of Saint's chest around Nash's first shared breath. "We didn't die. We're back on the *Ambit*, and we're gonna be fine. You're gonna be fine." So rasped, it barely reached a whisper, and desperate. A prayer, as Nash hit the top of a five-count, pinched Saint's nose, and bent for another breath. Her spare hand went to Saint's chest, knuckles rubbing a line into his sternum.

"Is he dead?"

Jal's head snapped toward the sound of Bitsie's voice, and Eoan couldn't have said who was more startled to see who. "Bitsie, get back." Weak, the first time, but then: "Bitsie, I said get back!" It occurred to Eoan they'd never heard him yell at her before. Jal so rarely raised his voice to begin with, but *never* to her.

Her eyes went wide. "But I—"

A sharp, ragged inhale from deeper inside the shuttle, and Nash barely leaned back in time to avoid knocking heads with Saint as he spasmed upright. Didn't quite make it all the way to sitting before gravity and Nash's hand joined forces to push him back down, and the next few breaths were at once the most uncomfortable and most *welcome* sound Eoan had ever heard.

Saint coughed and rolled, gagging up spit and air, but a few swift thumps from Nash between his shoulder blades, and his lungs seemed to find their rhythm again. "Did I have a stroke," he managed after another few gulps of oxygen, "or do I taste lip balm? *Ow.*" He covered his ear, dodging away from Nash's pinching fingers and starting to ease himself upright, only to get dragged into an awkwardly angled, but heartwarmingly enthusiastic hug by Jal.

"Scared the shit out of me, old man," Jal said. "Can't do that to me. Don't you ever do that to me, you hear?"

"I'll certainly try." Hard to say if the tone was dry, or Saint just lacked the air for inflection, but Jal didn't seem to mind. He just hugged Saint all the harder, until Nash started batting at his arm.

"You're gonna break his ribs," she said. "Drop him. Drop the half-hypoxic XO, so I can make sure he didn't break anything important."

It wasn't the scolding that got Jal to let go, though. Not the swatting, either. No, Eoan imagined it was the sound of small footsteps retreating from the cargo bay. *Running.*

"Shit," Jal said, hands falling to his sides, then to the floor as he went to push himself up. "I gotta—I should go talk to Bitsie."

"Hold on that," said Eoan briskly. Something other than a runaway child had caught their attention. "There's another ship entering the debris field. I'm picking up a short-range comm burst from its location."

Saint pushed himself up straighter, stifling a wince with practiced resolve. "One of Gethin's?"

Instead of an answer, Eoan routed the comm burst over the cargo bay speakers.

"—icking up a handful of life signs from your direction." It was an all too familiar voice with an all too familiar drawl. *Raimes.* "So, I'm gonna take a guess and say I'm not just talking to myself."

Who's that? Jal mouthed. The comm was a one-way transmission, so no chance Raimes would overhear, but they appreciated his discretion.

Nash knew better. "Remember that cowboy councilor we mentioned? That's him—Captain Raimes. 'Cause when it rains, it fucking pours."

"Never had this many visitors," Perseus said idly. "Shame the place is kind of a dump now."

Eoan didn't quite know what to make of the *Pathfinder*'s AI, and at the moment they didn't have time to work it out. "There's more to the comm," they said. "Listen."

"From the looks of all this shrapnel, I reckon you might be in a bad way. Can't offer much help myself, but you stay put, and I'll send some your direction just as soon as I'm clear enough of this junk belt to get the call out." A pause, and Eoan skipped it ahead. "Not getting a clear lock on your position, though, friend—all the brash and bits floating around out here're screwing with my instruments. If you're hearing this, I'll be in range another half a minute. Drop me a ping, so I can tell get the cavalry better than a ballpark."

"Or so he can get a lock on our location and blow us out of the fucking black," Nash spat. "Somehow, I don't think we *want* his kind of cavalry."

Eoan waited for Saint to disagree, but he didn't. Deep lines set into his brow as he scowled, and after a beat he said, "Don't answer."

"Are you sure?" they asked.

He gave a stiff nod. "He shouldn't be here," he said. "Either he followed us from the Waystation without us noticing, or he knew where to find us. Whichever it is, I don't like it. He knows something."

"Well, shit," Jal said. "If he knows something, let's follow his ass. Maybe he'll lead us to Gethin. Right? It's better than the fuck-all leads we've got without him." He looked between Nash and Saint, and when neither gave any indication what they thought of the plan, he threw up his hands. "Come on! You heard Raimes—only another handful of seconds before he's out of range. We lose him now, we might not find him again."

"You mean *her*," Eoan said, trying for a gentle touch. They weren't sure they pulled it off, if Jal's wince was any indication. "You're not worried about losing *Raimes*; you're worried about losing *Regan*. But one doesn't necessarily lead to the other."

Jal's brows furrowed. Clearly, they'd confused him.

"What I mean to say is, Raimes isn't our only lead on Regan. Drestyn's nanites seem to be offline, unfortunately, but recall we did have a drone aboard the *Pathfinder*."

Nash, unsurprisingly, seemed to be the first to get it. Unsurprising not because the others were slow, of course, but because one's lips were still faintly blue, and the other kept dribbling blood on his coat from an open head wound. Jal and Saint might need more time to process. "Cap, you tricky little sneak. You got the drone on their ship?"

There it was. Jal and Saint caught on quickly after that. "Wait, really?" Jal turned as if to look at them, only to remember he didn't know where to look. They hadn't bothered with a projection in all the bustle, and they couldn't have gotten a decent one aboard the shuttle anyway. Didn't have the angles. The lack of a projection didn't curb Jal's enthusiasm, though. He beamed, every ounce of his relief and surprise and gratitude on full display, as if it never occurred to him to try to dampen them. "That's fucking—*thank you*."

"It's only good for location, unfortunately," said Eoan. They didn't want to get his hopes *disproportionately* high. "The signal isn't strong enough for me to control the drone or stream any sort of audiovisual feedback, and I'm afraid if I tried to amplify it I'd give it away. Found a nice little out-of-the-way spot for it before the ships got out of range"—in the midst of their desperate search of the *Pathfinder*'s ruins, because what good was nigh-unlimited processing power if they didn't put it to use—"and with any luck, they won't find it for a good long while."

"But if the signal's weak, then can we really rely on it for tracking?" Saint had a particular way of asking questions, sometimes, when he knew *Eoan* already had an answer and just wanted to be filled in. A cadence. A calm. This was one of those questions.

He was right, of course. "The tracking beacon's a simpler program. Doesn't require input from me, and doesn't have to transmit anything more complicated than here I am." They wouldn't need amplification for that. It would do the job. "And it shouldn't give away the drone; it broadcasts in my native programming language, which on account of its . . . maturity"— they liked that rather a lot better than *obsolescence*—"shouldn't register on any of their signal scanners. Or if it does, they should write it off as clutter."

"I can hear it," Perseus said, with something strangely like nostalgia in his voice. "That's you, is it? Only, it . . ." A chuckle over the shuttle's speakers. "It sounds a lot like me."

Oh, the *questions* they had. They imagined Perseus had a few questions of his own as well, and Eoan was almost as interested to hear his as to ask theirs. Later, they promised themself. For now, "We're agreed, then?" they said. "Because Raimes is out of range, and we're running out of time to close the gap. We let Raimes go, and we follow the beacon." On a choice like this, they all had to agree.

One by one, with stilted nods, they did.

"Agreed," Saint voiced for all of them. "We get Gethin first. Whatever Raimes's role in this is"—and Eoan knew what it cost him, every time, to admit Raimes might have a role in this, but he did it anyway—"we'll deal with it once we've got Regan back."

"And we *will* deal with it," Nash said darkly. "I'm tired of this *are we, aren't we* bullshit—if the Guild's gone rotten, I want to fucking know. Understood?"

Saint, with an awfully heavy sigh for a man whose lungs had just remembered how to work, nodded and let his head hang low. Not quite resignation; rather, a reluctant acceptance. The deeper down this rabbit hole they went, the harder it became to believe *someone* wasn't dirty.

Eoan just hoped, at the end of it all, their people might still come out clean.

"So, that's settled," Jal said, wiping his hands on his thighs. Sweaty palms, racing pulse; after everything they'd been through, he had to be running on fumes, but he still ran awfully fast. Too much left for him to worry about: whether Drestyn would make good on his promise, whether Regan could hold out a little longer, whether Bitsie was all right, whether they'd make it in time. Hard to imagine how he could have all that on his shoulders and still have strength to stand, much less smile—albeit weakly—at Saint and Nash. "We good here? I really gotta go talk to Bitsie."

"Hold up," Nash told him.

"That *we good* was rhetorical."

Nash ignored him, grabbing a flat foil pack from her medkit as she stood and stepping over Saint's outstretched legs to get to Jal. Gloved hands—Eoan hadn't even seen her put them on, but there they were—tore open the pack and, without much in the way of warning, swabbed clean a spot on Jal's temple and stuck a small, thumbnail-sized patch on it. "Don't touch that," she warned, when Jal reached up. "It's a microtomography scanner. Pocket CT," she offered by way of simplification, at Jal's blank stare. "You took a knock on the head and lost consciousness, so you get to wear that until I'm good and satisfied nothing's bleeding in there. I've put that brain-shaped lump of schist in your skull on ice before, and I'd like to keep that a once-in-a-lifetime experience." She gave him another once-over and nodded to herself. "Anything else I should know about? Broken bones, bullet wounds, or the like?"

"No, ma'am."

"Then I bless this mess." She waved him off. "Go forth and damage control."

"That's it?" Saint asked from the floor. "You're not gonna check him out?" He started to get up, but Nash's sternly pointed finger promised unspecified but deeply unpleasant consequences if he moved another muscle.

Wisely, he stopped.

"No, I'm not," she said. "Because there's one of me and two of you, and *of* the two of you, he's the only one genetically designed to take a licking and keep on ticking. So I'm going to be too busy checking *you* out, Mister I Stopped Breathing and I'm Bleeding Like a Stuck Pig."

"Think I prefer McBlastinshit," Saint muttered under his breath.

"Anyway, what else do you want me to do? Check his pupils?" Nash turned back to Jal. "That patch'll tell me if something goes hinky in your attic, but you start feeling dizzy or nauseous, start seeing double, or start getting more than your baseline level of confused, don't keep it to yourself. Oh, and." She bent by her bag and tossed him a small box of gauze. "You might want to clean yourself up before you hunt down Bitsie. I think we've traumatized her enough for one day, don't you?"

Jal grimaced, but he pocketed the gauze. "Just take care of him, all right?" he said, with a nod to Saint.

She offered a small, tight smile. "I always do."

JAL

Perk of being back on a small ship was, it didn't take much to find somebody, even if they didn't especially want to be found.

Freshly cleaned up, with a change of clothes and some clumsily applied dermapoxy under the bandage on his brow, Jal made his way to Bitsie's room. Seemed like the place to start. "Little bit?" he called, leaning his shoulder against the doorframe. No answer, but that wasn't really a surprise. "Mind if I come in?"

A pause, then: "I don't know."

"You don't know if you mind?" He let his head tip against the doorframe, too, relishing the cool kiss of metal against his temple. The drums behind his eyes had found their groove, *bang, bang, bang*ing in time with his heartbeat. "That's all right. Don't mind waiting for you to figure it out." He'd wait out there as long as it took; he just needed to make sure she was okay. Or at least as close as she could manage under the circumstances.

For a long time, she didn't speak, and he didn't try to make her. In the silence, though, he heard rustling on the other side of the door. Footsteps, shuffling closer and closer, until the door slid open.

"Hey," he said, smiling down at her. She stood just a couple steps back from the doorway, head and shoulders buried in a blanket she'd brought with her from home. It'd been her mama's before hers, and maybe even their mama's before that, and it showed its age. All sorts of mismatched patches in all sorts of colors, set against a blue not too far off Jal's favorite jacket. Sometimes he wondered if that was why he'd liked the jacket so much, back when he was on the run. Why he'd gone to the trouble of swiping it, when he'd already had too much trouble to begin with.

Because it reminded him of *home.*

Bitsie's red-rimmed eyes shined in the hall lights, her red nose twitching around a sniffle and red cheeks disappearing behind her sweater sleeve as she turned to shuffle back to the bed. *She's been crying.* He'd known she might be, but seeing it still felt like a swift kick in the chest. Watching her sink onto the floor beside the bed, knees up to her chest and arms wrapped tight around them, until she damn near disappeared into the blanket . . . it made his throat ache.

"Can I join you?" he asked her gently, and got a twitch of her head he'd choose to take as a nod. His bad leg gave him fits the whole way over to her—and shit, listen at him; sounded like the old man, with his *bad* this and *busted* that—but he hid it as best he could. No reason to give her something else to worry about.

She didn't speak as he eased down beside her, but when he raised his arm, she ducked in underneath it and let him bundle her in close. "Is Saint okay?" she asked against his shirt.

"Seems to be" was the best Jal could do. He'd have to trust Nash to see to Saint; Jal had his own seeing-to to do. "What about you?"

"What about me?" Bitsie didn't raise her head when she answered. Easier to talk into his chest, he guessed. "I didn't even *do* anything. Mom's out there with those people, still. You and Saint, you almost died. And I—" A tremor rippled through her, hard enough that Jal could feel it. "I couldn't do a single goddamn thing."

He couldn't even bring himself to scold her. "I know," he said instead, tugging off his specs to rub at his eyes. It was dark enough in Bitsie's room to leave them off, so he tossed them on the bed and left them. "Sometimes that's the hardest thing there is." The helplessness. The guilt. The relentless pressure of *what if, what if, what if,* knowing all the while there was nothing you could do to change things. He knew what that felt like, and he'd have lived the nightmare on that ring ship ten times over if it meant Bitsie'd never had to learn. "I'm so sorry, little bit." Sorry he'd yelled at her. Sorry he hadn't brought her mama back. Sorry she'd had to think, even for one minute, that she'd lost everything.

He didn't know if that was the right thing to say or the wrong one, but whichever it was, it broke something. Broke it apart or broke it loose, because the next thing he knew, Bitsie was throwing her arms around his middle and clinging like it was the only thing she could do. Like he was the only thing she had left.

"You almost died," she said. "You're supposed to come back. You're *always* supposed to come back, but you almost didn't." It had the weight of a realization. A child's belief that everything would be okay, giving way to a grown-up's understanding that sometimes it wouldn't. And as much as he'd wanted to protect her from that, maybe he couldn't. Maybe he *shouldn't*. She'd grown so much in the years he'd been away, and on some level he hadn't wanted to see it.

She deserved to be seen, though. Stubborn and strong and almost thirteen, with her mama's mind and maybe some of her uncle's grit, and a fire inside that was so big and special that it could only be *hers*. She deserved to be that person, and whatever that person grew into, and he realized there under that threadbare blanket that he had to *let her*. He could protect her from a lot of things, but not from growing up. That was the way it was meant to be.

Jal's eyes stung, tears welling no matter how hard and how fast he blinked to clear them. "I tried my best, Bitsie," he told her. He wanted to tell her *I'll always come back*. He wanted to promise her that, because she deserved an uncle who could promise her that, but he couldn't. Not with everything that lay ahead of him, and maybe not with all the things that lay behind. The only thing he could promise her was the truth. "I'm *always* gonna try my best to get back to you, I swear."

He couldn't ask her to be okay with that. She shouldn't have had to be, and he wouldn't make her pretend like she was. Better to let her hold on while she could, and he held on right back, brushing his fingers through her hair as she sniffled and scrubbed her eyes with the corner of her blanket.

"You know," he told her softly, "we used to do this a lot when you were little."

She let out a misty little laugh. "Commiserating in the dark?"

He chuckled. "Pretty much. Don't know if your mama ever told you, but you were one fussy baby. I mean *fussy*." A smile tugged on his lips at the memory, even as Bitsie jabbed a finger into his side. "Swear if you weren't eating or sleeping, you were steaming mad about something. I used to watch you a lot in the evenings, when your mama was working. We traded shifts, see—she had you days, I had you nights. Course for a while there, I wasn't much older'n you are now, so it's a wonder that turned out all right.

"You'd do this thing, though, where you'd just—" He tried to mimic baby Bitsie's patented scowl, but he knew he couldn't do it justice. Bitsie lifted her head to look anyway. "—screw up your little face and start grumbling like this tiny old man. Never did scream. No, you'd just grumble, and your little face'd get redder and redder, and you'd look up at me with those big green eyes like *dammit, Uncle Jal, I'm tellin' you clear as I can. Why aren't you getting it?*

"Some nights, I'd grumble right back at you. Just two tired fools babbling back and forth at each other 'til we babbled our-selves to sleep. Or some nights, we'd sit around listening to the radio. You *loved* that thing. Probably older'n Saint's relic of a coffee machine, but we'd wrestle with the tuner for hours 'til we found something you liked, and you'd clap and give me this big gummy grin like I was some kind of hero."

"I don't remember the radio," Bitsie said quietly.

"Yeah." He scratched his eyebrow with the back of his knuckle and dutifully *didn't* scratch the microtomo-whatsit. Not because he was a grown-ass man with self-control, but because he was terrified Nash would somehow know and staple it to his skull. "Things got a little tight sometimes. Your mama wound up having to pawn it around your first birthday." Jal still remembered that day. Regan had tried so hard not to look defeated, leaving with the radio and coming home with a month's worth of rations, but he'd known. Seventeen years old, and he'd seen his sister bear up every day under a weight that would've crushed people twice her age with twice the help she had. Even when things had gotten better, when they'd *made* them better, he'd never forgotten that. The mining company might've given him his muscles, but he'd learned his strength from her.

Jal gave Bitsie a squeeze and thumbed a few stray tears from his eyes. "I tell you what, little bit, we had a couple of rough nights after that. Most you'd ever hollered in your whole life, and I swear I tried everything I could think of to get you to stop. Fed you, walked you, bounced you, and you just kept giving me that same look. That same *why aren't you getting it?* Until I guess I finally did."

He didn't know exactly when he'd started singing to her— which in that long string of restless nights it'd been that he'd sat down by the counter where their radio used to be and started humming one of the tunes that made Bitsie smile. He didn't even remember the words of the original song, only the melody. But he remembered the words he'd *given* it, over years and years of singing it as she drifted off to sleep.

"You remember the song?" he asked her. It'd been years since he'd sung it. Not since before that last mission with Gethin's crew. When he'd come back, Bitsie'd been so much older. Three years felt like a lot to him, but for Bitsie, it'd been a quarter of a lifetime, and he'd been afraid twelve was a little too old for lullabies. "Probably blocked it out, I reckon. Ain't ever been much of a singer, so I—"

But Bitsie started to hum. Just a simple, repeated melody, higher than he remembered, but then again, she was awful little for a baritone. *"There's a girl with starlight eyes,"* she started quietly, under her breath, *"and a smile like the sun . . ."*

Even after all those years, the words came back like breathing. *"And a heart that shines like diamonds,"* he sang with her, and kept on as she trailed off and tugged her blanket in around them both.

> *"She's my little starlight one.*
> *My sweet girl with starlight eyes,*
> *Oh, she means the world to me,*
> *Pray her days be filled with wonder . . ."*

He paused, a quiet laugh in his chest and a smile tucked against Bitsie's hair. *"But right now, it's time to sleep."*

Her eyes hadn't changed since she was little. Still big and green and bright, and his heart still swelled when they looked at him. "We're going to get Mom back, aren't we?" she asked softly, and with those eyes of hers staring up at him, staring *into* him, he didn't dare lie.

"Yeah, little bit," he said. He didn't know if that was the truth, he really didn't. But if it wasn't? He'd make it so. "Yeah, we will."

CHAPTER FIFTEEN

DRESTYN

Isaiah used to be a quiet man.

Growing up in the fields of his parents' homestead parcel, he hadn't had much time for talking. Crops to tend. Debts to pay. Rise early, work hard, and if you still had strength to use your mouth at supper for anything more than chewing, then you hadn't worked quite hard enough. That was what his father always said.

If his father was right, then Isaiah's brother *never* worked quite hard enough. Lleyton used to say he spoke enough for both of them, so his quiet-mouse little brother wouldn't have to bother, but they both knew better. Lleyton just couldn't help himself. Like a dam always *this close* to bursting, he just had so much inside of him—so much to say, so much to share—that he had to let it out a little at a time, or risk every bit of it breaking loose. His brother, the poet. The artist. The dreamer. Isaiah went to sleep every night to the sound of Lleyton's voice, talking about what big plans he had for the two of them. Talking about a future beyond those sorrel fields.

Isaiah wasn't like his brother; he couldn't see much future beyond the next sunrise. But he liked to listen. Share a bit of Lleyton's dreaming, if only until the sun came up.

Their parents died when Isaiah was thirteen.

They went together, more or less. One right after the other, not even a week apart, and it didn't really matter who went first. As far as Isaiah could tell, both their hearts stopped beat-

ing at the same time; it had just taken one a little longer to catch
the rest of the way up.

The day they put their parents in the ground, Lleyton had
cried enough for the both of them, too. Isaiah had never gotten around to thanking him for that. Their parents had been
good people. Hard workers. Kind. Naïve, yes, but you couldn't
blame the hens when the foxes got in. That was just the way of
things. They still deserved tears over their graves, and Isaiah
hadn't had any to give.

They'd gone back to work that very next morning, him and
Lleyton, and the day after that, and the one after that. Worked
the fields until their fingers bled and their bodies started breaking down. Until Isaiah stopped growing, no matter how much
supper Lleyton tried to sneak from his own plate onto Isaiah's.
Until their muscles ached so fierce and loud that it kept them
up at night. Two pairs of hands trying to do the work of four,
because the company didn't care that their parents were in the
ground. They sent their condolences two days before the first
late payment notice, and that, too, was just the way of things.
Some men feasted, and other men starved, and Lleyton spat
and cursed those company men, but Isaiah? He stayed quiet as
he'd always been. It was easier that way.

They lasted two more years like that, before the company
called in their homestead loan. *Default.* The man at their door
in his nice suit and shiny shoes, he said it like a crime. Like
murder. Like theft. And that shiny man and his shiny officers
treated them like criminals. Dragged them out of their parents'
house, past their parents' graves, off their parents' land, and
that was when Isaiah finally understood: it had never been their
parents' land. They'd worked it, bled for it, raised it up from
nothing like another son—like a *favorite* son—but it had never
really been theirs, and it was never meant to be. They were just
another piece of equipment, tending the company's crop.

Isaiah turned sixteen in the debtors' barrack of a refinery

rig, hands blistered from roustabout work and ears still ringing from the whir and grind and chug of so many different machines in so many states of disrepair. It was hard work—harder than the homestead, and grimier, and harsher, but in some ways, Isaiah thought, it was better. They'd spent those last years on the homestead with a sword over their heads, but now, the sword had already fallen. The worst had already happened. All he had to do was work hard and keep quiet, and for Isaiah Drestyn, that was the easiest thing in the world.

Not so for Lleyton. For all Isaiah got quieter, Lleyton got louder. Louder about the broken-down machines, about the unreported accidents. About docked rations and overtime, air quality and medical care. He got loud, and he got friends, and he got them loud, too. Got them to stop working so hard, and stop keeping so quiet, because he still saw them all as people, and he still thought they could make the *company* see them that way.

The first time the strikebreakers came, they beat Lleyton so bad he couldn't get out of bed for three days. Bruised his jaw. Split his lip. Cracked his ribs. They were the quietest three days of Isaiah's life—and the *longest*.

Everybody's got a choice, little brother, Lleyton had said that fourth day, dragging himself out of bed with a black eye and a limp. The work wouldn't wait—not the company's work, and not Lleyton's. *Sometimes a choice is* all *you've got, so don't you ever let anyone take yours from you, and don't you ever try to take somebody's from them.*

So, when the strikebreakers came a second time, Isaiah made a choice: he kept quiet. He kept quiet all the way to the strikebreakers' bunks that night. He kept quiet as he snuck inside. And he kept quiet, *so* quiet, as he slit their throats with a carpenter's knife.

The company never suspected him, and Isaiah never told a soul. Lleyton, though . . . he looked at Isaiah differently after that. With sadness. With sympathy. Not a violent man, was

Lleyton; he believed he could win a war with words and principles, with protests and pamphlets. He believed he could win with human fucking decency.

But the company believed it could win with bullets, and at the end of the day, they had it right. Decency didn't change the company's mind when the machines started spewing black smoke and shrieking like banshees—rusted heralds of death, disaster, ruin. It didn't stop them sending in *peacekeepers* when the workers refused to take up their posts. It didn't stop that redheaded ranger with the pitiless eyes from shooting Lleyton dead outside the work zone doors, and as he held his brother's blood-soaked body and heard those very last crackling, wretched sounds leave his lips, Isaiah made another choice:

Isaiah used to be a quiet man.

Drestyn would speak enough for the both of them.

Still, sometimes silence had its uses, and even after all these years, Drestyn hadn't lost the knack. He came to without a sound, tongue still buzzing from the piezoelectric sting of a couple of stun rounds, boots dragging on the ground behind him.

"Bastard's heavier than he looks," grunted the one to Drestyn's left. Drestyn didn't dare open his eyes to look at him— conscious men got attention; unconscious ones got left alone, at least for a time, and Drestyn would take every second they'd give him—but he didn't need to. He could glean enough about the speaker and his partner from the senses he *did* have at his disposal. The uneven angle of his shoulders, one pulled higher than the other in his escorts' grip, said the speaker was taller; but the firmer grip squeezing bruises into Drestyn's right bicep said the speaker's partner, the one on the right, was probably stronger. The partner's boots beat a syncopated rhythm against the grated floors; not quite a limp, but he favored one leg to the other. Right to left. A weak knee, maybe. He tucked the information away.

The sounds gave him a good sense of where he was, too. The

way the speaker's voice echoed, it had to be the cargo bay; nowhere else big enough on most ships for that kind of reverb, and probably not many other places they could walk three-wide. The cold air stank of peat and fermenting fruit, of sweat and fuel— the kind of smell you carried with you, whether you wanted to or not.

The speaker's partner grunted and shifted his bruising grip higher up Drestyn's arm. "Quit bitching and help me with him." The partner had a voice like rusted hinges, rough and creaking. "XO said to get him to the brig tout fucking suite, or do *you* want to be the one trying to wrangle him when he shakes off those stunners?"

"Gruffy can kiss my ass," the first speaker muttered. "He gets to scarper back to the other ship after that shitshow. Bet you his ass is halfway back to home base by now; it's you and me that've got to deal with Captain Gethin."

"All the more reason to do our job and get scarce."

The pneumatic hiss of an automated door hit Drestyn's ears, and the speaker and his partner turned Drestyn sideways to wrestle him through a doorway. Something popped in his shoulder, an elastic snap of pain that rippled all the way to his fingertips and back, but he breathed through it. No tensing. No wincing. Anything could give him away—turn him from a harmless lump of flesh and sinew into a person again. A threat. The longer he could play dead, the better lay of things he could get before they clammed up and reached for their stunners.

They walked him sideways down a short hall, and another hiss marked another door sliding open up ahead. Drestyn marked another *X* on the map taking shape in his head. Had to work up his own, since he doubted they'd be kind enough to provide him one if he asked. *Yes, excuse me, could I see a deck plan for your entire ship? Entry and exit points, security cameras, et cetera?* Probably ought to apologize for killing half a dozen of their friends first.

The temperature dipped a few degrees on the other side of the second door, and then a few more when they dropped him to the bare metal floor. It was a deeply unnatural feeling, letting himself fall. All those reflexes, practiced and inborn, telling him to catch himself, shield his head, find his feet, but he forced them all down. Silent and still. What were a few small indignities to a man like him, if it meant getting what he needed?

He repeated it to himself as a sort of anchor—*a few small indignities, a few small indignities*—as the cold bite of metal touched his back. A knife, but it mostly ignored his skin in favor of his shirt. The blade cleaved the fabric straight up his spine, and as they tugged his shirt away, the cold of the air pressed itself against Drestyn's skin in uneven patches of sensation. Most of the burns hadn't eaten through his nerve endings, though there'd been times he'd wished they had; but the scars had deadened them as they healed. He felt pressure, heat, pain, but something as subtle as a few degrees' chill didn't register.

The cuffs did. They clapped around his wrists, and he felt as much as heard something clip through the middle of them before they started to pull. Taut, first, then up, up, up, until his arms stretched above his head, and he had to let them take his weight again. Not a very natural position. Joints strained. Ligaments popped. Muscles burned, not with the effort of tensing up to take the pressure, but with the effort it took *not* to, as someone yanked his boots off his feet.

"Fuck," said the first speaker. "Get a load of this guy." Something hard like a baton, or a length of pipe, prodded Drestyn's bare ribs. "Not so scary now, are you?"

"Leave him, Rodri," said the partner. "Cap'll wake him up when he's ready to talk."

"This fucker killed Rory."

"You didn't even like Rory," said the partner.

"Doesn't matter if I liked him. He was my cousin. It's the fucking principle of the thing."

From somewhere behind him, Drestyn heard a laugh. Feminine, husky, with a dryness bordering on caustic. *"Principle?"* It sounded muffled, as if spoken through a thin door. A pane of glass. Drestyn didn't know that voice, but if it belonged to who he *hoped* it belonged to then it was damn good to hear it. "What do you knuckle-dragging slag nuggets know about principle?"

Knuckle-dragging slag nuggets. Drestyn had to fight a smile.

"You want a turn, girlie, keep talking," said the first speaker. Rodri, Drestyn presumed. It was all the presuming he had time to do before something swung into his stomach with enough force to knock the wind out of him. He barely stopped the sound before it left his lips. Barely stopped himself from tensing. *Breathe,* he ordered his lungs. In and out, slow and steady, and he managed two or three rounds before the next blow came, this time against his hip. No crack of bone, no snap of soft tissue, but pain rolled through his leg and side like a cresting wave. Even with his eyes closed, spots bloomed at the edges of his vision. Fractals of blue and green, crystalizing the darkness. Still, he breathed. In and out, slow and steady. "Damn, this guy's really out."

"We got him with three stun rounds. What'd you *expect?*" snapped the partner. "Now would you put that damn thing away? You kill him before Cap gets a chance at him, you're gonna end up like Ori. You want to end up like Ori?"

Judging by the silence, things hadn't gone so well for Ori.

"This ship's down two-thirds of a crew because of this fucker," said Rodri at last. "And we're just supposed to let that go?"

Another smile threatened Drestyn's charade. He took no pleasure in killing, not even in killing assholes, but he needed every advantage he could get. A ship down most of its crew? That was good news.

The partner grunted again. "He'll get his," he said. "Cap'll have him singing like a bird."

"Not likely," said the woman in the cage.

"One more word out of you," Rodri snarled, "and I'll—"

"Leave it, man." The partner's uneven footsteps beat a path back to the door. "Let's just get the fuck out of here before the captain comes. Don't want to know the kind of mood he'll be in when Gruffy gets him up to speed."

Gruffy. Rodri. Ori. Gethin. Drestyn never forgot a name, and he'd be sure not to forget theirs. Never knew when one could come in useful. *Gruffy. Rodri. Ori. Geth—*

Another blow, this time to the back, rocked Drestyn forward on his chains. A parting shot, from the sound of things, and Drestyn waited until he'd heard the hiss of the first door, then the second, before he let out the wheeze he'd smothered behind his teeth. *Dammit.* Pain was familiar; he knew how to deal with it when it came, and he knew how to weather it until it went.

It still fucking *hurt*, though. Waves of hurt, ebbing and flowing, and for a time he might've drifted with it. Carried out to a sea of black, drowning in the ringing in his ears, and he didn't try to fight it. He'd milked as much from his ruse as he could; no harm in catching his breath, getting his bearings, until the tides finally receded.

He didn't know how much time had passed before he opened his eyes, but his hands had gone cold, and his fingers tingled like sand shifting under his skin. Blinking through the bleariness, he scanned the dim-lit room around him. Not so much a brig as a repurposed supply room, from the looks of it, but they'd really leaned into the décor. A chair sat against the wall to his right, bolted to the floor, with restraints dangling from the back and arms that probably could've told all manner of stories—just not ones anybody'd want to hear.

A bit of shelving lined the opposite wall. Small crates, a fairly daunting medkit. A glance up, neck straining at the awkward angle, revealed another set of cables like the ones Drestyn hung from, and a single flickering light dangling between them. Hard to say if the flicker was poor upkeep or just a bit of scene-setting. Drestyn *did* understand the importance of showmanship. *Love what you've done with the place,* he thought wryly. One part clutter, two parts torture chamber. *That's what we call* all-purpose.

Seemed he had an audience, too. Beady eyes of cameras watched from every corner, and whoever'd installed them had gone to no trouble to hide them. They *wanted* the people in that room to know they were being watched. Wanted them to feel trapped and scrutinized in their cruel little cage. For the *ambiance.*

It took a bit of doing to spin around. The balls of his feet barely touched the ground, arches already cramping from the strain of holding him up. Anything to take a bit of weight off his shoulders, let him catch his breath.

Ah. There were the cells. Two of them, one in each of the back corners. The remaining two walls of each cell were clear silica, no doubt reinforced, with scuffs and scratches and discolorations that, like the restraints on the chair, probably held stories that didn't bear repeating.

In one of the cells sat the woman, staring green-eyed and defiant at him from a tangled sheaf of blonde hair. Bruises mottled her face, and her bottom lip had a split nearly straight down the middle, but she seemed to think it worth the pain and effort to scowl at him.

"Thought you might be dead," she said. If she had any strong feelings about it one way or the other, her tone didn't give it away.

He mustered a small smile. "Thought the same of you," he replied. "You *are* Regan Red, aren't you?"

"Is this the part where I pretend I don't know who you are?"

"You could," Drestyn said. Each word took an effort, but he tried not to sound like it—like the stretch of his arms above his head and the still-throbbing ache of Rodri's swings didn't exact a price for each breath. "But I get the feeling we don't have much time before a very unhappy captain comes to ask me some very pointed questions, and I think we'd be better served skipping straight to the good bits. Don't you?"

"I don't know, watching that brick-headed shit biscuit whale on *you* for a change might be a high point of my week," said the woman he'd decided was definitely Regan Red. Seemed the brother was the soft-spoken one of the family. Drestyn liked her. "I take it the hostage exchange didn't go to plan?"

"Depends on whose plan," Drestyn replied. "Have to say, I really wasn't sure you'd be here when I got aboard."

"Yeah, well, the escape attempt's still a work in progress."

"No, I meant—"

Her eyes narrowed. "I know what you meant," she said, sitting up straighter against the corner she'd wedged herself into. The movement must not have agreed with her; she winced and bit her lip, stilling for a beat while she waited for the pain to pass. Then she carried on like she hadn't stopped at all. "You thought they'd kill me once they had you." She breathed a laugh through her nose. "Kind of a self-important prick, aren't you?"

"Your brother has said something to that effect."

"Before or after you shot him and drove him off a rooftop?"

Drestyn would've sighed, if he'd had the wind to spare. *Reset.* "I told Jalsen I would try to protect you, if you were still alive."

"I don't need your protection."

Five, ten minutes ago, he might've written it off as bravado, but now? "I'm starting to think you might be right." After the way things happened on the *Pathfinder*, he'd worried about her losing her value to Gethin, not just as trade for Drestyn, but as bait for her brother and the rest of the *Ambit* crew. For all he knew, Jalsen was dead in the wreckage of that titanic ring ship, and Eoan didn't strike Drestyn as the type of captain to fall for the same trick twice. They'd barely fallen for it the first time.

Outnumbered, out-positioned, and it had still taken a run of sheer bad luck to get them backed into a corner. No, Gethin had to know he wouldn't come out nearly as well the next time he tried to cross them, which meant Regan's uses as a hostage were running perilously low.

But what if Drestyn hadn't seen the full picture?

"I get the strangest feeling I've underestimated you, Miss Red," he told her slowly. Not a mistake he made often. "Gethin doesn't just want you for leverage, does he?"

Regan didn't answer. Her fierce stare gave nothing away, and dared him to try to press her. *Try me,* said that look of hers. *You'll lose.*

That was all the confirmation Drestyn needed. "You know something." A relief and a revelation, to feel everything slotting together at last. He'd come aboard looking for missing pieces, and he'd found one in the most unexpected place. "Something even your *brother* doesn't know about." He wouldn't have asked Drestyn to leverage his information for Regan's safety, if he'd known Regan had information of her own. "That's why Gethin beat you."

"He was putting on a show for my brother," Regan replied stonily.

"Your face, maybe." The split lip, the bruised cheeks—those were the sort of wounds you made for someone else's benefit. A worried brother and his loyal crew. "But not your . . . *ribs,* is it?" The wince he'd noticed earlier suddenly had context. *Watching that brick-headed shit biscuit whale on you for a change,* she'd said. "*For a change.* I take it you've had a turn on the tether?" He gave his cuffs an illustrative tug. "And I take it he didn't get what he wanted from you."

"It's one of my superpowers," Regan replied with a tart smile. "Disappointing assholes. Want to try?"

Under different circumstances, he'd have liked to get to know her. She reminded him of all the best people in his life:

his brother, his crew. She and Marei would've gotten on like a house on fire, if they didn't try to kill each other first.

Drestyn stubbornly smothered the pang that came when he thought of them. Marei. Pabel. Rigby. He hadn't seen them since Lewaro, and he *missed them*. He'd tried not to. Four months, he'd tried not to think of them whenever he saw Saint and Nash together in the brig, because missing people meant caring for them, and caring for them made it harder to do the job—to put the many before the few, when they felt like *his* few. When he knew about the wildflowers Pabel kept pressed between the pages of a journal. About the sweet tooth Marei pretended not to have. About the names etched into the necklace Rigby wore. He'd fought beside them, yes, but he'd also laughed beside them. Slept beside them. *Lived* beside them.

He didn't like the idea of doing this without them, but maybe it was better this way. This wasn't the mission they shared. This was *his* mission, and his alone, and he'd see it through to the end if it killed him.

At least this way he wouldn't take them with him.

"You need to tell me," he said. "Whatever it is you know, whatever it is Gethin wants from you, when we get out of this, you have to tell me what it is."

Her jaw muscles twitched beneath a bloom of color. "Because if I don't, you'll leave me here?"

"Because my brother was a good man, and they killed him for it," he answered tightly. "And now they're trying to kill yours." *They may have already succeeded.* He couldn't tell her, not yet. Not because she didn't deserve to know, but because he *needed* her. He needed her focused, level, reliable, and he couldn't speak for her, but when he'd lost Lleyton, he'd been none of those things. Instead he said, "You and I may not have much common ground, Miss Red, but I know we have that. They've hurt people we love, and they need to answer for that. I intend to make them, but to do that, I need to know what you know. So I'm asking you, *please*. For them." *For our brothers.*

Regan said nothing at first, gave him nothing but that piercing stare, and he counted off the seconds in his head. *One, two, three.* Running out of time. With the cameras, Gethin would know he was awake, and he wouldn't leave it long. *Four, five, six.* Always, always running out of time.

Then he saw it—not an expression in and of itself, so much as a softening of the one already there. Gentling eyes. Uncurling lips. As the hiss of the door sounded behind him, she seemed to give the barest hint of a nod.

It would have to do.

"Surprised you two are getting along so well," said a voice Drestyn had never heard, but somehow knew. In his marrow, in his blood, in the charred parts of him he'd lost to the flames that day in the refinery, he *knew* it. "Didn't you shoot her baby brother?"

Turning hurt worse, this time. Like nails in the soles of his feet, and even the faintest shift of his weight on his shoulders frayed the muscles and sinew, but it didn't stop him. He distanced himself from it. Pain was a feeling just like any other—an itch he'd learned to ignore, no matter how insistently it gnawed at him.

Gethin hadn't changed.

In small ways, sure. The cut of his hair, the lines of his face, the clothes that he wore: they weren't a perfect match for the picture Drestyn had carried all those years. The eyes, though, they hadn't changed. Small and pitiless, set deep beneath a heavy brow that furrowed even as Gethin smiled. If those eyes had ever spilled a tear, they'd long forgotten how.

Drestyn ached to remind them.

"Hate to interrupt your sewing circle," Gethin said, clapping Drestyn on the shoulder. The force of it spun him again, a full three-sixty that set Drestyn's teeth on edge as pain ripped across his arms. Just a feeling. Just an itch. He got his feet back under him and raised up on his toes enough to steal a few easier breaths. "Hope Blondie didn't give you too much of a preview of how this works. I think it's better with a little *surprise*." Nothing as gentle as a pat, this time; Gethin's fist hit just below the center of Drestyn's chest, hard enough to knock the wind out of him, and for a handful of seconds Drestyn couldn't get it back. Couldn't make his lungs expand, couldn't make his diaphragm open to let the air in. Couldn't *breathe*.

Gethin's hand found his shoulder again, squeezing too tight. "Normally, I'd slow-walk this a little," he told Drestyn. "Ease you into it. Maybe start in the chair, work my way through a few fingernails before we graduated to the shoulder-stretcher here. But I'm on a timeline."

Drestyn rasped a laugh. "Got somewhere better to be?"

"Hot date?" Regan called from the cell. Drestyn didn't know what she thought she was doing, cutting in; and he didn't know if it was a good idea or a bad one. Gethin wasn't a total unknown, not after the refinery, but Regan had been with him for much longer, and had seen this particular side of him far more times.

He was sort of inclined to follow her lead.

For now, Gethin didn't really react. "Don't take it personally," Gethin said. "If it were up to me, I'd love to spend some quality time together. Got about a dozen dead crew members to thank you for."

"I only got six," Drestyn replied. "Hate to take credit for somebody else's work."

Regan laughed again, soft but scathing. "Jal's friend's a pretty good shot. Shame you weren't there to see his work up close, Captain."

A twitch at the corner of Gethin's eye—Drestyn barely caught it, before a kidney shot sent him twisting again. Pain spasmed through his middle, and he gagged on the taste of spit and stomach acid, but as he made it around Regan's direction he managed a smile. *Touched a nerve.* He'd seen it.

She ticked an eyebrow up faintly, as if to ask if he was sure.

He gave a quick twitch of a nod, before the momentum brought him back around to Gethin. *Keep going.* He could take the hits, if it meant finding an angle to work, and he already had a couple starting to take shape.

Gethin grabbed his chin, tipping his face up to bring them eye to eye. "You know who I am, don't you?"

It was as much a question as a taunt. Something small, disarming, to break the ice. *Interrogation one-oh-one*, Drestyn thought, *with a sociopath's panache*. He decided to play along. "You're the ranger that killed my brother," he said. He leaned into *ranger*, and watched for Gethin's reaction.

He got one. A slash of a smile cut its way across Gethin's face—a deeply unsettling expression, for no readily identifiable reason. It had all the trappings of a smile. The bowing lips, the flash of teeth. It had *dimples*, even. But it was a smile the way a hotel room was a *home*: a pale imitation, at best; and a mockery, at worst. He dropped Drestyn's chin and clicked his fingers sparse centimeters from Drestyn's nose, like he wanted to make him flinch.

Drestyn gave him that, too.

Gethin's smile stretched wider. "I knew it," he said. "I knew you saw me that day. Everybody else out there, they scattered like roaches from a flashlight when the shooting started. But not you, little brother. We locked eyes, and I knew you'd be trouble. Should've taken you out right then."

The bullet scar on Drestyn's shoulder gave a phantom twinge. "Seem to recall you tried. And missed." He wheezed between words, tugging on his cuffs to gulp in a few more breaths. Bodies weren't meant to hang from their wrists like that. Threw everything out of line. "Maybe . . . if you'd been . . . standing closer."

"Gethin here's more of a *lead from behind* kind of guy," Regan said sweetly. She was better at it than Drestyn—the taunting. Subtle and saccharine and *viciously* sarcastic. "Aren't you, pumpkin?"

It earned Drestyn another punch, but it was worth it to see the red creeping into Gethin's face. He didn't fluster easily, but if they could boil the frog by degrees, then all the better. They needed him *distracted*. Distractions bred mistakes bred opportunities, and they needed opportunities.

"Who else knows?" Gethin said.

"Knows what?"

"Come on, little brother, we were on the right track. Don't go dragging this out now."

Another punch, and Drestyn swore he felt ribs crack. Break, maybe. The next breath wrung itself out of him. Spit dribbled onto the floor beneath him—just spit, for now, no blood. No pink, no red, no problem. He wrestled a few times with the next inhale before he managed to say, "What happened to *quality time*?" His head felt like it weighed twice what it should've, but Gethin got a fistful of his hair and yanked it up like it weighed nothing at all.

"Told you, little brother—not up to me."

It was a jab, every time. *Little brother. Little brother. Little brother.* No, not anymore, and Gethin knew it. He'd stood at the far end of the crowd Lleyton had gathered—dozens of them, there to listen to Lleyton the way Drestyn used to in their tiny homestead bedroom, when his big brother dreamed his dreams aloud—and he'd *chosen*. He'd chosen to aim at Lleyton, and he'd chosen to pull the trigger, and he'd chosen to rip every one of those dreams from that hot refinery air and burn them all to *ash*.

Gethin went on, unaware. "Cap's got a real bug up his ass about you, and now I'm stuck digging it out. Don't you get it, you screwy little shit?" Gethin said. "This is *your* fault. All this mess, it's because you people can't just keep yourselves to yourselves and fall the fuck in line like the rest of us. Always making a fuss, always sticking your noses where they don't belong, and then you act like you're the victims when it blows up in your faces." He dragged a thumb over the scars on Drestyn's cheek and sneered at his own sick joke. "You couldn't just be *grateful*. You won the prize, little brother—you got to *live*. You could've just stuck to your backwater rallies and your pissy little pickets, and we'd have never darkened your doorstep again. But you had to go and make a name for yourself. Isaiah fucking Drestyn, anti-fucking-hero to the anti-fucking-establishment. You had to go and get yourself *caught*, and now you're back to being my goddamn problem. And you know what I do to my problems, don't you, little brother? So do yourself a favor, and I'll do you one in turn. I'll do you the same one I did Lleyton." Gethin jabbed two fingers into Drestyn's chest and leaned in, close, to whisper against the shell of Drestyn's ear, "I'll make it fucking quick."

"But see, I've got a problem, too," Drestyn told him through his teeth, reaching up to twist his fingers in the chains of his cuffs. Metal bit into his palms, ripped open calluses that had spent four months going soft in that brig on Alpha Librae.

Gethin leaned back. "And what's that, little br—"

Drestyn pulled himself up by the chains, swinging a knee up into Gethin's chin and stepping the other one up onto Gethin's shoulder. Just a half second of lift, but it was enough to get at the clip on his cuffs, and Drestyn came down hands and all on top of Gethin as the man fell. Pinned him to the ground and got the cuffs' chain across his throat, and Gethin's choked-out grunt of surprise barely made it to Drestyn's ears as he leaned all his weight onto that chain.

He stared into those small, cruel eyes—the eyes from his nightmares, from his memories, from the worst fucking day of his life—and watched as they welled with tears. Frightened, the way Lleyton's had been as his blood had pooled beneath him on the refinery floor.

"My problem," Drestyn whispered, "is you chose the wrong fucking brother."

A quick twist of his hands, and Gethin went slack beneath him. Regan was right—he was a man who fought his battles from afar. A captain who stayed safe aboard his ship while he sent his crew to die. A murderer who killed a peaceful man from the other side of a sniper's scope. A coward who'd made it this far only because he'd fallen in line. Kept his boot on his people's throats, while someone kept theirs on his.

"What the hell did you do?" Regan snapped as Drestyn searched Gethin's body. No gun—chickenshit, sure, but too smart to bring a loaded gun into a brig with the likes of Drestyn—but he had a shock baton in his belt, and a quick search of his boots yielded a small knife.

"I got what I needed from him," Drestyn said. "You heard him—he answers to someone. Somebody else is calling the shots."

"And you didn't think to ask him *who*?"

"He wouldn't have given us a name. And if he had, we wouldn't have believed him." But no name didn't mean Drestyn had come up empty. Turned out, Eoan's trick had worked a treat: let Gethin talk, and he'd talked his way right into what Drestyn wanted to know. He'd said *Cap*. Wasn't just a boss he answered to; it was a *captain*. A captain *of* captains, and the way he'd flinched when Drestyn brought up the rangers at the refinery . . . didn't take much to connect those dots. This wasn't just some rogue band of rangers, like he always used to think. Wasn't just mercenaries with connections, either. No, this went deeper. Higher.

This was someone in the Captains' Council.

He stood, telescoping the shock baton with a flick of his wrist and taking a swing at the bulb overhead. It shattered, plunging the room into pitch dark, and Drestyn took the three steps he'd mapped out to wedge his shoulder against the doorframe. "His men will be here soon," he told Regan evenly. "Keep low. Make yourself small."

The first hiss of the pneumatic door down the hall, and he'd timed that out, too. The steps between *Xes* in his mental map. He took a deep breath and let it out just in time for the second hiss, this time for the storage room door.

"What the—" Rodri started, and he ended with a shout as Drestyn grabbed his wrist and yanked it backward around the doorframe. Bones snapped. His gun dropped, and Drestyn dropped with it, digging Gethin's knife into the inside of Rodri's thigh and dragging it all the way down. Arteries were an imprecise science, Marei liked to say; you want to nick something important, you cut until you run out of meat.

He'd definitely nicked something important. Blood ran like an open tap, soaking Drestyn's arm and shoulder as Rodri fell. He hit the ground just in time for his partner to make the doorway, and by then, Drestyn had Rodri's gun up and sighted. He had the light on his side—looking at two well-lit targets, while they squinted into the dark.

Rodri's partner died squinting, a neat hole between his eyes and a heavy thud to mark his passing. Three down. If Rodri's *two-thirds of a crew* was to be believed, that left maybe one or two more to deal with before they had control of the ship.

"No keypad on your door," Drestyn said as he turned back to Regan. In the weak light trickling in from the hall outside, she didn't look afraid. She hadn't moved, wedged with her back against the corner and her hands behind her, shoulders and arms flexing like she was trying to pull them out from something. "Must be remote access. I'll see if maybe one of their GLASS pads can—"

A third hiss, but when Drestyn turned to the hall, he didn't see anything.

Regan cleared her throat. "They can," she said. By the time he'd turned back around to her, she'd rolled to her feet and made it to the door of her cell. The *open* door. A small, hand-held GLASS dangled from her fingertips as she stepped the rest of the way out. "And they did. I told you the escape attempt was a work in progress."

Drestyn was . . . well, impressed would've required a certain degree of understanding he didn't have yet. "How did you get that?"

"They had to move me from their main camp," she said. "Nicked it off one of Drestyn's men in the shuffle."

"He didn't notice you'd taken it?"

"He . . ." A grimace flickered across her face. "Let's just say he wasn't using it anymore. Had to listen to that one there"—with a nod to Rodri—"punch the keycode in a few times on his before I got the tones right, but I'm a comms specialist. Sort of have an ear for it." She stashed the GLASS in the pocket of her jogger bottoms—he hadn't noticed before, but she looked like she'd just rolled out of bed and straight into a hostage situation, with a faded T-shirt several sizes too big and makeup smeared around her eyes—and went to slide past him, but Drestyn caught her and pushed Rodri's gun into her hand.

"You might need that."

"I've never shot one." She didn't seem ashamed of it, but she didn't seem proud of it, either. It just was.

He offered a small smile. "If you can steal a GLASS and crack a keycode by ear, I'm reasonably sure you can work it out. Just"—he positioned her hand on the grip and set her finger along the trigger guard—"try to make sure I'm *not* on the other end when you squeeze the trigger."

"Don't tempt—" But before she could finish the joke—at least, he *hoped* it was a joke—her expression shifted suddenly.

Surprise or alarm, he couldn't tell, but a half second later, it hardened into resolve.

The twitch of her finger was the only warning he got before she fired.

A grunt of pain behind him broke off with the *thud* of another dropping body, and Drestyn glanced back to see a third man in the doorway, sprawled flat and unmoving in a growing puddle of blood. *Well done, Miss Red.*

She didn't look especially triumphant, blanching as a smaller, crimson inkblot bloomed across the fallen man's chest. Her throat worked around a thick, uncertain swallow, but Drestyn couldn't judge. The night after those strikebreakers, he'd thrown up half his stomach. "Did I kill him?" she asked.

Drestyn didn't bother to check for a pulse; he just stooped to grab Rodri's partner's gun, rose, and fired two shots into the body of the third man at the door. "No," he told her. "I did." Whether he had or he hadn't, he *had*. There'd been too many killers made of this mess already. "Come on, stay behind me. I think I know a few people who'll be glad to know you're safe."

He started to walk, but a hand on his arm stopped him. "Wait," she said, and when he turned around to face her—

She punched him in the jaw. Really put her hips into it, too; he spat blood as he straightened, tonguing a fresh cut in his cheek. He must've made a hell of a sight, all scarred up and smeared in another man's blood, but Regan squared her shoulders and stared him down like she'd seen worse.

"That was for my brother," she told him, and only the shine in her eyes and the harshness of her breathing gave her away. Helpless, seething fury, every bit of it earned. "Don't think I'll ever forget what you did to him. What you're *still* doing to him."

Drestyn swallowed copper, and it stuck in his throat. *Does he have nightmares?* he wanted to ask. *Does he wake up thinking he's still falling?* The way Drestyn woke up with the fires still burning behind his eyes. With the screams still ringing in his ears, and the taste of choking black smoke festering in his lungs. Was it Drestyn's eyes that haunted Jal, the way Gethin's had haunted him?

"You don't just want to punch me," he said instead. He knew that fury, too. If she'd tucked Rodri's gun against his chin and squeezed that trigger, he wouldn't have blamed her for it.

"No," she said. "But my brother's a good man, too. If I did any worse, I wouldn't be doing it for him; I'd be doing it for me. Just like what *you* want to do to the people who killed Lleyton."

It felt so strange, to hear her voice shape his name. Not sneering, like Gethin. Not clinical, like Eoan. She said it softly, with reverence. With *sympathy*. And as he held her gaze, he realized she was right. It had never been about his brother. Parts of him had died with Lleyton, but worse, parts of him *hadn't*: parts had lived on, mangled and ruined and bleeding. A killer, trying to do a dreamer's work. "It's not for him," he admitted—to himself, more than to her. "When I find whoever Gethin answered to, when I kill them, it'll be for me."

Of all the things she could've done, Regan *smiled*. Her eyes shined, and her hands shook at her sides, but she pulled him into a hug like she knew him. Like she understood him. "For *us*," she whispered fiercely against his ear. "It'll be for *us*." When she let him go, her smile was gone, and something determined had taken its place. "We clear the ship, we comm the *Ambit*, and then . . . then, I'll tell you everything."

CHAPTER SIXTEEN

EOAN

They waited until the others had gone to sleep to make the call.

They knew they shouldn't do it. Even comming from a spoofed ID on an encrypted back channel had risks; a good enough technician taking a close enough look could trace it back to the *Ambit*, no matter how many precautions Eoan took.

But they *had* to. For the first time in as long as they could remember, they simply couldn't *help themself*. The ship just got so still when everyone went to bed. None of Nash's chaotically efficient tinkering in the engine room. None of Saint's comforting routine of chores and exercise and reminding Nash that she could not, in fact, survive on tea and meal bars alone. Even Bodie would disappear for a while—slink off into some corner of the ship where Eoan couldn't find him, not to emerge until time to harass some breakfast out of his human crewmates.

They had no distractions; that was the problem, they decided. A basic trace to run, a set of vitals feeds to monitor, and they curled their consciousness around each of those four heartbeats like a hand cupping a flickering candle in the dark, but it wasn't *enough*. It couldn't banish the worry that clung to the corners of every thought, steadily gnawing its way inward with each passing second. Worry about the crew they'd nearly lost on the *Pathfinder*. Worry about the friend they'd nearly lost in the explosion on Alpha Librae. Worried about the relentless, vicious knowledge that it wasn't over yet, and in the echo chamber between their quiet ship and their unquiet mind, the worry grew and grew. How did humans *live* with this? How did they sleep, with so many troubles?

Perhaps they didn't. Eoan thought of Nash in the engine room, tinkering into the twilight hours of the morning, because she couldn't bear to close her eyes. They thought of Saint pacing the halls at night, checking every latch and readout and darkened corner until he'd satisfied himself enough to return to his quarters, then getting back up and doing it all over again.

Eoan couldn't tinker or pace, but without quite meaning to, they found themself in the bridge, listening to the ring of an outgoing comm. *An experiment,* they told themself, as they waited. That felt better. It was a risk to make a call, yes, but it was a risk for the sake of *understanding.* This newfound emotional sensitivity . . . it had put their crew in danger, on the Waystation. When they'd heard about the explosion at the Captains' Council meeting, they'd gotten caught up in it, and their focus had lapsed, and surely a good captain would do whatever they could to stop that happening again. They needed to learn to manage it. Needed to learn what made it better, what made it worse, and as the comm rang, and rang, and rang, they knew—no, they amended; they *hypothesized*—that this would make it better.

On the seventh ring, Torsten answered.

"Well, I'll be damned," he said, and even the sound of his voice helped dull the sharper edges of their distress. Deep and robust. *Healthy,* if a little haggard. They wished they could've seen his face, but a video comm would've been chancier. Instead, they pictured his face, his broad grin and smile lines, as he continued, "You really *do* remember the old days, don't you? When I got a ping from the *Vigor*'s ID, I half-expected somebody'd be tellin' me about my ship's extended warranty."

The *Vigor* had been their old ship, long since consigned to the scrapyard after one too many too-close calls. Its ID would've been returned to the pool and redistributed, so they doubted it would draw attention; they'd just hoped he would still remember after all these years.

Torsten never let them down.

"We shouldn't talk long," they said, though it pained them to say it.

"I'm surprised we're talking at all," said Torsten. "Tried pinging you a half-dozen times, figured you must've gone dark. You heard about the explosion, right?"

"I did," they said. "I'm sorry, I should've reached out sooner, I just . . ." *I'm scared.* The realization brought every other thought screeching to a halt. Thoughts of caution, thoughts of discretion—all of them, frozen in place by that singular moment of self-awareness. *I don't want to lose anyone, and I think I might, and I'm scared.*

"Eoan?" Torsten's voice had gone soft, searching. He'd always been the man who got his people home safe, who charged boldly into danger so his siblings-in-arms wouldn't have to. But more than that, he'd always been a *friend.* "You all right over there?"

For all they'd changed, these last few months, they still didn't like to lie. "I'm not sure," they admitted. It felt strange to say it aloud, but it felt *right* to say it to him. They loved their crew. Saint. Nash. Even Jal and Bitsie. Eoan loved them and trusted them, more than they'd ever loved or trusted anyone.

But sometimes, honesty came easier with distance. With an old friend, who'd seen some of their worst days and best days and days they'd sooner just forget. They didn't have to worry about losing Torsten's friendship, losing his respect; it had been a constant for so many years, through so many things, and that bred an altogether *different* kind of love, and an altogether different kind of trust.

The silence that settled between them settled comfortably. A pause between moves at a tabletop game. A breath in a story they knew he'd finish telling. "Is there anything I can do?" he asked finally.

They felt themself smile, even without a projection; it was an emotion, they'd decided, as much as an expression. A warmth. A relief. "Just tell me you're all right," they said.

Torsten chuckled. "I told you, didn't I? Goddamn tardigrade." They thought they heard the scrape of his callused palm over his beard. A small wonder he hadn't rubbed his chin as bare as his head. "Cuts and bruises, that's all. Bad hip's giving me fits, but that probably just means it's Tuesday, Thursday, or some other day that ends in a *y*. Give me a few days, I'll be back to stompin' around, annoying the piss out of everybody, mark my words. Although," he began, sobering, "I *am* a little curious why I got the head of Union security breathing down my neck. Heard something went down on the Waystation—lot of folks seem to think you had something to do with it."

"Ah."

"*Ah*. That's all I get?"

"That's probably all you want," Eoan replied. "The less you know, the better."

"I ever strike you as the *plausible deniability* type?"

Eoan made a noncommittal sound. "I ever strike you as the *destroy my friends' Guild careers* type?"

"Well, there was that time on Mars."

"That was *your fault*, as I recall."

Torsten chuckled again, deeper and merrier. "Oh, right. The old thinker's not what it used to be. Which is a real shame for that Officer Casale," he added offhandedly.

Eoan knew better. Torsten didn't do *offhand*. "Torsten," they said slowly, "what did you do?"

"My job, of course. Told Officer Casale that the Guild would be pleased as peach pie to assist in any way we could, and I invited her to join me on Alpha Librae so we could put our heads together." It sounded proper so far, but Eoan could hear the *but* coming, as Torsten sighed. "I'm just afraid I'm not the savvy young buck I used to be, and these *manhunt* things can be so damn tricky—I'm just all left feet. Ought to keep her out of your hair for a bit, at any rate."

It's all thumbs or two left feet, they thought, but as ever, they couldn't bring themself to correct him. "Torsten," they began, but they didn't know whether to thank him or scold him. They settled on "You didn't have to do that. You could get yourself into a lot of trouble."

"Pelton Five," Torsten replied bluntly. "I missed my exfil, and you ducked orders and came looking for me. Would've died on that shithole if it wasn't for you, and I seem to recall you getting into a good bit of trouble in the bargain," he added. "The Sverdrup mines. The outbreak on Brigham Three. Those pirates on Bell Station." He paused. "You want me to keep going, 'cause I just poured myself a glass of whiskey and I could do this all night. I owe you one, Eoan. Or ten. Or twenty."

"I haven't been keeping score," they said.

"Hogshit," Torsten replied, with a grin in his voice. "Still the same bad liar you always were—and that's a compliment, by the way."

"And you're still the same obstinate ass you always were." They couldn't have said it fonder if they'd tried. There'd never been any changing his mind once he'd made it up. They'd always admired that about him, for all the trouble it had gotten them into along the way. *The best kind of trouble.* There'd be no shaking him. "Will you at least promise you'll be careful? For my sake, if not for your own."

"Cross my heart," said Torsten. "But whether you like it or not, Eoan, we're in this together, and I'm gonna help you however I can. So just let me, okay? For old time's sake." They heard him finish his drink—the click of teeth against the glass, and a slow exhale after he swallowed—and before they got the chance to argue, he said, "See you around, old friend," and ended the call.

For old time's sake. He really was a stubborn ass.

Despite that—*because* of that—they found they did feel better as the silence and the stillness settled in again. Torsten was all right, and he wanted to *help*. Loathe as they were to draw anyone deeper into this maelstrom, they couldn't help exulting in the knowledge that they weren't alone. Their crew still had friends in the universe. And no matter what they'd been through, no matter the fresh scars and bruises, they still had *hope*.

.   .   .

Not long after that, Eoan heard Saint stirring in his cabin. The creak of his mattress, the resigned sigh of someone who'd chased sleep and come up short—they carried just far enough for Eoan to pick them up on the mic arrays in the bridge. "I can feel you out there wringing your hard drives," he called through the door. "You wanna come in, or do I have to get up and come out there?"

No sense arguing. A bit like Torsten, Saint could rarely be swayed once he'd made up his mind about something, so they projected into his quarters and settled into the armchair in the corner. Their feathery chiffon shawl struck a strange contrast to the fabric of the chair, style against substance, but they'd always rather liked that. The *distinction*. They'd spent so long trying to emulate humans, they enjoyed differentiating themself, now and again.

For all its simplicity, though, Saint's room was one of their favorite places on the ship. It had a warmth they'd never quite been able to trace. Could've been the old paper books on the shelves behind his bed, or the patches sewn into the softness of the armchair, or the strange contrast of military neatness and the odd creature comfort.

Or perhaps, they thought, as Saint smiled a weary, blood-shot smile at them, it was just the man who lived there.

"You should be sleeping," they told him.

He didn't deny it. Instead, he shifted himself up against the shelves—they pretended not to notice the hand pressed gingerly against his side, and he pretended not to notice them pretending not to notice—and waved his other hand at the door. "Might as well open that up. The others'll find their way up here soon enough."

Do you know something I don't? they might've asked, if they'd been talking to anyone else. But this was Saint, and for all he liked to pretend otherwise, Saint *knew things* about his people.

They opened the door with a purely theatrical wave of their hand and nodded at his side. "Nash said you'd make it."

"Unless I'm fucking stupid about it." He gave a wry twitch of a smile. "Think those were her exact words."

Eoan would've preferred a little more information, but like the privacy protocols in the nonpublic areas of the ship, they took their crew's medical privilege seriously. Not their place to pry, and with Saint, they didn't especially feel the need. He weathered wounds like coasts weathered storms: frequently and stubbornly. But they trusted him to tell them if it became a problem, and they trusted *Nash* to stop it becoming one in the first place.

"Any noise from our friend in the cargo bay?" Saint asked.

"Your friend?"

Saint shrugged. "He did give us a ride. Don't get me wrong—not saying we throw open the firewalls and give him run of the *Ambit*."

"Naturally." As the saying went, it wasn't paranoia if your last software-savvy houseguest uploaded a geocidal supervirus that nearly killed two-thirds of your crew.

"Naturally," Saint agreed. "Just curious how he's doing. And how you're doing," he added, with an arch of one heavy brow.

Nearly the same question Torsten had asked, but the answer didn't come quite so easily. *I'm not sure.* They knew he'd accept the answer. He'd respect it. He wouldn't judge it. Still, it wouldn't come. The thing was, with Saint, they *wanted* to be sure. It was their job to be sure. "Asks the man with a hole in his side," they said instead.

"A patched hole."

"A hole, nevertheless."

"Careful, Cap, you're gonna hurt my feelings," said Nash from the doorway. Eoan had caught her on the sick bay cameras just a few moments earlier, but they hadn't seen the need to warn Saint. Evidently he'd already known she'd be coming. "They're right, though. That hole's still a hole, McBlastinshit, so be nice to it."

"And it'll be nice to me?" Saint offered with a chuckle.

Nash snorted and dropped herself on the corner of the built-in desk by the door. Saint usually kept it pretty full, between his notebooks, gun maintenance, and the odd trinket, but there always seemed to be a bare space on the end where Nash liked to sit—enough to let her scoot back toward the wall and kick her socked feet up on the edge. "Yeah, no. That thing's gonna hurt like a bitch for a couple of weeks whether you baby it or not. But *I* might be nice to you."

Saint's turn to snort. "If you start being nice to me, I'll know I'm in trouble."

"Fair enough."

A soft cough from the doorway, and there were the Reds. Jal didn't have quite the same nonchalance about letting himself in as Nash had, hesitating even once Saint waved them in.

"Sorry," he said. "Didn't mean to interrupt or anything, just—"

"Couldn't sleep," Nash finished for him, flicking a wave down at the bleary-faced twelve-year-old trailing behind him. "Yeah, join the club. We've got . . . I don't know, what have we got?" she asked Saint.

"Bad manners," he replied, with a pointed look at her foot on his desk. He shook his head and started to reach for his blankets, like he meant to straighten them out for Jal and Bitsie to sit on, but he winced mid-lean and got a sock to the face for trying. "Would you keep your feet to yourself, you heathen?" he hissed at Nash, though he didn't try for the blankets again.

No need to, anyway. Jal was there in an instant, hesitation giving way to his bone-deep need to be *helpful*. He got the blankets straightened out and, after a quick glance at Saint as if to confirm it was okay, settled himself at the foot of the bed with his back to the other wall.

Bitsie didn't need quite the encouragement, climbing up onto the bed beside Jal and curling up against his side. The pillow marks on her cheek said maybe she *hadn't* had quite the same trouble sleeping, but they couldn't imagine Jal leaving her alone after the day she'd had. After the day they'd *all* had.

"She'll be back asleep in a few minutes," Jal said, tucking the blue blanket Bitsie had worn in like a cape a little more snugly around her small shoulders. "Just heard somebody moving around in the hall, thought maybe . . ." He trailed off, though Eoan could imagine what he might've said. *Maybe someone else might want company.*

The small shape that came skittering through the door spared him trying to finish. Unlike Jal and Nash, Bodie hadn't registered on a single sensor before he'd darted through Saint's door, and he didn't stop until he'd leapt onto the bed and onto Jal's outstretched legs.

"Damn it, cat, you're not supposed to be on the bed," Saint grunted, but his heart wasn't in it. His heart rarely was, when it came to his little band of strays. It was one of the things Eoan loved most about him.

Bodie gave a huff and a flick of his stubby tail, before stretching himself out in the dip of Jal's thighs like he belonged there. Jal, they suspected, wasn't doing much to discourage the notion. He smoothed a hand through Bodie's fur, and Eoan swore his shoulders sank lower out of their hunch with every pass of his fingers.

Terrible mouser, good cat.

"Great, gang's all here," said Nash, as if it was inevitable. Maybe it was. Something about a bad day always brought them all together—a kind of gravity, pulling them toward center. Toward *safe* and *steady*, and of all the places they could've gone, Eoan knew it wasn't coincidence they'd all wound up in *Saint's* quarters. "Welcome to the monthly meeting of Insomniacs Anonymous. Plus that asshole," Nash added, with a nod to Bodie. "Pretty sure he just comes for the donuts. Look at him. Lazy fucking bread loaf." And when Bodie peeled open an eye, she stared right back at him. "Yeah, I'm talking about you."

Bitsie gave a soft, sleepy laugh against Jal's arm. "He does look like a bread loaf," she said. "With spots. A moldy bread loaf. Bodie the Moldy Bread Loaf."

She giggled again, and Jal giggled with her—albeit in a *very* different octave—and shook his head. "Little bit, you are *done*," he said, ruffling her hair with his feline-free hand. "Just close your eyes, try to get some sleep. I'll wake you up if something happens." He didn't tell her what the next day would bring; the truth was, none of them knew. They had a heading, trailing Gethin's ship with hopes of carving out another chance, but no way to guess when or where that might be, or what it would look like.

Still, they half-expected him to try. *Something's different.* A faint shift in the dynamic, an unspoken acknowledgement. They seemed *synchronous*, he and Bitsie, in a way they hadn't before the *Pathfinder*. As though they hadn't quite found their new rhythm, but had at least acknowledged that the old one had changed.

Eoan felt inexplicably proud.

The room went quiet for a time after that. Trying to let Bitsie nod off in peace, yes, but also just . . . comfortable in each other's presence. Trading glances. Catching their breath. Eoan watched Saint's chest rise and fall, and Nash's tense frame slowly unfurl like a fern frond, and Eoan felt like they breathed with him, and relaxed with her, and a little more of that worry eased away.

"I spoke to Brodbeck," they said after a time. None of them looked surprised, or especially unhappy, as if it never even occurred to them that Eoan would do anything to put them in jeopardy. Nevertheless, Eoan explained, "I was careful; used an old data drop point and a spoofed ID, so I doubt anyone would've picked it up, much less traced it back to us."

"Is he all right?" Jal asked.

"As much as could be expected," they said. "He wanted to let us know Casale sounded the alarm, but he's running a bit of interference."

"Shit," said Nash. "Remind me to send the guy flowers."

"More of a whiskey man, as I recall." Saint turned to Eoan. "You trust him?"

Under the circumstances, Eoan knew the weight that question carried, so they gave the most honest answer they could. "Without question." And given their programming directive, Eoan didn't do that lightly.

Saint, of anyone, must have understood that. "Whiskey it is, then." And with that settled to his satisfaction, he let his gaze drift sideways to Jal. Bitsie's breathing had evened out, her frame gone slack as Jal settled her more securely against the cradle of his chest. He handled her *so carefully*, traces of uncertainty threaded through overwhelming affection, as if he didn't fully know how to hold something that precious. As if he didn't fully believe he *should*.

A chime from the desk next to Nash cut the moment short.

"It's your GLASS, Saint," Nash said, twisting to snatch it up off the other corner of the desk. "You've got a new message." The proper thing probably would've been to toss it to Saint and let *him* look at the message on *his* GLASS, but Eoan's crew never claimed to have much grasp of propriety. "Who the hell's

BBFB? And seriously, I thought we went off-network. Am I the only one not phoning home? What the fuck."

"We *are* off-network," said Eoan. The data drop they'd used to reach Torsten had been three layers of back channel, *none* of them Guild; and when they'd taken their transponder offline, they'd done the same for every comms system and connected device on the ship. Nothing on the *Ambit* was connected to any Guild, Union, or Trust network, so any contact would've had to come *directly*, through a private connection. "If someone's messaging him, they must know his personal terminal ID."

Wounded side, if not forgotten, then at least steadfastly ignored, Saint rose from his bed. "Give that here."

But Nash ignored his outstretched hand as another message popped onto the screen. "The shit?" she said. "Gethin's dead?" The message said as much. Short bursts in urgent capitals, like someone was sending in a hurry, or from an unfamiliar system.

BBFB—GETHIN'S DEAD.

NEED A RIDE.

COORDINATES BELOW.

As they read, another message popped up below it.

DON'T SHOOT.

Curious—and wary, and hopeful, and *really*, how did humans get anything done with so many feelings clanging around all the time—Eoan switched briefly to the receiver they'd locked onto the stowaway drone's position. Emotional or not, you couldn't beat an AI for multitasking. "Gethin's ship does appear to be slowing down," they told the others. A quick bit of math, and they added, "At their current rate of deceleration, they should stop at those coordinates."

"Weird choice for a merc on the run," said Nash.

"That's because it's not Gethin," said Saint, voice rough. The hand on his side had gone from hovering to holding, and his face had paled half a shade. *Unless I'm fucking stupid about it.*

Suddenly, Nash's diagnosis seemed an awful lot more prescient. He didn't stop until he got close enough to swipe the GLASS from Nash, who probably could've kept it without much trouble, but she seemed to be in a sporting mood. "Don't see a sender ID, but *BBFB*? That's definitely from Regan."

"Backstabbing backwater fuck bumpkin," Jal said, rousing Bitsie with a nudge. He *had* promised to wake her up if something happened, and he seemed intent on keeping his word. "Raise up a little, little bit."

Bitsie stirred, but sleep had stolen her coordination, and Jal mostly had to lift her off himself. Up he went, crossing the room to Saint in a couple of quick strides and peering over Saint's shoulder at the GLASS. "She called him that behind his back for a while after I got home."

"And to my face before that," Saint said, with a grim slant to his mouth that said he thought he deserved it. "Wasn't exactly her favorite person after I quit looking for Jal. Pretty much told me to go fuck myself when I gave her my terminal ID—just wanted her to be able to call if she needed anything. This is the first time she's ever used it."

"Assuming that's her using it," Nash said. "Not trying to rain on anybody's parade, but we got no vid feed, no return ID, and it's not like Gethin hasn't already played puppet master. Are we sure it's her?"

"Mom?" Bitsie had apparently caught on to the proceedings. She sat up, pushing herself to the edge of the bed. "Is that Mom?"

Eoan answered Nash's question first. "If we're *not* sure, we'll need to get that way quickly. We're closing in on them. Much longer, and we'll be in range of their ship's onboard defense system." Eoan had seen enough explosions for one day, thank you.

"It's her." Jal's tone brooked no argument. "I mean, we took out a dozen or so of Gethin's guys on that ring ship, right? Can't have too many left aboard, and between her and Drestyn . . . they could've gotten themselves loose. Taken control of the ship, slipped us word on whatever terminal they could get into. I know Regan, and I wouldn't put it past her. Or Drestyn, either," he added, with a touch less enthusiasm.

Nash held up a finger. "Counterpoint: we get in close and cozy with that ship, and a still-very-alive Gethin kicks off Trap Part Two. I don't know about you guys, but personally? Wasn't a big fan of Trap Part One."

Saint ignored them both and turned to Eoan's projection. "What about the drone?" he said. "Any way you can get a hold of it while we're still outside of weapon range? Get us eyes inside."

"It'll be close," they said. "But I should be able to boost the signal enough, yes. You know, though, that the stronger I make the signal, the more likely it is they detect it." If Gethin *did* still have control of his ship, they could end up exposing their one surefire way of finding him.

"It's a risk," Saint agreed. All his earlier fatigue had given way to a straight spine and flinty eyes. To resolve. "But we've got to take it. If there's a chance we get Regan back, we've come too far not to try." He turned to Nash. "You good with that?"

A genuine question, seeking a genuine answer. Saint might've outranked Nash on paper, but in every way that mattered, they treated each other like equals. Like family.

She held his gaze a long few seconds, before she finally slid off the desk with a deep, exasperated sigh. "Ah, what the hell," she said, brushing imaginary dust off her kaleidoscopically colorful boxer shorts. "Can't win if you don't play, right? I'm in. Let's 'Big Brother' their asses, see what's what."

"It's her," Bitsie said, in an uncanny echo of her uncle. Same conviction, higher register. Her spine pulled every bit as straight as Saint's as she rose to her feet, blanket drawn tightly around her shoulders. "I know it's her. I *know* it."

Eoan so hoped she was right.

"I'll sync up with the drone as soon as we're in range and let you know the moment I have something," they said. "Shouldn't be long. You should get yourselves ready."

"For what?" Jal asked.

"For anything, miner boy," said Nash, clapping him on the arm as she passed to retrieve the sock she'd thrown. "Way shit's been going, be ready for anything." With a wave, Nash spun on her one socked heel and left the room.

Jal followed slightly slower, letting an impatient Bitsie through first before he turned back to Saint. He didn't speak, and Saint didn't either. Even so, Eoan got the sense each said something to the other—something too uneasy, too cautious, too *important* for words.

When at last Saint nodded, a flicker of a smile chased itself across Jal's face, and he followed Bitsie out into the bridge looking just a little steadier than he had before.

"He believes in you, you know," they told Saint, once they were alone. Them and Saint, the way this had all begun. "However you think you've failed him, and whatever his sister's feelings on the matter, he *does* believe in you."

Saint grimaced. "I know."

"That bothers you?" they asked.

"Everything about this bothers me." Not much *getting ready* for Saint to do—he'd slept in jeans and that fraying black sweater Nash hated—but he had his gun belt and his shoulder brace to don. A practiced, time-honored ritual. "Regan's out there with one psychopath or another, might be a rat in the Captains' Council, and we have no fucking clue where any of this leads." He stopped, bracing his hands on the desk and letting his head hang.

Eoan felt . . . privileged, in a way. Heartbroken, to see him so worn down; but honored that he would *let* them see. That with them, he could allow himself this moment to be something other than strong, other than sure, other than the Ranger Toussaint who never faltered.

"I don't, either," they said. Suddenly, it seemed so silly, the things they hadn't wanted to say. *I'm scared. I'm not sure. I'm fallible. I'm* human. Saint was as much their equal as Torsten. As much their partner. As much their *friend*. And he deserved their honesty just as much, if not more.

"I don't know where this leads, or how this ends, but for what it's worth . . . I truly believe we'll be all right." Not just because they had to believe it, but because these people— their crew, their friends, their *family*—made believing so much easier.

They wished they could touch him: lay a hand on his shoulder, pull him into a hug. But all they could do was wait beside him until he raised his head, and offer a smile that they hoped conveyed all the same things. "We're alive. We're together. As long as we have that, we have everything we need to come out the other side." They caught his gaze and winked. "Unless we're fucking stupid about it, right?"

Saint laughed. A short, breathy bark of a thing, but definitely still a laugh, and as Saint straightened to cinch the last strap on his shoulder brace, Eoan felt better. They felt like they'd given him something, this man who gave the rest of them so much. A bit of strength to borrow, for as long as he needed to borrow it.

"Come on, dear," they said. "Chin up. We're in range for the drone and haven't been blown out of the sky yet. I've actually got rather a good feeling about this."

There probably weren't a lot of *good feelings* to be had for the man with the bullet wound and maybe a half hour's sleep in the tank, but Saint took a breath, let it out, and, as was his way, got ready to soldier on. "Yeah, all right," he said. "Just let me know when you've got eyes inside."

"Already done," they told him brightly. Not the best connection, but they'd managed to steer the drone up out of its cozy little corner of Gethin's cargo bay, and they had its video and audio feeds streaming right before their proverbial eyes. Bit of jostling, bit of interference, but as they caught sight of an open doorway in the hold of Gethin's ship, a grin slowly spread across their face. "Oh, Saint," they whispered, "you're going to want to see this."

They showed the others, too, but by then it had become something of a moot point. They'd already taken the *Ambit* in closer—close enough to dock their berth bridge, relaying instructions over the drone to try to speed and smooth things along. Wouldn't do to get this close, only to botch it at the finish line with a bad link-up.

Jal, understandably, was the first at the air lock door. Bitsie trailed behind him at a pace more suited to little legs, though she still wound up at the front. "Uncle Jal, you're fidgeting."

"Sorry, little bit."

"You're still doing it." And he was, in fact, still doing it. Shifting his weight from foot to foot, the way he did when his nerves told him *move*, and he couldn't quite stop his body listening. Flattening Bitsie's jacket collar, too, and straightening it, and then reflattening it, and then restraightening it, until it stuck up worse than it had when he'd started and Bitsie caught his hands in hers. "You saw the video," she said. "It's going to be okay."

"Listen to mini-miner." Nash joined next, drifting in with a mug of tea. Once she'd seen the drone feed, *she'd* made for the kitchen. "She's smarter than you."

"Don't I know it," Jal said earnestly.

Nash made a face into her tea—still learning how to pick at someone who *agreed* with her half the time—but she perked up a bit when Saint joined them at last. "Hey, so, *backstabbing backwater fuck bumpkin*," she said by way of greeting. "All that bitching and moaning about McBlastinshit, and we had *fuck bumpkin* on the table? Regan sounds awesome."

Jal mustered a pale smile. "Yeah, she is," he said. Then,

quieter, like he was afraid to speak it too loudly into the universe, "Can't wait for you to meet her." Still anxious, the poor thing, but they couldn't blame him. He'd been through an awful lot to get Regan back—more than any of them. If he didn't trust it until he had her in his arms, then they supposed the best they could do was hurry that along.

"Bridge is secure," they said. "First transfer, inbound."

"Deep breaths, miner boy," said Nash. "You pass out before the door opens, that's gonna be a real awkward reunion."

"Shut up," he muttered. No bite, just something to pass the seconds as they stretched themselves ever longer. Not many left now, but each one must've felt like an eternity to him. Time dilation in response to stressful stimuli—deeply fascinating science, actually. Somehow Eoan doubted he'd appreciate it as much as they did.

They gave him something he *would* appreciate instead. "Opening the air lock," they said, and as that door slid open, every horror of the last few days was suddenly, unequivocally *worth it*.

"Mom!" Bitsie's voice broke with a sob, and she was in her mother's arms before the first tears fell. Regan met her halfway, sweeping her up in a hug so fierce it carried her off her feet, and Jal did the same to them both. Got his arms around his whole family, his whole *world*, and held them like nothing else existed.

"I'm so sorry," Regan told them, one after the other, pressing the words into kisses against their heads. "I'm so, so sorry."

Jal let them down, but he didn't let them go. "Are you okay?" Shaking hands skimmed bruised cheeks and brushed sweat-damp snarls of hair from Regan's face, never settling in one place, like he didn't trust his eyes to check her over. "Did he hurt you? Either one of them, did they—"

Regan caught his hands and held them. "I'm okay, Jal," and her voice didn't waver despite the tears still rolling down her cheeks. She had a power to her, Eoan thought. A resilience impossible to imitate or replicate. It had to be *earned*, and however she'd earned hers, she carried it in every piece of her. The proudness of her shoulders, the height of her chin, the shine in her eyes. It took someone special to stand beside a man like Jal, not just with his mutations, but with his *history*, and still look strong. Smudged makeup and blotchy, bruised cheeks, but she still had such a radiant smile as she kissed her daughter's head. "I'm okay now."

Eoan would've liked to give them more time; no question they'd earned it, the three of them, after all they'd been through. But a red flash above the air lock cut the moment short, and there was nothing Eoan could do. "Gethin's ship is detaching from the bridge," they said. The *Ambit*'s air lock slid closed automatically, seals engaging with a hiss.

"Well, that's rude," said Perseus through the shuttle speakers. "Sorry, am I supposed to be quiet? Not really sure of my role here." Which, neither was Eoan. "I'd shake your hand, miss, but they blew up my arms back on my ship. My old ship, not my new one. The *Valorous Starship Shuttle Number Three*. Still workshopping the name. Now, about that bridge—"

Saint, who had held back by the hall, turned suddenly and started off toward the front of the ship. "Drestyn's running," he said. "That son of a bitch." But before he made it more than a few steps down the hall, Regan stopped him with a shout.

"Wait!" She pulled away from Jal and Bitsie, jogging half the distance to Saint and only slowing when he turned back toward her. "Let him go."

"We can't do that." Saint started off again, but this time Regan caught up and grabbed his arm. That he didn't wrench it away said more about his self-control than his mood, Eoan thought. "Dammit, Regan. I don't know if he did you a good turn back there or what, but Isaiah Drestyn is *not* the kind of man you just *let go*. He damn near killed your brother, and more importantly"—though he didn't say it like he believed it really *was* more important—"if we don't take him back to the Union, undo all the shit we did to get here, then we've got no way out of this hole we've dug ourselves into. You understand that? Never mind whatever kind of homicidal shitstorm he'll let loose when he gets wherever he's going."

"I know where he's going!" Regan snapped. "You bullheaded son of a bitch. I know who he is, and I know what he did, and I know where he's going and what he means to do when he gets there. And to tell the truth? I've got half a mind to let him."

Saint rarely got caught wrong-footed, but Regan seemed to have a knack. He opened his mouth to answer, but snapped it closed before he could say whatever he'd planned to. His fists clenched at his sides, and his nose flared around a long, deliberate sigh. "You're sure you know where he's going?" he asked finally, placing each word carefully at the end of the last. Saint *did* sometimes lose his temper, but flustered and furious as he was, he seemed to realize the folly of losing it on his oldest friend's newly recovered sister. Discretion, valor, et cetera.

Regan held her ground like she'd done it before—which, she probably had, given their history—and nodded. "I do."

"He told you?" Saint pressed.

"He told me enough. And I told him some, too."

Another breath, another sigh, as the bridge finished retracting and the ship formerly known as Gethin's skittered away into the black. "Well then," Saint said, "it sounds like we've got a lot to talk about."

CHAPTER SEVENTEEN

NASH

They set a course for Alpha Librae. "I know it doesn't make sense," Regan said. "Or I don't know, maybe it does. I've been stuck in a dinky little dungeon box for fuck knows how many days, so I'm assuming there's been some developments."

"Four days and change," said Jal, head ducked low and hands in his pockets, looking like he'd just confessed to murder. Nash, for one, thought a five-day turnaround on an impossible rescue mission was pretty damn impressive. Of course, *she* preferred to leave martyrdom to the professionals.

Looking at you, McBlastinshit. Standing there all upright and shit, pretending like he *didn't* want to crawl into a hole with a fistful of nerve blockers and a fifth of blur and sleep until his side healed up. He could maybe fool the others, but he'd have to try a lot harder to fool the lady who'd forcepped a bullet away from his spleen. *Dumbass.*

"Maybe we take this conversation someplace with seats?" Nash suggested, deliberately not looking Saint's way. If he thought she'd suggested it for his sake, he'd go all stoic-y machismo about it, so she nodded at Regan instead. "This one needs about two liters of water and something to eat that looks like a vegetable, and it's not like we haven't got the time to kill." Even with a few hours' travel under their belt, they still had about twelve hours before they got to Alpha Librae. Plenty of time for conversating *and* planting their asses someplace slightly less vertical.

Saint narrowed his eyes at her—yeah, okay, not an easy man to fleece, and she wasn't exactly queen of the grifters, but she deserved points for trying—but before he could argue, Jal went and smiled one of his golden boy smiles and opened his golden boy mouth.

"I'll fix us something." He said it like nothing would please him more. "Sandwiches or something, I mean," he qualified, rubbing the back of his neck sheepishly. "Ain't much of a cook, but I can manage something half-decent between a couple pieces of bread."

"Wow, don't oversell it." Nash snorted, but damned if Saint didn't head for the galley, with Regan and Bitsie not far behind. *Not bad, miner boy.* The satisfied curl of his smile behind the others' backs said he knew it.

He and Nash bumped fists before he followed his family down the hall, and as he jogged ahead to beat Saint to the pantry—lest the stubborn son of a bitch get any ideas—it struck her once again: that pesky, meddlesome thought that maybe, just maybe, she liked having Jal around.

"Sorry, Percy," she called on her way out. Didn't feel quite right, leaving him out of everything. The cargo bay might've been roomier than the brig, but so long as the AI couldn't leave, that didn't make it any less of a cell.

"That's all right, mam," Perseus said through the shuttle's external speakers cheerfully. "Being on your own a century or two, you learn to enjoy your own company."

Talk about your positive mental attitude. "I'll swing back by when we're done, how about that? You and I can brainstorm a little, maybe do something about that propulsion system you don't have." If the *Pathfinder* had taught her anything, it was that a backup vessel comes in handy.

She'd nearly made it out the door when he called, "Wait!" So she did. "*Percy,*" he said slowly, as if testing the word. "Is that a nickname, mam?"

He sounded so hopeful, she *had* to nod. "Sure is," she said sincerely. Cap was right to be cautious, after what Anke'd done to them; Nash would be the last person throwing stones at that particular glass house. But that weird-ass AI was the reason Nash's people made it back in one piece. Far as she was concerned, that made him something awfully damn close to a friend. "Is that all right?"

A flutter of energy drifted across her augments, fizzing and bright. *Happiness.* Anyone who said machines couldn't feel didn't know machines like Nash did. They made more sense to her than people ever would. "It's wonderful, mam," Perseus— *Percy*—replied. "It's absolutely wonderful. Thank you."

No, she thought, as she dipped her head and started back into the hall. *Thank* you.

By the time she reached the galley, Jal had turned the counter into his own personal deli. Peppers, tomatoes, some leafy greens from the grow room below deck, all set out with a container of spiced lentil spread and a loaf of bread. Somehow he'd persuaded Saint into a seat at the table while Jal got some coffee going, so either Jal was a magic fucking unicorn, or Saint was *exactly* as tired as she thought.

Regan probably could've given him a worn-out run for his worn-out money. She'd settled in the seat farthest from him, Bitsie right beside her, and Nash had clocked at least one smothered yawn since Nash walked in. Regan's hand trembled as she raised her water to her lips, drinking long and deep until she'd nearly drained the cup.

"Huh, is this what it feels like when people actually *listen* to my advice?" Nash asked, swiping the cup to refill it with a pointed look at Saint. "Weird. I almost feel like a doctor or something."

"Or something," Jal muttered.

She snatched the towel off Jal's shoulder—he didn't actually seem to be using it; knowing him, he'd just seen Saint do it enough times, he thought it was part of the galley uniform—and belted him on the ass with it, skipping away from his blind swat without spilling a drop of Regan's water.

Regan glanced between them as Nash sat the cup back down, brow wrinkling faintly. Not a bad look, but not a good one, either. Whatever. Nash was tired of weird looks and indecipherable people. If Regan needed to get something off her chest, she didn't seem like the kind of lady to hold it back on Nash's account.

It must not've been that important, because Regan shook her head and said, "I'm going to tell you everything I know. You'll probably have questions, and I may or may not have answers, but I'd appreciate if you'd let me get through it all first." Direct, but not harsh. Nash had an inkling Regan had planned out exactly what she wanted to say and exactly how she wanted to say it; any audience participation would just muck things up.

As Jal went back to slapping sandwiches together, Eoan materialized in the corner he'd just vacated. "Understood," they said, then gestured patiently with an outstretched hand for Regan to continue. "Whenever you're ready."

Another swig of water, and Regan began. "It started with Jal's bodycam footage," she said, eyes closing briefly in pain—the special kind of pain that came with knowing someone you loved had been hurt, and you hadn't been there to stop it. They all knew the sting of it. Even Bitsie now, and didn't that *suck*. "First time I saw it, I could barely—I didn't exactly notice much." Not a bad recovery. She'd kicked off a staring match with her cup, though, tracing the rim with short, paint-chipped fingernails. Sometimes, to get through something, you just had to put your head down and *get through it*. "You'd just reached out after Noether, and I know you said I shouldn't watch it on my own," she added to Saint, "but what else was I supposed to do? We were halfway across the spiral when we got the news, nobody knew if Jal would pull through, and I had *days* on the shuttle before I could even see him.

"So, I watched it. Then I watched it again, and again, and again, and I don't remember which time it dawned on me, but I realized that Fenton wasn't just talking to himself, that scum-sucking sack of schist. There was someone else on the line. Somebody *told* him to leave my brother there to die, and I wanted to know who."

With a frustrated sigh, she spread her hands. "Of course, you know how that panned out. Even by the time the hearings rolled around, they still hadn't managed to run down the other side of that conversation. Bunch of corrupted files where the crew's bodycam footage and comm recordings should've been—some kind of *equipment failure*. I know you guys tried to find it, too. I know that. And I know you brought my brother back to me, and I know you saved all those people on that station, but at the end of the day, you're still *rangers*. You still fly under the same banner as the people who left my brother on that rock to die, and he wouldn't have even *been* there if one of you hadn't—"

Jal's fist hit the counter, rattling the cutting board and sending a tomato rolling away down the counter. "Regan." He didn't shout, but there was a warning in his voice just the same—a warning, and a plea. *"Don't."*

The damage had already been done, though. Across the table, Saint had gone board stiff, expression shuttered and flat. They all knew how that sentence was supposed to end. *If one of you hadn't left him in the first place.* Even Nash, who'd never been party to the whole story, knew enough to know how deep that had to cut. Could damn near hear it sliding between Saint's ribs, reopening all those raw-edged old wounds that'd never quite managed to heal.

Regan had every right to think it, was the thing. The Guild *had* used her little brother up and thrown him out like scrap, and Saint *had* left him behind to join Eoan's crew. Both those things were objectively true, and as the sister who'd raised him and lost him and grieved him, what obligation did Regan have to try to see past all of that? If it'd been Nash sitting there in her seat, she couldn't say she'd have done things any differently.

But fuck her for saying it anyway.

Regan looked guilty, at least, though it might've been less about upsetting Saint, and more about breaking her and Saint's unspoken little détente. Two people who were the face of each other's worst days, stuck together by the sheer goddamn misfortune of loving the same man. They played nice because they didn't want to hurt Jal.

"You two are worse than my parents," Nash muttered.

Saint seemed to shake himself off, grunting a quiet thanks as Jal passed him a coffee mug. "Thought you said you grew up on a commune station," he said to her.

"Did I?" she replied. "Yeah, well. I refuse to abandon the entire pantheon of bad parent jokes just because I didn't have any. It's called an imagination." She turned back to Regan, ticking up an eyebrow. "So much for *no interruptions*, huh?"

Jal glanced uneasily between Saint and Regan as he set the plate of sandwiches down on the table. "Can we maybe skip to the part where you tell us what's going on?"

A dash more guilt—on her face, and on Saint's—and Regan picked up one of the sandwiches and started back in. "Long and short of it is, that's why I asked for placement in the communications division on Alpha Librae. I've got the background, so I didn't think anybody'd look too closely at the request, but it gave me access to all the archived recordings. Every second of comms from every sanctioned Guild mission, going back decades.

"At first I just wanted to dig up that one file. But when I

couldn't find that, I expanded the search. Started looking through every entry for that whole crew. Figured if they'd covered it up once, maybe they'd done it before. Must've been hundreds of hours of recordings to comb through, but what the hell. Everybody's got to have a hobby, right?" She gave a weak shrug and finished picking the rest of the crust off half her sandwich, before passing the crustless wedge to Bitsie, like it didn't even occur to her to eat until her kid had food, too. Nash really didn't know *what* to make of her.

Bitsie didn't really seem to *want* the sandwich, but she took a few bites—when your mom's been kidnapped and held hostage for a few days, you humor her and eat the damn sandwich—and got up to put the kettle on. The littlest Red had definitely taken an interest in Nash's tea stash; after the Waystation, Nash had watched her hop up onto the crate-turned-step-stool and spend a solid fifteen minutes opening the cannisters and sniffing, before she'd painstakingly measured out the mix she'd wanted.

It was kind of awesome, actually.

Saint didn't drink anything that didn't come from a tap, a bottle, or a bean, so Nash didn't get a lot of chances to share her collection. Let the kid help herself; to Nash's surprise, she didn't mind sharing.

This time, though, Bitsie grabbed *three* mugs from the cabinet: one for herself, one for her mom, and, with a small smile at Nash over her shoulder, Bitsie pulled one down for her, too.

As Bitsie got the kettle on, Regan continued, "Anyway, fast-forward a few months of late nights, a stronger contacts prescription, and enough coffee to permanently pickle my adrenal glands, and I'd only made it through about a quarter of the files, but I had something.

"I'd found a few other outages—not always equipment failure, like the spiel they gave about the scav site, but an 'accidental' systems purge here, a bad file conversion there. Most of the crew changed a little from one time to the next, but one person was listed as active on every single one of them. Martyn Gethin. Which I know is sort of an anticlimax under the circumstances—was for Drestyn, too, on account of he'd just finished"—she reached over and covered Bitsie's ears with her hands, whispering the rest—"snapping the sadistic fucker's neck with his bare hands."

Bitsie batted her hands away, and Regan let her, continuing after only a quick break for water and a bite of crust. "I looked into the missions a little bit, and I'm sure you'll be shocked to hear the reports all passed muster. Couple of smuggling shutdowns, a warrant for some kind of scav warlord, some peacekeeping ops—pretty much your standard mission fare for a Guild crew. Apart from Jal's bullshit desertion story," she added.

"Which nobody *knew* was bullshit," Jal said pointedly. He gave her and Saint *both* the hairy eyeball on that one. At least, she thought he did; kind of hard to tell with the specs. The effect was kind of ruined anyway, what with Jal trying to play peacekeeper with half a sandwich crammed in his mouth. Nash had forgotten how much the guy could really pack away without stress killing his appetite. Now that he had his sister and nobody'd died in the process, the human garbage disposal made a ravenous comeback. "So it's nobody's fault if they did or didn't believe it, and we're just gonna keep moving right on through to the next part of the story."

Evidently, the *no interruption* rule didn't apply to him. In Regan's defense, three years without hearing your brother's voice probably made it hard to tell him to shut it.

"Well, like I said, the reports were pretty much spotless. But Jal said something at the hearing—something about how they were there to shut down a trafficking ring, but he didn't actually see any signs of trafficking when he went inside. And if they lied about that, then maybe they lied about the others, so I started doing a bit of digging off the normal channels." Which was, in Nash's experience, shorthand for a stroll through the dark web.

Damn, sis, she thought. Had to admire the resourcefulness.

"Wasn't a lot to work with, but that *warlord* . . . op specs made her sound like some kind of mass-murdering insurrectionist, but I found loads of people saying differently. *They* said she hadn't killed anyone. That it was part of her religion or something—not a single casualty on any job she'd ever pulled. Which, correct me if I'm wrong, takes her squarely out of y'all's jurisdiction, doesn't it?" She didn't have as much of an accent as Jal, but it kept sneaking in there when she got going. "*Neutral preservation of human life.* If nobody's dying or headed that direction, it's not your business, right? Otherwise, you're just hired guns like every other mercenary in the spiral."

Saint's jaw twitched, but he managed not to say anything. Maybe because he was trying to behave, but also maybe because she was *right.* The Guild had a code, and that code kept them from advancing any interest but the safety and security of as many lives as possible. They didn't chase thieves, they didn't guard shipments, they didn't come running when the Trust rang its prissy little bell. They were neutral.

At least, they were supposed to be.

"So I'm thinking," Regan went on, "that all those reports I found are just as full of shit as the one for Jal's mission. That if the warlord wasn't a warlord, then maybe the peacekeeping missions weren't to keep the peace, and maybe the smugglers weren't smugglers—at least, not the kind of smugglers you rangers are supposed to care about.

"I mean, think about it. The Guild's got resources that mercenaries don't have, and you can go places the mercenaries can't go with the kind of impunity that mercenaries can't take advantage of. Why *wouldn't* someone want to use that? And I know it'd break your oath, but do you really think someone like Gethin is gonna wring his hands over a broken promise?" She shook her head. "No, I *know* he was up to something shady. I knew it the second I found out about the warlord, and I thought—" Her expression shifted, darkening. With a sigh, she leaned forward, head in her hands and fingers in her hair. "I thought someone else needed to know it, too. I thought it was just Gethin, and I could tell the Captains' Council, and maybe they'd stop sitting around with their thumbs up their asses and actually *do something* about the devil on Fenton's shoulder. Jal deserved that. The Guild *owed him* that.

"So, I took it to the council. Bundled up everything I'd pulled together, put a nice little bow on it, and spammed the shit out of every council terminal on Alpha Librae. Figured one of them had to see it that way." She sighed. "That was probably ten, eleven days ago. Gethin's men came for me less than a week after I sent it, and I guess you know the rest. So, Jal?" She turned toward the counter, where he'd settled in to eat his third sandwich—and sneak pieces of it to Bodie, who'd cozied up on the counter beside him, the stub-tailed mooch. If Jal *did* stick around, they were gonna have to put the damn cat on a diet.

Jal paused mid-bite and, apparently catching on to the seriousness of whatever Regan was about to say, set his plate and sandwich to his other, catless side. "Why're you looking at me like that?"

"Because I know you," she said, voice roughening. She'd held it together this whole time, made it all the way through the meat of it with her composure intact. But here, at the end of it, she started to fray. Something worse than guilt crept into the lines of her face, like spiderweb fractures spreading through glass. "I know what you must've thought when they took me."

Nash didn't need to see Jal's eyes to know he'd averted them; he'd ducked his whole head. Now *there* was a man who couldn't stand to be on the spot. "My fault," he said, mouth barely moving to shape the words. "It was my fault."

"But it *wasn't*," Regan told him, rising from her seat. "That's what I'm trying to tell you, Jal. Gethin came for me because *I* gave his name to the council. Because I'd found something I wasn't supposed to find, and I'd told people I shouldn't have told, and they were afraid of who else I might tell." She stopped in front of him. "I should have told you what I was doing. I thought . . . I thought you needed time to heal. I thought I was *protecting* you, but when they took me—God, Jal, I knew I'd made a mistake. None of this was your fault, you understand? None of it." As she cupped his face between her hands, Nash felt the sudden urge to look away. This felt . . . private. Necessary, like debriding a bad wound, but not something that needed witnesses.

She turned to Bitsie instead. Her eyes had gone watery, sandwich mostly uneaten on her plate, and Nash saw guilt there, too. *This is what you were trying to tell me before, wasn't it?* The secret she hadn't been sure she could tell, while Jal was away on the *Pathfinder.*

Quietly, Nash moved to the table and settled a hand on Bitsie's shoulder. "It's okay," she whispered, squeezing gently. She'd had a secret, and she hadn't known who to tell, and that was okay. It wasn't a twelve-year-old's job to make sense of the world. "Everyone's okay."

As Regan pulled Jal into another hug, Nash gave Bitsie a nudge toward them. Something broken, reassembled—that was the way it was meant to be, Nash thought. Seeing the way Saint looked at the three of them, she guessed he agreed.

"So, it's someone in the Captains' Council," Eoan said, with a certain finality to their voice. A question answered.

Good. They'd danced around it long enough. *If it scurries like a rat, and squeaks like a rat, let's just call it a fucking rat.* "Someone in the Captains' Council who was on Alpha Librae eleven days ago," Nash said. "Timing all lines up. That'd be about a day before Fenton's ship left—plenty of time to rig a malfunction, if they realized they needed to start trimming all the loose ends."

"So, that leaves us five candidates." And look at Saint, getting on board. He wasn't happy about it; every shred of him radiated displeasure. He was Saint, though. Just because something sucked, that didn't stop him doing it. As it had been, so would it ever be. "Three, now, with the bombing, and that's *if* we're counting Brodbeck. Then there's Raimes and—" He glanced over at Eoan.

"Karim," Eoan said. "Saad Karim was the other survivor. If we're to assume Regan's suspicions didn't make it off the satellite, then yes, it would be one of those three."

Fuck, but it almost felt like they had a plan coming together. "My caps are on the asshole that *didn't* get blown up," said Nash, raising a hand, only to wince when Saint cleared his throat. "Not to be insensitive."

"No, because sensitivity's what you're known for," Saint muttered. If he hadn't had a mug of steaming coffee in his hand and a very underqualified dermapoxy patch holding his insides *inside*, Nash would've boxed his ear for that shit. But he did, so she didn't. See? *Sensitivity.* "Considering where we're headed, I'm going to take a wild guess and say Drestyn knows everything you've just told us."

Regan, who'd let go of both her little and her not-so-little loved ones, crossed her arms and nodded. "Just about," she said. "And he also seems to think that whoever's pulling Gethin's leash—whoever *was* pulling his leash," she amended, "had something to do with killing his big brother. Seems to have taken that kind of personally. Which." She glanced over at Jal. "Have to say, I can relate."

"Is that why you told us to let him go?" Eoan asked, tilting their head. Curiosity, pure and simple. Regan was *new*, and Cap loved themself a novelty. "Because you agree with him?"

"Yeah, sis, maybe let's don't side with the screw-loose agitator with murder on the mind," Jal said under his breath, and got an elbow in the ribs from Bitsie for it. Man, Nash loved that little gremlin. Smart like her mom, half-feral like her uncle, and no patience for anybody's bullshit. "Sorry, that wasn't fair."

"Wasn't *un*fair," Regan allowed. "But no, that's not why I told you to let him go. That man . . . there's something *broken* in him, you understand? Deeply, fundamentally broken, and he hides it better than you'd think someone could, acts all reasonable and polite, but what I saw on that ship . . ." She shook her head, scrubbing at her eyes like she wanted to erase something sketched onto the backs of them. Didn't seem to work, though; just squeezed a bit more red into the lurid rainbow of bruises on her cheeks as she raised her head again and said, in a forced-steady voice, "I was afraid if we didn't let him go ahead of us, that he would go *through* us. And I couldn't risk that, not right now."

Not with your family aboard. Nash got it. "Live today, fight tomorrow," she said, and Regan dipped her head in a nod. "And we *are* gonna fight, right? Somebody's gotta do something about this turncoat councilor, or else he's bound to keep coming at us, but I don't think hanging back and letting Drestyn kill the hell out of him's really our style."

"Is warning the councilors off the table?" Jal asked.

Saint took a swallow of coffee and nodded. "We warn any of them, they might accidentally tip off the turncoat."

"Or *be* the turncoat," said Nash.

"Or that," Saint agreed. "But that raises another problem: we don't even know if the horse we're betting on is at the station. Last we saw Raimes, he was hauling ass out of the junk belt."

"Raimes isn't on Alpha Librae?" Regan asked.

Jal shrugged. "Could be where he was headed back to," he

said. "I mean, it'd make sense, right? If he's the guy, his big fireworks show missed half the councilors on the station. Well, didn't *miss* them, but you know what I mean."

Nash translated for him: "He's two for four on his whack-a-councilor scorecard."

Jal shot her a look. "You are not a nice person."

"Yeah, well, that's what we've got you for, miner boy."

"He's got a point, though," Saint said. "If I'm Raimes, and assuming I've got two or three brain cells to rub together, I know I've got two stationary targets at Alpha Librae. I also know those two targets might draw some others." He gestured around at them with his coffee mug. "Look where we're headed right now. Drestyn, too. Raimes has to know we're onto *something*, and he's got to know there's enough breadcrumbs leading back to the Captains' Council that it'd be our next stop."

"All roads lead to Rome," said Eoan. "Does seem appropriate, doesn't it?"

"End where you start." Saint nodded, mouth twisting wryly. "Of course, it means he'll have the home field advantage. We've got to be on everybody's shit list by now—it's gonna make moving around the satellite a hell of a lot harder for us than him. Especially when we aren't one hundred percent on who we're really moving toward. Way I see it, we're in the same boat as Drestyn: don't know who we're gunning for, just know they're probably holed up there."

"Ah." Eoan held up a finger. "We may actually have a *slight* advantage there," they said. "In no small part thanks to Drestyn, in fact. And you, Miss Red, of course." They extended the rest of their fingers on their outstretched hand, and dozens of scanned documents appeared above the galley table. Each twitch of each finger moved a different document to the forefront of the projection, skimming through them so quickly that Jal let out a queasy little groan and looked away.

How's that concussion treating you, big guy? Still no brain bleeds, but that didn't mean he'd escaped a banger of a headache.

Eoan noticed—because Eoan noticed pretty much everything, yeah, but also because there wasn't much subtle about a giant blond miner trying not to cack on the countertop—and slowed the skim to a slightly more reasonable pace. "Ledgers from Yarden's Redweld files," they said. "I've been reindexing the documents since I spoke to Drestyn, trying to isolate the ones that might have anything to do with Kepler. I got the impression that might be the connection our turncoat was worried about."

"Ah, shit." Nash got it now. "You think the Redweld Leak didn't just spill the *Trust's* dirty laundry." If their turncoat councilor was dealing with the Trust under the table, especially out in the frontier, Yarden might've kept some dirt on him, too—something that, with the right intel to pair it with, could be traced back to him.

Jal whistled as the documents kept scrolling. "That's all on Kepler?"

Eoan nodded. "Yarden had a surprising amount of paperwork on it, actually."

"Guessing Yarden missed the *burn after reading* memo," said Regan.

"Oh, I'll bet he got the memo," Saint said. "Probably made sure to print those docs in triplicate. That's where all the *good* blackmail is."

"Quite right," said Eoan. "See this ledger? It's dated just one week after the refinery fire. There's a payment, there, to the Guild."

Nash whistled. "That's a lot of zeroes," she said. "Think it might be time to up our rates."

"Especially if you're charging double." Regan had pushed away from the counter, stepping right up to the end of the table to trace a fingertip along two of the projected documents. Eoan blew them up bigger, just the two of them. "This number, here—I recognize the format. It's basically an invoice number, right? Ties the Trust's payment for a contract to the mission file." She glanced over at Eoan. "I'm gonna go out on a limb and say this one lines up with the Kepler mission?"

"And the limb would hold," said Eoan. "Officially, it's listed as a peacekeeping mission. Riot control and recovery after the refinery fire, only to hear Drestyn tell it, the Guild forces arrived *before* the fire. Another one of your mismatched reports," they said.

"I never made it back that far," Regan replied. "But it seems to fit."

"Wait, though," said Bitsie, coming up to join her mom at the table. "If this one is the payment to the Guild, then what's this one over here?" She pointed to the second ledger. To Nash's eyes, they looked almost identical. Same price tag. Same format. The only difference she could see was a single string of numbers, in the same place the Guild's invoice number would've been.

Eoan smiled. They had a lot of smiles, Eoan did; this wasn't one of the happier ones. "That's the question, isn't it?" A flick of their hand, and dozens more documents surged up from the table to join those two. Each in pairs. Each almost identical. "It looked like an accounting error at first," Eoan said. "Some kind of duplicate payment, or one of the Trust's tricks to keep the auditors occupied during tax season. But there's dozens of them," they said. "All exactly the same: one payment under the Guild file number, one payment under a different number. Not the same number across all of them, unfortunately; could make it more difficult to trace the number back to any one recipient, especially if they're only shell accounts.

"Nevertheless, I could give it a whirl. Always wanted to

try forensic accounting. Seems like fun." And there, Eoan's smile curled a shade higher. "How's the saying go? *Follow the money.*"

Saint's mug *clink*ed down on the table, chair creaking as he leaned back in it. "Fuck," he swore, and his hands only half-muffled it as he scrubbed them down his face. "That's what this is, isn't it? All of it—just another backroom deal with the Trust. They've got *rangers* doing their dirty business like a bunch of privateers."

"That's what it looks like," Eoan said, not unsympathetically. It sucked for them, and it sucked for Nash, realizing that something like this could've been going on under their noses the whole time. They liked the Guild and what it stood for—what it was *supposed* to stand for—and they hated the thought of all that getting twisted into another way for the Trust to screw people over.

But Saint? For Saint, it was worse. He didn't just *like* what the Guild stood for; he *believed* in it. He'd taken the mission and folded it into himself like the flag on his shelf in its little glass case, because that was what he did. That was how he lived: defining himself by the causes he served. The cause was him, and he was it, and over the years, she and Eoan had gotten so much closer to helping him untangle the two, but he wasn't there yet.

Nash didn't know what to say to him. Eoan didn't seem to, either, smile long gone and replaced with something strained.

Jal, though. Jal, that fucking sunbeam personified—he pushed off the counter, marched right up Saint, and said, "Fuck 'em." Never mind Bitsie and her mom and whatever vows of good behavior he'd taken, he put his hands on Saint's shoulders, he looked him in the eyes, and he told him in no uncertain terms, "Fuck 'em for what they're doing, and fuck 'em for thinking they can get away with it, because it stops now. *We* stop it, right fucking now."

Nash didn't think Jal cared about the oath, and she didn't think he cared about the caps or the conspiracy or the goddamn principle of the thing. At the end of the day, Jal cared about people. He *only* cared about people, to the exclusion of everything else, and whichever councilor was behind this, he'd hurt Jal's people.

That was a big fucking mistake.

A heavy, poignant silence settled into the seconds. A beat. A breath. But then, Saint brought a hand up to cover one of Jal's, nodding firmly. "We stop it," he said, and she could hear in his voice that he meant it. That he *believed* it, if only for all their sakes.

Nash decided, then and there, that Jal would always have a place with them on that ship.

"I'll start the trace," said Eoan, with audible relief. Some puzzles even *they* couldn't solve, but they had one they could. "Regan, if you happen to remember any of those files you found—"

"I remember all of them," said Regan. "I've got copies of every comms file in the archives with Gethin's name on it backed up to my vault drive; I can give you access. I'm assuming you don't want to link up to any Guild networks if you can help it."

"Frankly, I'm not sure I could if I wanted to—not without some inside help, and I'd rather not bring Brodbeck into this if we can help it. Without him. . . ." Eoan gave their version of a shrug, which was really just a wrinkle in their shawl and a faint air of annoyance. "I expect by now they've blocked all of our access to Guild systems."

"Guild tends to frown upon nicking prisoners," Nash supplied, by way of explanation. "Especially out from under the Union's nose in the middle of one of the Union's main bases."

That got an eyebrow tick, but Regan seemed to understand it was a story for another time. "Well, between your ship's archives and mine, we should be able to make do," Regan said, and she was probably right. Perks of having an AI captain and a metric *fuck-load* of digital storage space: Eoan backed just about everything worth having up to their own local drives. "And if there's anything I can do to help you nail this bloodsucking shit louse, Captain, it would be my genuine pleasure."

Nash raised a hand. "So, just to clarify, we *are* swearing in front of the kid now?"

Bitsie snorted. "You never *stopped*."

"Touché." Bitsie was probably about half a decade shy of recruitment age, but she was another Red who Nash wouldn't mind hanging out with again sometime, if they didn't all die screaming and bullet-riddled. Nash had been so . . . guarded, back on Alpha Librae. All those months, when she wasn't on Drestyn babysitting detail, she'd holed up in her engine room and buried herself in machine parts and hand tools, and she *knew* why. She was self-aware enough for that, at least, even if she wasn't always self-possessed enough to do anything about it.

She'd let someone in, with Anke. Someone new, someone different, someone interesting—she'd taken a chance and let herself get close, and she'd been burned so spectacularly that she still felt the sting of it. Every time she saw that damn lavender plant, still growing steadily in one of the guest bunks; or saw the mug Anke had favored in the cabinet; or thought, even for one second, about *trying one more time*, it burned all over again, and it wasn't a pain she knew how to deal with. It wasn't a callus she'd ever had to have.

Then along came this knobby-kneed little *kid*. Her whole life had just been upended, and she had all the reasons in the world to close herself off to everything and everybody, and she just . . . *hadn't*. She'd looked at Nash—foul-mouthed, caustic, unapproachable Nash—and she'd decided *that's someone I want to trust.* Someone she wanted to pay attention to, and learn from, and reach out to, even when she couldn't reach out to her own uncle.

Maybe Nash could stand to take a page out of her book.

She cleared her throat, flashing Bitsie a smile. "So, we've got a plan, then?" she asked. "I mean, like, *our* version of a plan." Half-cocked, half-assed, and half-put-together, but if it had even half a chance of working, then it worked for her.

Eoan nodded. "We're full burn to Alpha Librae," they said. "Gives us a little under twelve hours in transit, which gives Regan and me some time to see about narrowing our targets. If we can, excellent."

"If we can't," Saint joined in, "then there's three councilors and three of us. We'll make it work. *But*—we gotta land first. By now, word's got to have made it back to the Guild about Drestyn and what we did on the Waystation, so I'd say it's safe to assume we're not headed for a friendly welcome."

"Guessing the Guild's not gonna fall for that *aid ship* trick we pulled on Lummis," said Jal.

Nash shook her head. "Paint's gone to shit from the junk belt anyway. Couldn't pull it off if we wanted to."

"So like as not, they'll have guns on us the second we clear the air lock," Saint continued, unperturbed. The man had a mission again; long as he had that, he'd be fine. They'd worry about what came after, *after.* "And that's if they even let us *through* the air lock. Can't do much about the councilors if we're stuck in orbit."

He made a good point. The *Ambit* was pretty damn recognizable, and they probably weren't *anybody's* favorite people right about then. Jailbreaking a would-be mass murderer tended to have that effect on people.

"We need a way in on the down-low," she said, mulling it over. "Something the Guild won't shoot on sight. Ideally something they won't even know is us." And she'd no sooner said it than the answer came to her. Wouldn't be an easy sell, but these were her people. If they didn't have faith in her, who would? "You know, actually? I think I might have an idea."

CHAPTER EIGHTEEN

EOAN

Rangers swarmed the *Ambit* the moment it docked on Alpha Librae.

"Well, this is a fun development," said Regan, glancing up from the holotable just long enough for a quick head count through the view port. She actually had—reluctantly—gotten a few hours of sleep after she'd given Eoan access to her vault drive, but she'd since settled into the bridge to help Eoan with their little research project. Quite the dab hand at it, it turned out. Probably all the practice. "Thirteen rangers and a purple-haired warrior queen. You guys must've really gotten on somebody's naughty list."

"They're on *everybody's* naughty list," Bitsie said. With the others otherwise occupied, she'd joined her mother in the bridge, frowning at the rangers from the console. "For the good guys, you make an awful lot of people mad."

True enough. They'd given the Trust a proper poke in the eye with the Deadworld Code, and their budding careers as jail-breakers probably hadn't won them any favor with the Union *or* the Guild—even the parts of it the councilor's conspiracy *hadn't* touched. If there really was a triumvirate, like Drestyn said, Eoan imagined they'd pissed off every part of it.

Never let it be said they weren't thorough.

"*How* sure are we they're not just gonna blow us up?" asked Bitsie. "Because they look like they want to just blow us up."

"They're supposed to look that way, dear," Eoan told her,

projection smiling down from next to Bitsie at the console. They probably wouldn't keep it running much longer; too many other demands on their attention, and there'd soon be even more. For now, though, Bitsie seemed to like having someone to look at when she talked. A small comfort, but a comfort nonetheless. "They don't want anyone leaving this ship without their say-so, and they want us to know it."

It was what they'd been afraid of: surrounded the moment they landed, welcomed as enemies in their very own home. "But we still have friends here."

"Friends don't usually greet friends with a firing squad," Regan pointed out, without looking up from the audio wave visualization she'd brought up on the holotable. Fascinating to watch her work, actually; the methodical way she dissected the sounds, like threads from a weave, but with a nuance Eoan hadn't managed to replicate. Science and art. Engineer and virtuoso. Eoan could see why her family admired her so.

"Fair," Eoan said. "But our conspirators have gone to an awful lot of trouble to hide what they're doing; they wouldn't bother if they didn't have people left to hide it from. Take us, for example. Take *her*," they added, with a tip of their head toward the *purple-haired warrior queen* making her way through the rangers. She came right up to the back hatch of the *Ambit*, the only one in the bunch without a gun in her hand or a scowl on her face.

"Captain?" Casale called, voice a shade hoarser than Eoan remembered—a parting gift from Nash, they expected. A fair trade for the bruises on Nash's ribs. "Can you hear me?"

Wasn't often they got to use the ship's external projectors, but this seemed as good a time as any. A few of the rangers startled when Eoan's projection appeared just a few steps to Casale's side, but Casale didn't so much as blink.

"Believe it or not, Casale," Eoan said, by way of greeting, "it's actually very good to see you." Even if they did still have friends among the Guild, it would be hard to know who they were until they'd worked out which councilor had it out for them. Raimes didn't have much of a following, as far as they knew; but someone like Karim, who'd been a well-regarded member of the council for the better part of three decades, would've had a much wider reach. No way to know how far the rot had spread until they knew its source.

Casale, though—she and her people had a vested interest in getting Drestyn back to the Union, and as the saying went, *the enemy of my enemy. . . .*

"I expect you're here for Drestyn?" they said. Even if Torsten *hadn't* made good on his offer to lure Casale off the *Ambit*'s trail, it made sense that she'd double back to Alpha Librae. They'd made sure she couldn't follow them, so she'd had to *find* them. With or without Torsten's interference, where better to start than the nerve center of the Guild?

Casale gave a stiff nod. Definitely a sore neck, and Eoan could just make out the colored blooms of bruises faintly ringing her throat. Nash wasn't the type to relish something like that, but a small, petty part of Eoan would relish it for her. "If you have him, give him to me. I'll put in a good word with your people."

"I'm afraid we're quite beyond that," Eoan said. Good words, bad words . . . they wouldn't make a difference now. "And we don't have him anyway. We haven't for a while." They studied Casale's face for her reaction, but one never really came. "You don't look surprised."

"Something stinks here." Casale's nose wrinkled. "You? You don't stink."

"That's . . . encouraging."

Casale shrugged and jabbed a thumb over her mountainous shoulder. "Not so encouraging," she said. "They're still going to arrest your crew."

"I expect that's why they're here, yes."

"You expect." Casale nodded again, as if she'd just answered a question for herself. As was so often the way, one answered seemed to lead to another one asked. "So why did you land?"

"They were getting quite insistent about it," said Eoan.

"So leave."

"I can't do that."

"If you wanted to protect your crew, you would have left," Casale replied. "Not brought them here to be arrested. Either you're a shit captain, or." Casale lowered her voice, nearly to the limits of what the *Ambit*'s external mics could pick up, and concluded: "Or your crew isn't here." And if Eoan could hardly hear her, they expected none of the rangers could.

Encouraging indeed. It would've been just as simple for Casale to share her theory with the others; might've even earned some grace with the Guild. Perhaps she had her own motives for keeping it to herself, or perhaps they really *did* have friends on Alpha Librae. It hardly mattered, either way. Friends or no, allies or enemies, Eoan's crew would do what they always did: what needed to be done.

And they'd already gotten started.

A slow smile spread over Casale's face. "No," she said, still so soft it could hardly be called a whisper. "Not a shit captain at all. You're the *distraction*." Eoan didn't bother denying it. No need to now; they'd gotten what they wanted. "Where's your crew, Captain?"

"Now, Casale," Eoan said, with a slow grin of their own, "what kind of distraction would I be if I told you that?"

NASH

Exactly five minutes before the *Ambit* docked on Alpha Librae, the *Valorous Starship Shuttle Number Three* had touched down on an emergency landing permit. Perseus gave a hell of a performance about faulty propulsion and a duct-taped oxygen stack, and port security had been so tied up with the fugitive Guild ship that'd just entered their airspace that they'd pretty much just waved the shuttle on through.

"Sounds like the jig is up," Perseus chimed over the comms as Nash, Jal, and Saint made their way into the concourse. Eoan hadn't been thrilled to patch him into their network, but Nash had held her ground. *I'm not asking you to believe in him; I'm asking you to believe in me.* After Anke, she'd spent so long questioning her own judgment, but not anymore. Not with her friends' lives on the line. She trusted Perseus to help them, not just because he'd yanked their asses out of the fire twice now, but because she trusted *herself* enough to make that call. So, dammit, she stood by it. And to her relief, her friends stood by *her.* They'd gone along with her plan, and so far? So good.

"Ah, well," said Perseus. "It was fun while it lasted. Very exciting stuff. Do you do this sort of thing often?" He sounded delighted by the prospect.

Nash wished she could share the enthusiasm. "There's usually more shooting," she said, aiming a glance back at Saint. He walked in the middle of their trio, and Jal brought up the rear, hovering his preferred half step behind Saint's bad shoulder. "But stay tuned. I get the feeling that was the *easy* part."

That feeling had been with her since they first dreamed up their half-baked little shell game. Board the shuttle outside Alpha Librae airspace, follow the *Ambit* in at a distance, and let Eoan hog all port security's attention for as long as they could manage before they had to dock or risk getting gunned down. *No pressing our luck,* they'd all agreed. Not with Bitsie and Regan aboard. All they needed was enough of a distraction to get them through the proverbial door; the rest was just bonus.

It'd been a long shot from the jump: the kind of plan you come up with when you're fresh out of *actual* plans. She should've been elated they'd even gotten that banged-up old shuttle to fly—with less than twelve hours to work and only

her own scrap stash to use for parts, they damn near hadn't—
never mind that they'd managed to land, debark, and make
it halfway to their respective targets. That was some god-tier
good luck.

For all that, she still couldn't shake that damn *feeling*—a
gnawing, cancerous unease spreading under her skin. It tasted
like rot and cortisol on the back of her tongue, buzzed in her
molars, crawled on prickly legs across her nerve endings. It
grew, and grew, and kept growing with every step she took,
until it stopped being a feeling at all, and sprouted a whole
goddamn thought.

This one's gonna cost us.

It already had. Bruised ribs and bumped heads and bullet
holes. Whole days with little to no sleep and whole years' worth
of belief systems cracked open and scrambled like eggs on a hot
plate. They'd sweated and bled and cried, lost each other and
found each other and *fixed* each other. They'd been pushed to
their limits and then some.

And now this? Unknown enemies in unknown numbers,
their misfit crew of screwups and strays against the whole fucking *spiral*—at their sparkling best, it would've been the hardest
job they'd ever pulled. Like this, she didn't know what it was,
but she knew it wouldn't be pretty.

She also knew they didn't have a choice.

"All right, gents, let's get this show on the road. Miner boy,
we're coming up on your exit." Three of them, and three targets to secure: Karim in the sick bay, Brodbeck in his quarters,
and the server room to get Eoan access to the satellite's systems.
They needed their eye in the sky. And the halls. And pretty much
everywhere else Eoan could slip their sneaky little digits without
getting shut the hell out. "Think you can remember your way
around?" All the time he'd spent cooped up in there, she'd have
hoped so.

He cocked a wry grin and shifted his specs on his nose. Apart from the adversarial patches on his coat, he didn't look like a man about to head on a mission. Didn't suit up like Saint, with his gun belt and his brace; didn't load up like Nash, with her pack full of goodies and her Very Serious Pigtails. He was every tool he needed, wrapped up in a stolen blue coat and a sweet pair of shades, and somehow, in spite of the goofiness and the guilelessness and the general goddamn *goodness* of him, she trusted him to get the job done.

"Oh, I think I'll manage, glowworm," he said. "Just let me know when Cap's in the system, and me and ol' Karim'll have ourselves a nice little chat. Assuming nobody's tried killing him yet."

"And assuming he doesn't try killing *you*," Saint said gruffly. "Remember, kid—until we know for sure that Raimes is the shot-caller, you treat Karim like it's him. Keep him alive if someone comes gunning for him, but don't turn your back on him. For all we know, they could all be in on it."

Nash whistled low, weaving through a cluster of passersby as the three of them neared the MEDICAL PLAZA sign looming overhead. "Damn, McBlastinshit. Really leaning into the conspiracy angle now, aren't you? Didn't know you had it in you."

"Just don't want anybody getting a knife in the back when they're not watching it." *Or when I'm not around to watch it for them.* He didn't say it, but she knew he was thinking it. Shit, they were *all* thinking it. Splitting up hadn't exactly been their power move lately. "Just be careful," Saint told him. "We passed Gethin's ship in the docks on the way in, so we know Drestyn's lurking around here somewhere. Raimes, too, probably, and a fuck-ton of Guild security that's not gonna want us anywhere near the councilors. If something doesn't feel right—"

"None of this feels right," said Jal, as they came to the split. "But we do what we gotta do, right? We'll be fine." If he didn't believe every word he said, then it was the best lie he'd ever told them. Maybe he *had* to believe it. Had to just put his head down and keep planting one foot in front of the other, because you didn't survive the things he'd survived by stopping to *think*. He just kept moving.

Whatever it takes. "Hey, miner boy?"

He'd already started down the hall, but he turned on his heel to look at her without breaking stride. "Hey, glowworm," he shot back.

"Don't get caught," she said.

"Don't get dead," he replied.

She flicked him a salute, and he flicked one right back, and as he turned and faded into the crowd of passersby, she told herself it wasn't goodbye.

"He'll be fine," Saint told her, like he could hear her thoughts just as clearly as she could hear his. "Kid's a survivor." He fell in beside her, all straight-backed and stalwart, and she could almost pretend this was like any other mission. Them against the world, bring it the fuck on.

Almost.

"What about you?" she asked. She had a little while longer with him, before she had to split for the servers, and he had to split for the council's quarters. A minute, maybe less at the pace they'd set. *Not enough time.* Bar the doc, Nash had never known another human being as long as she'd known Saint, and it *still* didn't feel like long enough. "Are you gonna be fine?"

No, whispered that gnawing, festering feeling. Its teeth got sharper with every step. She could see it—the thin sheen of sweat on his brow, the hitch in his gait. Pain didn't care how tough you were or how deep you shoved it down; it always found a way to make its presence known.

"I will," he said, eyes fixed firmly forward and mouth fixed firmly flat. *Atten-hut, soldier!* That expression was as much a uniform as the gun on his hip. "I have to be."

She shouldn't have been surprised. She *wasn't* surprised, because this was Saint, and Saint was *always* fine, even when he wasn't. No, she was *angry*, suddenly and violently. It licked hotly up the back of her throat as she reached up to mute her mic and did the same to his. This had been a long time coming, and she didn't know if she'd get another chance. "You're a fucking idiot, Florence Toussaint," she said. "And if you die, I will *never* forgive you."

For a moment, the uniform slipped. The soldier gave way to her best friend—her *first* friend, after she'd lost the doc and lost her way. The guy who picked at his guitar when he was thinking, and always insisted the best cure for a bad mission was a big pot of stew and a dinner around the galley table. He'd always had her back, and he'd never shied away from all her sharp edges, and after years of butting heads and rubbing elbows and living in each other's pockets all the time, she didn't know what she'd do without him.

"I'll sure as shit try not to," he said, aiming for a smile and missing the mark.

"I don't believe that."

His sorry excuse for a smile fell. "Nash . . ."

"No," she said. "We don't have long, and if I don't say this now, I might not get a chance. You've been looking for a way to die for as long as I've known you, and me and Eoan—we've done our level best to stop you finding it. I've patched you up more times than I've fixed our damn ship, and I'm glad to do it, Saint. I am. I'm glad to put you together again as many times as it takes, because you're my best fucking friend, and I love you. *I love you*, you stubborn jackass. And I'm *scared*." She grasped for the anger, for all its soothing heat, but she couldn't find it. It'd burned itself out and left her with nothing but cold. "I'm scared that this time I'm not going to be able to fix you. That you're finally going to find what you've been looking for all this time, and there's gonna be nothing me or Cap or Jal can do to stop it. It'll be down to you. Your choice. And I'm *terrified*, okay? Because I don't know what you'll choose."

She'd nearly lost him twice already: the first time on No-ether, and the second on that damn ring ship. Even the unkill-able Ranger Toussaint had to run out of lives eventually.

Saint opened his mouth, but nothing came out. Pain creased the corners of his eyes—from the gunshot, and the bruises, and the pure abominable punishment he'd put his body through the last few days, yeah. But a different kind of pain, too. The pain of wanting to argue and knowing you couldn't. They didn't lie to each other.

It was Eoan's voice that broke the stalemate. "Nash? Saint? I'm not reading you on comms."

Time's up. Wasn't just Eoan: they'd nearly reached their crossroads, her and Saint. Up at the intersection ahead, a few storefronts down the walkway, she'd go right, toward a mainte-nance access point, and he'd go left, toward the lower branches of the residential sector, where the members of the Captains' Council hung their hats when they were on station.

She swallowed hard, clearing the lump in her throat. "As your friend, it's not my job to tell you what to do. That's never been our thing, and I'm not gonna start now. As your doctor, though, it *is* my job to tell you this is fifty flavors of bad idea. Brodbeck's security's gonna shoot first, and maybe skip the questions altogether. And they might not be your only com-pany."

Drestyn was gunning for one of the councilors, and since they only had a firm bead on two of them, she split their odds fifty-fifty between Karim and Brodbeck. Never mind what-ever Raimes the Sketch-Ass Cowboy was getting up to. Unlike Gethin's ship, Raimes's rockhopper hadn't been in the main port, but Alpha Librae had enough secondary and tertiary docks scattered around that Nash was still betting they'd find him skulking around on the station somewhere. All in all, she'd put their straits at *pretty fucking dire*, even without Saint's internal organs springing a leak. Which was not, unfortunately, outside the realm of possibility.

"So I'm gonna say this again," she told Saint sharply, "and you're gonna hear me through whatever Manly Martyr Medley you got playing on loop in your brain: that patch job on your side's the only thing holding it together, and it's not made for this. You get hit in the wrong place, you move the wrong way, you push yourself too hard, that dermapoxy's gonna split, and you're gonna start bleeding just as bad as before. Maybe worse. And if I can't get to you in time, if I can't stop the bleeding . . . Saint, you *will* die."

"I know," Saint said. "But—"

"There's not a *but* here."

He gave her one anyway. "But you cleared me with Cap," he finished. It wasn't an accusation, but a question. *Why?*

She slowed as they reached the intersection, twisting around to pull him into a clumsy, crooked hug. She wasn't any good at them, but he was. He wrapped his arms around her and tucked his chin on her shoulder, and she stood up on her toes to tell him the truth she couldn't tell him to his face:

"Because the only thing that would kill you faster than letting you come with us is making you stay behind." Her eyes burned as she leaned back, but she managed a smile. Probably wasn't any better than the one he'd given her before, but he returned that, too. "Go kick some ass, McBlastinshit."

He kissed her head and gave her one last squeeze before he let her go. "Go give 'em hell." And as they parted ways in the concourse, she told herself *that* wasn't a goodbye, either.

A quick tap on her earpiece, and Nash's mic went live again. "Sorry," she said. She didn't bother with an actual excuse; Eoan would've seen through any she gave, and she tried not to bullshit the captain any more than she bullshitted Saint. "We're back, and I'm at the maintenance access." Just a plain-ass door in a plain-ass nook, but to hear Regan tell it, that'd be her gateway to the promised land.

As if on cue, Regan spoke up over the comms. "Lock's keyed to maintenance ID badges, but you should be able to—" She must've been watching the bodycam feeds, because she paused as Nash pulled her plasma torch from her pocket and made about three seconds' work of the lock. "—scorch the everloving shit out of it," she concluded neatly. "Oh, I'm gonna have to get one of those."

Nash wouldn't say she felt *better* as she tucked the torch away, but she definitely felt a little more herself. "And they say diamonds are a girl's best friend." A nudge, and the maintenance door swung open to the inner workings of the satellite. Like night and day, going from the *sanitized for your consumption* painted walls of the hallway to the bare metal and pipes of the maintenance corridors, but for Nash? Give her the guts any day. "All right, Red One," she said to Regan, "tell me where the hell I'm going."

JAL

The medical plaza itself wasn't that tricky to get into. Plenty of people coming and going, and the Guild didn't have the people power to lock the *whole* place down. He'd made it into the main lobby—which was about as cozy a place as it could be and still let them hose it down with disinfectants every other day—without anyone so much as asking his name, and posted himself up by one of the vending machines to wait for his cue.

"*Red One?*" he said as he deliberated over the candy bars. Not a lot of health food for a sick bay vending machine, but he guessed anybody spending too much time in that lobby, with its *three* separate waiting rooms circling the round check-in desk, probably had bigger problems than the snack selection. He tried to imagine Regan and Bitsie waiting in some of those plasticky seats while the docs took a second crack at fixing his leg, but it just reminded him again how hard those months together had been, no matter how happy they'd been to have each other back. The snacks were less depressing. "Now hold up, glowworm. How come I get *miner boy*, and she gets *Red One*?"

"Because she's cooler," Nash replied ruthlessly. "And because you call me *glowworm*."

"Your hair glows, and I know, like, *three* bioluminescent animals. You wanna be *jellyfish*? You can be jellyfish. Hey, jellyfish."

"Hard pass," said Nash.

"*Glowworm* it is then." He cast a glance around the room and caught a few more eyes than the last time he'd done it. "Hey, gonna need y'all to speed things up on your end. I stand here a few more minutes, somebody's gonna start thinking I wandered out of a ward."

"We're almost there," Nash said. "Just another minute or two. Try to blend in."

"Sister, I'm about a head taller than everybody here, wearing shades inside and looming by the snack machines like I ain't ever seen a candy bar in my goddamn life. Think we're *past* blending in." He needed to keep by the machines. The machines split the difference between the doors to A Ward and B Ward, and judging by the handful of officers posted outside B Ward, he was willing to bet that was where he'd find Karim. *Burn unit's a hell of a place for a bad guy,* Jal thought. If Karim had set that bomb, either he'd done a piss-poor job, or he'd *really* wanted to sell it.

Nash scoffed down the line, with a creak of what sounded like old hinges and a grunt of effort. "Hey, remember when you didn't talk much? That was nice. Let's"—another grunt—"go back to that, huh? Or maybe you want to be the one cramming your giant-ass body into this tiny-ass ventilation shaft."

"You'd have to squeeze him out like toothpaste," Saint muttered, and Jal laughed before he could stop himself.

A couple of the guys by the B Ward door turned and looked at him, and he mustered his best *don't mind me* smile and went back to the vending machine. "Did I say a few minutes?" he whispered under his breath. "Let's say seconds. Seconds feels better."

"I'm shimmying as fast as I can," Nash hissed. More banging echoed under her voice, rhythmic like steps, but with an extra pair. Knees and elbows. "They don't exactly make these things easy to break into, you know. *Fuck*, it's cold in here. Gonna freeze to the walls."

"Lick one, I dare you," Jal said.

Nash's teeth had started chattering. Server rooms were cold; the cooling systems *for* the server rooms were *frigid*. "Regan, how do you feel about being an only child?"

Jal half-expected the joke to land badly, given the givens, but Regan laughed. God, it was good to hear her laughing. Even if it was just about his future murder at the frostbitten hands of one very pissed off Nashsicle. "You're almost there, I promise. Good news is, the cold kept screwing with the sensors they tried to put in the vents, so as long as you don't trip anything *inside* the server room, nothing should pick you up. You see that grate up ahead?"

"I see it," said Nash. "That the server room?"

"That's it. Grate's reinforced; it'd take your plasma torch to get through it, and I'm pretty sure that'd trip something inside. But you said you had something small enough to fit through there?"

"With room to spare," Nash replied, with an audible grin and an even *more* audible shiver. Good old Chiclet Junior. Jal didn't really get tech, but he was starting to appreciate Nash's knack for it—especially when, after no more than a handful of seconds, Nash said, "Junior's in position. Cap, you got a signal?"

"I believe so," said Eoan. "Jal, dear, are you ready?"

Jal reached up and took hold of his specs. "Whenever you are."

"Go in three, two, one." At the bottom of Eoan's three-count, the whole lobby went dark. Damn near pitch black, save the emergency exit lights—not near enough for anybody in the lobby to see by, but plenty for Jal. He yanked his specs down around his neck, and he'd never seen clearer. He could make out every detail of the doorway guards as they squinted around. A couple of geniuses were already reaching for a flashlight or a GLASS, but genius or not, the dark did things to normies. Reached into the deep, animal parts of their brain and said *danger, panic, run*. Throw in a loud sound—a shove to topple the vending machine, and another to get the one beside it—and even the smart ones lost their shit a little. They startled apart, a few jolting toward the sound and the others jolting away, and in the seconds it took them to unclench their assholes and scrounge up their wits, Jal'd already bolted through the gap.

"I got a fuck-ton of doors here, Cap." And a fuck-ton of people in the hall, only about a handful of whom actually seemed to know what to do. See, killing the lights wasn't just about the *dark*; it was about the confusion. Sure, yeah, they could pull out a GLASS or squint up at the exit signs, but that didn't stop them wondering why the hell the lights went out and how the hell to get them back on, and while they were busy wondering about all that, they *weren't* busy wondering about the stranger weaving through the halls. It was as good an advantage as surprise.

Unfortunately, it didn't last much longer.

"Shit," he hissed as he clocked a couple more uniforms heading his direction down the hall. They had that cantering sort of jog and their heads on a swivel, like they knew something was up, just didn't know the *what* or *where* of it. "Where am I going, Cap?"

"The door on your right," they said, and he didn't ask questions. They said right, he went right, and found himself in what looked to be a supply closet with a real confused-looking cleaner in the middle of straining for a bottle of something on the top shelf.

He held up a finger to his lips, peeking up through the glass window on the door to watch the uniforms go past. With the guys in the lobby, that made *nine* warm bodies in B Ward. *Don't get caught.* Nash's sign-off was sounding like better and better advice. *Just keep walking, fellas. Just keep walking.* He held his breath as their shapes passed beyond the door, and a few seconds more for good measure.

"You're clear for now," said Eoan. "But go quickly."

Quickly. Right. Seemed to be the order of the day. He mouthed a *thank you* to his closet companion—and, as an afterthought, swiped the bottle of cleaner she'd been reaching for off the shelf and set it on her cart—before ducking back out into the hallway.

"Guessing there's more where they came from?" he asked, voice low and taut. Blackout infils were sort of his specialty, but this one was weird. So many *civilians*, and he didn't know whether to avoid them or walk right past them. Didn't know which might be plainclothes security, and which might be nurses and doctors on their way to do something important, and which might be visitors on their way to *see* someone important. He picked up the pace—not quite a jog, but headed that direction, as he scanned the hall ahead. *Cap's got eyes*, he reminded himself as he neared the intersection by the nurse's station. *Something I need to know, they'll tell me.* But that was strange, too. Giving himself over to somebody like that, trusting they'd steer him right . . . it was good, knowing he could;

but mother of God, it was hard. Every step felt like he was back on that Noether rooftop, headed for an edge he couldn't avoid.

Eoan had his back, though. "Incoming on your left," they told him, just in time for him to turn and face the other way. No closets to duck into this time; he felt exposed, counting down the seconds as the footsteps approached. "Hold," Eoan said, and at the very edges of his periphery he saw two more uniforms. Place was swarming with them—had to be every ranger on the station, split between that welcome party at the docks and the two councilors. They were getting closer. Only a few steps now. Any closer, he wouldn't have near enough of a head start to get clear. "They won't make you, Jal. Just hold your position." Leaning against the corner, hands in his pockets, trying to look casual with his heart beating out of his chest. No engagement; those were the parameters. That was what Saint said, and Jal *wanted* to do what he said, not just because of the double-digit Guild security that'd run his ass down at the first sign of trouble, but because this was how it was supposed to be. This was a *team*. A crew. A family. Jal hadn't been a real, functional part of one since before he'd left for that scav site mission, but he wanted so badly to try.

So he held. Held, and breathed, and willed his heart to stop beating so loud as the footsteps drew closer and the officers passed not two arms' length from him. Yeah, all right, maybe killing the lights *was* a little bit about the darkness. Outside the beam of their flashlights, he was just another shadow.

They passed him.

"Good," said Eoan. "You're clear for now. Head down the hall they just came from, and Karim's door will be halfway down on your right."

"Any signs of Drestyn or Raimes?" he asked.

"Not in the medical plaza," they replied, "but I'm running a search of the satellite as we speak."

Jal swore. "Means they're probably headed your way, old man." And so was Jal, just as soon as he got Karim squared away. "Anything else up ahead, Cap?"

"Should only be two more officers to contend with, right outside Karim's door, and a doctor inside. Not sure you're going to be able to slip past these two undetected."

"Think you can handle a two-man takedown before they can call for the others?" Saint asked, like he hadn't taught Jal how to do it himself, back when Jal was still a greenhorn recruit.

He shook off the nerves—actually *shook*, because it helped, and Nash wasn't there to give him grief for shaking himself out like a wet dog. "I'm rusty, but I ain't that rusty," he said. "Though if you've got any other tricks up your sleeve, Cap, I wouldn't mind a couple extra seconds."

"Couple extra seconds, coming right up." Down at the very end of the hallway, some kind of alarm bleated out from one of the rooms. Sounded like a monitor alert, high and shrill, but he didn't have time to investigate. Couple extra seconds, Eoan promised, and that was what he got, as the guards instinctively turned toward the sound. Meant they didn't see him coming until he had them both by their collars, and under different circumstances he'd have liked to be gentler than cracking both their heads together like a pair of unripe melons, but he knew his strength. Knew how hard he could go before he did any lasting damage, which was fortunately at least a little bit harder than it took to knock them out.

"Sorry," Jal told them, as he dragged their limp-sack bodies through the appointed door. Not that they were awake to hear it, but it made *him* feel better. "But hey, where better to get a concussion than in a sick bay, am I—wait." He'd just cleared the door, and that was when he caught sight of the doctor Eoan had warned him about. Big son of a bitch, and even with his face half-hidden by a surgical mask, he had something kind of familiar about him. The eyes, Jal thought, dark and half-buried under a brow that made Saint's look downright gentle. "Don't I know you?"

Apparently so. He just barely had time to duck before the knife he hadn't seen the guy draw buried itself in the wall behind his head. Somehow that was what did it; turned out dodging projectiles made for a hell of a context clue.

"You're Gethin's man." Gethin's second-in-command, from the *Pathfinder*—the asshole who'd nearly blown him and Saint to smithereens. Guy about split the seams on his scrubs, hunched over the far side of Karim's bed with a needle in his hand. *Bettin' that's not an antibiotic.* "The fuck is that?" Karim didn't stir, even as the Second grabbed his IV line. Dead to the world, save the beeps of the monitors and the twitch of his eyes behind their lids. "Hey! Get away from him!" The Second didn't listen, though, just stuck the tip of the needle into Karim's IV and started on the plunger.

Well, fine, then. Time for a fucking rematch.

CHAPTER NINETEEN

JAL

"The hell's going on?" Saint's voice boomed down the comms as Jal vaulted over Karim's bed and slammed the Second into the far wall of the room. Felt like running headlong into a stack of bricks. "Kid, you okay?"

Good question. Jal got a second to find his feet as the Second recovered, but he spent them on Karim's IV instead. Yanked it from his hand, tape and all. He had no idea if it'd help, or if he'd gotten it too late, but he had to try.

The effort cost him a kick to the chest from the Second that knocked him backward over the bed again, ass over teakettle. Fuck, the guy was strong. Strong enough to give Jal a run for his money, and significantly better armed. By the time Jal'd rolled back up to his feet on the other side of the bed, the guy had two more knives in his hands. Jal's only saving grace seemed to be that he wanted to do this quietly, or else he got a feeling he'd be staring down a barrel instead.

Not that it bought him a hell of a lot. Another knife whipped across the room, burying itself in the door as Jal dove sideways behind the monitors. Not much cover, it turned out, in a hospital room. Couple of shit chairs and a monitor stack.

"There's a call button on the end of the monitor." Yeah, it was always going to be weird hearing Regan's voice on a mission. Two halves of his life colliding, with dizzying effect.

He was too busy ducking another knife to answer, but Nash did it for him. "He can't," she said. "He hits that call button, shouts for help, there's a good chance it's a nurse or doctor that comes through that door first, and if this guy's one of Gethin's, he's probably not sweating the collateral damage."

Exactly. Eventually, the noise would bring someone running anyway, and Jal needed to make damn sure Mister Second-in-Command was down—or at least out of knives—before that happened, or good people might wind up dead.

"He can't just fight that guy by himself!" Worry pulled Regan's voice taut, and Jal couldn't blame her. If the roles had been reversed, he'd have been beside himself, and she didn't *know* this side of him. He'd tried his damnedest to keep them separate, the sibling and the soldier, and maybe that hadn't been fair to her, but it was too late to clear things up now.

It was Saint, this time, who cut in as Jal reached around the stack for the knife buried in the front. Never pass up an opportunity to level the field; Saint had taught him that. "Kid knows what he's doing; just let him do it."

Wasn't really a pep talk, but it kind of felt like one. *Kid knows what he's doing.* And he did. This part? This made sense. The fighting, the danger—somewhere along the way, that'd gotten easier than the other stuff. Couldn't play house with the family he loved, but give him a knife and a big motherfucker to use it on, and he reckoned he could handle himself just fine.

Only, Jal wasn't much of a knife-thrower. He shoved the knife in the back of his belt and grabbed the closest chair instead, hurling it one-handed at the Second's chest. *Always aim for center of mass, kid.* It'd been a lesson on bullets, but Jal reckoned the same basic principles applied.

The Second was quick, but not quick enough to dodge it, so he brought up his arms to shield his head, and Jal saw his window and *took it*. Didn't try bounding over the bed this time, but ran and slid around the foot of it, hooking a kick at the back of the Second's legs.

The Second went down. Outstanding. He went down swing-ing, though, which was a little *less* outstanding. Flung the chair sideways and caught Jal in the side of the head with it, and bells started ringing between his ears as Jal scrambled to knock it aside and close the gap. There was nothing graceful to it. None of Nash's art or Saint's skill, just a bunch of genetically modified muscle and a vague notion what to do with it.

Jal managed to get on top, throwing the chair aside and swinging a right cross hard as he'd ever swung a pick. The Second didn't break apart like all those mountains of stone, though; his head snapped sideways, then it snapped right back, and he threw a punch just as hard into Jal's side and tried to buck him off.

Jal locked his knees and held on fast. Threw another punch, and another, until blood painted his knuckles—his blood or the Second's, he couldn't be sure. Didn't hardly seem to matter, as another fist cracked into his ribs. He'd gotten his knees around the Second's waist, where most of the knives seemed to be com-ing from, but it meant he couldn't pin the man's arms. Couldn't keep him from matching Jal blow for blow, neither one of them brave or stupid enough to stop punching long enough to grab for something a little more decisive.

It was a beating, pure and simple. The Second bucked and rolled, got in a few swings with Jal underneath him, and Jal reversed and did the same. Wasn't about who could land the most hits; it was about who could take the most punishment.

Thing was, Jal'd been *made* to take a beating. His ribs didn't crack, and his fingers didn't break, and when Second started slowing down, Jal didn't. He hit harder. Brutal, howling, des-perate hits, because this man had tried to kill him, and he'd gladly try again, and he wouldn't stop at Jal. These people— they wanted *everyone* Jal cared about. His loved ones were their loose ends, and he didn't want the violence, but if bloody knuckles and broken noses were the only way this ended, then so fucking be it.

"Jal." He barely registered Regan's voice. Barely registered the burn in his arms or the ringing in his ears. "Jal, stop! It's over!"

But it wasn't. It was never over. Not when his old crew'd left him for dead. Not when they stopped the Deadworld Code. Not when the hearings ended, or when Gethin took Regan, or when the ring ship blew, or when Saint stopped breathing on the shuttle floor. It didn't end until they *ended* it, so even if he had to do it with his bare goddamn hands, Jal was *going to end—*

"Kid, that's enough!" A command this time, sharp and coarse, and it reached someplace deep in Jal's core and grabbed hold.

Jal stopped, and the Second didn't get up. His head didn't rise. His hands didn't lift. He lay there on the hospital floor, face so broken Jal barely recognized it, and it took a whole handful of seconds before Jal even saw his chest rise.

"I—" His throat stuck, tacky and sore like he'd been shouting, but he didn't remember making the sound. Blood painted the backs of his hands, ran warm down the side of his face, soaked the knees of his jeans as he staggered to his feet. "I—" *I didn't mean to.* But he had. He'd meant every punch. *I had to.* Maybe so, or maybe he could've stopped sooner. He didn't know.

I think there's something wrong with me.

"Deep breaths, miner boy," said Nash, just like she'd said back in Regan's cabin at the start of all this. *Deep breaths.* "You're okay, but you need to make yourself scarce."

He nodded, half-numb, even though there wasn't anybody there to see it. Just him and four dead-to-the-world men, and a door that seemed about a light-year away. He started toward it anyway, wiping his nose on the back of his sleeve and his hands on his pants.

"Think it's safe to say Karim's not our guy," he said hoarsely. If there'd been any room left to doubt, he'd no sooner staggered out the door than Karim's monitors started to sound. Tritone and discordant, broken beyond all repair, but not, apparently, beyond their purpose. And even in the dark, people came running. Scrubs and white coats, their flashlight beams stinging Jal's eyes. "Check the needle in the floor," he told one of the white coats as she passed. She looked at him strangely, but he pressed on. "Think they dosed him with something. I thought I got it in time, but—"

"Jal, dear, the officers are incoming. You need to go." Inside Karim's room, the lights flickered back on as the doctors got to work. "They'll do their jobs. Now *run*."

Turned out Jal was still pretty good at that, too.

SAINT

"Headed your way, old man. What's your position?" Kid must've been hauling some serious ass, because even *he* sounded winded. Better, though. More himself than a minute ago. Christ, Saint hated this—his people scattered around the satellite, each of them worn out and beat down and tearing at the seams. Nash wasn't supposed to be afraid for him, and Jal wasn't supposed to be afraid of himself, and Saint wasn't supposed to be too far away from either of them to do a damn thing about it.

But the universe didn't run on *supposed to*, and as far as Saint could tell, the only way out of this shitstorm was through it. *So we get the hell through it.* He sped up, ignoring the warning pang in his side. His pre-deployment nerve blockers were wearing off, but it didn't matter. He'd brought spares, and he had faith in Nash's handiwork, even if she didn't. It'd hold long enough. *He'd* hold long enough.

"About to hit the life support facilities," he said.

"You're not the only one," said Eoan. "I've got six warm bodies moving into the facility from the lower levels."

"So much for the easy way in." Saint didn't know what he'd expected. Nothing about this had been easy. Why start now? But a little surprise security coverage didn't change anything. Couldn't take the elevators; way too likely he'd get jammed up if anyone realized he was in one. And switching to the stairwell would've meant backtracking half the length of the sector. The life support bay cut straight down the middle of the sector with linkups on every floor—it was the cleanest, fastest shot they had at Brodbeck's quarters, so inbound security be damned, that was the way he'd go. "I'm good, Cap. Get the door."

"No, fuck that," said Nash. "I'm less than six minutes out from your location. Just wait, and I'll back you up."

"Not sure there's time." Eoan beat Saint to the punch. "I've got the camera feeds on Brodbeck's floor, and I'm counting six more officers down between the life support bay and his door."

Fuck. "Drestyn?" Saint asked.

"Could be. Or it could be Raimes, or it could be both. I can't get access to the interior cameras to confirm." Agitation clipped Eoan's voice short. Wasn't just the not knowing; they went way back with old Brodbeck. That was their friend in there, and for all they knew, he was dead or dying or sharing quarters with one or two of the deadliest men in the spiral.

No time to wait for backup, then.

"The door, Cap."

"You'll be outnumbered," they said.

"I know."

"I can't ask you to go in there."

"Thing is, you don't have to." As the light on the lock flashed from red to green, Saint grabbed those spare nerve blockers from his belt, tugged the caps off with his teeth, and jabbed the whole kit into his side. A sharp sting, a rush of warmth, and a sudden, gaping *void* of sensation spread through his side. Could've been the relief that made his pulse jump, or it could've been the bonus epinephrine, but either way, *he had this.*

The door swung in on a metal walkway circling the wall of the bay—one of five, plunging way the hell down to the bottom of the bay and connected by bare U-bent staircases at near-even intervals. Pipes and tubes and half-width catwalks threaded between a half-dozen massive tanks, all in different shapes with different labels, with a general theme of *don't touch this.* They'd done up all the railing in what Nash liked to call *lawsuit yellow,* so probably not the kind of place you wanted to be screwing around.

Also, probably not the kind of place for a gunfight, but it couldn't be helped.

The first shot pinged off the wall by his head, and Saint didn't wait for the second. He bolted for the first set of stairs, grabbing the railing and throwing himself over the side to the next flight down. Landed hard. Barely felt it. *Nash, you beautiful little genius.* The jump brought him level with the first ranger, standing on the other end of the platform with his gun still sighted on the doorway.

Saint shot between two of the tanks and put him down—at least for a few minutes, until the stun wore off—as a new set of boot steps clanged up the stairs beneath him. Two shots from that one, but they burst apart on the grated metal under Saint's feet. Piezoelectric round. Sparks spewed, and Saint bolted toward the tanks, bracing his boots on some of the pipes and twisting around to fire a couple shots at ranger number two. They had numbers in his head. Just numbers, not names, not faces, not stories. Easier that way. Two down, four to go—

A flash of movement on the next walkway down, and Saint had a perfect angle to put the third guy down before he'd even clocked Saint's position. *Three to go.*

On the other side of one of the tanks, a pipe led straight to the next tank down. "Sturdy?" he asked Eoan.

"Sturdy enough," they replied.

Worked for him. He got a hand around it and slid down, as a few more shots pinged off the tanks around him. Looked like a light show in there, all those sparks flying, but if he was still alive and conscious, he'd call it a win. He jumped off the tank back onto the walkway, where number four was coming up the stairs. Smart guy. He saw Saint and doubled back to the lower walkway, stopping under Saint's feet and holding there. No way he could shoot Saint, but no way Saint could shoot him—not a bad move, if you had reinforcements coming.

"We have you surrounded," called number four. "Put your weapon down."

"Shoot the blue pipe," Eoan told him.

He didn't question it. Just aimed, fired, and hit the target. Steam erupted with a hiss from the broken pipe, and number four was probably too far away from it to get scalded, but he wasn't too far to get *spooked*. He staggered back with a yelp, and the second or two it took him to recover was the second or two Saint needed to jump another flight of stairs and get his arm hooked around the guy's neck from behind.

Across the way, number five came running around the walk-way, only to freeze when he saw Saint's arm around his bud-dy's throat and Saint's gun tucked against his temple. Another time—or, rather, *more* time—and he might've given the guy a chance to drop *his* weapon, but seconds were precious, and triggers were faster. One shot for number five, and Saint shoved number four away and put a round between his shoulder blades.

"One left," said Eoan. "One level down, far side of the walk-way."

"Copy that." He holstered his gun, ran at the rail, and jumped across to the bottom-most tank in the bay. Not the quietest landing, but as the guy on the other side brought his rifle around, Saint jumped over to him, knocked the barrel aside, and swung a hard right cross into his jaw. More than one way to stun somebody.

"I think you broke his jaw, dear."

"He'll live. Look, he's already getting up." Saint switched number six's rifle to nonlethal and put a round in the guy's chest, and the guy went back to doing his best impression of a rag doll. "Now where the hell's my exit?"

"Straight ahead through that green door," said Eoan, and Saint dropped number six's gun, redrew his own, and took off toward the fuzzy-edged block of green straight ahead.

"How are we looking for backup?" he asked.

Jal made a disgruntled sound. "Still a few minutes out."

"How are we looking for not bleeding to death?" Nash shot back.

Saint touched a hand to his side, unsurprised and more or less unbothered when his fingertips came away red. Wasn't soaking through his clothes yet. Not an emergency. "Still a few minutes out," he answered wryly.

"That's not funny," said Nash.

The corner of Saint's mouth twitched up as he nudged open the door and cleared the corner. "It's a little funny," he said, then, "Looks clear, Cap."

"You're clear all the way to Brodbeck's room," they said. "The officers in the life support bay must've been on their way to your floor."

"Question is, *who sent them*?" Those men could've been answering to Brodbeck just as easily as Raimes. Calling for help, or stopping help from coming—either way, Saint had a feeling he was about to find out.

An uneasy prickle started between his shoulders as he passed the body of the first ranger. No blood. No visible gunshots. "If this is Drestyn's handiwork, he's changed up his style." Saint still remembered the roomful of dead mercenaries they'd found on Noether, lined up neat like corpses in a morgue. The man claimed to have his morals, but he didn't shy away from a body count. Not when those bodies made the mistake of standing between him and what he wanted.

Had to be Raimes, then. Had to be. But something about it just didn't *sit right*. Stunning them, instead of killing them—it meant more witnesses. More messes to clean up. After everything that bastard had put Saint's crew through, Saint had a hard time believing Raimes would have hang-ups about a few more dead rangers.

"That's Brodbeck's door, up ahead," said Eoan quietly. Didn't really need to be said; the handful of bodies scattered around outside it sort of set it apart from the others. Seemed more like a lead-in to what Eoan *really* wanted to tell him. Or, as it turned out, *ask* him. "You're sure you want to do this? Jal can be there in under five minutes."

"And your friend could be dead in under five seconds." Since they were pointing out the obvious. Wasn't just about Eoan's friend, either. They'd lost three councilors already, and depending on whether Karim pulled through, they might've lost a fourth, too.

If they had to lose a fifth, Saint wanted it to be the crooked son of a bitch that started all this.

Another breath. A hard blink to chase the spots away. A finger on the trigger. "Open the door," he whispered.

Eoan opened the door.

No gunshots this time. He might've preferred that to whatever the hell he walked in on. He saw Brodbeck first, hunched against an old armchair with one hand half-raised in the air and the other pressing hard against his right shoulder. Blood wept between his fingers, spreading down the front of his sweater and smeared on the back of the armchair. Real paper books lay scattered around his feet, with a medal display so full that it was hard to believe they could all belong to one man. Looked like they might've been on the shelf once, but like Brodbeck had fallen into the shelf and knocked them all off. Getting shot did tend to take a man's balance.

The rest of the room filled in more or less at once. A couch. A writing desk. A handful of open doors, like somebody had been smart enough to sweep it for backup before Saint arrived. If Saint had to take a guess, he'd say he had that *somebody* right in front of him.

Midway across the room, Raimes stood with his back to Saint and his gun to Brodbeck. Saint could only make out his face in profile, smooth as polished oak. Damn near apathetic, like holding another councilor at gunpoint was just something he might as well be doing that day.

Except his eyes. His eyes gave him away—that particular shade of stormy green the skies turned right before a tornado hit. That face said *this ain't personal*, but those eyes said otherwise.

Drestyn, Saint saw last. Tucked in the nearest corner like he was, he must've been the latecomer to the party, but he'd certainly caught on to the theme. He had a gun of his own—nothing quite so flashy as Raimes's revolver, but in that man's hands, it'd get the job done just as well—aimed at the back of Raimes's head, but he hadn't moved his finger from the trigger guard yet. Not quite ready to shoot. All told, it was like something out of a cartoon. A standoff. Only, the guns didn't look quite so shiny in the cartoons; and the men didn't look quite so *vicious*.

Took him all of a second to absorb the scene, and maybe another half to decide what to do about it. One squeeze, one shot, and Drestyn dropped before he knew what hit him. Only way to outgun a man like that was to never let his finger touch the trigger.

Neither Brodbeck nor Raimes flinched, though that *take cover* stare of Raimes's did flick back Saint's direction. His thin lips twitched. Might've been a smile, but it could've just as easily been a snarl.

"I'd say it's good to see a friendly face," said Raimes, in his slow, twanging drawl. Still sounded half-drunk, even stone-cold sober. "But you're not looking mighty friendly there, *Saint*. You mind pointing that gun someplace else?"

Saint hadn't even waited for Drestyn to finish hitting the ground before he'd turned his barrel on Raimes. "You first," Saint said.

"That's not gonna work for me. So, here's my counter: I shoot this scheming sack of shit, then I walk my country ass over to that fine tray of blur on that desk, pour us both a drink, and you let me tell you a little story 'til he comes back around."

There it went again: that itch between his shoulder blades. That *birds stopped singing in the woods* feeling like something just wasn't right. "Until he comes back around?"

Raimes's brows furrowed, then relaxed as his mouth shaped a little *ah*. "I see," he said. "What we have here is a good old-fashioned misunderstanding. I didn't put that hole in your friend; that was your blacked out buddy over there."

"Bullshit," said Brodbeck, wincing as a fresh well of blood oozed between his fingers. Wasn't a kill shot, and Saint figured Raimes—and Drestyn, on the off chance Raimes was telling the truth—could manage one of those at this distance with his eyes closed. More likely, somebody just hadn't wanted Brodbeck going for that piece on his hip.

"I didn't," Raimes insisted, like repeating himself would make a difference. "Though I'd have been well within my rights to do it if I had. He's playing you, Saint. If he ain't, then you're on his side, but I don't think you are. I think you and I want the same thing here. If you'd just give me a chance to explain."

"Then put your gun down."

"Let's *all* put our guns down," Brodbeck said. "I think enough people have gotten shot today, don't you?"

Raimes's finger twitched on the trigger. "Oh, I think we're still one shy." A twitch, but no squeeze. No bang. Not yet. Saint's heart still jumped into his throat, though. His own finger still twitched. Fifty-fifty he got his shot off before Raimes did.

"Put your gun down," Saint repeated. "That's twice. I won't ask a third time."

Seconds ticked by, and Raimes didn't move. *Nobody* moved. Brodbeck stood there bleeding and breathing; Raimes stood there with Brodbeck in his sights; and Saint stood with his finger on the trigger, each watching the other two and not daring to blink.

Then Saint saw it—the faint dip of Raimes's narrow shoulders. A beat later, as his finger fell to the trigger guard, his eyes flicked back one more time to Saint.

BANG!

Happened so fast, Saint barely clocked it. That one glance, that one split-second's distraction, and the next thing Saint knew, Raimes was staggering back, hand to his belly. Didn't stop him raising his revolver again, but the next shot did. One to the thigh, and Raimes dropped like a hanged man with his rope cut.

"Shit," Brodbeck swore as Saint went to kick Raimes's revolver away. He held onto it, though. Held on tight, for a man with so much blood soaking through his clothes. "Draw's still half-decent, but my aim's gone to shit without my bifocals," Brodbeck said, checking something on his own pistol. The sight, maybe, or the safety. Saint didn't see, exactly, and he didn't look close enough to find out; too busy kneeling to try to pry the revolver from Raimes' callused fingers.

"—ing to y—" Raimes rasped, pulling against Saint's grip.

His thumb slid above the grip, until it released the cylinder of his revolver. "He's—" And finally, as the cylinder dropped from Raimes's gun, Saint saw what he'd been trying to show him.

Those were nonlethal rounds in Raimes's revolver.

Comprehension sank like an anchor in Saint's gut. He understood. Too late, he understood, as Raimes strained up and hissed against his ear, *"He's lying to you."*

Raimes couldn't have shot Brodbeck even if he'd wanted to. And if Brodbeck had lied about that, then . . .

The crack of a gunshot interrupted the thought, and he never got to finish it.

EOAN

"Saint?" Eoan tried again. They'd been trying since his comms went silent, only moments after they'd opened the door, to no avail. "Saint, dammit, *respond*!" They had no eyes inside the room. No ears. Nothing moved outside the hall. They had *nothing*. "Jal, can you go any faster?"

"Going as fast as I can, Cap!" But they swore he found some new reserve of speed, tearing through the crowd around the elevators like a man possessed. "What the fuck happened?"

"I don't know," they said. "His comms went dead the moment he stepped through the door. Bodycam, too."

"Some kind of Faraday setup." That was Nash—problem solving in a crisis. Eoan looked for answers, Nash looked for solutions, and Jal . . . Jal looked for *Saint*. "Have you still got the feeds outside the hall?"

Nash had no sooner asked than everything went dark. Every camera across the station, all at once. Only, no. No, it wasn't the cameras. It was Eoan. "I've lost access to the satellite's systems. Someone's shutting me out." *No, no, no.* They tried to slip back in, but they ran up against a wall. Tried a backdoor, same result. It was like it was anticipating them. Like it knew where they'd go and what they'd try, and had already set itself up to stop them.

But Raimes couldn't know that. Raimes couldn't know *them*, not that well. Nash could've. Saint, maybe. Their friends, their teammates, their crew, they might know how Eoan worked well enough to orchestrate such a targeted defense, but—

Oh.

A horrible thought. A horrible, hideous, *heartbreaking* thought, but suddenly, it made the most terrible sort of sense. "He knew about the transponder," they said. Regan startled as they materialized in the bridge, clearing the projections above the holotable with a sweep of their hand and pulling up a set of transcripts instead. They switched the comm feeds to ship wide only; they needed to think. They needed to process. And they needed not to distract their people in the field while they did it.

"We've been doing this wrong," they told Regan. "*I've* been doing this wrong." The accounts, the recordings—all those intricate, impossible little puzzles. They'd drawn Eoan in, appealed to the fundamentals of their programming: that craving for mystery, for intricacy, for discovery, when the truth lay in the simplest of facts. They'd just missed it. Overlooked it, and wasn't that so sublimely, catastrophically *human*? "Brodbeck knew about the transponder."

"I don't understand," Regan said. "What about the transponder?"

"Someone accessed the Guild's transponder archive, used it to track our ship. We thought it was Raimes—that he'd worked out where we were headed and warned Gethin we were coming to get you. It was *Brodbeck* who told us the logs had been accessed. He commed right as we were leaving Lummis to let us know, but—"

"But how would he have known to check the access logs?"

Bitsie finished softly from the console. "Unless *he* was the one who accessed them."

It had been right in front of them. The log entry was masked; it could've been *anyone* with councilor-level clearance. Torsten had to have known Raimes had left when he told Eoan about the transponder codes. Had to have known they'd look into it and make the connection—the repository access and Raimes's sudden flight from Alpha Librae—and it had been so easy to believe it. The cowboy. The rule breaker, talking to Drestyn against regulation and slipping away on an unsanctioned mission with no word of where he was going or why. Torsten had told them a story, and Raimes had made it so easy to believe him.

Perhaps, they thought, it was all the easier because they'd *wanted* to. They'd known Torsten for decades. Their friend, their colleague—they'd trusted him, because they'd wanted to trust him. But now, they looked as suspicious as Raimes. How many rules had they broken in the last few days? How many people had *they* told about *their* mission when they'd slipped away from the satellite? Torsten, with the right combination of words and history and cheerful malapropisms, had steered them down the same path to the same result: hunted and distrusted by the very people they'd sworn to serve beside. By the very institution they'd been trying to protect.

They'd believed.

At the core of it, that was Torsten's greatest advantage: belief. The people's belief that the Guild was incorruptible. Their crew's belief that the oath they'd taken meant something to everyone else who'd taken it. Eoan's belief that an old friend was a *true* friend. He'd taken those beliefs, and he'd *used* them.

"Christ, Cap, what's going on?" Jal ground out. He'd reached the door to the life support bay, with Nash not far behind him, and he hadn't slowed a bit. Half-mad and half-wild, he flung himself over the railing like he didn't even *see* the five-story drop to the bottom. Like it didn't even occur to him that he could fall, or that the fall could hurt, when his body was riddled with scars to say otherwise. He caught the rails of the next walkway down, then dropped, and caught, and dropped, and caught, until he hit the bottom and sprang forward without ever breaking pace. "C'mon! Keep us in the loop here."

As Jal turned the corner and kicked open the door to Torsten's quarters, Eoan couldn't find their voice. There was no one inside. No Saint, no Torsten, just a toppled bookshelf and two puddles of blood seeping into the vintage handloom rug.

Jal drew a shuddering breath from the doorway, comms and bodycam crackling as he took a step over the threshold and back again. Uncertain. Uneasy. Unsure what to do next, now that he'd run out of running to do. "They're not here," he said. "They're not fucking here. Raimes, that son of a bitch, he must've—"

"It's not Raimes," they said at last. Firm and definitive, because as horrible as the knowing was, at least they finally *knew*. "It's Brodbeck." It felt wrong to say it, but as they scanned the room in all its damning emptiness, they realized something very much worse. "The turncoat is Brodbeck . . . and he has Saint."

CHAPTER TWENTY

SAINT

The cold came first—a bone-deep shiver to shake him out of the dark. Swamp rat that he was, Saint had never managed to get used to it. Seemed a little late to try now.

Pain, though . . . pain, a man could get used to. He could *use* it, so long as he could keep his head on straight and pay a-fucking-ttention. The strain in Saint's shoulders and the sting in his wrists said his hands had been tied, tight, behind his back. The throb in his jaw, drilling up into the roots of every tooth in his mouth, said somebody'd hit him with a shock round. And the burning in his side said the nerve blockers were wearing off. More than a twinge, less than the blisteringly hot *fuck you* of an unmedicated hole in his gut, so he'd probably been out somewhere between a quarter and a half hour. Tack that on to the unmistakable chill burrowing into his bones, and Saint had a pretty good idea where things stood before he even opened his eyes.

They'd brought him to the brig, down in the secure ward. Coldest place in the whole satellite, just like he remembered, but the *view* had definitely changed. From his spot on the floor, tied to the base of the console in the middle of the central hub, all he could really make out at first were feet. Five, six pairs, beating a patrol around the room. Coming and going from the blurred-out edges of his vision, all shined-up boots and regulation laces. Those weren't mercenaries looking down on him; those were *rangers*. The thought hit like a bad shot of blur, but he choked it down much the same. Head on straight. Pay attention.

He wasn't the only one tied to the console. A shoulder bumped his, and for a heart-stopping second, he thought, *Jal? Nash?* But it was too short for the kid, and too tall for Nash, and before Saint could wrestle his chin far enough off his chest to see who that left, the answer volunteered itself.

"Nice of you to finally join us, Ranger," said Drestyn, with a certain slur to his voice like he hadn't quite shaken off the stunner round, either. "Just in time. The councilor here was starting to get impatient."

For a half second, Saint still thought of Raimes. Habit, before the memory of what'd happened in that room caught up with him. *He's lying to you.* It hadn't been Raimes; it hadn't *ever* been Raimes, and everything he'd done . . . it all looked different now.

They'd all known Drestyn was important—the hush order, the pissing match for first dibs between the Trust and the Union—but Saint's crew hadn't worked out *why* until they'd gotten Regan back. Call it distraction, call it prioritization, call it bad goddamn judgment; it was what it was, and they were past the point of changing it.

If Raimes had worked it out sooner, though, or at least had his own suspicions about the goings-on in the Captains' Council, then what he'd done made sense. Fenton's escort blows just hours after Drestyn's transfer off-satellite? Raimes had to've figured Drestyn was on somebody's to-do list. So he hauls ass after Casale, and lo and behold, there's the *Ambit* crew, swiping Drestyn and stealing away like bandits in the black. They'd thought he found them in the junk belt because he'd known where to look, thought it would've been damn near impossible for someone to follow them that far, that well, and not get caught.

But maybe Raimes could've. Man was a legend in his own right. A loose cannon, more swagger than sense, but you didn't make the Captains' Council at his age just because the Council wanted you somewhere they could see you. If he was the kind of ranger who could earn a badass reputation in a whole *legion* of badasses, the kind of ranger who could ferret out a decade-old conspiracy before anybody else caught on, then he probably *was* the kind of ranger who could pull that off.

It made it that much harder to see him lying just a few steps away, unmoving, in a puddle of his own blood. A good man, gone, because he had the misfortune of being the smartest one in the room.

Saint raised his head a little farther, by degrees. Slow movements kept his vision from blurring quite so bad, kept the bile from climbing up his throat. He had a little red puddle of his own going, down by his hip—must've torn the rest of Nash's patch job, or else one of those rangers had torn it for him. He got the feeling they hadn't taken any great pains to get him down there in one piece.

For his efforts, Saint finally locked eyes with the *real* turncoat: Torsten Brodbeck, a consummate son of a bitch. He stood there at the back end of the hub, not too far from Drestyn's old cell. Had his head high, back straight, hands clasped behind him, and a crisp white bandage peeked out from the open collar of a gray uniform coat—a captain's uniform. A councilor's uniform. Felt like spit in the eye, seeing that Guild patch on Brodbeck's shoulder. Wasn't enough for him to break the oath; had to do it with the banner on.

"You keep your wedding ring on when you cheat on your wife, too?" Saint said.

Brodbeck arched a thick, gray brow at him. "Is that what you think I'm doing, son? *Cheating?*"

"I think you're a goddamn parasite." A tick in a gray coat, fat on the blood of Saint's siblings-in-arms. Jal's blood. Saint looked at Brodbeck, and he didn't see conspiracies; he didn't see some sweeping sense of betrayal. He saw that video from the scav site. He saw Fenton's face, when he'd wrestled Jal's bodycam away.

He saw the scars on Jal's belly, and bruises on Nash's ribs, and tears in Bitsie's eyes, and Raimes lying dead on the goddamn floor. And Eoan . . . God, Eoan had *loved* this man. The molten anger pooling in his gut didn't belong to Saint, or his oath, or his beliefs; it belonged to *them*. "And I *know* you're not leaving here alive."

A chuckle from beside him. "Careful, Ranger. I think I'm starting to like you," Drestyn said. Wasn't hard to imagine what *he* saw when he looked at Brodbeck. After all this time, he'd finally found the man who'd ordered his brother's murder. Saint had a sneaking suspicion a little thing like three-to-one odds and a pair of zip cuffs wouldn't discourage him from settling that score.

Good for him.

Brodbeck ignored Drestyn, face drawn tight with something an awful lot like disappointment as he finished buttoning his coat. "You've got this all twisted, son," he said. "I'm not a parasite. I'm the medicine. If it weren't for me and them"—he gestured around at the other rangers—"the Guild would've shriveled up and died years ago. *Neutral preservation of human life*—it sounds good on paper, I know, but neutrality don't pay. You know how many crews out there are struggling just to break even? Bounties don't pay like they used to, nobody wants to turn out their pockets for peacekeepers, and half the jobs worth doing get snatched up by mercenaries before the council gets around to rubber-stamping them and throwing them in the pool.

"You see the problem? Everybody wants peace, but nobody wants to *pay for it*. If it weren't for Guild stipends, half our people couldn't afford the fuel for their tanks or the bullets for their guns. Now, you tell me—the hell kind of good could we do for the spiral if we couldn't even get our ships off the docks?"

Beside him, Drestyn snorted. "The hell kind of good do you do now, Councilor? Assassinating peaceful protestors, whoring yourself and your people to the likes of the Trust . . . your *good* ends in blood and ashes. I've seen it."

A nod from Brodbeck, and one of the rangers drove a boot down into Drestyn's gut. "You're a goddamn child," said Brodbeck, as he pulled his gun belt from where he'd hung it on the console by Drestyn's old cell. Shined boots, crisp belt—dressing for a ranger's funeral. Nearly a day since the explosion in the councilor's meeting; Saint reckoned Brodbeck had a ceremony or four to attend. "Naïve and idealistic, running your mouth about things you don't understand. The Guild saves lives." He turned to Saint. "I truly believe that, and I know you do, too. The spiral needs us. It needs people like you and me out there keeping the lines clear and uncrossed, or else the whole universe would split at the seams.

"But we need things, too. We need to eat. We need to keep the lights on. And whether you like it or not, and whether it jibes with how you think things *ought* to work, sometimes that means playing ball with the people that pay. Shit, son, you think I enjoy working with the likes of Yarden? You think I agree with the bullshit politics of a bunch of spineless, silver-spooned C-suiters? I wouldn't trust them with a bucket of water if their own grandmas were on fire. But this isn't about principles. Not yours, not mine, not theirs. This is about *capital*. Always has been, always will be. We need the caps, they've got the caps, and that means we need them. There's no Guild without the Trust."

"That's an excuse," Saint snarled, shifting up straighter against the console. Made his side burn like a swarm of hornets, but he swore he felt the zip cuffs go a little looser. One loop around his wrists, pulled taut by the tension in his shoulders. If he could steal another few centimeters, he might could slip it, but his shoulders were already stretched to their limit. He gritted his teeth. "Just a bullshit justification you use to keep doubling your caps off the Guild's good name."

"It's the God's honest truth," Brodbeck replied. "It's ugly, and it's shameful, but it's the way things work. That's balance. You ask me, that's the Guild's real oath. Fuck neutrality; we keep the scale level, and sometimes that means thumbing it one way or the other. For every Deadworld Code, there's a Kepler, and vice goddamn versa. Good and bad. Can't have one without the other, not if we want the Guild to survive.

"You should know, I respect the hell out of you and your crew. What you did on Lewaro, saving that whole station? And bringing in this fucking cockroach, to boot," he added, with another nod toward Drestyn. No kick this time. From the sounds of things, Drestyn had barely gotten his breath back from the first one. "That's something to be proud of, no matter what has to happen here. And you and I both know what has to happen.

"If I let your people go, you'll turn that bulldog determination on me and mine. You won't stop until you've busted up everything I've spent decades building, and I can't let you do that. The work's too important."

"The *caps* are too important, you mean." Saint shifted again, higher, and the tendons and ligaments in his shoulders damn near drowned out the pain in his side. Right on the edge of tearing; he knew the sensation all too well. All that scar tissue in his bad shoulder, ready to split.

Brodbeck gave him a pitying look, like a good dog gone rabid. Like it wasn't Saint's fault, but it wasn't Brodbeck's either. Some things just had to be done. "I told you, son: you can't have one without the other. And if we're not here when the next Isaiah Drestyn comes, the next Otho Yarden, the next *Deadworld Code*, who will be? The Trust? Hell, if it's not the scavs, the mercs, or the agitators starting shit, it's them. The Union's got their moral high ground, sure, but a bunch of labor license desk clerks and collective bargaining negotiators aren't gonna bust up a militarized trafficking ring or take down a warlord.

"You get it? I'm the solution. *You're* the problem. You and your crew, you're the ones gumming up the works, and if I don't deal with you, you'll take the whole Guild down with you."

"You keep doing this, it's not gonna *be* the Guild." Not the one Saint signed onto. Not the one the spiral needed. In a universe bought and paid for by the Trust, the people needed protectors who couldn't be bought. Who lived outside the influence of Trust and Guild alike, and put *people* before power in a way the Trust and Union didn't.

Brodbeck's mouth turned down at the corners. "But it'll be *a* Guild," he said. "And that's better than nothing, so here's what we're gonna do." He reached into his breast pocket and pulled out a little case. "I'm gonna reactivate your comms, let your people work out where you are, now that you're good and settled, and they're good and frazzled. When they come, we're gonna finish this. For what it's worth, I'll make it as quick and painless as I can, and I'll make it look good. You three, you were bringing Drestyn back to his cell when he got the better of you. You didn't make it, but you managed to eject the high-security pod. You did the right thing in the end—gave your lives for your Guild, for your siblings-at-arms. As far as I'm concerned, that part's true. It's just a shame you didn't know about the bomb he'd put on your ship."

Saint's blood coursed with a different kind of cold. "There's civilians on our ship, you twisted son of a bitch."

"Regan and Briley Red." Brodbeck nodded. "I know, son. But that Regan, she started all this. Coming to the council, telling them about the missing recordings and the off-the-books missions . . . I knew it was just a matter of time before someone got curious and dug a little deeper. I'd been careful, but with all Yarden's files floating out there and a goddamn firsthand witness"—with a wave toward Drestyn—"I knew it wouldn't be enough. Then the cowboy over there starts sniffing around,

L. M. SAGAS

breaks Drestyn's hush order, starts cozying up to the Union escort team when the transfer comes . . . I did what I had to, to protect the Guild, and I'll do it again. I'll eat those sins, because that's what it takes. Because I'm a fucking *soldier*, son, just like you, and we do what we've got to."

On that, at least, they agreed.

NASH

Jal had tossed every centimeter of Brodbeck's quarters.

In his defense, he'd at least waited until Chiclet Junior finished sweeping the place and Nash had knocked out the Faraday transmitter blacking out all their comms signals. When Junior came up with nothing, and with Eoan still wrestling their way back into Alpha Librae's systems, there wasn't much else he *could* do. No leads. No convenient trails of blood droplets or boot prints to follow back to their XO. Just a room in ruins, Brodbeck in the wind, and two bloodstains soaking the rug—one, a match for Dalton Raimes; and the other, blessedly smaller, for Florence Toussaint.

Should've just waited for us, idiot, she thought, smothering a curse as Jal broke something in one of the back rooms. She was pretty sure he'd given up actually *finding* something, with all that searching, but he just couldn't seem to stop trying. *Why didn't you just wait for us?*

"Nash?" Eoan's voice broke the damning, relentless silence down their comms. "I've got something."

Nash's heart did a funny trip-step. "What is it?"

"Saint's comm signal—it just went live again. The mic's down, but I've got a location. He's in the high security ward of the brig." They didn't deliver it like good news.

Probably because it wasn't. "Brodbeck's using him as bait."

"I expect so," Eoan agreed. "It's almost certainly a trap, and a good one at that—only one way in. No backdoors. No surprises. We come in through the lift, or we don't come in at all."

"And they'll probably have a cheery little firing squad waiting for us when we do." Nash swore under her breath. "Seriously," she said. "Just *one* stupid bad guy. One dumb-as-dirt, squash-for-brains bad guy, that's all I ask." She'd had it with clever enemies. They didn't always win, but they always made it hurt. *Then we'll just have to hurt them worse.* "All right, what's our play?"

The chaos in the back room had cut out, and Jal appeared in the doorway. Or, *through* the doorway, then the sitting room, headed for the hallway. "We get Saint," he grunted. "That's the play."

She grabbed him before he could pass her, shoving him back into Brodbeck's room. "And you've worked out how to do that without getting fucking *aerated* by however many goons Brodbeck packed into that brig?" she shot back.

"Nash is right," said Eoan. "This isn't a time to leap before we look. We'd be fools to think Gethin's crew were the only ones Brodbeck had under his command. Any ranger on this satellite could be one of his, and that means we have to assume we're woefully outnumbered."

"Numbers or not, if we don't go get Saint, they'll kill him." Jal started for the hall again, and again, Nash pushed him back.

"Not necessarily," said Eoan. "At least, not immediately. If Brodbeck just wanted you dead, it would've been much simpler to send people down to kill you in his quarters. He wants you *there*—all of you, together. Somewhere he can control everything. Clean up the mess, set the narrative, make sure the story is the one he wants to tell. Seems he's rather good at stories." Something bitter soured their voice, aimed inward as much as out. They hated Brodbeck for what he'd done, but they hated themselves for missing it.

Nash knew the feeling.

"We've got time to be smart about it," she agreed, but even as she said it, that scraping snarl of wires in her gut cinched tighter. "But we don't have much of it."

Jal turned to her, hands clenching at his sides. "The hell's that supposed to mean?"

Fuck it. "It means Saint got shot on the ring ship," she snapped. "Not clipped, not grazed—full-on, bullet-through-the-meat *shot*. I patched him up as best I could, but a wad of dermapoxy and a pressure bandage isn't gonna hold up in a fight." *Hadn't* held up. That wasn't a *call the coroner* bloodstain on the rug, but it was a lot. More than enough to worry that their XO had more urgent concerns than Brodbeck's timeline.

"You knew he wasn't fit for the field?" Eoan asked coolly. Reminded her of Saint's voice, all sanded down and smoothed over, when he wanted to blow a fucking gasket. "And you cleared him anyway."

"I did." No apologies. No regrets—at least, not yet. "He asked me to clear him, so I did, and he asked me not to tell you, so I didn't. Either of you. You can be pissed at me later, but I'd do the same for any of you." Because it wasn't her job to make choices for people. Not even for the people she loved, and not even for their own good. Her job, her *only* job, was to do her damnedest to help them survive the consequences, and that was what she'd do. *Not letting you die on me, McBlastinshit. Not today.* "What matters is, if his wound's reopened, then right now, he's bleeding to death. Only question's how fast, and whether we can get there in time to do something about it. So you wanna bitch about doctor-patient privilege, or do you want to put our heads together and save our fucking friend?" It wasn't really a question; she knew their answers before she ever even asked.

"We save our friend," said Jal, and that wasn't hope or optimism or wishful thinking hardening his voice; it was sheer goddamn *resolve*. He'd tear the station apart with his bare hands to get to Saint, and stars and skies help anyone fool enough to get in his way, because he'd tear them apart, too.

For all his faults, Jal was kind of great like that.

"We're agreed, then," said Eoan. "Saint's been there for all of us when we needed him, and I'll be damned if we can't do the same for him. *Without* getting ourselves aerated."

Nash flashed a vicious grin. "That mean you've got an idea to get us in, Cap?"

"Oh, I'll think of something. You just get to the brig." All crisp and polite, but damned if Eoan didn't sound a little vicious, too. This was it. This was Nash's crew. These were the people she'd chosen to live beside. Fight beside. And no matter what happened, it was the best choice she'd ever made.

Brodbeck, though . . . he'd made the wrong choice. He'd made a fucking *mistake*. Betraying the Guild, lying to them, that was two strikes. But taking Saint? *Their* Saint?

They would set his whole fucking world on fire.

SAINT

It was getting harder to keep his eyes open. The temperature of the brig hadn't changed, but he'd gotten colder. His limbs had gotten heavier, as the red stain on his side spread and spread, like sand pouring from the top of an hourglass.

He hadn't realized he'd started to drift, until Drestyn kicked him awake again. "Work to do, Ranger," he said, in that quiet, cutting way of his. "There's still work to do, and we don't leave jobs unfinished."

"There's no *we*," Saint growled.

Drestyn gave a wry, airy huff. "Keep telling yourself that."

"Leave him be," said Brodbeck, not unkindly. "His work's done. He doesn't need to see what's coming."

What's coming. Like it was inevitable. The elevator doors

would open, Brodbeck's people would open fire, and that'd be the end of Saint's crew. Wouldn't be long now. Jal and Nash had already hit the elevator, but Saint had lost track of the seconds since one of Brodbeck's rangers told him. Tried counting, lost his place. Drifted off and crashed back to himself, like a piece of driftwood caught on the tide. That was the real mindfuck of blood loss—the unpredictability. The slow loss of control.

He tugged on his restraints and welcomed the fresh flash of pain. *Stay awake.* An order. A promise. His people were good and smart, and they'd figure a way out of this; he had to believe that. And he'd help them. Whatever it took, whatever their plan, he'd help them.

If it was the last thing he did.

"You angry, yet, Ranger?" *Ranger, Ranger, Ranger.* Even whispered in Saint's ear, it felt like a taunt. Drestyn's split lips peeled back in an unholy smile, twisted with scars and pure, practiced *rage.* Jal'd had it wrong—that man wasn't a preacher. He was something else. Something that'd crawled out of the flames, broken in ways there weren't words to describe, and pretended to be human. Crawled, like Saint had crawled from that army hospital back on Earth. Pretended, like Saint had pretended every fucking day since he'd lived and his squad had died, because all those ghosts in all those graves wouldn't let him just lay down and die. "You'd better be angry. You'd better be *furious.* And you'd better be ready," he said, with that brimstone smile. "Because the fight's not over yet."

"Captain, they're here," said one of the rangers, just a beat before the light above the elevator flashed blue. Saint had to strain to see it, head turned to the limits of how his spine could bend, but he couldn't look away as the elevator doors started to open.

Be ready. Ready to fight. Ready to die. Ready to do whatever it took to keep his people alive, because he didn't have anything left. *Be ready.* He twisted his wrists in the zip cuffs, testing the strain as his shoulders howled. *Be ready.* And he was, until the door finished opening.

There wasn't anyone inside.

"What the fuck?" said the ranger who'd spoken earlier. Saint restarted his numbers. One. One of six, and Brodbeck made seven. "That's not possible. They blacked out the elevator feeds, but we saw them get on, Captain. We saw them get on, and we never saw them get off, and there's no goddamn way they could've hacked the feeds. I'm still showing everything locked down tight. They should be there."

"Well, they're not, are they?" Brodbeck barked. "So go figure out where the fuck they are."

Number One and his buddy—call him *Number Two*—shuffled onto the elevator, guns drawn with nowhere to point them, so they pointed them everywhere. Did a sweep inside the car, until they made it back around to face the hub, and Number Two swore. "You've got to be shitting me." He reached up, and Saint heard the rip of peeling tape before Number Two came away with a strip of it. Even if Saint were at his best, he wouldn't have been able to make out the writing on the front of it. Not from that distance. But he didn't have to. "*Behind you,*" Number Two read from the tape.

It didn't matter where they stood; every last one of Brodbeck's rangers turned and looked over their shoulder. Just a glance, but it was enough. Two shapes dropped through the ceiling of the elevator, straight down onto the rangers still standing inside. They went down, hard, and as their heads bounced off the floor, Jal and Nash sprang up. Jal went right, quick as a blur, tackling the nearest other ranger—Number Three—into the wall; and Nash came up with that first ranger's gun, aimed straight at Brodbeck's heart.

Brodbeck didn't falter. "Pull that trigger, your friends die."

Jal still had his guy pinned against the wall, but the three other rangers had gotten their guns up and aimed, one for each of them. Jal, Nash, and Saint.

"Right," Nash said, scathingly sarcastic. "Because if I don't, you'll let them live. Try again, shithead." Her aim didn't waver, but her eyes did. They went to Saint first, a split-second once-over. Bloody, bound, but conscious and biding his time. Then over to Raimes's body, still and lifeless on the floor, and a strange look passed across her face. Confused, then curious, then . . . contemplative.

What's in your head, Nash? She had something brewing up there; Saint knew the look. Same look she got when she came back with a bag full of junk parts and a grin. Same look she got when something wasn't working, and she thought she'd found the fix.

Brodbeck didn't know that look. He didn't know that *woman*. If he did, he wouldn't have smiled like that. "Because if you don't put your gun down," he said, "I'll tell my people to stick a bunch of hull-punchers to your ship and blow it off the docks."

"Casale might have something to say about that," said Eoan, through the external speakers of every earpiece on their network. Jal's. Nash's. Saint's, still held in Brodbeck's callused hand. "We're not without friends here, Brodbeck." He'd never heard Cap's voice like that, vicious and seething. Loathing.

"I'm sure you're not," Brodbeck replied. "But I've got more of them, and they've got better toys. Casale can't save your ship, or the people on it," and that bastard looked dead at Jal when he said it. *The people on it.* His family. He'd fought his way back from hell to get to them, and Brodbeck kept using it against him. "But these two can. Your people stand down, Captain, and I'll let you take Briley and Regan and leave this place."

"He's lying," said Jal, pressing his arm harder against Number Three's throat. The guy was nearly the same size as Jal, clawing and punching and kicking with everything he had, but he didn't have prayer against a pissed-off mutant miner with his family on the line. Jal didn't budge. "Man can't open his mouth without bullshit falling out."

Jal was right. No way Brodbeck would leave a thing like that to chance, and Nash had to know that. She'd faltered, from time to time, same as the rest of them—misjudged the wrong people for the right reasons. But of all of them, she was the only one who'd never *truly* put her faith in anyone or anything that didn't fucking deserve it. She wouldn't start now.

"Just shoot him." Drestyn hissed.

"I don't care about them," Brodbeck pressed. "A little girl, an AI past its expiration date, and a grieving sister who hasn't stopped crying wolf since her brother went AWOL—nobody in the spiral's going to side with them over me, so I'm willing to let them go. You die, they live, and the Guild survives. That's what all this is for—everything I've done, everything I'm doing, it's to keep the Guild alive. It's to *save us*, so we can keep saving the people who need us. Isn't that what you signed on for? To lay down your lives for the mission. So, do it. Put the gun down and let this be the end of it. Nobody else needs to die."

"You do," said Drestyn, and Saint felt him shift against his arms. Working at his cuffs, and Saint didn't know how he meant to break loose, but he had a suspicion he would.

Whatever you're doing, Nash, do it quick.

As if she'd heard him, suddenly, Nash lowered her gun. She lowered it all the way to the ground, sliding it away from her as one of the three remaining rangers shifted around to cover her again. Smart move, getting the console between herself and all the guns in the room, but Saint didn't know what good it'd do her. The gun skittered across the floor, until it bounced off Raimes's body a half-dozen steps away. No way any of them could reach it in time to do something with it.

But as the ranger—Number Four—got her in his sights, she caught Saint's eyes. No words, not even a wink, but the twitch at the corner of her mouth said everything he needed to hear.

Now.

A sharp jerk, and Saint dislocated his bad shoulder. Hurt like a bitch, but it gave him the centimeters he'd needed. The cuffs went slack enough to yank his hand free, and as he dove for the feet of Number Four, a gunshot split the air.

It came from *behind* him.

Raimes. Only one it could've been, and Saint had written him off, but of course Nash knew better. Nash, whose biomech implants could pick up a sparking wire in the bridge from all the way back in the cargo bay; who'd never bothered to check for a pulse in all the days he'd known her, because she didn't have to. Raimes could play dead all he wanted, but he couldn't fool her, and just like that, *they* had the numbers.

Raimes dropped Number Four with a well-placed shot before Saint could reach him, so Saint grabbed Four's gun instead. Let his momentum carry him into a slide and put a bullet in the back of Number Five while Jal, with a shout that filled the whole damn ward, lifted Number Three and hurled him into the last of Brodbeck's rangers. Wouldn't kill either of them, but it sure as shit kept them from getting a shot off. He and Nash closed in on the pair, but movement out of the corner of Saint's eye stopped him following suit.

Brodbeck. He'd drawn his sidearm and fired a shot—right at Drestyn. Christ, Saint hadn't even seen him break loose from his cuffs. Hadn't seen him snatch a gun, either, but the ranger Saint had put down was missing a weapon, and Drestyn was on his feet and closing on Brodbeck. The bullet tore a trench in his arm, but Drestyn didn't stop, and Brodbeck did the only thing a half-decent shot like him could do, in a shoot-out with a deadeye like Drestyn.

He ran.

Ran for Drestyn's old cell, and Drestyn ran after him. A few wild shots pinged off the wall around him, but Drestyn didn't even try dodging them. He didn't care if he died. Hell, maybe he was already dead. Maybe he'd died with his brother, a couple of scared kids on a homesteader's debt, bleeding and burning for someone else's caps.

Later, Saint might say *that* was why he followed: because Drestyn was half-mad with fury and likely to get himself killed before he ever put Brodbeck down, and Saint couldn't risk letting Brodbeck get away—letting him lock himself in a cell until reinforcements came, or whatever other fallbacks he had in his pocket. This didn't end unless Brodbeck was stopped, and it *had* to end. Saint's people wouldn't be safe until it did. That was what he'd say, if he made it out of this alive. That he did it for them. It would even be true. In a way, everything he did was for them. But the bigger truth was this:

He was so fucking *angry*.

He threw himself after them, as the light above the entryway flashed red. A straight line of sight down the hall showed him Brodbeck, already in the cell and beating furiously on the console inside. Every cell had an interior panel—a fail-safe, in case some unlucky guard or a maintenance worker got themself locked inside. Unhackable, uncrackable, and hidden so well you'd never find it unless you already knew where to look.

Of course Brodbeck did, and of course he had the code to use it. What he didn't have was a strong enough head start. Drestyn slipped in as the door started to close, but Brodbeck was waiting. Not much of a marksman, but the man could fight like the devil, and even Drestyn couldn't make a ninety-degree shot around a reinforced alloy wall. Saint heard a shout, and the clatter of a gun, and then he lost sight of them as he sped for the closing door. Not much space left. Not much time.

He jumped through just before the doors sealed shut, but his legs gave out on the landing. Pain seared white-hot up his side, blurring his vision as Brodbeck got a hold of Drestyn's bloody arm and flung him into the wall. Experience and brute goddamn strength, pitted against quick and furious and *fearless*. Drestyn didn't even make a sound as he hit, bouncing off the wall and barely managing to get his hands under him before gravity put him on the ground.

Brodbeck didn't give him the chance to get his bearings. A kick in the ribs took Drestyn off his hands and knees, rolling him halfway across the cell floor to the other corner.

He realized his mistake about a half second after Drestyn did—or, at least, that seemed to be about the time he saw the gun in the floor. Drestyn's or Brodbeck's, Saint didn't know, but there was another one on the floor by Saint's feet.

Bloody arm and broken ribs be damned, Drestyn dove for the nearest gun. Brodbeck, too, and with the benefit of two feet under him and all his bones intact, he looked like he might reach it first.

Until Saint fired a shot.

Didn't shoot for Drestyn; didn't shoot for Brodbeck. He shot the ground in front of the gun, and like the rifles in the life support unit, the bullet broke apart in a shower of sparks. Ricochets were a hell of a design flaw in a close-quarters satellite.

Brodbeck stopped. Reasonable thing to do, at gunpoint. Didn't panic, didn't flinch, but he stopped where he stood, because he was smart enough to know the next one could just as easily go into his head. At this range, even with the world swimming, Saint wouldn't miss.

His problem was, Drestyn wasn't quite so reasonable. He didn't panic, either. Didn't flinch. But he didn't *stop*. He reached straight through the sparks, hands all bloody from where the cuffs had bitten into his skin, and Saint's shot hadn't even finished echoing before Drestyn got his fingers on the grip.

That got Brodbeck moving again, diving onto Drestyn and grabbing for his arms. "Shoot him!" Brodbeck shouted, trying to pin Drestyn's gun hand to the ground, but his grip kept slipping on all the blood. "Goddamn it, we're on the same side! We want the same thing! You're a good soldier, Saint, same as me."

Saint had the shot. Drestyn had nearly slipped loose, but for another second or two, Saint had the shot. *You're a good soldier, Saint.* That was what he'd always been. When he was eighteen years old, trudging through swamps and woods with snipers' beads on his back; when he was Jal's age, begging his CO to let him re-enlist after the ambush that killed his squad and tore him to pieces; five years ago, when he signed onto the *Ambit* and a life as a ranger he thought for sure would kill him . . . through all that, he'd been a good soldier. He'd followed his orders. He'd fought for his cause. He'd risked his life for the people he served, and the people he served *with*, because he'd thought it meant something. He'd thought *he'd* meant something, even if it was only as a piece of something bigger.

Now he understood. The world didn't need people following orders. It didn't need people fighting for causes. It didn't need the Guild. Not his version of it, and not Brodbeck's. The world needed fixers, like Nash; and explorers, like Eoan; and protectors, like Jal. It needed good people, not good soldiers.

You're a good soldier, Saint. He swallowed, finger shifting from the trigger. "No," he said. "Not anymore."

As he lowered his gun, Drestyn raised his. Saint made himself watch, made himself *witness*. He'd promised to see it through to the end, and with one shot, Drestyn ended it.

All at once, the room flashed red. *Warning* red. Over at the fail-safe panel, text scrolled across the tiny screen.

"Ejection protocol." Drestyn's face was a mask of red on red—flashing lights on shining blood. Somehow there was something almost peaceful about him as he wrestled Brodbeck's corpse off himself and rose to his feet. "Bastard must've had a dead man's switch. He *really* wanted us gone, huh?"

"Saint?" Eoan's voice crackled from somewhere Saint couldn't pinpoint, until Drestyn bent and pried a tiny piece of plastic from the ball of Brodbeck's fist. Saint's comm piece. "Saint, dear, they seem to have triggered—"

"The ejection protocol," Saint finished for them, tipping back against the wall. His legs didn't want to hold him anymore. His fingers lost their grip on his gun, and when he pressed them to his side instead, fresh blood welled between them. Too much of it. He'd lost too much. He'd *taken* too much. "I know, Cap."

"Nash and Jal, they've cleared the hostiles in the hub, and I've got control of the elevator. I'm holding it down for you, but we've only got a few minutes to get you all to the lift, and I can't seem to access the cell door."

"Brodbeck hit the override, and I don't know his code." Had to be his. Same one to open as to close, and damned if that wasn't the quickest fucking karma he'd ever seen. *That's what you get for letting Drestyn execute a whole-ass human being.*

Eoan didn't seem to see the irony in it. "Then we'll get you out another way. Saint, dear, step away from the door. Nash is trying to short out the servos holding the panels closed—" A couple sparks flew from the override panel before the whole thing went black, and Nash cursed a blue streak in his ear. A happy one, he thought, but it was hard to tell with her sometimes. "And then we should be able to pry it open manually."

"In a few minutes?" Saint said. He didn't make a habit of doubting them, because they'd never made a habit of disappointing him. But just this once, he wasn't sure they could pull it off. He wasn't even sure he wanted them to, not if it meant risking their one shot back to safety.

Jal growled, and Saint could picture him on the other side of the door, fingers dug into the lip of one of the door panels like a shallow pocket of a cliff face. Give him time, and Saint knew he could probably manage it, but it sounded like time was in short supply. "Dammit, old man, we have to try!"

"No, kid, you don't." He expected it to be harder to say, but it was suddenly the easiest thing in the world. Easier than keeping his eyes open. Easier than keeping his feet under him. He was just *tired*. Tired of the cold, tired of the pain, tired of picking himself back up after every fucking body blow. There'd been a question in his head since he'd first woken up in that army hospital. *How much can you take?* Every fight, every scar, every new and horrible loss, that question was always there. *How much can you take?* And every time, the answer had been the same: *Just a little bit more.*

Not this time.

"Just get yourselves to the elevator," he told them, even as he heard them struggling on the other side of the door. "Please. Get yourselves safe, before it's too late."

"We've got time," Jal insisted. "Just—just get off your ass, okay, and help us. We need you." His voice broke, and Saint wanted to blame it on the struggle of moving that much metal, because the thought of letting Jal down again, even to try and save him . . . he didn't think he could bear it. "Drestyn! If you're in there, help us get this fucking door open. You want a ride topside, it's yours. Whatever you want, it's yours. Just *help us!*"

Then, softer, Nash spoke. "I told you that you'd have a choice, McBlastinshit." He knew what exertion sounded like in her voice, but he knew what tears sounded like, too. He heard them both. "I *told* you, and I know I said it'd be up to you, and I meant it. You get to decide."

"What?" Jal snapped. "No, fuck that."

Nash kept going, though, voice thick with so many emotions that Saint had to close his eyes. "If you tell me right now that you're done," she said, "that what you *want* is for us to leave you down here, then we'll do it, even if I have to drag Jal kicking and screaming to that elevator. Because we owe you that. You've *earned* that, Saint. Our trust. Our respect. But—" Her voice cracked, and he heard the click of her swallow even through Jal's protests. "But I don't want to lose you, okay?" she said, softer, smaller, and Saint wanted nothing more than to hug her again. To gripe at her about spare parts on the galley table. To bump his head on another macrame planter she'd stuck out in the hall. To dodge another handtool when he'd gotten on her bad side. "I know you're exhausted, and I know you're hurting, and it's your choice," she told him, and he knew she meant every word of it. "But please, Saint . . . choose us one more time."

"Please," said Jal.

"*Please*," said Eoan, crisper and clearer than either of the others. How many times had that voice dragged him out of the dark? How many times had Eoan offered him a hand, a *chance*? "One more time, dear—not for us, but for yourself." Saint wasn't sure he'd ever heard what *certainty* sounded like from Eoan. Until now. "You're more than a ranger. You're more than a soldier. You're more than an oath and a banner, and you always have been. You're our *family*, Saint, and we need you to *please. Get. Up.*"

His family. His clueless kid on a transport ship, with a ratty deck of cards; his would-be thief who could fix the whole goddamn universe with a plasma torch; his incredible captain who always saw potential—in things, in places, and, most importantly, in *people*. He'd lost the Guild, but he still had them. Just outside that door, begging him to fight just a little longer. Begging him to just *get up*.

He could hardly stand. His hand slid against the wall, slick with his own blood, and he'd barely gotten upright when his knees went. *Get up.* Another try. Another fall. *Get up.* Another. *Get up!*

He'd started to fall again, when a hand seized his wrist and pulled him back up. "You get it, now, don't you?" Drestyn said. "It was never about a cause." And as Saint hooked his fingers onto one side of the door, Drestyn did the same on the other, and slowly, the door started to open.

"It's going!" Jal hollered, and Saint could *see* them now— him and Nash, on the other side. Fingers bloody and teeth bared, but they grinned so wide when they saw him that he forgot how much it hurt. "Come on, come on, come on!" As soon as they got it open wide enough, Nash let go with a hand and reached through to grab him. If Jal felt the extra weight, the extra strain, as Saint let go and stumbled through, he didn't show it. He just dug in his boots and shouldered the load, with a strength that lived as much in his heart as in his genes. "Your turn, Preacher," he said. "We got thirty seconds. Let's go!"

As Saint turned back to help Drestyn through, though, he saw something in his eyes that made him stop. "You fight for people," Drestyn told him, with a soft, scarred smile. "Remember that."

Then he let go.

On his own, even Jal couldn't hope to hold the door. It shuttered closed, and somehow Saint knew that'd be the last he ever saw of Isaiah Drestyn.

"No!" Jal, God bless him, dug his torn-up fingers back into the door to try to open it, but Saint pulled him away. Drestyn had a choice of his own to make, and he'd made it. His reasons were his own, and in spite of everything they'd done to each other, Saint respected it. Respected *him*.

"We gotta go, kid."

Ten seconds. The light above the elevator door flashed red, and Nash tugged his arm over her shoulder while Jal broke off to help Raimes. Didn't have a drop of energy left between them, but they ran like they did, until they cleared the elevator door and dropped in a heap against the back wall.

"Going up," Eoan chirped, and from his back on the floor, half on top of Jal with Nash half on top of him, he watched the elevator doors slide closed on the secured ward for the last time.

Good fucking riddance.

A crackling cough drew his attention to the other side of the elevator, where Raimes drew himself up against the wall with a handkerchief from fuck only knew where pressed against his middle. He didn't look much livelier than he had when Saint thought he'd died, but he had the same half-stunned grin as all of them. "So," he said, "is this how y'all usually wrap things up?"

The three of them traded looks, and they might've had some bullet holes and broken bones and bloody hands between them, but damned if they didn't laugh.

"Oh, Captain," said Eoan, with a laugh of their own. "We're just getting started."

EPILOGUE

JAL

The *Ambit* spent another two weeks on Alpha Librae before the satellite doctors cleared Saint to fly, and another week after that before *Nash* did. Between the sick bay visits, the council depositions, the nights he spent staring at the door like Gethin himself would come busting through it, nothing really went back to normal. Jal wasn't sure it ever could.

He wasn't sure it *should*.

Things were settling, though. Bitsie went back to school. Regan went back to work. And at the end of those three weeks, Jal made his way out to the docks to see the *Ambit* off the way he'd planned to the first time around. Unfortunately, somebody'd beaten him to the punch.

"Much as I appreciate all your help, y'all are leaving a hell of a mess behind, here," Raimes was saying, leaning against a stack of crates at the bottom of the *Ambit*'s cargo bay ramp. Might've looked more casual, if not for the brace around his thigh and the walking stick hanging from his secondary holster. Jal was pretty sure it wasn't doing him much good there, but Nash had given up harassing him about it. Seemed she reserved her threats of staples and glue for the *real* special people in her life.

Not that those people actually heeded them. *Those people* mostly being Saint, who definitely hadn't been cleared to move crates aboard, but who couldn't stand to lounge around and watch other people work. And his *system*, Nash. They were fucking up his *system*. To which she'd muttered something about *her* fucking up his system if she saw him carrying anything heavier than his coffee cup.

God, Jal was gonna miss them.

Eoan's projection stood with Saint and Nash at the top of the ramp, smiling down at Raimes with a fondness he wasn't ready to call friendly—if only because Eoan didn't seem quite ready to call anyone else a *friend*—but might be headed that direction. "If you need help, you only need to ask," they said. "But this is a place for rangers of the Guild, and it's not our place anymore."

"It could be," said Raimes. "Turns out, now that those accounts and shit tied everything back to Brodbeck, I'm no longer the *most* hated man on the Captains' Council. Though I expect those winds to change any day now. Bet you Karim'd put in a mighty good word for you, too." He didn't really try to sell it, though. He had, and they'd turned him down, and he might've had his own way of doing things, but he at least respected theirs. He wanted to fix the Guild from the inside; they wanted to fix it from the outside—it, and everything else broken. Sounded like a hell of a job, to Jal, but if anybody could do it? It'd be those three. "I'm just saying, I've got my hands full. Got about a decade's worth of archives to comb through and a full-ass house to clean, and we still ain't turned up that security pod."

Jal couldn't have said why, but he kind of had a feeling they never would.

Nash just snorted from her perch on the nose of the *Valorous Starship Shuttle Number Three*. Seemed she and Percy still had some plans for it. "Oh no, they're making you work for a living. How terrible."

"Ghastly," Perseus agreed through the *Ambit*'s speakers. Eoan hadn't given him full access, but they'd agreed it wasn't right to keep the guy cooped up in the cargo bay all the time. He'd done them one too many solids for that. "Downright unethical."

"Yeah, yeah," said Raimes, with a crooked smile and a shake of his head. No hard feelings. "Had to pitch you one last time. But you stay in touch, you hear? I might have some jobs for you, 'til I work out what's what and who's who around here." *Until I know who I can trust.* They all knew he was thinking it. Knew the kind of burden he'd taken on, trying to shepherd the Guild back to rights. Jal wasn't sure it was possible, or if it was even worth trying, but he admired the hell out of Raimes for giving it a whirl. "Y'all don't be strangers. Now, if you'll excuse me, I've got an appointment with a certain purple-haired she-terror."

He dipped in a bow—not bad for a man who'd been gutshot less than a month ago—and turned on his heel, nearly running into Jal on his way out. "You change your mind, Red?" he asked, arching an eyebrow. "Not too late. Train ain't left the station yet." Before Jal could answer, though, off he went, whistling down the gangway and twirling his walking stick around his finger.

When Jal looked back up, Saint had started toward him, but he stopped a few steps down. "Regan," Saint called, in about as awkward a *hello* as two people could manage having never slept together. "You, uh. You going somewhere?"

Jal turned and took in the duffel bag on Regan's shoulder and the backpack on Bitsie's back. "Uh," he started eloquently—maybe his third career could be speechwriting; wasn't like the first two were roaring successes—and that was as far as he made it before she caught his arm and started pulling him off to the side.

"Give us a minute," she told Saint, and as Saint put his hands up and stepped back aboard, she turned to Jal. "Sorry we're late," she said. "We had some packing to do."

"I can see that." And just when he'd thought he couldn't get *more* confused, she swung the duffel off her shoulder and held it out to him. "Regan, what—?"

"I know you, Jal," she said. "I've known you since the day you were born, and I wouldn't trade a second of our lives together for all the caps in the spiral. You're one of the strongest, sweetest, most *sincere* people I've ever met, and I love you so, *so* much. You know that, right?"

He glanced over at Bitsie, trying to work out what he was missing here, but all he got were watery eyes and that same bittersweet smile. So much like her mama. He only wished he knew what was *wrong*.

"Did I do something?" he asked, reaching up to brush a tear from Regan's cheek. More just fell to take its place, and she didn't try to stop them. Beside her, Bitsie hiccupped and wiped her face on her sleeve, and when he knelt to hug her, she threw her whole weight into him. "What's all this, now? Come on, hey, did you bring them something?" He wiped her face with the hem of his shirt and smiled. "You wanna go give it to them?"

"The bags aren't for them, Jal," Regan told him. "They're for you."

His stomach sank. "What?"

Regan squatted down, too, brushing a few strands of hair from his face. "You don't have to go with them," she told him gently. "But I think you should."

"No, I—Regan, I just got here. I just found you guys again."

"And you won't lose us," said Regan. Her hands shook a little as she cupped his cheeks. "We'll always be here, and whenever you're ready, we'll be waiting for you, I promise. We're your family, Jal, and that's *never* going to change. But we're not your *only* family now. Those people on that ship, they *love* you, and you love them—"

"I love you two more."

Her face softened, breathtakingly and *heartbreakingly* fond. "Jal, sweetheart, you've got love enough to share. You always have. I told you: I know you. But I think . . . I think it's taken me this long to *understand* you, since you got back. The things you've seen. The things you've been through. You've changed, little brother, and that's—that's okay," she told him, smiling through the tears. "That's *beautiful*, because it means you survived. It means you made it back to us.

"Now, you just need a chance to make it back to *yourself*. Not to the person you were before, maybe not even to the person you are right now, but the person you want to be. You deserve that. You deserve to be happy, and safe, and surrounded by people who love you in a place you feel like you belong. And you'll always have that here, whenever you want it. Whenever you're ready for it. *Always*. But right now, I think that place is with them."

It was blessing, he realized, not a banishment. Permission that he loved them too much to ask for, and that they loved him too much not to give.

"You . . . you're sure about this?" They'd lost him, too. They'd grieved him. They had as many reasons to want him to stay as he had to *want* to stay.

And yet.

Bitsie pulled her backpack off her shoulders, and when she tugged their patched-up blue blanket out to press into his hands, he felt his eyes well behind his specs. "It's okay, Uncle Jal," she said, with far too much wisdom for her age. She'd be the best of all of them, mark his words. The kids always were. "And sorry we sort of sprang it on you. We just figured this way, you couldn't get all shit-scared and bail."

"*Shit-scared?*" Jal surprised himself with a watery laugh as he turned to Regan. "That's *your* daughter."

"That's *your* niece," Regan said, reaching over to ruffle his hair.

"And that's your ride." Bitsie cut in with a nod toward the *Ambit*. "I know they like you and all, but I don't think they'll wait around forever." She wiped her face again and widened her smile. "So? What do you think?"

Jal had never been much of a thinker—just wasn't in his DNA. But for the first time in a long time, he knew what he *felt*. Relieved. Grateful. Loved. And, as his decision settled warm and solid in his chest . . . *hopeful*.

He hugged them both and kissed their heads. *Not a good-bye*, he told himself. He wasn't leaving them, not really. Wherever he went, wherever that wild-ass crew of used-to-be rangers took him, he knew he'd always find his way back.

"Reckon I could see if they've got need of an extra hand," he said, shouldering his bag and his blanket and stepping out from the crates. "What do y'all say?" he called to the others. "Got room for one more?"

"There goes the grocery bill," Nash groaned, but when he made it up the ramp, she was waiting right there with Saint to swing an arm around him. "Took you long enough, miner boy."

"About five years late, by my count," Saint said, giving Jal's shoulders a squeeze. He seemed lighter now, somehow. A little bit lost, but a little bit found, and maybe that was the best way to be. "But God, kid, it's good to have you."

Eoan was the last, gracing him with a smile as real and fond as the others' arms around him. "Welcome to the *Ambit*, Jalsen Red," they said.

It felt like *welcome home*.

END

ACKNOWLEDGMENTS

To those who read the acknowledgments in *Cascade Failure*, this next bit's gonna look kind of familiar. A cosmically big *thank-you* to Mom, Dad, Meagan, Andee, Lara, and Remy, for being the kind of family a nerdy little bookworm like me is lucky to have. To Claire, Courtney, Jessica, Laura, and Jules—you're every shade of awesome under the sun, and I'm thankful for your friendship always. Thanks to Jen, my editor, for seeing this rowdy little story's potential and working her editorial magic to get it there; and to the rest of the team at Tor, whose incredible work and support have made this series what it is. To my agent, Sara, I'm so grateful for your guidance and advice on this wild ride. And to you guys, the readers—from the bottom of my heart, thank you so much for letting me share this story, this crew, and this universe with you. I hope you've enjoyed the adventure as much as I have.

ABOUT THE AUTHOR

L. M. SAGAS is an author of rowdy, adventurous science fiction and fantasy stories full of characters who live hard and fight harder. She writes to give folks a few good laughs, but has been known, on occasion, to tug a few heartstrings along the way. When she isn't writing, Sagas daylights as an intellectual property attorney in Nashville and moonlights as a dirt-smudged gardener, breakfast food enthusiast, and professional pillow to the world's snuggliest shelter pup. *Cascade Failure* was her debut novel.